"LOOK! THEY COME!"

At his comrade's shout, Nul turned to see firvolkans, a dozen of them or more, tumble from the tunnel. Jeremy had just enough time to send a bolt from his crossbow into the leg of one of the leaders, while Nul hacked at the thigh of another.

Nul weaved in and out among the enemy, seeking to hamstring the creatures, to run them through, to harry and delay them. He turned from a fallen foe just in time to see a club descending toward him. He dived to one side, and the club gave him a glancing blow, sending him crashing to the cavern wall. He lay there stunned and was only dimly aware of a hand grabbing his ankle. Then the firvolkan was running through the tunnels, dragging him over the rough stones. Nul's head smashed into the ground, sending and explosion of light through his skull, then all was darkness. . . .

NUL'S QUEST

BRAD STRICKLAND

A SIGNET BOOK

NEW AMERICAN LIBRARY

*This book is dedicated
with love
to
Jonathan and Amy*

ACKNOWLEDGMENTS

Many thanks to all those who helped:

Elizabeth Conklin
Tonya Cox
Richard Curtis
Tom Deitz
Thom Hartmann
Michael Langford
Jack Massa
Klon Newell
Greg Nicoll
John Silbersack
Barbara Strickland
Lamar Waldron
Wendy Webb

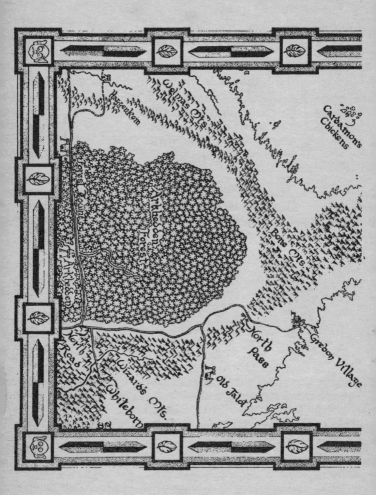

CHAPTER 1

"TURN, HELL-HOUND, turn!"

The usurping king, a tall man in the first years of a sturdy middle age, froze, his eagle face stern. Slowly he turned to face his younger challenger, who stood panting, sword drawn. Between clenched teeth, the elder man said, "Of all other men I have avoided you. Back, away! My soul already is too much charged with your blood."

Shaking his head, circling, steps wary as a great cat's, the younger man murmured, "I have no words; my voice is in my sword, you bloodier villain than speech can describe!"

With an inarticulate cry, the two clashed, swords glittering in the blue blaze of wizard-light. The crowd in the dark began to murmur encouragement to the younger man; but Jeremy Moon sank lower in his seat and groaned at what he had done.

The combatants broke apart, gasping. The elder sneered, "You lose your labor. Your keen sword might as easily cause the invisible air to bleed as draw blood of mine. Go, find some vulnerable foe; I bear a charmed life and cannot be slain by one of woman born."

Beside Jeremy, strangely shaped little Nul, sitting on four fat cushions to make him tall enough to see the spectacle, breathed hard. "Trick?" he whispered to Jeremy.

"Just watch."

On stage the younger actor was triumphant: "Then despair of your charm, and let the demon whom you have served tell you: Bernor was from his mother's womb untimely ripped!"

1

Mutters of surprise and appreciation rippled through the audience as Kernow, the overly ambitious king, reacted in anger and defiance. Another exchange, and then the maddened usurper thundered, "Lay on, Bernor; and damned be he who first cries, 'Hold! No more!' "

Jeremy's cheeks burned in the dark.

But the mummers finished the play and were rewarded with an earthquake-rumble of applause, signaled in the Great Hall of Whitehorn Keep by the enthusiastic native custom of stamping feet. The chief mummer, he who had essayed the role of Kernow, beamed, scanned the audience, and beckoned to Jeremy Moon. "Come," he said grandly, rolling his rich voice over the treads of approval. "Good folk, I give you the author of this new and best tragedy!"

Jeremy, feeling the hot blood rise into his face, shook his head, but from her aisle seat Kelada urged, "Go on! They want to see you!"

Somehow he stumbled up to the stage, mounted it with the help of two smiling actors, and turned to give the hundred and twenty playgoers a weak, sickly smile. They drummed the floor with loud heels as Jeremy waved to them. Then, blessedly, the wizard-light in the hall brightened and the heavy purple curtain—a theatrical innovation Jeremy had only lately introduced—fell. The players burst into hoots of jubilation and release, and "Kernow" —the dignified leader of all the mummers, a man from the south known as Winyard—threw an arm around Jeremy's shoulders. "By the everlasting moon! A triumph, lad! You've done rare work."

"Not really," Jeremy demurred. "I told you at the beginning, I'm only translating from another language—"

Bernor, still dashingly noble in his costume, but close up a rowdy and blond young man with a roguish smile, thrust two flagons of wine on them. "A toast!" he cried, laughing. "Drink a toast to *Kernow*, our author's latest triumph!"

"No, really, I took the whole thing from another play called *Macbeth*—"

"A toast, a toast!" Winyard boomed. "Lad, we leave next week for a year's tour; and at the end of that, your name will be honored in every city of Cronbrach!"

"Every enlightened city, anyway," grinned an elder actor. "Who knows what the benighted provinces will make of this new form of play-acting?"

Winyard roared his objection: "Nonsense! With such a genius as a writer of plays, and, if I may say, with such wonderful mummers to present them—" A chorus of cheers agreed with him. "I say, then, that Jeremy's fame is a thing of certainty. All of you now, and lustily—a toast to our young author: Jeremy Moon!"

A chorus of voices took up the cry, "To Jeremy!" and Jeremy glumly drank. Winyard clapped him hard on the back, making him cough. "You're a marvel, lad, nothing less. Devised this whole new method of presentation, written three wonderful plays for us—you'll have more for us next season, won't you?"

"Oh, yes," Jeremy said. "That is—I suppose—"

"Good! Good! More wine!"

The players, pausing only long enough to accept the spoken appreciations of the departing audience, swept him into their chambers for a riot of praise, laughter, and wine. It was a long evening. When the night was more than half over, Jeremy became aware that he was lying on a pile of cushions, his head delightfully pillowed in the lap of Selura Colt, a raven-haired beauty of an actress, as he tried with wine-thickened tongue to describe the part of Juliet he planned to write just for her. Unfortunately, just at the most heart-wrenching point he had to rise quickly and throw up.

By the time he had recovered, Selura was kissing a young fellow who had doubled in two roles, and Jeremy was feeling considerably less festive, anyway. Slipping away—not a hard task, with most of the cast drunk or getting there—he staggered down a long echoing corridor, up the eastern tower stairway, and to the rooms he shared with Kelada. For some reason it took him several tries to open the door. He stumbled in and found Nul and Kelada seated before a comfortable fire. Carmon, the first month of sleets and snows, was upon them, and the weather outside the castle was chilly. "Sorry," Jeremy muttered, slumping into a chair. "Players wanted to celebrate my artistic trumpet. Triumph, I mean."

Kelada, sitting in the adjoining chair with her feet drawn up under her, reached for his hand and squeezed it. She gave him a sleepy smile. "Everyone loved it," she whispered. "I'm very proud of you."

"Well, that's reasonable," Jeremy said. "You trained as a thief, after all. Takes a thief to know a thief, somebody said. No, that's wrong. Takes a thief to do something else. Steal Shakespeare, maybe." He hiccuped.

"I was trained in an honorable profession," Kelada playfully objected. "Not in lying."

"Who's a liar?" Jeremy closed one eye, making the room spin a little faster.

Kelada gently shook his hand. "You told me you were, back in your world. You practiced advertising, you said. As far as I can tell, advertising is nothing but lying."

"'S right," Jeremy murmured. "Not like writing plays, huh?"

Nul, seated on the hearth in front of the fire, said, "Liked the witches."

"Go on with you," Jeremy said. "Your favorite's *Midsummer Night's Dream*, 'cause you're in it."

Nul, a creature not quite chest-high to Jeremy, with a disproportionately large head, round amber eyes, and a coat of soft, short gray fur, grinned, displaying an alarming white crescent of teeth. "Puck the pika," he said, pronouncing *pika* as "PEE-ka." The little fellow chuckled. "Lord, what fools these mortals be," he quoted. "Good play, too, Jeremy. Better if Puck was real pika, not human boy dressed as one; but good." Nul's spirits seemed to decline suddenly, and he shifted his seat so that he could stare into the fireplace blaze. "Impossible, though," he said as if to himself. "Only one pika now, and he no mummer."

Jeremy, watching Nul's dark silhouette against the yellow flame, felt a pang of remorse. "We'll look for your people in the spring," he said carefully, trying not to slur the words. "I promised."

Nul sighed. "Late," he said, stretching like a cat. He slipped off the hearth and stood, his arms long and spidery, his legs short and bowed. "Good night, Jeremy, Kelada." He limped past a sofa and a blocky walnut table to the door and out into the hall.

As the door closed, Kelada touched Jeremy's cheek and with a playful finger ruffled his short brown beard. "What's wrong?" she asked softly.

Jeremy rested his head against the chair's high back and sighed, the taste of his own breath sour on his tongue. "Nothing. Everything. It's not like I thought, that's all."

"You're going to be famous." Kelada smiled.

"False pretenses. Gonna be famous on false pretenses. You don't really understand, that's what. See, I'm just translating the stuff, that's all. It's not really mine. And somehow the translation never measures up to the original."

"Everyone loves it."

"Yeah, well, lot they know." Jeremy looked broodingly at Kelada. She was small, just chin-high to him, her elfin face framed in a soft fall of blonde hair. Her gamine charm was in no way spoiled by the slight but noticeable curve of her abdomen. Their child was due in early summer, and she was beginning to show. "It's okay now," he grumbled. "When I can do *Macbeth* and *Midsummer Night's Dream* and *Measure for Measure*. But what about in ten years, hmm? I'll be down to *Timon* by then. And it's damned hard to find Thaumian parallels to the Earth characters, too. If Barach hadn't told me about Kernow and Bernor—"

"What difference does it make? If not for you, no one would ever see these wonderful shows."

"Yeah, but that's not the point. See, I'm supposed to be this great wizard. How great am I? Ask Nul. His whole family, his tribe—hell, his people, all disappeared in a war. I promised back last summer to help him find them. Have I done anything about that?"

"The Bone Mountains are far to the north," Kelada said. "Winter's no time to go there. There's plenty of time in the spring, as you said."

"Think so? I dunno. I have the worst feeling that time is short." A tremendous yawn felt as if it were going to split his head. "Ah, I'm tired."

"Come to bed," Kelada said, and she led him that way. He fell into bed beside her and passed into a deep sleep almost at once. Much later in the long winter night he awoke with a furred tongue, a pounding hangover, and bitter reflections on his odd fate. He sighed and resigned himself to a session of pondering; his head would not let him get back to sleep, and, anyway, the night was already far advanced.

Jeremy Sebastian Moon, the émigré from Earth, was not so well advanced, at least not in his studies of magic. For nearly a year now he had been a resident of Whitehorn, the mountaintop palace of Mage Tremien, and a student of Barach, a once-powerful mage now bereft of magic himself but, with his rich store of years and magical knowledge, a remarkable teacher of magic. It could not be said that Jeremy was an unwilling student, or that Barach was less than a patient and thorough teacher; still, somehow the lessons never seemed to increase Jeremy's skills very much, and sometimes they produced results that were downright dangerous.

"You have the natural lack of control of any young magician," Barach had observed to him more than once. "In your case, of course, there is a complicating factor."

That had been one drizzly fall morning as Jeremy, on hands and knees, tidied up after the most recent disastrous lesson. "And what would that factor be?" he had asked the old mage.

"It's your curious blending of *mana*, of potential magic. On the one hand, you have the forces of Earth, strange magics whose nature and limits are hidden to me. On the other, you have absorbed some powers of Thaumian magic, which have in turn been altered and changed by your proper self."

"I still don't think," Jeremy grunted into the woven-rush carpeting, "that rocks should explode." He fished a shard of granite from under the sofa and passed it up to Barach. "There's a piece. What happened?"

Barach, a wizard in his robust late middle age—about a hundred and sixty, from what Jeremy had gathered—furrowed his brow, nearly obscuring his eyes beneath bushy gray brows. "I see nothing unusual in the stone itself." The gray fragment, maybe four inches long, was smooth on one side, splintered and white on the other.

Barach flicked a few pebbles loose from the broken side. "The fault is in your spell, I'm afraid, Jeremy. The first component, *unshaping*, was so unexpectedly strong that the second, *remaking*, never had a chance to operate."

"It unshaped itself, all right," Jeremy grunted, sinking onto the sofa with a squeak. He had materialized the furniture for the tower apartment himself in an effort to make the stone-walled rooms seem more homelike, but with indifferent success. The sofa was a pleasant shade of blue, for example, but it was protected by a permanent cold, slick glaze of clear vinyl, a detail Jeremy had not had in mind at the time. "A piece shot through the window. Hope it didn't hit anyone."

Barach studied the broken pane with a judicious frown. "No. The trajectory's wrong. It will land in the snow outside the curtain wall."

"If it comes to rest. Remember the book."

Barach chuckled. "Ah, yes, your first success. You tried to levitate it and it flew away. Where's it been seen most recently?"

"About a month ago it was migrating south across the Green Dales. Do you know it makes nests?"

"Nests?"

"In printery towers, out of old poems and broadsides."

Barach chuckled. "That reminds me of a story. The mage who invented the printing spell, one Gustav Tzoner, was once approached by a young man who asked to be taken in as apprentice. Tzoner wished to know what his qualifications were. The young man, wishing to impress the master, boasted that he could read all languages known to man and could thus work translation spells to aid the print-mage in his endeavors.

"Tzoner doubted the young man's word and produced a short document written by Hrunston the Obscure, the last surviving member of the Stzelly Wizards, and the last speaker of their bizarre tongue. He passed it to the young man and asked him if he could read it.

"After a few moments' study, the aspirant nodded, all confidence. 'It's perfectly plain,' he told Tzoner.

" 'It is?' the astonished mage asked. 'What, then, does it say?'

" 'It says the great magician Tzoner won't be taking an apprentice this year,' the young man replied, and bowed himself out."

Jeremy smiled politely, got up, and placed the fragments of rock he had retrieved on top of the television set. The shattered stone joined a great many other pieces of failed experiments, for he used the TV mostly as a table to put shards and flinders on. It was a handsome model with a twenty-five-inch screen in a glowing walnut console, but once again Jeremy's magic had gone somehow awry, and it would pick up only one episode of *I Love Lucy* on Channel 6 and on Channel 13 only a *Huntley-Brinkley Report* from September of 1961. "Thanks for the history lesson, anyway," he told Barach. "Kernow and Bernor were just what I needed. Of course, in my version, Kernow's going to have a wife."

Barach shrugged. "It happened six hundred years ago. Kernow may have had a wife in reality; no one remembers. Certain it is that he slew the rightful king of Alderland and took his place, however."

"Just as Macbeth slew Duncan."

"Well, if teaching you history helps you with your hobbies, I am glad to do it. Now you can complete your play?"

"To world acclaim."

World acclaim. Yes, that was what he had said with a grin only last month; and now he had the acclaim, and its taste was as ashes in his mouth.

Kelada tossed in the bed beside him, her own sleep restless. He felt a deep pang, compounded of love, guilt, and despair. It was one thing to be a magician in a strange quasi-medieval world when the hurly-burly of battle raged, when one confronted the terrible Hidden Hag of Illsmere and her even more terrible master, the Great Dark One; but when the adrenaline of combat had subsided, when the reality of day after day of study and discipline sank in, why, then the daily round seemed hardly more exciting than his old life back on Earth, as advertising copywriter for the Taplan and Taplan advertising agency in Atlanta. And, somehow, concealing his own meager talent in the stolen plumage of Shakespeare made it all worse, no matter what the elated players—or the dazzled playgoers—thought.

Despite himself and his thumping head, Jeremy smiled when he remembered the gingerly astonishment that the players had displayed when he first began rehearsals for *Midsummer*, more than three months back. "You mean we speak?" Winyard had asked, the concept clearly amazing to him. "Instead of our performing the action in dumb show while the Narrator reads the poem, we actually *speak*?"

Fortunately, all the actors had taken turns as Narrator, and they had readily retentive memories. Within a fortnight they had the play down fairly well and could declaim in loud, if not exactly high, style. They surprised themselves at the simple innovation of spoken lines, finding their excitement growing at every rehearsal.

They were astonished, too, by the staging, the creation of a new theater—a proscenium theater with a curtain, instead of an arena with the dumb show surrounded on all sides by the audience. Jeremy supposed he should feel some sense of accomplishment, but there was only a vaguely empty, cheated feeling. Still, would he willingly return to his old way of life? Well—to be truthful, he didn't know.

Sighing, Jeremy closed his eyes and lay in the dark wondering what, if anything, would ever make him happy.

An apprentice magician's lot is not a happy one.

Jeremy carried the honorary title of "mage" as a reward for his services in the Hag's Uprising, as the brief war that had taken place the preceding spring had come to be known, but an honorific is no proof against the enthusiasm of a merciless teacher like Barach.

The very morning after the play, almost as soon as dawn had begun to redden the east, Barach summoned Jeremy from his warm bed beside Kelada out to the courtyard, where the younger man was expected to perform a strenuous series of calisthenics, hangover or no. When Jeremy complained, Barach, who was muffled in a thick fur robe and wore as well a fur hat and gloves in contrast to Jeremy's light breeches and shirt, simply observed that he who chose to ingest poisons must live with the consequences.

Grunting and sweating, Jeremy submitted to the exercises with bad grace. Still, he acquitted himself better than he could have hoped. After months of this regimen, his body was in better shape than it had ever been in the old days; better even than during his swim-team days back in college. His five-foot-eleven frame had grown spare and hard under Barach's tutelage, and his endurance was better than it had ever been. Despite his thumping head and lurching nausea, Jeremy went the distance, and after an hour of running, pullups, pressups, and weight lifting, he felt somewhat better.

The sun was up by then, gilding the turrets and towers of Whitehorn and filling the winter sky with a deep blue. The large moon, past full, barely showed above the western wall, pale silvery-blue in the light of day. The air Jeremy drew in was crisp and cold, headier in a way than the wine he had drunk the evening before. His breath puffed out in visible wisps of vapor as he and Barach walked a round of the courtyard.

"You are troubled," Barach observed.

"Worried," Jeremy said. "And something more. Dissatisfied. Ashamed, in an odd way."

"Yes, well, any young man occasionally overindulges—"

"I didn't mean last night."

Barach's shaggy eyebrows rose in polite inquiry. "Oh?"

"It's—I don't know. A feeling of something impending, something bad. What does Tremien say?"

"Nothing of ill omen. As you know, he and the Council are still trying to assess the strength of the Great Dark One, to learn how much the old adversary has lost in the past year. The lands of Cronbrach are serene." They paused near the great gates, which stood open. Far down the pathway, their progress speeded by the beneficent magic the great Tremien had laid on the ways of the valley, a small caravan made its way upward. Barach nodded toward it. "Festival days and Winter Market approach. All is well."

"I haven't seen much of Tremien lately."

"He is old. He tires easily these days. Though I think

he is somewhat more lively since the downfall of the
Hag. He liked your plays, by the way."

"I didn't know he had seen them."

Barach rumbled a deep chuckle. "A sorcerer as powerful as Tremien does not have to be present in body to
observe and hear. Especially in his own place."

Jeremy, still gazing through the open gates, murmured,
"Who are those people? Their dress is strange."

Barach shaded his eyes with his hand—hardly neces-
sary, considering the projecting tufts of eyebrows—and
squinted to the east. "Northlanders, I think. Odd folk
from beyond the borders of the civilized world. But they
bring trade stuff; ores and furs, special balsams and oils,
exotic spices. They are outlandish, but everyone is welcome in Festival season, and their wares will enliven the
Winter Market."

Jeremy shivered.

"Cold?" Barach asked.

"Yes," he said, and they turned to go in. But he
wondered if the chill he felt was totally external. Somehow he connected it not with the winter morning at all
but with the strangers, clad in shaggy auburn furs and
skin caps, who made their way beside their laden horses
up the trail to Whitehorn.

Winter Market was a riotous three-week period, a sort
of Thaumian Christmas and New Year's season, pulling
the farmers and artisans from their snug valley homes to
the cold mountaintop keep. Something in the air kept
people laughing and good-humored, even amid the bustle and confusion of a courtyard crammed to bursting
with temporary stalls and tents. The Northlanders, squat,
bronzed, broad-faced men and women with strange ac-
cents, were first to set up their wares and so had the best
spaces, just inside the great gate; but by the end of the
day they had been joined by a dozen other small groups
from the valley, and the next day saw even more come
in. The market actually began on the morning of the
third day, a morning of strong winter sunshine and clear,
biting cold.

Kelada and Jeremy strolled the rows of booths, admir-

ing the goods and the go of the sellers—and Jeremy
admired Kelada. Only a year ago she would have scorned
the clothing she wore now, a long green velvet dress and
decorative pale green capelet. Back then her clothing
had been for utility only, trousers and shirt and boots:
proper attire for a thief, but not for a court lady. But
now, her dress swaying gently as she walked, she was as
comfortable as any duchess, and more beautiful than
most.

A pair of Northlander jugglers made their way in and
out of crowds, stopping now and again to astonish their
audiences with wonderful feats: juggling a dozen sharp
daggers between them, a flashing figure eight of moving
steel, to the collective gasps of onlookers, or creating a
cascade of multicolored fire as they deftly tossed and
caught small balls of burning yarn, their hands moving
too quickly to take harm from the flame as they surrounded themselves with sparks, smoke, and the scent of
scorched fabric.

Musicians created a fearful wail of reeds and strings,
the fantastic, melancholy winter songs traditional to the
eastern coasts, where long nights and short days were
spent looking to a bleak gray sea; but there were some
foresters there, too, whose fiddle-like instruments reeled
off giddy dancing tunes, and there was a young red-
headed woman from a far southern town who sang of
love with a sweet and touching innocence.

Smells wove in and out of the music: crisp fish twists,
served hot from the oil in which they fried, dainty pas-
tries oozing sweet smallberry or kinze filling, musky per-
fumes imported all the way from the far deserts of
Akrador, the fresh piny aroma of the Northlanders' warming fire, the deeper scent of native hardwoods heating
food or people.

Kelada was delighted with the sheer busyness of it all.
"This is like home," she said, pulling Jeremy along by
the hand. "The city's like this all the time."

"One big festival, huh?" Jeremy said, glumly enough,
though he enjoyed Kelada's excitement.

"Oh, look!"

They paused before a small opening between tents,

where a stony-faced, middle-aged man presided over the antics of some trained animals. "What are they?" Jeremy asked, staring at the squirrel-sized flashes of brown.

"Tarrydals," Kelada said, squeezing to a better vantage point. "I've never seen tamed ones."

Jeremy, his head tilted to the right to gaze over the shoulder of a tall shock-haired farmer in front of him, made out at last that there were five of the little creatures—at first there had seemed to be at least a dozen, because they moved with startling speed. The tarrydals, light brown with darker brown tiger-striping, were built something like ferrets, though with more compact bodies. They were in almost constant movement, pausing only when their owner clucked a soft command.

"Dance," he said, and the animals capered around his legs, prancing and leaping with eye-blurring abandon.

"Climb," and they raced up his legs to his head, and made a pyramid, three, two, and one.

"Leap," and one by one they launched themselves from his head to a tent guy, from which they slipped to the ground.

"Now," their trainer said, "my animals are educated animals." A few people in the crowd laughed, and the trainer waved his hand as if shooing away a pesky cloud of gnats. "Yes, yes. Someone hold two coins, one small, one large."

The farmer in front of Jeremy produced a copper and a half-silver. "These do?" he said, holding them out on his palm.

"Ya, fine. Pick one of my animals."

"The bushy one with gray in the tail."

"Elza. Elza, get the best present."

The creature clambered up the farmer's trousers and shirt, onto his wrist, and paused to look at the coins. She picked up the copper, sniffed it, put it down, and then grabbed the half-silver. Clamping it in her jaws, she leaped to her master, thrust it into his breast pocket, and climbed to his shoulder. Then she chattered, a rapid-fire burst of squeaks and whistles. "Elza says 'Thank you for the present, Mr. Farmer.' "

Everyone, including the farmer, chuckled. Before the

show was over, Jeremy had himself contributed a silver to the trainer's treasury. Then he and Kelada moved on. He bought her a brooch of bderium, a deep red stone, and five yards of Tarkenien silk. They were just approaching the tents of the Northlanders when the commotion broke out.

It was a sharp curse at first, then a howl; and then everyone was moving in one direction, sweeping Jeremy and Kelada along willy-nilly. "Fight!" someone shouted. "Fight at the fur traders'!"

Jeremy had been holding Kelada's hand. He lost his grip in the tumbling press of the crowd, then lost sight of her as the crowd poured through an opening between two tents, pushing him ahead of her.

The tumult was deafening: shrill shrieks of women, the basso yells of men, an odd squealing that was neither man nor woman. It sounded like—

"Nul!" Jeremy shouted. "Let me through here." He shoved and pushed past turbanned and bare heads, shouldered aside travelers clad in fur and in silks, and finally burst through into the front rank.

A Northerner rolled howling and yelping on the ground, while his people looked on screaming and calling advice. Clinging fast to his back was the grotesque form of the little pika, his teeth clamped hard on the man's ear.

"Mate with it, Kushan," one of the men yelled, laughing. "You can skin your young ones and sell their hides for profit!"

The man tried to roll over and crush Nul, but the pika was too quick, always winding up on top and somehow beyond the reach of the flailing, grasping arms. But a younger man, his face scarred and grim, stepped forward with a dirk. "Time to put an end to this," he said, drawing back to strike.

"The party knife!" Jeremy yelled in English as the dirk flashed upward. "Fool your friends! Incapable of causing the slightest harm!" The knife struck, and the young man blinked as the blade, suddenly become rubber, bent without effect.

Those nearest Jeremy in the crush were aware that the strange young man among them had done *something*, had called out in an unknown tongue, and they suspected that he had thrown a magic spell. They melted back, and Jeremy was free. He fell in with the scuffling man and pika.

"Nul!" he coughed as the three of them tumbled in the dust. "Nul! Let go!"

"Killer," rasped Nul, but in doing so he released the clamp of his formidable teeth. "Let go. Kill him, kill him!"

The trader had no more fight in him. He scrambled on all fours to the edge of the crowd and turned, a hand clamped over his left ear. Blood leaked through his fingers.

The younger trader aimed a kick at Nul. Jeremy caught the leg, used its own momentum to bring it up impossibly high, and spilled the man on his back. The breath *chuff*ed out of him, and he lay dazed.

"Now," panted Jeremy, struggling to keep his grip on the writhing pika, "tell me what happened."

Nul chattered nonsense syllables.

"Nul!" Jeremy shouted. "It's me! Tell me what happened!"

The orange eyes of the pika glowed momentarily into his without even the slightest trace of recognition; then the little creature shuddered. Pikas did not weep, but Nul's eyes held a strange sheen. "Jeremy," Nul said in a soft and broken voice. "Oh, Jeremy—" he choked.

"Here," Kelada said from behind them.

Jeremy turned. Kelada held a fur, one she had evidently taken from a stack piled outside a tent.

"That's mine!" the wounded Northerner said in his throaty dialect. "My goods, and this—this demon—"

"Quiet," Jeremy said. "That looks like—"

"It's a pika hide," Kelada said. "Oh, Nul."

In his strangled, choked voice, Nul groaned, "My brother. Is my brother."

CHAPTER 2

THE EARLY DUSK of the cold months had fallen when Tremien saw them all in his study, a roomy, book-lined chamber with a huge stone fireplace in one wall and, opposite that, the large and cluttered desk of the old mage. Tremien, a spare old man with a nimbus of white hair around a bald pate, a great long white beard (though for all its length, a tidier one than Barach's), and keen dark eyes set deep in his saddle-brown face, spoke quietly but with cold fury: "What right have you to kill a thinking being in this barbarous way?"

"A lie!" shouted the scarred-face Northerner, a man named Ingorod. "My uncle had this fur of someone else!"

The older man, his torn ear now bandaged, nodded. His brown eyes were slightly crossed, and his broad dark face glistened in the light of the fire. "I traded for it," he said in slow, thick speech.

"Revenge," growled Nul. Jeremy, holding onto the little being's shoulders, gave him an unobtrusive shake.

Behind them stood Barach and Kelada; Tremien needed no other guard in his own room, for there was nothing on Thaumia that could threaten him or stand up to his power there. The old magician stared hard at the two Northerners. "Kushan, you have come to Winter Festival at Whitehorn for many years. I have never found you to be a dishonest man, but I have never known you to be too slow in looking for a chance to profit. You will tell me everything you know of this skin—where you had it, and how you came by it." The penetrating eyes locked

16

with those of the younger outlander. "And you, Ingorod, will add nothing until you are asked."

No spell strengthened the speech—none but the indomitable will of Tremien, and that seemed enough. The heavyset Kushan scratched gingerly at his bandaged ear. "Well, that is easy told. My clan traps on the northern slopes of the Bone Mountains in spring and summer. Then in late summer we goes further north, up to the Twilight Valley. There we sells what we can. When we gets done with that, we hires a ship and come south for the rest of the seasons of fall and winter, selling until it's time to go north again."

"My people lived in Bone Mountains," Nul said. "In caverns under the mountains. You know, Mage!"

Tremien waved a quieting hand. "Yes, Nul, I know. The time for you to speak is not yet. Please listen with us."

Jeremy felt a tremor pass through the pika, whether of rage or of grief he could not tell. But Nul subsided into silence.

"Continue," Tremien told Kushan.

"Your little, uh, friend's wrong," the big man shrugged. "We didn't take none of his kind in the traps. Never seen nothing like him."

"Then where did you come by the fur?"

"In the cursed Twilight Valley!" shouted Ingorod. "I told my uncle we shouldn't have gone there."

"Hush, cub," growled Kushan. "This is between elders." He scratched again at the bandage. "The lad's right, though. We come into Twilight Valley along after their harvest time—you know it comes early away up there—and done some trading with the people. Not much, because, well, you know the Valley. Hardly ever gets real cold there, far north as it is. Not much of a market for warm furs. But we done well enough, and we was just getting ready to go on down the river—what a plague's the name of that river, nephew?"

"The Friddifor."

"Can't seem to get my tongue around it noway. Down the river we was going, until we'd come to the fishing port off in the east, you see, where we'd get our boat. We was in a hurry, too, 'count of the robbers—"

"Robbers? In Twilight Valley?"

"I guess they was robbers. Folks kept telling us not to travel in the dark, or somebody'd grab us sure. Must've been robbers. Well, to cut a long tale short, as the gramarten said when the beshrike grabbed him, one of the women in Twilight Valley comes to me with this gray fur. Never seen nothing like it, not me: soft as moleskin, smooth, and shot with that one white blaze. What, she says, you give me for this? So I traded her some foxes for it, enough for her to have a robe made, and then we left that ungodly Valley behind us."

Tremien was silent for a long moment. Then he turned to Ingorod. "Is what your uncle says true?"

"Oh, yes," the younger man said. "The Twilight Valley is most ungodly."

Tremien sighed. "That is not what I meant."

"Well, it's true. They don't even believe in the use of good magic, do they? But the rest is so, too. The woman traded the gray fur for four foxes, all of them red, just like my uncle told you."

Behind Jeremy, Barach coughed. "Perhaps she may have mentioned where *she* obtained the—item?"

"She told some tale," grumbled Kushan. "I remember nothing of it. Just the skin was what I wanted."

Ingorod said, "She told us that the creature was found after the Valley people fought a battle with the underground hobs."

Tremien exchanged a startled look with Barach. "Hobs, you said?"

"Them's the robbers I said they told you of," Kushan muttered. "Didn't take no stock in the other name. Ain't heard of no real hobs in years and years."

"Hobs is what they told us," the young trader insisted. "They're tunnelling, like, under the town. Some of the men of the Valley decided to run 'em out with smoke and fire. They shot at those they could with arrows. The thing wearing this fur came out of a hob-hole, and the woman's husband killed it. They'd never seen anything like it, so he decided to skin it."

"When was this?" Tremien asked.

The young man looked at his uncle.

"Season ago, I guess," Kushan said. "We'd traded there last year, and this woman never said nothing to us then about a special fur."

Tremien asked several more questions, but neither trapper could add anything significant. At last the old mage rose wearily from his chair and paced the room, from the fireplace to the high-arched windows, where he stood drumming his fingers for a few moments before retracing his steps. At last he stood silhouetted against the fire, his arms behind his back. "I sense no deception," he said slowly. "But if what you say is true, it is doubly heavy news. The first part is that hobs may yet linger in the far north, something that has been rumored but never believed. The second woe is that I have done my friend a great disservice. Nul, I apologize to you. If your people, or some of them, still live, it was wrong of me not to discover them before this terrible event."

Barach said, "Tremien, you blame yourself too much. You know as well as I that the Fridhof Mountains have a certain uncanniness about them. The stones themselves are hostile to our powers. And as for the people of the Valley—as an old story has it—"

"Not now, my old friend," Tremien sighed. "We have a puzzle, it seems. Kushan, Ingorod, you may go. I will pay whatever losses you have suffered; but not for the hide, for it is that of a creature like yourselves, one blessed with a mind. My guard will take charge of that. Barach, Jeremy, Nul, stay with me. And Kelada, if you wish."

"Yes," Kelada said. "I will stay."

The two trappers left them alone in the chamber. "Sit," Tremien said. All but Nul sat in the chairs scattered about the room; the little pika sat on the high stone hearth, staring into the flames. After a long pause, Tremien said, "I suppose there can be no mistake?"

"Nah, nah," grunted Nul, his voice still husky. "Brother Jare. Older than me. Same father, same mother."

"But you are sure?"

Nul gave Tremien a surprisingly angry glance. "Know

my own brother, Mage. Same streak of white in coat. Same scar on shoulder. Sure."

"I had to ask, my friend."

Nul turned back as if seeking solace from the flames. "Nul know. Sorry for way I spoke. Is heavy feeling in my heart. But how came Jare to be killed among hobs?"

"Excuse me—what are hobs?" Jeremy asked.

"Jeremy, this will be new to you," Tremien said. "Or much of it will be, anyway. You are aware of the long war between the Great Dark One and we of the northern continents. However, I do not know if you have heard much of the invasion we suffered some forty years ago."

"I have heard only a little about it," Jeremy said.

"We are not yet up to modern history in his studies," Barach added.

Tremien nodded, swept a palm back over his bald spot. "It was open war that time. The armies came in fog and mists, shrouded even from my seeing, until their ships were close enough to grate on the sands of our shores. Most of the soldiers were men, but some were hobs—creatures of the south, whether natural or of magical origin I do not know. The hobs were ruthless fighters, enormously strong, astonishingly quick, and with no fear in them. It was with the greatest difficulty that we dealt with them; though in the end, they seemed to have vanished utterly through no doing of ours.

"We overcame the master of the armies, a man named Ursulun: a man, I believe, more than half possessed by the Great Dark One. At that time, the hob armies simply fell apart; scattered like so many leaves in a high autumn wind. Many of the hobs died in the next few days, for no cause that I could see. Except that the will driving them was not their own, but flowed in them from the Great Dark One, through the medium of Ursulun."

Tremien sighed again. "You have heard from Nul how I found him. He had been captured and enslaved by a farmer of the northlands, in the fields between Arkhedden Forest and the Bone Mountains. The farmer and his family died in the wars; and when Nul attempted to return to his own people, he found their tunnels and caverns empty. He joined my service because he had nothing else to do, no one else to turn to; and I promised to help him when the war was over."

Nul stirred by the fire. "You tried, Mage Tremien," he murmured. "Nul not blame you."

Tremien gave Nul a brief, almost fatherly smile. "We did try, Nul and I. We descended into the caverns, but found them bleak and deserted. Nul showed me his own family's den, but even there, where they had lived for so long, I could not sense their living presence. I believed them all dead—then."

Kelada was frowning. "But Nul's brother must have lived until last season, if the trappers were telling the truth."

Tremien nodded. "I was wrong. A thing which has been known to happen more than once, although it never fails to irk me. But at the time I did not perceive how I could be wrong, and so I falsely told Nul that his people were no more."

Jeremy was puzzled. Once, more than six months earlier, he had heard the Great Dark One, himself a wizard of great power, refer to Tremien as an old spider; and like an old spider indeed, Tremien seemed alert to every quiver of his web, which was all of his country, warded and threaded with invisible rays of subtle power. "How could you be deceived?" he asked.

Tremien gave Jeremy a melancholy smile. "I was fooled, I fear, by having lived too long amid magic."

"I don't understand."

"Tell him about the Twilight Valley, Barach," Tremien said, settling back into his chair and closing his eyes.

Barach shifted his weight slightly. "The Twilight Valley. Yes. The place where more than once I've thought it might be good to retire, now that I have no magic left. Jeremy, a good hundred and eighty leagues to the north of us, in the extreme north of Cronbrach-en-hof, is the Fridhof range—the Fathers of Mountains, we sometimes call them. They are high, barren, covered with snow most of the year. From them two ranges strike out, one going southwest, one southeast. The southwestern mountains are the Wolmas, where we traveled when we fought the Hag. The southeastern ones are outside the windows there: the Wizard's Mountains, named after my old friend here."

Jeremy nodded. "Yes, and the Bone Mountains are the union of the two ranges, running north to the Fridhof Mountains. I've studied geography."

"Patience," Barach said. "Recall what happened to the bird who rose too early. What you may not know is that the Friddifor River cuts through the Fridhof range from east to west. Surrounding the river is the Twilight Valley. Some quirk of the land gives it a cool, even climate all year around; long cold winter, though not bitterly so, short spring and autumn, brief warm summer. It is not a bad climate for certain types of crops. In the early years of Thaumia, some people settled there. But they quickly moved away again."

"Why?"

"They discovered that their magic did not work there. And they were accustomed to magic, by then; they did not realize how quickly spoken spells lose their vigor, and in those days they did everything by magic."

"A waste," Tremien murmured. "Their shortsightedness meant great hardship for later generations. Men are ever wont to use the good things of life all too fast."

"You mean the valley itself spoiled the people's magic?" Jeremy asked.

Barach puffed out his cheeks. "That was what the settlers thought. Now we know that the Fridhof Mountains are rich with veins of a strange stony ore. It damps magic, prevents it from working properly; in great concentrations, keeps it from working at all."

"Which made the valley attractive to certain of our people in later years," Tremien added. "Those who did not understand magic, or who feared it, or whose superstitions it upset. They found the valley a haven; and their descendants still live there to this day, in conditions of near-absolute mundanity."

"They are not friends of ours," Barach said.

"They side with the Great Dark One?"

Tremien shook his head. "Jeremy, the world is not so simple. No, the people of the Valley are not in league with the evil wizard of the south; but neither are they friends of ours. They live their own lives, sheltered in their valley, and wish no exchange, or at most only small exchange, with the rest of the world."

"But if there are hobs in the valley—"

"Exactly, Jeremy." Tremien opened his eyes. "They must be the ones who came in the invasion, or the descendants of the invaders."

"And if they live in the valley, or in the caverns under the valley, they are natural creatures, not magical ones."

"Not necessarily," Barach demurred. "After all, life itself is a manifestation of magic. It seems to be *verbal* magic, not *natural* magic, that is negated by the Fridhof mazerite—that is the name of the stone. If Tremien went there, he would not cease to be Tremien; but his ability to cast spells might lessen or even fade altogether—though I suspect that it would take great power to remove his magic completely. The hobs may very well *be* magic, but living in the Fridhof range they cannot *do* magic."

Tremien nodded agreement. "What Barach says is true. But whether the hobs are natural or magical, I do not understand them, and cannot suggest a way of combating them."

"Have to go," Nul said. Jeremy looked at the pika. He sat on the hearth, his bandy legs drawn up, his six toes curled over the edge of the stone. "Have to go, mage."

"I know that," Tremien said. "But you do not have to go tonight, and you should not go until we have considered this matter."

Jeremy looked at Kelada, saw understanding in her eyes, and said, "I will go with you, Nul."

Barach sighed. "I fear that months of peace have made me soft. I will come with you."

"You have no magic," Jeremy said.

"Precisely. Nor will you in the Fridhof Mountains. Perhaps you can teach me a thing or two about living without the aid of sorcery, eh?"

From the hearth Nul slipped to the floor. He stood before the two men. "Thank you," he said. "You friends of Nul. You will go. But first is something Nul must do."

"Yes," Tremien said. "The funeral."

*   *   *

A broad river, the Bronfal, flowed through the valley beneath Whitehorn, winding its way through groves of hardwood and tumbling now and again over rocky rapids. In the valley, within sight and hearing of the river, and within sight, too, of the castle on the mountaintop, Nul, Barach, and Jeremy buried the skin. The two men left the pika there, huddled in a woolen robe much too big for him, to perform a ritual of farewell that only pikas knew.

As they rode on horseback up the winding trail to the mountain summit, Jeremy paused to look back. He could see the hilltop and the grove of tremble-leaf where the grave was, but from here he could not see Nul. Jeremy turned his horse's head back toward the castle. "What do you think?" he asked Barach as they moved steadily along the trail.

"About what?" the older man asked, his face and his voice both bland.

"About Nul's chance of finding his people again. What if Jare was the last one?"

Barach shook his head. "Who can say? Where there's thunder there has been lightning, as the old saw has it; and where there was one pika, there may be more. Pikas, as you may have noticed, are a hardy folk. It is more difficult to kill one than you might imagine. I think as a race they would be hardy, too, with unsuspected reserves of strength and endurance. But it is bad that they are in the company of hobs."

"What *are* hobs?" Jeremy asked. The path tilted up now, toward the castle, framed against a gray cloudy sky that threatened sleet or snow, and the air was keen in his nostrils. "I've heard them described as soldiers, as abortions of nature, as monsters—what are they, exactly?"

Barach said, "Once a student asked his master, *What is fire?* The master told him to study a flame and find out. He left him alone with a candle, a flint, and a steel. Hours later, the master opened the door and said, *Well, student, do you know what fire is now?* And the student, sitting at the table with the candle wick still unburnt, the steel undisturbed, and the flint untouched, said, *As nearly as I can see, it's wax, string, metal, and a hunk of rock.*"

"Then no one knows."

"Well, there are some who know, I have no doubt. But not I. I can tell you what they are like: great hulking brutes with small heads, furred on the crown, neck, and shoulders. Eaters of the dead. Possessed of strength but little mind. Quicker than you would believe possible, and more silent. And deadly in a fight. But what they *are* is a different question altogether. Some say they were men, once, and that their souls have been taken from them by magic; others that they are, like the pikas, natives of Thaumia, not intruders as humans are; and still others that they are neither man nor beast but images conjured by the Great Dark One and given life by him. What is true is impossible to say. They were here in great numbers forty years ago. I fought against some of them myself, during the siege of lost Jalot; fought by directing the soldiers, you know. I fear I've never been good at hand-to-hand combat."

"What happened?"

"We lost Jalot. I'll tell you the tale someday, though it does me no honor. I miscalculated gravely; thought I could bring reinforcements by means of the travel-spell. A few of us got out, but the Great Dark One was disrupting all enchantments. My spell was misdirected, and my party was cast far into the wilderness. By the time we had made our way out—well, that is a tale for another telling."

"But the hobs?"

"We killed quite a few of them. Their bodies did not last; they went to liquid, then to dust, in the course of a day or so. There certainly was magic, and a foul one at that, in their decomposition. And later, when the army of the south had been broken, most of them seemed to fall where they stood and died."

"Most?"

"If the tale of the trappers is true, there must be some left in Cronbrach." A breeze sprang up, wafting Barach's gray beard over his shoulder. "That is evil to hear. And an evil thought, too: if indeed these hobs have gone underground, into the caverns and tunnels of the pika people, who knows how many there may be, or how

extensive their digging could prove? I do not know if
Tremien's power of perception ends at ground level; but
if it does, we may all face a much worse danger than we
appear to."

They made the last turn on the enchanted pathway—
its benign influence allowed them to make a full day's
journey in only a few minutes—and came in sight of the
great gate, guarded by the two animated sandstone gargoyles, Fred and Busby. This afternoon the gate stood
open, but Busby ritually cried out, "The travelers return!" in his grating stone voice.

"But the small one is not with them," Fred added.

Busby's head gritted sideways as he gave his companion a look even more stony than usual. "That was mine
to say. You announced their departure."

"But you left it out."

"Please," Barach said. "Remember the occasion."

"Sorry," they said in unison. Then Busby added, "Truly,
we are sorry. Nul has been a good friend to us. He has
talked to us often and long of the stalactites and stalag-
mites of the pika caverns, of the agates and rubies found
there, of the strata of limestone and shale that line the
walls with beautiful colors. And we felt sympathy with
him, since he, even as we, had no living kin."

"That's right," Barach said, pausing just before the
gate. "You both were carved from the fabled living rock
of the South Islands, weren't you?"

Busby reared back a bit, his lion-paws clenching the
orb at the top of the pillar, his great dragon-shoulders
thrown back. "Yes. Of course, Fred is only from the
Late Tertiary—"

"Old fogy," Fred grumbled. "Just because you happened to be from the Paleocene stratum—"

"Oh, quiet, the two of you," Barach said. Jeremy
followed him through the gate, but behind him he could
still hear the querulous, gritty argument being carried on.
The two men dismounted, led their horses to the stables,
and went inside the castle. Kelada waited for Jeremy in
their room.

"How was he?" she asked.

Jeremy shook his head. "Sad. Grieving. I'm sorry for him."

"Yes."

Jeremy sat beside her and studied her. Once Kelada had not thought herself beautiful, with her gamine figure and her elfin, broken-nosed face; but that time was past, and now, with the glow of motherhood growing round her daily, she was changing visibly. No, she was no longer a girl, but a woman; and her early charm was ripening into a more mature beauty. Her blonde hair, once hacked carelessly short, now fell amost to her shoulders, and her figure was more graceful, fuller. Her silvery gray eyes, though, had not changed; they still looked on life with an intense directness. "You were right to say you'll go with him."

"How did you know what I was thinking?"

She kissed him. "When did I ever not know? You still have something to find, Jeremy. Or something to prove, I don't know which. But Nul never deserted you when you needed him; and it would be wrong of you to desert him now. I only wish I could go with you."

Jeremy touched her lightly swelling stomach. "You have more important things to do."

Her warm hand covered his. "Yes. I knew you would forbid my going with you. And I suppose a fat thief would only be in your way." She sighed. "Do you ever worry about our child?"

"Oh, yes. All the time."

"There is so much evil in the world."

"But much good, too."

"What sort of life will he have?"

"Or she," Jeremy smiled. "I expect she—or he—will have a life like everyone else's: some happiness, some grief, and some things that have to be done for their own sake."

"If you'd stayed in your world, you would not have to worry about evil magic and the future of your child."

He drew her closer to him. "You are my world," he said. "And don't believe there is no evil magic on Earth. There are evils there beyond your counting; but good, too. It balances in the end."

"You sound like Brother Thomas."

"I'm no preacher," he said, and kissed her.

"No, thank heavens," she murmured, her breath sweet and hot against his face.

They made love, tenderly. For a few moments he forgot sorrowing Nul, forgot the hobs and Twilight Valley, forgot everything but the wonderful woman with him; and she seemed to lose herself in him as well. Later, softly, she whispered to him, "Come back safely from this journey."

"I will," he promised, his arm warm around her. "Our child deserves both mother and father."

"Don't forget that. Not ever."

"I never will," he said, but with a little tremor his heart misgave him.

The clouds outside grew more sullen toward evening, and a thin snow began to fall. Just after sunset Jeremy went out to the gates. He saw Nul on the path to the castle and waited for him, shrinking inside his fur-lined cloak and feeling the stinging impact as the tiny, hard snow lashed his face.

Nul, limping more heavily than usual in the cold air, trudged up to the gate and paused to clasp Jeremy's hand. The pika's own hands, three-fingered and small, were icy cold. "Better come in and warm youself," Jeremy said. The little creature nodded.

Barach met them at the entrance and took them along to his own apartments, in the central keep of the castle. His rooms were more like the most disorganized library imaginable than living quarters, with every wall lined with bookshelves and more books stacked knee-high in piles on the floor. But he had a warm fire burning and hot spiced wine for them all.

Nul accepted a mug gratefully and sipped from it. "Over now," he said. "Jare's spirit sent to after-land. May it find peace."

"May it find peace," Barach repeated gravely, and immediately Jeremy echoed the wish.

Nul clutched the mug with his three-fingered hands and drank again, more deeply. Jeremy sipped from his own cup, savoring the fruity, spicy warmth of the wine on his tongue. It was curiously soothing going down, and it brought to his stomach a welcome glow.

Barach set down his own cup on a low table, moved stacks of books from three chairs, and had them all sit. "Now," he said, "I think, Nul, you should tell us something of your people—and of Jare. It is only right that we know a little about them if we are to try to help you find them."

"Yes, yes," Nul said. He drank again, then set his cup down. He leaned far back in his chair, his little bandy legs dangling. His huge orange eyes closed. "Hard to remember it all," he said in a soft voice. "So long ago. I was just young pika then, maybe fifteen years old or so. Jare was older by ten, twelve years maybe. Pika people not keep birthdays like human people. Live longer, too. If Nul had other pikas around, lady pikas, he would just now be old enough to get mate for first time."

Nul fell into a deep study for a long while. Jeremy, not wanting to intrude on his silence, drank his wine quietly and waited. At length the pika opened his eyes; they seemed to look far away, seeing another time, another place.

"Pika-men marry many wives," he said. "Many pika-women, few pika-men. In my clan we have one father, three, four, many mothers. Many children, but only five male children: Jare and me, sons of Vall and Yaret; Zaf, son of Vall and Zolisat; Chag, son of Vall and Sagorel; and Tol, son of Vall and Tolinar. We have many, many sisters. Of all brothers, Tol was eldest; I second youngest. We live in tunnels beneath the Bone Mountains for all my life. Pikas are diggers, tunnelers; farm some on surface near cavern openings, fish and hunt some, but live underground.

"My clan one of ten big ones, maybe ten, twelve smaller ones. But called Tribe of Ten Clans, after main families. Pika-people used to be more numerous than sands of river, more than stars in sky; but we have dwindled with passing of years. Now the Tribe of Ten Clans the biggest settlement we knew of in all of north. Live there in caverns for many years.

"How I lost them I have told you: first became trapped by farmer, then war came. Nul hide in barn, under straw, when hobs come through from north. Hobs kill everyone: farmer, wife, daughters, sons. Kill horses." Nul shivered. "Eat all," he whispered.

Barach began, "If you don't feel up to talking—"

"Nah, nah." Nul slipped from the chair and poured himself more wine from the pewter decanter warming before the fire. He put the cup on the table, scrambled back into the chair, and reached for the wine. He took a long drink. "Never feel like talking about hobs. But have to." He drank again before resuming his story.

"I hide many hona in barn, all day, all night, next day. Then hobs gone. They search house for more people, but not barn. Had slept in barn. I hurry back north to cavern entrance in side of Two-peak Mountain. Just small entrance. I have to squirm through.

"Path from there leads down and down. Traveled fast, running as much as I could. Got to meeting-place cavern: cold, empty, no fire, no lights. Evil smell, thick smell of hobs.

"Hurried on to home den. All rooms empty, cold. No blood, no sign of fight; no pika, either. I young then, just a child; very scared to be in cold, dark place that feel so wrong. So Nul left caverns."

The pika fell silent for a long time. Barach urged him gently: "Then you came back out?"

Nul nodded. "Hungry, cold, weary. Found human soldiers. Stole food. Stayed close to camp. Then Tremien catch me, scare me. But he became my friend."

Jeremy said, "Nul, how many pikas in all were in your tribe?"

"Pika-people not count same like human count. But I guess maybe two hundred, three hundred pika-people in all in Bone Mountain caverns."

"And elsewhere?" Barach asked.

"Used to be tribes in Wolmas, on other side of Haggenkom. Not hear from them in long time. Used to be tribes in south. But if they still there, they go underground for good now. No human has seen pika in many, many years."

"If we could find the others, could they help us?" Barach asked.

Nul considered. "Nah, nah. Pikas very independent. Not have anything to do with others. Our tribe started when father of grandfather quarreled with family in Wolmas, moved followers to Bone Mountains. Pikas have long memory for quarrel. And how you find pika if pika does not want to be found? Even Nul could not."

"Then we're on our own," Jeremy said.

"Well," Barach rumbled, pushing himself up from his chair, "that may not prove too terrible a handicap. We have come through some tight spots, the three of us together. Let me find a map." He went to a shelf and began to rummage through folded papers and parchments.

Nul finished the last of the wine. "Pikas not use magic much. Just little bit of mining magic, finding magic," he said. "Tremien, he tried hard to find traces of them; but some other magic, evil magic, overlaid all trace of my people."

"Mining and finding? I don't understand. What magics do pikas use?" Jeremy asked.

Nul shrugged. "Spells to find gemstones. Spells to give light. Spells to help dig. Small spells for underground life, that all. Nothing big."

"Some of their magic is inborn," Barach explained, looking up from a handful of folded papers. "Instinctive, almost. Other types are spoken."

"What will you do if you find your people again?" Jeremy asked Nul.

"Not know." Nul shook his huge basketball of a head sadly. "Not know. Want to find them alive. Want to belong to family again. It long and long now. Father and mother be very old if alive. Even Tol be a middle-aged pika now, maybe hundred years. As old as Nul's father was back then. Maybe whole family very old now. But Nul want to find them."

"Here we are at last," Barach said, bringing a thick folded map to the fireside. "Jeremy, give us a little light, if you please."

Jeremy obliged with a quick incantation in English. It produced wizard-light, a sourceless cheerful glow that threw into clear illumination the stacks of books, the intricately molded wine pitcher, the table, the ornate wooden chairs. Barach swept the empty cups and some stray books off the table and spread the map. It was in very large scale indeed, showing Cronbrach in much greater detail than any other chart Jeremy had yet seen.

"Here we are," Barach said once more, his pudgy finger coming down on an isolated peak in the Wizard's Mountains. He ran his finger north and west. "And here, Nul, was your home. Now, as you see—" his finger swept farther north— "the Bone Mountains really are just the southern spur of the great Fridhof range. And here is the Friddifor River, which flows through Twilight Valley." The old wizard traced the stream from west to east, where it emptied into the sea. "Very far north; I do not think we should risk traveling overland, even with the aid of the travel spell."

"It must be close to the edge of the world," Jeremy said.

Barach stared at him, his tangled gray eyebrows raised high in surprise. "What do you mean?"

"Well, the world is flat—"

Barach burst into laughter. "Flat! Wherever did you hear that?"

"I—I think Kelada told me."

The old wizard's eyes danced. "Jeremy, your wife is a very fine woman, and I think highly of her, but, bless her, she is not very educated. The world is a sphere, Jeremy; it's round."

Jeremy's cheeks burned. "My world was round, too."

"Haven't you noticed the globe in the—no, I suppose you haven't. Flat indeed!"

"Hey," Jeremy protested, "Thaumia is so different from Earth in all other ways that it seemed to make sense. As much sense as magic, anyhow."

"Sorry, Jeremy. I meant no insult," Barach said. "But let us get back to business: the travel-spell could take us with certainty to the Bone Mountains, perhaps, but no farther north than that."

"The, uh, anti-magic ore." Jeremy hoped he wasn't completely ignorant.

"Yes, quite correct. As I mentioned, the stone is called *mazerite*—the substance that impedes magic. There is a sort of field above the Fridhof Mountains that does not exactly negate all magic, but at least alters it in unpredicatable ways. If we attempted to travel directly to the Valley by the travel spell, we might wind up far at sea, or even on another continent altogether. The spell would *work* after a fashion, but we could not control it."

"How we go then? Long, long journey by land," Nul said. "In winter, two, three month anyway."

"The alternative is to go by sea," Barach said. "Dale Haven may be reached by the travel-spell—it's about five days overland from here, south and east—and there we may find a ship to take us to Fridport. The harbor there is often ice-choked in deep winter, but this time of year it should be open." Barach's finger returned to the mouth of the Friddifor. "Here's the port. Now, the valley is narrow here, at the place called the Gray Falls, as you see; but once you pass the falls here, it broadens. This is our goal."

"How long?" Nul asked.

Barach stroked his tangled beard. "A coasting vessel, heading north. I should say we'd make a speed of twenty leagues a day, at the least, and possibly a little better. Perhaps seven to ten days to Fridport. Then three or four days to the Valley."

The pika stared hard at the map. "When we leave?"

"As soon as we can be ready," Barach said. "But let us not be overly hasty. We go into the unknown, Nul. The people of Twilight Valley are rather like the pikas— they keep to themselves and rarely speak to outsiders. They will be sure to distrust us at first; and, to tell the truth, I hardly know how we will be able to deal with them. They are very different from us: self-willed mundanes in a world of magic. Even their tongue is strange."

"Nul will find a way to make them listen."

"But even if they listen," Jeremy warned, "they may not wish to help."

In a grim voice, the pika only repeated, "Nul will find a way."

* * *

They left each other past midnight. Jeremy went back to his tower room; Nul descended to the little chamber on the ground floor where he stayed. Alone, the pika wrapped himself in a blanket—his neglected fire had been out all day—and sat on a ledge by the window. His window, low to the courtyard, looked out to the north and west. He could see little, for the night was dark and the curtain wall here was only a few paces away from the castle wall. But he heard the ticking of the snow as it blew against the glass, and he felt the aching cold just beyond the thin panes.

His thoughts were nearly as dark and bitter as the night outside, full of memories, wishes, half-formed regrets. He began, very slowly, to rock back and forth to some inner rhythm, his mind wandering paths long forgotten, his heart feeling heavy in his chest.

If only I could speak all the sorrows of my heart, he thought to himself in his own tongue. *My brother Jare. If only the words would come for me, as they do for my friend Jeremy, like a flight of beautiful birds; if only they would obey my will as they do his. Then what mourning I would make for you, brother.*

Nul wore his usual winter outfit of brown leather breeches cut to accommodate his short legs, a tunic, and an overcoat. His feet were enclosed in soft leather boots, nearly shapeless things. He tugged them off and clenched and unclenched his six long toes. Pikas never wore shoes, ordinarily. Or human clothing. But then, in their snug underground homes, they never got cold.

Nul shivered and pulled his feet in under the blanket. *I am more than half a human*, he thought to himself. *I have lived too long among them, have become too used to their comforts. How do they see me, I wonder? Foolish, pitiable, lame dwarf. And how would my people see me? Mockery of alien flesh, wearing alien apparel.*

He sat that way for a long time, gently rocking, huddled gratefully in the warmth of the blanket. At last he sang, in a hoarse, whispering voice, a simple and plaintive tune that he remembered his father singing at his uncle Thol's burial so long ago. Now and again he had to pause to remember the pika words, but always he found them somehow, and the wavering voice would take up again the burden of the farewell song.

At last, the funeral dirge finished, Nul slumped before the dark window, wrapped in the blanket and wrapped almost as much in dim and misty memories of days long gone. Somehow, before dawn arrived, he fell into sleep, where he and Jare raced through narrow tunnels, splashed through underground streams, played in the flashing light of rubies that burned in their secret hearts with a ruddy fire.

CHAPTER 3

PREPARATIONS HAD TO be made for the journey: packing, planning, and plotting, as Kelada called it. Jeremy decided to wear the same type of thin, light mail he had worn on the expedition to the Hag's Valley the previous spring, and he would take with him the crossbow that even Captain Fallon grudgingly admitted he had mastered—though privately he hoped that no need for the weapon would arise. He had many questions to ask his teacher and his friend, but Barach closeted himself with Tremien, and Nul kept mostly to himself.

Jeremy did see the mummers off one cold, clear morning. A band of laughing gypsies they seemed, with their costumes and properties packed in half a dozen large, colorful trunks. Selurà Colt wore a robe of whitest fur, in startling contrast to her black hair, and she gave Jeremy a warm goodbye kiss; Kelada was not there, and at the moment he was glad she was absent.

Then Winyard, his breath rich with his fortifying glass of wine taken at parting, gave him a bone-crunching hug of farewell. "You have done the profession proud, my boy!" he proclaimed in high style. In his dark furs and hat, he seemed a burly bear rather than a man, but his florid gestures and grandly eloquent voice gave him human qualities, too. "Depend upon it, Jeremy: by the turning of two years you shall be the talk of the continent, celebrated in every gallery from—"

"We're late, Master Player," a younger actor said.

"So we are. How the hona fly when friends are together, eh?" Winyard slapped Jeremy hard on the back

36

and in somewhat more tentative tones added, "As to the canon of new dramas, my young friend. You, ah, will have a few new, fresh, and, as these first three are, eminently actable plays for us come spring?"

"At least one." Jeremy grinned, hoping he had managed to follow at least most of the player's elaborate syntax.

Winyard bent so close that Jeremy could again smell the morning's cup, or more likely bottle, of wine sour on his breath. "With a—you know—a good part for—for a man of—of a certain bearing and nobility—"

"I have in mind a wonderful part for you," Jeremy assured the actor.

"Why, then, it's farewell! We are off to the southern provinces, my lad, to scatter your fame throughout the land. Wish us the best of speed and think of us in the dark evenings of winter. Back a bit, Jeremy."

Jeremy stepped away from the brightly colored pyramid of trunks and actors in the courtyard. Winyard, with his usual declamatory style, pronounced a cantrip, and with a *pop!* more felt in the eardrum than actually audible, the troupe disappeared. Jeremy shook his head ruefully. He'd known a few actors back on Earth, though none quite so enthusiastically hammy as this mummer, who could make a simple "good morning" sound like a funeral elegy.

And now the old rogue wanted a part for a man of bearing and nobility, did he? Jeremy grinned to himself. Well, Winyard was gaining weight; why not give him Falstaff for next season? Barach recalled no exact parallel to *Henry IV*, but the story of a young prince and an aged rascal was universal enough to carry, he thought. And if other audiences like *Macbeth*—no, Jeremy corrected himself, *Kernow*—as much as those at Whitehorn had, the acting company would indeed find a great demand for these newfangled plays.

Alone and lost in thought, Jeremy climbed the steps to the wall-walk and strolled to the great gate. Fred and Busby brooded there on either side of him, colossal figures of sandy red stone staring down at the road that wound up the mountainside. The valley below was brown with winter, the trees bare, the Bronfal glistening here and there with white patches of ice. The snowfall had been light in the valley, though the summit of Whitehorn bore a respectable cover already. This morning the air was so achingly clear that everything, from the skeletal trees to the scattered blue smoke-trails from the foresters' hearths, stood out sharply.

"Has Tremien said anything to you?" asked the grating voice of Fred, from Jeremy's right.

Jeremy gave the gargoyle a startled look. The great hooked beak had not turned toward him, and the carved eyes still stared down and ahead, but beyond doubt Fred had spoken. "Has Tremien said anything about what?"

"You'll find out," said Fred, and if stone could laugh, Fred did.

Tremien saw him that evening. Barach, as usual, stood by, his arms folded, his gray beard sunk on his chest. "I have tried to send a message to the town masters of the Valley," Tremien said to Jeremy without preamble. "I have failed."

"They won't talk to a wizard," Barach explained. "They seem to think it against their religion."

"Be that as it may," Tremien muttered, "my messenger, a captain of a trading ship, sends word that they refused to talk with him. I am afraid your group will be very much on your own. I am sorry; I wish there were more I could do." The old sorcerer wore a long white linen robe trimmed in burgundy-colored satin, and over that a surplice of green velvet tied at the waist by a red sash, a more colorful display than his usual fashion of dress. Barach, in a plain tan robe like a monk's habit, looked positively plebeian by contrast, and Jeremy, in his baggy blue trousers, simple white shirt, and pale blue vest, appeared odd and outlandish beside them—or so he thought to himself, at any rate.

"We will just have to get along on our own," Barach said reasonably. "Don't worry so much; Jeremy lived the first twenty-seven years of his life without magic, and I've almost gotten used to having none. You know what a stout fellow little Nul is at heart. Give us a bit of credit for what we are, Tremien. Among us we should do well enough."

"Permit an old man his little worries," Tremien said. He heaved a great sigh. "Anyway, there is no rumor of trouble in the north, nor has there been for these many years, and that may be a good sign; though the people of the Valley are certainly so uncommunicative that I do not fully trust a lack of news. I truly believe that any hobs left there came with the invasion forty years ago; or at least that their sires and dams did. And I have begun to fathom, I think, the reason why they have lived while their fellows died."

"I wondered about that," Jeremy said.

Tremien turned his back to the fire, warming himself. "It is all very simple—and so hard for a cunning old fool like me to guess. In the battles around the Bone Mountains, the hobs were driven back time and again; indeed, the larger part of their army had vanished well before the general fall of the Great Dark One's forces.

"I now believe that, bested in battle, they fled underground, perhaps taking Nul's people as prisoners as they did so. And if they traveled north and came at last to rest in caverns beneath the Fridhof Mountains, they would be beyond any magic, ill or good."

"I think I see," Jeremy said slowly. "If the Great Dark One destroyed all his army when failure seemed imminent, he did so by spell. If the hobs were protected by the, uh, un-magic field—"

"Then they may have survived. And they may even believe the war is still raging," Tremien said. He shook his head, his long white beard swaying gently to the motion. "Transmute and ensorcel it! Had I guessed this earlier, our course would have been clear: take an army into the caverns of the Bone Mountains and pursue the quarry north. But I failed to guess the secret, and now we have long since lost that chance. The three of you will be unable to fight the hobs alone; your best hope is to win the people of the Valley to your need, to let them help you deal with the hobs and their danger."

Barach put his large hand on the old man's shoulder. "Old friend, you worry overmuch. Remember the tale of the race bewteen Hari and Melnanor: Hari vowed he would run the straight track, and Melnanor said he would look for the best of the way. Hari's path led over boulders, down ravines, and up steep slopes; Melnanor's was easy but long. And they both arrived at the same time."

"Yes, Barach," Tremien acknowledged, "there are separate paths to the same end; and perhaps, after all, diplomacy will be best. Still, I blame myself for not having acted earlier."

"You had great concerns, Master," Jeremy said. "If not for you, there would be no reason for this quest, for the Great Dark One would long ago have overthrown the north and all that's fair in it. No one, human, hob, or pika, would then be living to wait our coming."

"It is kind of you to say so," Tremien said. "Mage Jeremy, take my caution with you: do not attempt your strange magic of Earth when in the Valley. It is a curious sort of magic, and still not fully under your control. It might work, or work after a fashion, even in the caverns under the mountains; but then again, it might not, and in any case it would make enemies of the Valley dwellers at a time when you, Barach, and Nul sorely need friends."

"I will be careful."

"See that you are. The Great Dark One somehow put a bit of his power into the hobs, and I cannot imagine what foul deeds have been done in his name and his memory in the fastnesses of those caverns."

"We will leave tomorrow," Barach said.

"So soon?" Jeremy asked.

Tremien turned to warm his hands once more. "Pray it is not too late," he said into the fire. "Jeremy, there is one other thing: you will find a box on the desk. It is my gift to you for this journey."

Jeremy gave Barach a suspicious look, but the bearded, bland face showed no emotion. The young man walked to the desk and found there a large box made from thin wood, a chest perhaps one foot by two and about six inches deep. He opened the chest and took out a long gray hooded robe.

"I wore that long ago," Tremien said without looking around. "Ages before you were born. It has a virtue of warmth that is no imposed spell but part of its nature; it may be useful in the realms of snow and ice. See if it fits."

Jeremy donned the robe, found that it fastened down the right side with a series of intricate hooks and small gem-inset buttons. It felt wonderful, light and somehow extremely comforting. He cinched a blue sash in the manner of a belt and said, "It fits perfectly."

Tremien turned then. "So it does. Most handsome you look in it, to be sure. Far more handsome than did I, I expect, though she who gave it to me was kind enough to tell me otherwise." He smiled, an old man's smile of recollected joy. "Well, peace to her spirit, and long rest. Take care of the robe, for my sake and hers. It is warmer than you would think; and it may have other virtues about it as well, for all I know. May it serve you well!"

"Thank you, Master."

Barach cleared his throat. "Don't you think Jeremy should know the rest of the news?"

"The rest?" Tremien frowned. "About what?"

"Our companions," Barach prompted.

Tremien's white eyebrows rose. "Bless me, I had quite forgotten! You will have guides, Jeremy, should you be forced to venture underground."

"Guides? Who?"

Tremien blinked. "Why, Fred and Busby, of course. Dear me, I should have told you."

Jeremy tossed restlessly, fell asleep late, and awakened early. The good weather held, as he saw with a glance out of the window: the sky overhead was velvety black, spangled with frosty stars. While he stood at the window, Kelada came up behind him and put her arms around him. "You will be careful," she said.

"Always."

"I wish I could come too."

He took her in his arms. "Somebody has to stay and help Tremien run things."

"When did he accept anyone's help?"

Jeremy kissed her. "Look at it this way. If you're here, you know I've got to come home safely."

For a time they did not think or speak of the journey. But eventually the sun rose, and Jeremy dressed himself warmly. He carried most of his travel things in a pack; folded in it now too, and taking up surprisingly little space, was the robe Tremien had given him.

The castle was astir by the time Jeremy and Kelada came down. Tremien seemed to have a hundred obscure relatives and loyal retainers, and at any given time half of them or more were actually living in the castle. This morning, however, Jeremy and Kelada did not join them for breakfast in the main dining hall, but ate a quiet meal with Barach, Tremien, and Nul in a smaller private room. Jeremy tucked in with a will; among the animals imported to Thaumia from Earth were swine and chickens, and this morning he enjoyed a double helping of bacon and eggs, together with plenty of milk and slabs of toasted brown bread spread with butter.

"This husband of yours has been in training too long, Kelada," Barach observed with an amused expression. "See how he pigs himself!"

"The body needs fuel," Jeremy responded with a greasy smile.

Nul, more silent than ever, hardly even looking up from his plate, ate his breakfast of bread and fruit—he ate flesh only occasionally and some time before had sworn off fish. He was dressed for the road, too, in leather coat and woolen trousers, with somewhat heavier boots than normal on his three-toed feet. Tremien, his attention focused on the little pika, was likewise quiet throughout the meal.

When all had finished, they went out to the castle gate. The morning was bright but decidedly bitter; Jeremy, his pack resting comfortably on his back and the crossbow slung over his left shoulder, found himself wishing that he had taken out the cloak before leaving the warmth of the castle. Barach wore a fur coat and hat, and even Tremien had slipped into enveloping furs. They all stood in sunlight before the gate, where from atop their pillars the two gargoyles glared down.

"Now," Tremien said. "Your companions will join you." He pronounced an arcane incantation couched,

Jeremy was sure, in some obscure tongue for greater efficacy, and it drifted away from his lips in clouds of shining vapor.

The gargoyles began to move.

Fred stretched himself like a cat, the stretch beginning at his head, arching through his neck, bowing his back, and leaving by means of his hind legs and tail. Busby seemed to swell and puff and then to shrink in on himself. Both gargoyles began to climb head-first down the outer wall.

"This is ridiculous," Jeremy said. "How can those huge—" He broke off. The gargoyles were climbing toward him, but they seemed at the same time to be receding.

"They're shrinking!" Kelada cried.

They were indeed shrinking. The size of two healthy draft horses at the top of their pillars, they were only man-sized halfway down; pika-sized three quarters of the way down; and cat-sized when they bounded free and landed on the frosty ground. Jeremy laughed despite himself.

Now that they were small, he could for the first time see differences between Fred and Busby. Both were composite monsters, with reptilian shoulders and hindquarters, the forequarters and paws of some great cat, and raptor-like heads and beaks; but Fred's features were more like those of a hawk, lean and keen, while Busby's face looked like an eagle's, sterner of eye and somewhat more hooked of beak. "Holiday," Fred grated, and his voice was still that of grinding stone. "It hasn't come too quickly for me, I promise you."

"Not holiday, youngster," Busby admonished. "Quest. Questing is serious business."

"You two behave yourselves now," Tremien said. Turning to Jeremy, he confided, "They can be a confounded nuisance at times, but they may be of great help. Like the mountains of the north, these two are made of naturally enchanted stone, and they have their own abilities that will come to your aid on demand. They need not sleep, eat, or drink; they will prove good sentinels. And once you are underground—if you are driven to that extremity—you may find they have other skills and powers as well. But no magic is sure in the far north, so I commend them to your care, Jeremy, and to yours, Barach. May they serve and guard you well!"

"Too much talk," Fred complained, prancing like an impatient cat. "Let's be off."

"Patience, gatekeeper," Tremien said. "Now: all ready? Last farewells, then, and take with you our best wishes. Jeremy, wish Kelada well; Barach, my old friend, fare you well, and use my gifts and advice to best advantage; and most of all, Nul, may your seeking end in joy. Now, make ready." Tremien and Kelada backed away, and Tremien pronounced a special variant of the travel-spell that Winyard and his acting troupe had used: in this case modified into a sort of send-spell that would transport non-magical beings like Barach, or alien ones, like Jeremy and Nul—and even stone ones like the two gargoyles, as it appeared.

The swirling colors of the spell enveloped them all. Jeremy felt the odd sensation of falling and spinning, and they were on their way.

Instantly (from Tremien's point of view) and almost an hour later (from their own), the travelers popped into existence again. Jeremy's ears crackled from the change of pressure: they had traveled from a mountainside to sea level, and for a moment the pain was intense. Then he swallowed and it passed.

"Well," Barach observed, "we're all here."

Jeremy blinked at his surroundings. "Here" was a sandy hillside overlooking a crowded little seaside town and harbor and, beyond that to the east, a great wrinkled gray sea. They were a mile or more from the town, but even at this distance they could see the bustle and movement in the streets as men and animals hurried to and fro. A forest of masts showed on the far side of the town, ships docked at piers, no doubt; beyond them, in the harbor itself, more ships waited at anchor, wooden sailing vessels broad in the beam and round in the prow.

"Mica," pronounced Busby from somewhere down at Jeremy's feet. The dwindled gargoyle sat on his haunches and in his forepaws held up a glittering piece of mineral the size of a small coin. "The sand's rich with it."

"Mostly quartz sand," Fred added, nosing the ground. "Very smooth from wave action—"

"Here, you two. I think you had better stay out of sight," Barach declared, stooping to pick up both gargoyles. "Umph! You're heavier than you look. Jeremy, do you want Fred or Busby?"

"Ah—Fred," Jeremy said, for the younger gargoyle's personality somehow seemed more compatible with his own. The ex-wizard carefully handed over the gargoyle, which indeed felt surprisingly heavy in Jeremy's hands. It was a curious sensation, holding the creature: the gargoyle was hard as stone and yet mobile, alive, under his touch. "I suppose you could ride in my pack," Jeremy said.

"Aww . . ." Fred whined. "Couldn't I pretend to be a statue or something?"

"Later," Barach said. He was already dropping Busby into the huge floral-patterned carpetbag he carried. "And no noise out of you, now."

Jeremy slipped Fred into his backpack and felt the straps take a new bite into his shoulders with the increased weight. They started downhill, and Jeremy noticed that Nul, who also wore a pack, was carrying and using a short staff. The pika's limp, under the combined problems of weight and the descending slope, was noticeable. Jeremy felt a twinge of guilt; Nul had suffered torture at the hands of the Hidden Hag of Illsmere, and the limp was the memorial of that bad time, a time when Jeremy had had to turn his back on one friend to save all the others.

But Nul bore up stoically enough, and before long the three travelers came to the outskirts of Dale Haven. The salt scent of the ocean was strong here, along with the smells of fish, tar, and alcohol. The buildings were all two or three stories tall, top stories often projecting out over the cobbled streets, sometimes by several feet. Barach seemed to know their destination, and Nul and Jeremy fell into step behind him. The streets were busy: carts drawn by donkeys or horses rumbled over the cobbles, loudly when empty, groaningly when laden with wares bound for storage houses or for market. Cats abounded in the streets, somewhat surprising Jeremy; whereas oxen, cattle, goats, swine, and sheep seemed to have made the transition from Earth readily enough back in the dim past, the smaller domestic animals were scarce.

But here cats were in more than abundant supply: tabby cats, black cats, orange cats; short-haired cats and long-haired cats; sleek fat cats and scrawny ear-torn skulkers. Once a larruping hound appeared, scattering a hissing group of five or six felines; then, as if proud of himself, he trotted alongside Jeremy for a while, head high and chest swollen. Jeremy grinned. The dog was of no particular breed, a medium-muzzled mongrel with short brown hair, much like the farm dogs his grandfather had been inclined to adopt back in the hills of North Georgia long ago. "Hey, pup," Jeremy said softly in his own language. The dog looked up, ran out a dripping pink tongue, and grinned. But then he spotted another cat, sneaking into an alley, and bayed off after new quarry.

Jeremy looked around. They were deep in the town now, following crooked blind streets and attracting the occasional notice of passers-by, who seemed to regard Nul with a sort of bemused interest. Pikas had always been rare, so that was no wonder. Indeed, the surprising thing was that Nul attracted so very little attention; but then, Jeremy told himself, strange sights must be common in seaports everywhere.

"Finally. Here we are," Barach said, drawing up short. Before them was an inn, tidy and small, bearing a signboard that pictured a sinuous sea serpent rearing above a ship tiny by comparison. "The Sea Dragon. The owner owes Tremien more than one favor, and he's been put in charge of finding us passage. A man named Abdaliel."

They entered the common room, a room panelled in some light wood and floored with rush-strewn stone. A dozen or so tables were scattered about, and in the morning light from the bay windows Jeremy saw they were all unoccupied, save for one at which a man dozed, face on the board, arms outflung, drunk or sleeping off drink.

A bell tinkled overhead as Jeremy closed the door. A moment later a fat, bald little man, his chin just frosted with a closely clipped gray beard, came bustling in, drying his hands on an apron. "Bless me, if it isn't Barach!" he exclaimed, throwing wide his hands.

Barach dropped his carpetbag ("Oof!" grunted a stony, muffled voice within) and embraced the man. "Abdaliel, as I live! How are you keeping, fellow?"

Abdaliel pushed back to arm's length. "Well, well. Well enough. And this is the young gentleman Tremien spoke of? Jeremy Moon, was it? Outlandish name! Abdaliel, young sir. I've a special request for dainty food for the father-to-be! And Nul: still thirst for my ale, do you, pika?"

Nul grinned. "Good ale," he said.

"Good! He calls my ale merely good! Why, you miserable fur-bearing ape, you know my ale's the best in the country. Has to be. Has to be. That's my speciality, you know." Abdaliel turned his attention and his bright blue eyes to Jeremy. "Enchantments of food and drink. Increase the quantity, enhance the quality. Why, I kept an entire army fed once, did I not, Barach?"

"Indeed you did, old friend. A strange war that was, where our men went into battle thin and ready and came out fat and indolent!"

"But here, you need to settle into your rooms and have somewhat to eat. After that there'll be some time for yarning, eh? Your passage is all arranged; no, news of that later. For now just know that you'll be spending the night under my roof, and tomorrow night out on the broad ocean, God help the three of you. This way, this way. Best rooms in the Haven I've saved for you."

The rooms were indeed good ones, small but orderly and neat—shipshape, Jeremy thought to himself. In fact, everything about the little inn, from its pegged furniture to the low ceilings and, on the second floor, its round windows, reminded Jeremy of sailing ships. But instead of a hammock his room boasted a soft bed, and the floor was steady enough beneath his feet. As he unslung his

pack, Jeremy wondered for a fleeting second how well
he'd stand up to a sea voyage; a cabin cruiser on Lake
Lanier was the closest he'd ever come to such a thing
back home, and he suspected somehow that experience would bear little resemblance to a trip aboard a real
ship.

He dropped the pack on the bed and for a moment
shivered as it moved of its own accord. Then he almost
laughed aloud. He had forgotten Fred.

"Out of there," he said, opening the pack. A beaked
head poked out, glanced around, and then emerged, and
after it the gargoyle's long body.

"Stuffy," Fred commented as he went through another
luxurious head-to-tail stretch.

"I didn't think you breathed," Jeremy said.

"I can smell. It smells stuffy." The gargoyle leaped
from the bed, landing on a round brown and yellow
bull's-eye rug with a muffled crash.

"Watch that!" Jeremy said as he carefully stood his
crossbow in a corner. "You'll have Abdaliel in here
complaining about noise in a minute."

But Fred was inspecting the fireplace. A small fire
burned there, more for appearance's sake than for utility, since the weather in Dale Haven was considerably
warmer than that on the shoulders of Whitehorn Mountain. "Good solid granite, well worked," Fred pronounced.
Then he jumped right into the fireplace, the flames licking his sides.

"Hey!" Jeremy shouted. "You'll burn yourself!"

"Humpf. It would have to be a hotter fire than this."

Jeremy squinted through the flames. "What are you
doing? Eating *soot*?" The gargoyle, stretched across the
flames, appeared to be doing just that, rasping his tongue
over the deposit at the rear of the fireplace.

"Cleaning. Hmm. Firebrick of southern make. Good
quality, too; looks like a white clay base, with a mixture
of—"

Jeremy rolled his eyes. "Get out of there."

Fred left the fire, a little reluctantly, Jeremy thought.
His sides were streaked with smoke, and he left little

black footprints on the rug. "Now wait!" Jeremy ordered. "Look what you're doing."

A ewer and basin waited on a stand at the foot of the bed. Jeremy wet a cloth and scrubbed the gargoyle as well as he could. "You're going back into the pack," he told the creature.

"Aww . . ."

"Unless you have any better idea."

"Statue?"

"You'll be still?" Jeremy asked in what he hoped was a stern voice.

"Sure. I'm still day in and day out at the castle."

"Strike a pose."

The gargoyle sat on its haunches, curved its tail around its bottom and up the side of its left hind leg, and as an afterthought raised its right forepaw in a gesture of feline menace. "How's this?"

"Fine," Jeremy said. "You want to be on the mantel?"

"Aww . . ."

"Where, then?"

"So I can see out the window. Please."

Jeremy moved the washstand to the portholelike window and set Fred on it, turning him this way and that. "Good," Fred said, when Jeremy had adjusted his view.

"Stay," Jeremy said before he left the room.

Nul, in the room next door, had stripped off his coat and his boots—he always seemed more comfortable barefoot—and lay on the bed with his hands clasped on his stomach. "Rooms good," he said as Jeremy entered. "Ale, too, when Abdaliel has it ready. You like."

Jeremy nodded. "Well, we're off tomorrow. I hope we find your people, Nul."

"Nul hope so too." The pika raised himself to a sitting position. "Tremien very good to me," he said slowly. "You, Kelada, Barach, all very good. But not my own people, you know? Always in here—" he touched his chest— "is a longing to see them. Or to know they dead."

"How will you feel if we do find that out, Nul? That all your people are dead?"

The orange eyes dropped. "Bad. But worse if I not

know at all. That what I fear: long journey, nothing at the end of it. That would be worse than the other.''

Someone rapped at the door, and Jeremy opened it to find Barach. "That gargoyle," the old man said as he came into the room. "He broke his blessed little piece of mica, and I still haven't heard the end of it. 'If I hadn't dropped him so hard. If I'd wrapped his mica for him.' I wonder if my idea was a bright one, after all.''

"I had a little trouble with Fred, too. He seems to be, ah, restless," Jeremy said.

"We ought to do something with them." Barach sighed, sinking into the room's one vacant chair. "They *are* restless, because all this is new to them. They've been animate before, several times, though never to my knowledge in such reduced size. But always before they had duties of war, protection of the castle, to keep them busy. Now they're apt to get into mischief—and to cause us all sorts of problems.''

"Is our mission—well, secret?" Jeremy asked.

Nul barked his hoarse laugh. "Anything Tremien does secret.''

Barach smiled indulgently beneath his gray moustaches. "Now, now, Nul. Watch your manners. But it is true that our old friend believes in caution. I don't think the Great Dark One, or any of his spies, could possibly know of or be interested in our journey; still, you never know. It's like the old story of the frog and the pitcher—''

"No story," groaned Nul. "Barach's stories all make pika's head hurt.''

Barach sniffed. "As you wish. I was only going to observe that it's as well not to let everyone know of our purpose or even of our journey.''

"How about this?" Jeremy asked slowly. "I could work up an illusion-spell on the two gargoyles. They're about the same size and general build as some of these cats I've seen around. I can cast a glamour that will make them appear to be cats. Then they can have more freedom of movement without attracting too much attention.''

Barach thought it over. "Good," he said. "Of course, I do not know whether the enchantment will hold as we near our goal. I suspect that it will fade, in fact. But for

our stay in the inn and our journey by sea, yes, that
seems a good notion. Shall we work out the parameters
in your room?''

"Nul?"

"Go, go," Nul grunted. "Nul sleep little bit then eat.
Then time for ale."

They left him on the bed. "I'm worried about him,"
Jeremy confided in the corridor. "He's so lifeless."

"He has many fears, and yet he will not show them,"
Barach said. "Pikas are very strong people, Jeremy; but
sometimes it is not good for even a strong person to be
too secret. We must let him open himself to us, when the
time comes and he is ready. That, I think, may prove
truer friendship than this or any journey we may undertake. Well. I'll fetch Busby and meet you in your room."

It took the rest of the morning to work out the spell in
Presolatan, the standard language of this part of Thaumia,
and to translate the terms into English. Jeremy had discovered long ago that his gift of words, his ability to
write ads, stood him in good stead here; for in Thaumia,
which seemed made of magic and matter as Earth was
made of energy and matter, spoken spells could trigger
sorcerous changes. True, all the changes tended toward a
kind of mundane entropy in the end; but the change was
so small and gradual that it made no appreciable difference in the short run.

It was true, too, that once a spell was spoken and
completely worked, it lost its virtue. Spells like Walther's
Fast Travel were special ones, Great Spells painstakingly
worked out so that each time a travel cantrip was pronounced, it formed only a minute part of a much vaster
spell. One day, though, all the virtue would be at last
used up, and someone else would have to spend long
years working out another unimaginably intricate series
of sounds to create another travel-spell.

As for Jeremy, his language and his skills gave him
certain strange advantages. If English speakers had ever
journeyed to Thaumia—and it seemed certain that some
had, to judge from the names of certain places, domestic
plants, and animals—then their language had taken no
hold. Jeremy's contemporary American was a whole new

dialect here, and as such it had great potential for triggering magical reactions.

Jeremy's training as a copywriter also helped. Magic spells, after all, had to have a certain shape and weight to work properly; and the structure of advertising language seemed to work nearly as well as the poetry Barach favored. True, Jeremy's ability to control his magic still was touch and go; but he had used his spell-casting to get out of several tight spots and his confidence in it was growing.

Jeremy and Barach decided not to attempt any actual change in the gargoyles, for the shaping of living matter—even of living stone—was an exhausting and very tricky process indeed; it had driven the Hag mad, Barach thought. But illusion was much easier. In the forenoon ona Jeremy pronounced his new spell, and Barach grunted appreciatively as the figures of the two gargoyles seemed to shimmer and soften. "That will do," Jeremy's teacher said.

The gargoyles blinked green eyes at each other. Fred had become a fluffy tiger-striped orange cat; Busby was equally furry but a gray tabby in appearance, with a blaze of white on his chest and a black capital *M* between his eyes. "Ho," Fred snorted. "You're funny."

"You're a sight yourself," growled Busby.

"Get the glass from the wall," Barach said.

Jeremy took the small looking glass from its nail over the spot where his washstand had originally stood. The gargoyles admired themselves extravagantly.

"Now," Barach said, rising from his seat on the edge of the bed, "be off with the two of you. Run through the streets if you please. Count the blessed cobblestones. Sort them and arrange them to your hearts' content. But be back at the inn here by midnight! Understand?"

Jeremy opened the window for them. With wonderful alacrity, the two dropped to the projecting porch roof below, leaped from there to the branches of a bare ash tree, and went whirling down its trunk. They scampered off together, dodging the feet of dray horses and the rolling, rumbling wheels of carts. "I hope they'll be all right," Jeremy said.

"They will be," Barach assured him as Jeremy closed the window.

"I don't know. It's a strange city, and they're certainly strange cats."

Barach spread his hands. "That is true. However, do not overlook their advantages. They're bright, quick, and really pretty level-headed under it all. And besides, what, short of a sledgehammer, could hurt them?"

"True." Jeremy grinned. "I think I fooled myself into thinking they were cats."

"Ah," Barach twinkled. "Then you are like Gassoon the Conjuror."

"A story?"

"And a most instructive one. But let me tell it over luncheon, for I am hungry. And it is a story that Nul should hear, too. Why should I let you alone have all the benefit of my learning?"

"A question I have often asked myself," Jeremy replied gravely. He dodged out the door just ahead of the old man's kick.

Abdaliel set a good board. The common room was a cacophony of laughter and shouted orders when the three travelers came downstairs. "Local trade. Town-folk," Barach said to Jeremy's questioning look. "Most of them, anyway. Some sailors over there in the corner."

Following Barach's gaze, Jeremy saw the group, sitting at the table farthest from the bay window: a dark-clad company, a little exotic even for Thaumia with their baggy white caps, woolen sweaters, and loose-legged trousers, all in shades of blue from the color of midnight to a faded denim. They were eating with a will, laughing at occasional sallies of bawdy wit directed at the serving girls, and arguing among themselves in a good-humored way.

The rest of the company was more ordinary. Jeremy saw a few men and women in the robes of lower-level magicians, but most were simply red-faced, boisterous townspeople: shopkeepers, small farmers, fishermen. Abdaliel came bustling up. "Saved a table for you," he puffed. "In the chimney corner there. A bit quieter, I think."

The small table, shoved against the wall in the nook between the chimney and the kitchen wall, was indeed a little more private than most. They made their way to it, and Barach entrusted their meal to Abdaliel. "Whatever you think is good today," he said. "And some of that famous ale."

Nul, who had ensconced himself on a high stool so that he could comfortably reach the table, said, "Ale. Yes. Lots of ale for Nul, please, Abdaliel."

The innkeeper beamed. "Small as you are, Nul, you have a delicate taste in drink, if I may say so. The girls will bring your food and ale, friends." Abdaliel turned and bustled away, fairly radiating pleasure. As for Nul, he followed the departure with hungry (or perhaps thirsty) eyes.

Barach leaned a little closer to Jeremy, to be heard above the din, and confided, "It will be plain but hearty fare. Abdaliel was never one to scant his guests, and we are special friends. But you ate well at breakfast this morning. Be aware of that and moderate your appetite."

"I suppose that doesn't apply to you," Jeremy grinned. "In fact, it's obvious from your stomach—"

"I," Barach said with vast dignity, "am not a sorcerer in training."

The food was good, plentiful, and as hearty as Barach had promised: a steaming fish chowder (even Nul, who had given up on fish after having been forced to eat almost nothing else for several weeks, enjoyed it), followed by a roasted poultry dish with a delicately spiced flavor, vegetables (Jeremy recognized only green peas, glazed with a peppery white sauce, but the native vegetables were good, too), and—ah, yes—Abdaliel's famous ale.

"Wonderful," Jeremy pronounced after his first sip. The brew was deeply brown, rich and malty, robust and full-bodied. "Now, this I could sell back on Earth," he announced. "Barach, why don't the two of us set up a system of trade between Thaumia and my old home? You and I could grow rich by marketing this stuff."

Barach, who had just taken a long and appreciative drink, delicately wiped foam from his moustaches. "A kind thought, apprentice. But thank you, no. At my time of life, what use have I for wealth?"

"Another," Nul said eagerly, having drained his entire pewter stein, a little more than an earthly pint, at one long pull. His round, pointed black tongue licked his almost nonexistent lips.

Jeremy laughed and poured from the generous pitcher that Abdaliel's serving girl had left behind. "Well, if Barach won't join me in business, how about you, Nul? You'd be a terrific spokesman," he said.

Nul, savoring the second brew more slowly, frowned, his wide mouth flecked with foam. "Not understand."

"You would tell people how good the ale is," Jeremy explained. "You'd speak for the product. We'd put you on—television, I'm afraid there's no Presolatan word for that—"

"Tel-ee-viss-ion," Nul pronounced. "That English?"

"Yes."

Nul made a face. "Ugly language. Difficult words. Even harder than Presolatan for pika tongue to say. Anyway, Nul not good talker."

"I would write the words for you to say."

Nul took a long pull at his ale. "Nul tell people how good he think ale is. But you write words for him to say. So his words your words, not really his words. Right?"

"Right."

"Ah," Nul said. "Nul understand. More, like Kelada say, ad-ver-tis-ing. *Spokesman* is another word for *liar*."

Jeremy shook his head ruefully. "I'm afraid you've got me there."

From behind Jeremy came a gravelly voice: "What ya got there, inlander?"

Startled, Jeremy turned, his stein frozen halfway to his lips. One of the sailors, a grizzled, wiry figure in dark blue, stood behind him. Barach, who had similarly been taken by surprise, murmured, "What do you mean?"

The man badly needed a shave, and his eyes were more than a little bloodshot. He nodded his head toward

Nul. "That critcher there. What is it? Some kind o' southern monkey, now? Ya maybe looking to sell it?"

Nul growled.

Barach smiled, but his expression was wary. "You've made a mistake, sir. Nul is our friend, not our property."

The sailor shoved close beside Jeremy, put both beefy hands on the table, and leaned far over to stare at Nul. "Never seed the like, not me. Is it real, or one of them, now, stuffed critchers? Is it enchanted or something? Did ya somehow bring life to a old skin with—"

At the mention of *skin* Nul leaped onto the table and swung his heavy pewter stein. It caught the sailor by surprise, cracking against his forehead with a resounding blow.

With one angry voice, the sailor's companions sprang up. The man himself, stunned, shook his head as if in bafflement, and raised his head toward the pika. Nul hit him again, this time a hard downward blow.

Jeremy had leaped up, his chair crashing to the floor behind him. "Nul, no!"

But the stein had already found its mark again. The sailor collapsed to the table and slid backward onto his butt, then flopped to the floor. He rolled onto his stomach, grunted, and lay still. "Get him!" one of his companions roared, and Jeremy turned to see the other five sailors crowding toward their nook.

"Damn," he muttered. Barach stepped over the fallen man and closed ranks.

"Back, all of you," he said in a commanding tone. "This man offered our friend insult, and he is justly repaid. No great harm is done to him."

"Yah, well, he's *our* friend," returned the lead sailor, a truly imposing figure. Jeremy looked at the man's bulging arms with a sick, sinking feeling.

"I," Barach said quietly, "am a Mage and a magician of the Council, as my robe proclaims. Think again before you decide to fight us."

The sailors hesitated at that bit of news, looking at each other uncertainly.

"Mages bleed red," the leader growled.

But still they paused. The other diners had, quietly,

pushed away from their meals and unfinished ale and had moved to the front of the common room, where they stood watching, apparently unwilling either to take sides or to miss the promised brawl.

Jeremy was acutely aware that the three of them were hemmed in, caught between the sailors and the wall. Nul, still standing on the table, tried to shove past Barach and Jeremy. "Let them come," he growled. "Fight them all."

"Shut up," Jeremy whispered.

The standoff might have lasted seconds longer, had not the window exploded.

Jeremy at first thought the sailors had made a move, but he realized they were just as surprised as he; and then he saw a furry orange form scrambling across a table, leaping, landing with a thud on the next table, and leaping again. Through the open inn door roared a dog, either the one he had seen earlier or another just like it, ears flopping and mouth wide with the canine excitement of pursuit.

The cat caught sight of Jeremy and jumped to the floor. The dog bayed after it.

"My inn!" wailed Abdaliel from somewhere behind the crowd.

"Get out o' here!" one of the sailors shouted, slapping at the dog's nose. The startled hound yelped, did a somersault, and streaked yipping out the front door, tail between his legs.

"And you," the big sailor said, kicking the cat viciously.

The cat moved perhaps a foot. The sailor sat down hard on the stone floor, howling: "My toe! I busted my toe!"

"Oh, great," Jeremy sighed as the cat clambered up his leg and onto the table. "Wonderful timing, Fred."

CHAPTER 4

THE EPISODE MIGHT have ended differently had no harbor warden been attracted by the smashing glass. One was, however, and he loomed in the doorway. "Here, now, what's the row?" he asked, fingering his baton.

The sailors melted into the crowd—all but the two on the floor, one unconscious, the other cradling his injured foot. Jeremy gulped. The harbor warden was *huge*—beside him even the lead sailor looked almost normal. The crowd made way for him as he lumbered in.

Abdaliel was at his side in a moment. "Nothing serious, Hrawald. Just a little high spirits, ha-ha." His laughter sounded worse than any possible plea for help.

Hrawald, an enormous figure of a man with fiery hair and a blunt, broken face, slipped the toe of one boot under the unconscious sailor's stomach and flipped him as easily as Abdaliel could have turned a griddlecake. The sailor rolled bonelessly to his back and opened his mouth in a drunken, guttering snore.

"They started it all," the other sailor said, with a nod toward Jeremy and Barach. He had pulled his shoe off and was gingerly working his big toe back and forth.

"So you started it, eh?" Hrawald said, looming over Barach.

"Nonsense," Barach puffed, looking almost straight up into the warden's red face. "The man on the floor there came to our table and insulted us. We did nothing to him."

" 'Nothing' put those walloping great lumps on his head, then?"

58

"Nah!" Nul had finally managed to outflank Jeremy. "I do that."

Hrawald's head retreated backward as he inspected Nul with a dubious eye. "You did, eh? H'm! A different story, then. What did y' do it with?"

Nul held up his stein. It was battered almost flat on the side opposite the handle.

"Hmm," Hrawald ruminated. "I expect that would do it." His broad cheeks began to twitch. "So, you with the foot. This little whatever-it-is beat up your mate, that it?"

"Yah," the sailor said. He got up and tried his weight on his injured right foot. "Ow!"

"He stomp on your toes, too?"

"No. I hurt my foot by—" The sailor broke off and blushed through his deep-water tan.

"Go on."

"By kicking a cat," he murmured in a contrite tone.

Hrawald's belly began to twitch, too. "And where's the cat?"

The sailor pointed to the table. Hrawald peered around Jeremy's shoulder, and Jeremy himself looked back. Fred, still in feline guise, was industriously washing his paws. He stopped long enough to blink his great green eyes and murmur "Merow?" in polite inquiry.

"Soft toe and hard cat," Hrawald mused. "Well. What do we propose to do about this run-in?"

Barach sighed. "Let us just forget about it. I'll buy ale for all, and we'll call it even."

The unconscious sailor opened one eye. "Ale?" he said in the kind of voice that implied he would lapse again into unconsciousness if denied.

"That's what the gentleman said," Hrawald rumbled, stooping to grasp the sailor by the neck and set him upright. "Abdaliel, start drawing."

Abdaliel and his two barmaids had much ado to fetch and carry, Hrawald himself put away a prodigious quantity of ale. "At any rate," Barach observed philosophically, "Tremien's rich enough to afford it. Perhaps you'd better see Nul and, ah, the cat upstairs."

Jeremy saw the wisdom of the suggestion. He accompanied the pika up to the rooms, and Fred trotted along behind, his clumping steps louder than any real cat's had ever been. "Sorry," Nul growled. "That man—"

"I know," Jeremy said. "But Barach's right. Our trip may not be exactly secret, but we'd do better to avoid attracting too much attention."

Fred climbed up to Nul's washstand. "For myself, I believe that any creature that would kick another so much smaller deserves a little pain. However, it was partly my fault, and I am sorry as well," he said, though his voice held little contrition.

"What was the idea of running like that, anyway? That dog couldn't have hurt you."

Fred lapsed into his old gargoyle pose: out of habit, Jeremy imagined. "I thought it was a game. I saw the brown animal chasing other animals like my form, and so I thought it would be sport to let him chase me."

"Through the *window*?"

"A miscalculation on my part. I thought I was heading for the open door. I was looking back over my shoulder at the dog, you see—"

"No great harm done, I suppose," Jeremy said, thinking of the windows he had broken in his time. "Where is Busby?"

"Roaming the alleys, I think. He is much interested in the foundations of some of the older houses."

"As long as he's back by midnight."

Barach tapped on the door and came inside. "Eleven silvers," he groaned. "And some-odd coppers to reglaze the window."

"Is there any problem?"

"Not really. At least I hope not. The sailors are gone— went reeling away to a wine-shop, I expect, to see if they can get a little drunker than they are now."

"It what he said about skin," Nul said, sounding really unhappy at the admission.

"I know, I know." Barach stroked his beard. "It was a cruel thing to say, though spoken in ignorance. Well, no more of this. Tonight we'll have dinner sent up, I think. Jeremy, what do you propose to do with your time?"

"I hadn't thought about it."

"I have several old friends in Dale Haven I'd like to call on. If you wish, you and Nul can go with me."

"Nah, nah," the pika said immediately. "Nul stay in room. Sleep. Not get stared at."

Jeremy smiled. "It's kind of you to offer, Barach, but I'd feel in the way. I may walk around town a bit, if that's permitted."

"Certainly," Barach said. "Cronbrach is a free land. Just stay out of trouble."

"I'll go with him," Fred pronounced.

"Now," Barach said, "I *am* worried."

Jeremy and Fred strolled from the inn to the waterfront, where a forest of masts sprang up. The docks smelled wonderfully of tar, fish, spices, sweat, and salt. Men hauled and lifted bales of cargo from some ships; others sat idle, sails furled, flags barely moving in the soft harbor breeze. It was a sight that had been seen nowhere on Earth since the days of the great sailing ships, and it was an absorbing spectacle. Jeremy saw that the harbor was broad here at the town and narrow toward the sea, roughly key-shaped. As he watched, a three-masted ship, rigged fore and aft like a barque, sailed out into the ocean, leaning gracefully as it began to tack to the south.

A larger vessel was being rigged closer in to shore. Jeremy watched the sailors use magic spells—though at a distance he could not hear them—to witch the sheets up and through the blocks, then back down to the belaying pins. Fred climbed upon a piling and sat there staring out at the harbor. "Very great water," he said.

"The ocean. Haven't you heard of it?"

"Heard of it. Never seen it. When the original stone was brought to Cronbrach from the Islands it was uncarved, and I had no eyes to see with."

"Tell me about yourself," Jeremy said. "I don't believe I've ever heard about living stone."

Fred struck his habitual pose, which was not out of place for a cat. "Magic shows up in different forms," he said. "In one particular place on some islands far to the south, it showed up as living stone. There was never much of it: just one deposit, and that one not very thick. Both of us came from there. Once Busby and I were the same."

"You mean you shared consciousness?"

" 'Shared' is not quite the word; it says that there were two of us. But there was only one consciousness then. The slow awareness of stone. The ages of ice were our nights; the ages of sun were our days. Then a wizard, not Tremien, discovered us and taught us to speak. From us he had stories out of the ancient times, for he was thirsty for knowledge.

"In return, he asked us what we wanted. We wanted to be free to move. He showed us we could do that already—but we had no shape for movement. And so he quarried the block of living stone to bring it to a master sculptor here in this land. The sculptor studied for a long time and then began to shape it. Good as he was, there was one accident: we broke apart along an old fault line, and so he made two gargoyles of us, and since then we have had two minds."

"And you can move."

"Yes, when we wish. But the more we travel among humans, the less there seems to see. Forgive me, but you of flesh and bone are so—temporary. Things of stone like us, now—they endure."

Jeremy began, "I know one man who—" He broke off, suddenly aware that a stevedore nearby had paused in his labor and was looking at him. "Nice kitty," Jeremy said, petting Fred. Fred gave him an amused green-eyed look.

Damn, Jeremy thought, *it's a good spell; he even feels like a cat.*

The dockworker's supervisor yelled at him, and the man hefted a shaggy, rope-cinched bale of something to his shoulder and tramped off.

"Talking to a cat," Fred said. "He thinks your head has a little fault in it, maybe."

"He'd think worse if I were talking to a gargoyle," Jeremy said.

"What were you saying? Something about a man who was not temporary?"

"Oh. The Great Dark One. He's lived for thousands of years."

"An eyeblink to a good sturdy shale."

"Point taken. Let's go see what else we can see."

They passed a chapel where a wedding had just taken place. The bride and groom, both rosy-faced, stood in a circle of well-wishers, and little boys and girls darted in and around their elders, defying orders to settle down. They passed a gambling house where seamen loudly played nine-spot and argued over the bets; they passed taverns and warehouses, homes and shops. Toward sundown, Jeremy paused, looked around him, and confessed, "I'm completely lost."

"No matter," Fred said. "Follow me." He set off at a trot along the cobbles, his bushy orange tail held high exactly like a real cat's. The illusion was all but perfect, if one overlooked the clacking sound his paws made, the sound of stone against stone. Fred threaded his way through street after street, and before long pulled up short in front of the Sea Dragon.

"Thanks," Jeremy said as they went upstairs. "How did you do that?"

"The cobblestones guided me. I can find my way through any horizontal stratum," the gargoyle said. "Or in this case over one stratum of discontinuous rocks."

"Like Kelada's talent of never being lost."

"Something like that. At least when there's stone around."

Barach returned too, not long after sundown, and they had supper sent up to the rooms. True to his word, Busby came back just at the stroke of midnight. Jeremy and Fred settled into Jeremy's room for a few hours of sleep—or at least Jeremy did—before the coming of dawn and their embarkation for the Twilight Valley and whatever lay beyond.

Barach woke him the next morning well before sunrise. Jeremy washed, after a fashion, and ate a bit of cheese and bread by way of breakfast; then the gargoyles were stored again in pack and carpetbag (though it seemed to Jeremy rather cruel treatment, now that they looked like cats), and the three travelers went softly downstairs. The common room was deserted. The glazier had already replaced the broken glass, and through the bay windows came the faint gray light of earliest dawn.

"Abdaliel won't be stirring yet," Barach said. "We'll let ourselves out."

To Jeremy the door frame seemed alive with tiny cobweblike strings of pulsing color, pale greens and paler purples. "The door's warded," he warned.

"Of course it is; warded against thieves. Not against friends."

They passed through the magic spell without incident, though Jeremy did feel a momentary tickling and stinging. *Probably sensing that I stole from Shakespeare*, he thought; but if the spell did so sense, it at least permitted him passage.

The sun rose out of the sea as they neared the quays. "Our ship is the *Gull*, a coastal trader," Barach said as their footfalls echoed in the empty morning streets. "Not much by way of accommodations, but a sturdy enough vessel, if what Abdaliel tells me is true, and perfect for our purposes. It regularly trades with Fridport, and there will be nothing remarkable about its appearance there."

The wharves were just beginning to stir with life. Jeremy looked at the sailors, with their peculiar rolling gaits, and marveled at the variety of men he saw: some of sun-baked skin, some with gold rings in their ears, some with long beards curled in fanciful ringlets, most of them foul-mouthed and surly in the cold light of dawn.

"Here we are," Barach said, walking out onto a long wooden pier. "And there, if I'm not mistaken, is the boatman sent to fetch us."

The boatman wore a heavy cloak of some close-woven tan fabric, none too clean. He slumped against a piling, his arms crossed as if he were freezing, and as they approached, blew his nose over the side of the wharf into the ocean. "Passengers for t' north?" he rumbled as they approached.

"Right enough," Barach said. "You'd be with the *Gull*?"

"Boat's down below," the sailor said. "Stow that for you?" With considerable alacrity the man took packs,

crossbow, and baggage down. Nul got aboard the launch
first, taking long steps down the ladder with his short
legs; then Barach, and Jeremy last of all. He had a
precarious moment when the boat wanted to push away
from the dock, as all boats seem to do, but he shoved
with his foot and got into the launch without too much
ado. Barach had settled in the stern and held the steering
oar; Nul was beside him, the sailor amidships, and Jeremy took the prow seat. Following the sailor's instruc-
tions, he untied the launch and pulled the rope inboard.

They passed under exotic figureheads and the high
sterns of ships, for the *Gull* lay some way out. The
launch went swiftly over the water, and sometimes the
cables of the other vessels grated mournfully beneath the
keel, while others swept past only inches above their
heads. Before long they had cleared most of the dockside
traffic, but one fairly large square-rigged craft lay directly
ahead of them. Jeremy turned to ask Barach, "Is that the
ship?"

Barach nodded. "A good little craft," he said.

The *Gull* was a three-master, broad in the beam, riding easily on the tide. The sailor brought them alongside, and Jeremy scrambled up a rope ladder. A tall,
middle-aged man offered him a hand up, which he took;
then he turned to haul the baggage on board before
Barach and Nul came up. "Thanks," Jeremy puffed,
hefting the carpetbag. "I'm one of the passengers. Jeremy Moon."

"Ah. Are you now?" the man said without much
warmth. "I'm Arowan Redeker, master of the *Gull*. Give
the little'un a hand there; he's going heavy."

Jeremy leaned over and held his hand out. Nul stretched
up and grasped, and Jeremy hauled him up and in. His
wide mouth was set in a grimace of distaste. "Boats," he
grunted. "Water. Don't like 'em."

Barach scrambled up somehow or other on his own,
and the sailor, who had made fast the launch to a couple
of davit lines, was up a second later. "Here you are,"
Redeker said, still gruffly. "And not a bit too soon. Mr.
Garf, bring the launch up. Tide won't wait."

Jeremy looked around curiously. The deck was at first

glance a random clutter of boxes, crates, and coils of rope; but then he began to see some order in the chaos. The sailors went about their business in a matter-of-fact way, some already hoisting the anchor.

"Now, I'll be busy for a while," Redeker said to Barach. "And you'll be underfoot, like as not. Your cabin's aft, first on the port side. Go there until we're underway if you want to be of help. And take your luggage with you."

"Excellent suggestion, Captain Redeker," Barach said mildly. "Jeremy?"

"Sure," Jeremy said, slinging the crossbow to his shoulder and hefting his and Nul's packs. They went back along the deck—rolling only minimally in the harbor— and down a companionway. Barach opened the door to their cabin. "This is it?" Jeremy asked, stepping in. The entire cabin was perhaps half the size of one of the inn's rooms.

"Space is at a premium on a ship," Barach observed with patience. "It is said that Serodial of the West lived for all his life in a box only waist-high and so small that he could not lie at full length in it. Serodial, it is said, appreciated the simple things."

"He have to," grunted Nul, swinging a network of cords to and fro. "We sleep in those?"

Two hammocks were slung in an alcove to the right of the door, another in a similar recess on the left. One small porthole let a little light in. "We sleep in those," Barach confirmed. "And we sit in the two chairs, and we stow our gear in the chest against the bulkhead. Nul, you can probably sit comfortably on the chest if we pad it."

The ship lurched suddenly, and Nul almost tumbled. "What that?" he asked in alarm, his hands locked onto the hammock for support.

"I expect it was the sails," Barach said. He made his way over to the porthole. "Yes, we're moving."

They released Fred and Busby, stowed the packs and baggage, and waited. Fred was chattery, excited about the idea of a boat, but Busby was his usual disdainful self. The ship's rolling increased, and Jeremy began to feel decidedly queasy. "Do you think Redeker would mind if we went on deck?" he asked. "I think the air—"

Barach gave him a keen, appraising look. "I should think there would be no trouble with the captain if we kept ourselves out of the way. Nul?"

"I go too. Room awfully small."

Barach chuckled. "Do you mean to tell me that pikas suffer from a fear of close confinement? I thought you were burrowing creatures."

Nul shot an orange glance of irritation at the magician. "When burrows move up and down, it time to dig a new burrow."

They reached the deck and found a place near midships by the port railing. The countryside, flat and wooded, slid past, perhaps a mile or more distant. Behind them Jeremy could see the harbor and beyond it the gray cluster of the town. "Funny how small it looks from here," he said.

Barach swept an arm toward the shore. "Thaumia is not a heavily populated world. The cities of humankind *are* small, compared to the great expanse of nature. Somehow that always surprises people. It is said that once a moon-moth alighted on a great bronze temple bell, a bell almost the size of a small house. At the instant the moth touched the bell, a servant on the other side gave it a lusty strike with a huge hammer. The bell sounded out its great voice, and the moth flew away thinking, 'My! What a strong touch I have!' "

Nul, rather like a child, had hoisted himself up on the railing and hung on, his feet dangling free of the deck while he looked down at the foaming wake curling from the prow of their ship. He dropped back with a thump. "Moths think?" he demanded.

Barach rolled his eyes. "You explain it," he said to Jeremy, and went below, walking with a sort of staggering dignity across the rolling deck.

Jeremy shook his head. "Poor Barach. He speaks in metaphors and images. You take him too literally."

Nul shrugged. "Don't know metaphors or images. Just know what he say. Moth land on bell. Bell ring. Moth fly away thinking he ring the bell. Right?"

"Right."

"But what the point?"

Jeremy took a deep breath. His stomach still had not caught up to the coursing of the ship. "I think the point is that humans are like the moth. They feel self-important when they're not, really, not in the whole scale of the universe."

Nul seemed to ponder that. "Nah, nah. Not make sense. Look, moths important to selfs, right?"

"I suppose so—"

"Sure. Pikas important to pikas. Humans important to humans. Probably even hobs important to hobs. So moths important to moths. Not seem, but are. So why should moth not feel, what you say, self-important? Or human? Or even pika?"

"No reason in the world," Jeremy said, and leaned suddenly over the rail.

Nul lifted himself again, staring at Jeremy. "Why human do that?" he asked, but Jeremy could not for the moment give him an answer.

Arowan Redeker's gangly form was everywhere as they drew farther and farther from land. The tall captain had a rough tongue and a ready curse for any sailor who seemed to be slacking in his duty, and he seemed to be always at the center of a small eddying rush of men who would dart up to him, give him some incomprehensible report, and then dash away again to do whatever it was they did. To the uninformed eyes of a landlubber like Jeremy, that activity seemed mainly to consist of clambering up to the masts, tugging on various assorted ropes, and shouting at other sailors.

He began to feel a little better by midday—though not so well that he could think of lunch—and by afternoon, when the land was just the merest gray line on the horizon, he could walk fairly well on the deck. Nul had gone below to rest, and Barach had not returned, so Jeremy practiced his walking alone, wondering if he could formulate some magic spell to reduce the ship's confounding tendency to ride up one deceptive swell and then rush madly down the other side, only to tilt up again immediately.

So absorbed was he in the complex calculations of the three stages such a spell would require (the standard formulation, visualization, and realization) that Jeremy blundered into a thin young sailor who, even in the cool winds of winter, had stripped to the waist.

"Out of the way there!" bellowed a loud, rough voice, the captain's voice.

Jeremy muttered an apology to the sailor, who grunted and hurried past, trailing a ripe scent of sweat.

Redeker stumped over. "If you can't keep clear of working men, go below, sir."

"I told him I was sorry."

"That makes no difference." The wind ruffled Redeker's long gray hair—*give him a beard*, thought Jeremy, *and he'd look like Abe Lincoln on a bad day*—but it seemed to do nothing to cool his spirits. "This is no excursion craft. This is a working ship. You called yourself a passenger, but to me you're cargo. And if cargo gets in the way, we kick it." The captain spun away to bark something at yet another sailor, and Jeremy, hating the man thoroughly, retreated to his safe railing.

The sun was lowering over the almost invisible land to the west. Creaking sea birds, white and gray with black-tipped wings and great long orange beaks, wheeled overhead from time to time, and the slight fitful breeze seemed to die as the ship changed her heading slightly and ran before a clean wind.

Jeremy, almost hypnotized by the rush of the ship through the water, by the pitch and rise of the ship (smoother now than it had been—or else he was getting his sea legs), suddenly snapped fully awake. He looked around, frowning: men were in the shrouds, the helmsman at the tiller, the captain beside him, other men forward doing something arcane with ropes. Nothing had changed.

Yet something had.

He had *felt* something, had sensed it: a faint electrical sensation, a quivering of the hair on his nape and arms, a sudden tactile impression like tiny ants running over his skin.

That was the feeling of magic; and the magic he felt was operating close by.

But nothing had changed; none of the other men seemed aware of anything out of the ordinary. Jeremy, wrapped in thought, went down the companionway and found his fellow voyagers indulging in a most uncompanionable argument about some story of Barach's and Nul's hard-headed misinterpretation thereof. Fred and Busby, secure in their cat disguises, unless perhaps the sailors might expect them to catch a rat or two, had left to explore the ship and avoid the exasperated voices. Jeremy's entrance made no impression on the debaters.

He considered mentioning his sense of magic to Barach; but as he gingerly climbed into his ropework hammock (he took the higher of the two) and listened to the argument, he felt less and less certain about what he had felt. The afternoon sun had been bright on the water, the motion of the ship had been monotonous, and now, looking back, Jeremy was not entirely sure that he had felt real magic. Tremien, the old spider, was alert to every quiver of the magical web. Jeremy was not.

He told himself that it might have been a fleeting hallucination, a flashback to the agonized paralysis he had felt when the Hag of Illsmere had turned her fell powers on him. He did have such flashbacks, usually when he was on the verge of dozing off or was just awakening in the morning. And certainly now there seemed to be nothing amiss.

But he was abstracted all the same, and though he felt up to eating a little that evening he found it difficult to drop off to sleep in the swaying network hammock. The posture was odd, for one thing: his spine curved, his head and feet on a level; for another thing, he had a great deal to think about. Jeremy was still awake when Fred and Busby returned, stepping lightfootedly like the cats they seemed to be but producing thumping footfalls like the stone they were. He was awake even later, when Nul grunted out of his hammock across the way and went up on deck—to pee, Jeremy supposed, having learned that the rail was where one did it. Just when he was beginning to think he would never fall asleep, he finally did, eased into a deep drowsiness by the close air of the cabin and by Barach's gentle, sighing snores below him.

Nul had indeed risen to answer a call of nature, but not the kind that Jeremy had surmised. He found the ship coursing along under a sky thickly sprinkled with stars: cold blue, burning fiery red, and others more distant that seemed merely a powdery, gauzy vapor. Staring up at them, Nul shivered, not altogether from the chill of the air, but in part because of the wonder of it all, because of the blackness of night and the remote brightness of the stars.

But partly he shivered because the night *was* cold, and Nul huddled deep inside the thick woolen jacket he had thrown on. The sailors were not as active now—the ship was running well in an open sea and the captain, it seemed, was off watch—and so he went as far forward as he could, to the point of the bows, and there he gazed out into the night.

Horizon was almost lost in sky. There was a very faint glow along the world's rim, and closer to the ship came the occasional phosphorescent flash of fish leaping from the invisible sea; otherwise all was darkness.

Night, Nul thought, *is my cavern now. The stars my jewels. I am no longer a creature of burrows and caves.*

Once he had been content to live in the tunnels and dens of his kind; once being out in the open at night would have filled him with unease. But tonight the confinement of the cabin had grown too much, as oppressive as a closed tomb. Nul wondered if he had been civilized right out of his nature, if the normal life of a pika was now impossible for him.

He concentrated hard on remembering life underground and succeeded only in remembering his people. His father, who found such delight in the shaping of stone and gems; his older brothers and sisters, delvers of ores, workers in metals; his mother, who sang such sweet songs as her young ones drifted to sleep. He recalled others, too: the old pikas, male and female, who culti-

vated the subterranean gardens and more furtively the
above-ground ones, raising both the plants that shunned
the sunlight and those that died without it. Other than
the people, Nul could recall only fleeting impressions,
strongest among them the smell of water underground
and the sound of an unseen waterfall, a ribbon of top-
pling water in the living heart of a mountain.

It was like a dream.

Nul sighed. He tried to force himself to feel homesick;
but he could not. He could not find it in himself to miss
the caverns and the tunnels of his folk.

But the people—he missed the people.

That was what they called themselves: *pwyktwa*, the
people. Humans were *baligasir*, the clumsy ones. Or they
were called other things: the big ones, the earth-walkers,
the cruel ones, the plant-servants. It depended on how
contemptuous the pika speaking might feel about humans at the moment.

Plant-servant, for example: that was a human farmer.
Pikas grew crops in small, scattered plots, and it would
take a close inspection to see that the plants grew by care
and design, not by nature. But humans insisted on rip-
ping the flesh of the earth in rectangular patterns, in
building permanent dwellings close by, and in ministering
to the growing plants' every whim. Their farms owned
them, and the plants seemed to own the farms.

The right way to farm was the pika way. The human
way was a fool's way.

Except that, knowing humans as he now did, Nul
couldn't accept their foolishness as being real. Tremien,
for instance, was often absent-minded, occasionally abrupt,
but behind all that and above all that, he was wise and
kind. And Jeremy—well, Jeremy should have been born
a pika, Nul thought. Except that he worked his art with
words, not stones. "Double, double, toil and trouble,"
he whispered to himself, the very shapes of the words
delicious on his tongue.

Thoughts of all the deaths in Jeremy's play led to
thoughts of Nul's dead brother, Jare. Nul remembered
the cold shock of recognition all too well: one moment
he had been idling through the courtyard, bantering with

some of the winter merchants he knew well, and the next moment the world had fallen away beneath him. The pika skin had been spread out for inspection atop a chin-high stack of other pelts. The white blaze along the shoulder had told the whole story.

The rest—his leap across the stack of furs, his attack on the human peddler—was dim in Nul's memory. But the moment of knowing, of seeing, that was his forever. Especially in the night, in the dark. And for all it's sudden chill, that moment had lighted a fire in Nul that burned even now, and that needed revenge as its fuel.

The pika sighed. The ship drove on through the night.

He thought at first that the motion of the craft had lulled him to sleep when the voice spoke softly in his ear, calling his name. Then he realized that Tremien was talking to him, using the communication spell. He crossed his arms and whispered an acknowledgement. "Here, Mage Tremien," he said so quietly that no one, not even the sailor in the rigging overhead, could have heard.

But the old magician did. "Good. Are you alone?"

"Yah. Alone enough. Trouble?"

"You sense trouble?"

"Why else call Nul?"

After a moment of silence, Tremien whispered again from his study so far away: "You speak the truth, my friend. Often and often have I relied on you when trouble loomed. Now—I do not know. There is nothing certain to warn you of. But I feel misgivings in my heart. How goes the voyage?"

"Well enough." In a few words Nul sketched in all that had happened.

Tremien, when Nul had finished, sighed, "I do not like the fighting. Perhaps the men were only common sailors; perhaps they were something else. Be alert, my friend. Be the eyes and ears of Barach, who has such need of you."

"I will," Nul said simply.

"Then tell the others that you have spoken with me and that I have said all goes well at Whitehorn. Kelada has left us for a season; the healer Melodia asked her to visit, and for a month or so the two are at Melodia's farm."

"Is that all?"

"Winter Market goes on. We have had an early snowfall. Quite deep in the valley."

"It fine here."

"Well . . ." The old wizard seemed curiously reluctant to say goodbye, Nul thought, and the thought gave him some uneasiness.

"We be careful," he said.

"Very well. I am old, Nul, and sometimes the old must mistrust their premonitions; and yet I am worried about the three of you. Take no chances. Be very careful. And get news to me from Twilight Valley as soon as ever you can."

"Will, Mage Tremien."

"Then farewell."

The voice was gone, and with it the tingly, prickling feeling of magic at work, the feeling that always seemed to ruffle the fine hair on his face and neck. Nul took a deep breath of cold sea-scented air, rose, stretched, and started back along the starboard rail. He paused before he reached the companionway, gazing back into the dark. There, quite far off, a yellow light rode low, so low that at times it was obscured by an intervening swell. But it was only a spark, and a dim one at that. After staring hard at it for several breaths, Nul decided it was only a star, very close to setting. Or, if it were the light of a vessel, it was so distant that even his eyes, especially good in the dark, could not distinguish it from a star. In any case, Nul felt no foreboding about it, no premonition of evil.

That, he reflected, was one way that pikas were superior to men: they sensed only immediate dangers, not remote or imagined ones. Pikas slept soundly as a general rule.

Nul heaved a great breath and descended to the cabin to try to prove the rule.

The voyage was not especially eventful. They made good time, putting in twice at ports, very small ones hardly more than villages. The first time they did so, Jeremy asked Barach why Tremien hadn't simply sent them there instead of to Dale Haven. Barach explained that these were fishing settlements, usually without substantial sailing vessels, and that in this season they were visited only irregularly by traders.

Jeremy saw why. The first port was home to perhaps two or three hundred people, stocky, hearty souls bundled warmly against the increasingly bitter northerly winds. Everything stank of fish. Jeremy urged Fred and Busby to show some interest, but their attention had been caught by the peculiar black rocks of the area, and they engaged in a hot, whispered debate on the volcanic origins thereof. At length Jeremy, afraid that two talking cats might provoke some attention, sent them both to the cabin, where, presumably, they settled matters.

The second port was farther north and even colder. Jeremy, by now used to the motion of the ship and more confident of his digestion, didn't even go on deck during their brief stay there. Nul, who did, assured him that he had missed nothing. "Small nasty town," he pronounced. "Fish, fish, fish."

The ship made steady progress to the north. The days grew keen and sharp, the nights brittle with cold. The bright skies they had sailed under at first gave way to leaden ones, hung with folded clouds that spat stinging sleet. The sheets grew a frosty coating of rime. The bulkheads became glazed with ice. Still they drove on, alone on a tossing, choppy sea the exact color of the sky.

At length the ship's head turned a little more westerly than north, and on a dull, overcast morning Barach called Jeremy and Nul up to see the landfall. They stood at the port rail, gazing into the gray distances. "That jagged line?" Jeremy asked at length.

"That is it," Barach said. He was well muffled in furs, but even so his nose and cheeks glowed pink from the cold, and the chilly scats of wind stirred his gray beard and his tufted eyebrows as if they were themselves clouds.

"Mountains," Nul pronounced.

"Very high mountains," Barach agreed. "They come right down to the sea and march into it. We shall not be going directly in to Fridport, for the peaks of those mountains that have descended into the water jut up as rocks and reefs. Captain Redeker will have to maneuver us through such a maze as you have never imagined."

Busby had wandered up. He leaped to the rail and stared across the sea with them. "Funny mountains," he commented *sotto voce*.

Jeremy glanced at him. "Uh-oh. Look at Busby."

Barach squinted down. "The disguise spell is slipping."

The cat was still there, but it was a lumpy-looking cat now, a strange-looking cat. The fur on the shoulders seemed to blend together in a scaly kind of network, and there was something eaglelike about the head. "I think," Jeremy said, "that you had better remain in the cabin until we land."

"How do you feel?" Barach asked.

The gargoyle seemed to consider the question. "As I always do," he said at last.

"Then Tremien was correct in his surmise. The damping effect of mazerite will not affect magical creatures— only the exercise of verbal magic. Or at least we can now hope so."

The cold soon drove them below deck. When, late that afternoon, Jeremy returned alone, they had drawn much nearer the land. Looking out and up at it, he felt a quivering in the pit of his stomach: the mountains were *huge*. They were far higher than any he had seen on Earth, so tall that their peaks were lost, invisible in the clouds. They wore heavy white coats of snow on their northern shoulders.

The rocks, too, began to appear, dark pinnacles shooting up unexpected plumes of frothy white spray as the waves struck them, looking like geysers.

The sailors swarmed busily now, managing the ship like a spirited steed, easing it among the rocks with a delicacy that Jeremy hoped betokened skill and care.

Captain Redeker, swathed in a heavy cloak and hat, paused near Jeremy once. "With a good wind and good luck, we'll make port early tomorrow morning," he said. "We have these shoals to get through before dark, and then we'll take in sail." He stood beside Jeremy, resting his arms on the rail, gazing out at the rock-strewn sea. "Wanted to get her in tonight, but there's no hope of that now."

Jeremy nodded his thanks.

"Good thing you caught us when you did," the captain told him, evidently in a garrulous mood. "Not another vessel like the *Gull* in these waters, not this time of year. Wouldn't be surprised if we're the last craft to visit Fridport this season. Unless maybe the one that overhauled us is still there and stays after we leave."

"Another ship overtook us?" Jeremy asked, surprised.

"Oh, aye. Some nights back. Hailed her but her master was in a hurry and never answered."

"Do you think the other ship was headed for Fridport?"

Redeker gave him a gaunt, short-tempered stare. "Nowhere else to go, not for a vessel heading north in these waters. Didn't touch in at Grebon or Hevalomor, where we did. And north of Hevalomor it's either Fridport or the everlasting ice, that's all."

The helmsman called, and Redeker turned to go. Jeremy grasped the man's arm. "Wait," he said. "This ship—why didn't you tell us about it before?"

Redeker shook off Jeremy's hand. With a mirthless grin, he said, "You never asked me."

CHAPTER 5

FRED AND BUSBY took the news with their usual stony indifference to anything not of geological import. Nul shrugged it off, and even Barach the worrier appeared philosophical. "There is no law that says ships may not visit Fridport in wintertime," he pointed out. "And nothing that indicates this particular ship was a hostile one."

"True." Yet Jeremy had the old familiar feeling of impending danger . . . though at the moment there seemed no easy way of putting the feeling into words.

Jeremy sighed; there was simply nothing to be done about it, particularly if the *Gull* had entered the zone of no magic, as it appeared it had—both Fred and Busby were indisputably miniature gargoyles now, all their catness dissipated; and as Busby observed testily, they needed all their concentration to keep themselves in their dwindled state.

"You mean being small is your own magic?" Jeremy asked. "I thought Tremien shrank you."

Busby was almost curt in his reply: "No. Mage Tremien only released us from guard duty; we knew what had to be done and animated and shrank ourselves, of course, using our own magic. Tremien is no fool; he knew that any outside spell cast on us would wear off in these latitudes."

"For which," Barach said, "we should all be grateful. If our magic will not hold, then neither will an adversary's."

"Well, even a gargoyle's is having some trouble now. We have been small a very long time."

There was no regular meal that night, for sunset took them as the ship still navigated a tricky region of scattered rocks and shallows. The party made do with the same fare the working sailors ate, and as they all munched on dried meat and hard biscuit, the ship crept along for some time in a swiftly gathering dusk.

Finally, in the lee of a larger rock than most but well away from it, the ship dropped anchor and rode uneasily on the rolling swells. For the first time since their second day from port, Jeremy's stomach fluttered just a little to the swing and fall of the *Gull*. Nul had not become any more lively or talkative in the last days of the voyage, and Barach was uncharacteristically silent that night, even his fund of stories seemingly exhausted. Jeremy slept, though fitfully, until the pale late dawn awakened him. From the movement and the creaking, he sensed that the ship was underway already.

He decided to don the robe Tremien had given him, and he unpacked it. It fell from its folds gracefully with no trace of a wrinkle. Slipping it on, Jeremy belted it with the narrow blue sash. He was amazed at the thinness and lightness of the garment. Indeed, for a moment he wondered about its worth in such a climate. Though he did not doubt Tremien's word (and though he somehow took comfort from the mere fact that the old magician had once worn this same garment), Jeremy found it hard to believe that the robe, so finely woven and so insubstantial, could really keep him warm. But he reflected that the only way to test it was to wear it in the open, and so he clambered up the companionway and onto the deck.

His breath came sharp in his chest. The *Gull* had set what seemed a suicidal course toward an impossible landfall. Direcly ahead of the prow huge mountains of some pale purple rock, well glazed with ice, reared incredibly from the sea. His first impression was that the shoreline could be only yards away, and that the *Gull* was in imminent danger of running onto the rocks and foundering; but after a moment of panic, he realized that the ship was still many miles offshore. The mountains were simply huge—rugged and irregular cones whose snow-streaked sides plummeted sheer into the sea.

He made his way to the bow and stared at the sight. The sky was a pearly gray, scudding with high, almost luminescent clouds, and the air was utterly transparent, making even distant objects seem clear and close. Jeremy saw now that the ship was heading toward a chasm or defile in the mountainous rampart ahead. He could see, too, off to the left a chain of sharp-peaked islets and rocks, the outcroppings that the captain had navigated the evening before. He assumed a similar scattering of shoals and rocks lay somewhere to the right, where the other branch of the mountains went into the ocean. The ship seemed to be making for the vertical gash in the mountains on as straight a line as its crew could manage, which was in fact not straight at all: during the night the wind had swung around and now came out of the west, a head wind, hard and viciously cold.

Jeremy reached for a rope to steady himself and his hand closed on frost. Only then did he realize that Tremien's assessment of the robe had been correct: he felt perfectly warm, although his breath drifted away in thick vapor and the whole ship was a jewel of glittering ice.

The sailors worked harder than ever and cursed the weather. Before long it became clear that Redeker's prediction of a morning berthing had been far too optimistic; the broad-beamed *Gull* made headway only slowly, tacking and rolling as she made for the shore. Spatters of sleet rattled on the canvas now and again, and Jeremy had to brace himself to maintain his footing in the heavy weather.

The sea became even rougher as they neared shore, and Jeremy thought he could see why: the great westward-rolling swells of the ocean were funnelled inward by the two chains of rocks and rocky islands, and as the space they occupied narrowed, the rolling, spume-streaked waves became increasingly higher. The wind, a flat, cold knife slashing out of the west, sliced off the white tops of the waves and sent them straight back toward the ship in level, drenching sheets of salt spray.

For perhaps an hour Jeremy stood and watched the mainland gradually draw nearer as the *Gull* labored hard against wind and wave, but at last the roller-coaster sensation of riding up the back of a wave and plunging down the far side grew too unsettling for him, and he retreated to find his companions awake and packed.

"Land soon?" Nul asked.

"If we don't crash," Jeremy said, sinking into one of the two chairs bolted to the bulkheads and putting a hand out to keep himself steady. He swayed hard to port as the ship took another gigantic wave and began to wallow in the trough. "How Redeker plans to manage this I don't know."

"Trust to the professional man, apprentice," Barach said in hearty good humor. "It's like the story of the man with an acre of land and the crow with three legs—"

"Please," groaned Nul.

Barach threw up his hands. "Nul, you should form a settlement of the hopelessly literal. You'd have company enough in this unenlightened age."

"It might not be such a bad place at that," Jeremy said with rather a green grin. "Pretty attractive to me right now. Quiet little spot where people don't go off adventuring on ships that hardly seem up to the occasion. I don't know that I might not want to join such a settlement after this trip is over. Where are Fred and Busby?"

"Packed," called a gritty, disgusted voice from Barach's carpetbag.

"Just wait," Jeremy said in a somewhat louder voice. "I think you fellows are going to see all the rock your, ah, hearts desire. And soon, at that." Under his breath, he added, "I just hope the rocks aren't submerged ones."

Barach's trust in the professional hand proved well placed. A few simi before midday the *Gull* reached a calmer stretch of water. When the party went on deck, they discovered that the ship had negotiated a tricky turn and was now heading somewhat south of west in a well-protected fjord. A mile to their left and a bit closer to their right the walls of stone rose almost vertically, their sides festooned with frozen torrents and columns of ice.

"The cliffs get only an ona or two of sun a day," Barach observed. "And the days are getting shorter. By next month the sun probably won't even reach the southern rampart. Indeed, I understand that this entire anchorage sometimes freezes solid in the full depths of winter."

Jeremy did not answer his mentor's observations. He couldn't; standing there on deck, his head craned back to look at the dizzying reaches of vertical rock, he felt as if his heart were thumping away in his throat, and he was half afraid that if he opened his mouth it would leap out and dive overboard.

The harbor gradually widened, and before too long they were in a broadening bowl. Here the mountains did not plunge straight down into the water, but shelved, and they could see comparatively flat pebbled beaches off to their right. Barach pointed wordlessly ahead, through the cliffs toward another flattened beach. At first Jeremy could not make out what he was indicating; then he saw the town.

No wonder it was hard to spot. The buildings, low and squat but with steep-peaked roofs, were made of the same purple-gray rock as the mountains themselves. At this distance only the billows of blue-gray smoke showed that it was not a collection of enormous house-shaped boulders; as they drew nearer, they could make out quays and boats, most of them small fishing craft but at least one roughly the size of the *Gull*. Cold though it was, the ground around the town was almost free of snow. A very few struggling firlike trees cast a little shade, and some snow lay on the north pitches of the tall roofs.

"The mountains keep the worst of the weather off," Barach observed. "The Valley is even warmer; hardly any snow falls there, even in the deepest winter."

"What?" Jeremy said. He had not really been paying attention, and somehow he had lost the import of the old mage's words.

Patiently Barach repeated himself, and Jeremy nodded. He licked his lips. They felt dry, and somehow he had a curious, lightheaded feeling, as though Barach had begun to talk nonsense all of a sudden, but he said nothing of it to his companions.

Barach and Nul, chilled as the sun slipped from sight behind the mountains ahead, went below, but Jeremy, kept warm by the miraculous robe, remained in the bow, out of the way of the muffled, bundled, cursing sailors. The captain managed the craft in a masterly way. The harbor here, after one or two narrow dogleg turns, was almost as smooth as glass—well, Jeremy amended mentally, at least when compared to the chopping waters outside the bay. The town grew larger as the unnatural twilight deepened, and before long Jeremy could see a small boat making for the ship.

"Ah," Redeker snorted, pausing a few steps behind. "Agude. The pilot ket simis, after I have done most of his damned job for him. If he'd chensed falam at bay head, we could've been docked before nidis."

Jeremy frowned. The man's accent, already difficult for him, seemed to have grown much more pronounced, and some words, perhaps strange syllables of nautical import, had wholly escaped him. But the actions of the next few minutes carried meaning enough.

The boat drew alongside, a rope ladder snaked down to it, and a short, heavyset man with a broad, flat face and white chin-whiskers clambered aboard. He nodded to Jeremy, took a perfunctory look around, and went back to the helm.

Jeremy thought he would always remember the landing. Like her namesake, the *Gull* became graceful under the Northlander's touch, slipping nimbly toward a stone quay. The sailors leaped to his orders, and at last the ship glided in easily beside the dock, where more Fridporters waited to seize and make fast the lines thrown to them. The ship stopped, not abruptly but definitely, and there was a moment of quiet. In the flare of torches from the quay—for it was now quite dark—Jeremy saw the pilot smile for the first time, a broad, broken-toothed smile of pure pleasure at a job well done. Despite the enchanted robe he wore, Jeremy shivered a little at that moment.

They disembarked in a gloom that was more than

gathering night, for the Fridporters, unlike the inhabitants of Dale Haven, seemed a taciturn lot. One of them bore a torch and consented to take Barach, Nul, and Jeremy to an inn or something like an inn. Burdened with their luggage they followed, and only when they had come inside the one-story building and their guide had tossed back the hood of a heavy coat made of something like sealskin did Jeremy realize that their torchbearer was really quite young and a woman into the bargain. She spoke with a quick, nasal accent that garbled her words entirely, but Barach seemed to understand.

A boy of twelve or so, chattering the same incomprehensible dialect, took over the guide duties and led them to a room somewhat larger than their ship cabin, made cheerful by a crackling but odorous fire. Jeremy doffed the robe and carefully folded it before placing it on the foot of one of the beds. As he bent to warm his hands at the fire, a sickening oily stench washed over him, making him gag.

"What is that?" Jeremy choked.

Nul and Barach stared at him.

"The smell. What—" he broke off, confused. He had been speaking English.

Barach said something that he couldn't quite catch.

Concentrating ferociously, Jeremy said in Presolatan, "Something is wrong."

Barach replied very slowy and distinctly. "I did not think. You learned our language by magic spell. Remember?"

"Yes. In the Between. Kelada cast it." Jeremy felt tongue-tied as a bumpkin.

"It was verbal magic. The virtue of the spell is interrupted here. But you have spoken the tongue for almost a year. You have practiced well. You still have your memory."

Yes, but, damn it, speaking to Barach now was like trying to converse with a waiter in a Parisian restaurant on the strength of one year of high-school French. Jeremy's tongue felt thick and clumsy. "Should have paid more attention."

"That," Barach said, straight-faced, "is what I have always told you, pupil."

Their boy-guide had left. Nul, his face puzzled, said, "You talk funny. Like Nul almost."

Jeremy shrugged in helpless anger. "What to do?" he asked Barach.

"Do? Nothing to do, except to speak as clearly and plainly as possible. You are not *that* difficult to comprehend. And you do understand us, do you not?"

"Yes. If you go slow."

"Then we, too, will speak slowly. With practice and attention, things will improve. Now. You said something in your strange native language. What was it?"

"The fire." Jeremy had to think a long time to frame his question. "Why does it stink?"

"Ah. The smell? That's the fire, I expect."

Jeremy flushed, realizing now that the others had as much trouble with his words as he had with theirs. "I know. But why? Why does it smell that bad?"

"Oh, the reason? No wood around in these parts, you know; or precious little of it." Barach reached into a bin beside the hearth and withdrew some black, twisted, oily-looking thing. "They burn dried fatty fish here."

"We have fish for supper, too," Nul grumbled.

Barach assented, and Nul said something that was just too fast for Jeremy to understand. Barach replied in a querulously sharp tone, and of his words Jeremy caught only "fish," "drink," and "Nul."

"Please," he said, and both his companions apologized.

Supper was as bad as Nul had feared: salted dried fish, a coarse mealy bread that probably had fish in it, a few roasted potatoes, and a fiery wine. Jeremy drank too much of the latter. "Need to find out," he said after carefully planning his speech, "about the other ship. Can you ask?"

"I'll learn what I can," Barach said. "There will be some drinking around the fireside tonight. The people of the Valley come downstream to trade in Fridport, and there probably are some of them around. I will try to find a guide for the next part of our journey. At the same time I will ask about the other ship. Perhaps you and Nul had better stay here. Nul is all right when he's bundled up—he looks a lot like one of their young ones—but I fear he would attract attention indoors."

Nul gave some sharp and rude reply. Jeremy, who had been holding on to each word Barach uttered, did not catch it, but once again the two were off on a short argument. In despair, Jeremy threw himself on one of the three beds in the room. He discovered it was little more than a stout wooden table with a thin straw mattress on top.

They had released Busby and Fred from their luggage, and the two gargoyles were clambering over the walls, discussing, no doubt, the ages and compositions of the various stones; but to Jeremy their talk was just a high-pitched, grating chatter, much too fast for him to follow. Indeed, he could not even catch a word here and there. He felt almost like weeping in frustration; for the first time in months he had the sense of being lost and ignorant, and it was not a welcome feeling.

Barach took his leave and went down the hall alone. Jeremy, after composing a question in his head, asked Nul, "Do you know what we will do in the Valley?"

Nul frowned. "Understood most of that. What we do in Valley? First ask people of Valley for help. If they not give help, then find caverns. Nul go. You not have to go."

"You know we will all go together."

"It hard for you now. Not fair."

"Nothing in life is fair." Jeremy had leaned the crossbow against the wall at the foot of one bed. He reached for it, held it up. "This," he said, "I did not learn by magic."

Nul nodded grimly. He got up and opened his pack. From it he took two daggers, already keenly honed. Then he opened the carpetbag that Barach had carried. His short sword was inside it, a child-sized weapon, but one that Nul could wield expertly. "We who cannot talk well," he said slowly, "can let weapons speak for us."

Jeremy became aware of a tug at his trouser leg. It was Fred. He chattered something too fast for Jeremy to catch, and the young man gave Nul a hopeless look of confusion.

"Fred say he and Busby want out," Nul translated. "Need to return to proper size for little while. Go out among rocks, outside of town, away from people. All right?"

"Sorry," Fred said. "I forgot about your problem."

"I think it will be all right," Jeremy said. "Be careful. Don't be seen."

"We will be," Busby said. "And you take care as well. Perhaps you had better unbar a door for us."

The corridor led to the common room on the right, but a barred doorway far down it to the left appeared to lead outside. Jeremy and the gargoyles went down the hallway, and when Jeremy unbarred and opened the door, he found that it did indeed give onto a street now fully dark. Windows glowed here and there, but otherwise Fridport was locked in night.

The gargoyles sniffed the air. "We will go into the foothills not far west of town," Busby said. "We will become our rightful size tonight. We will shrink and slip back by dawn."

Jeremy carefully repeated the words, and the gargoyles dodged out into the frigid night. He shut and barred the door and returned to the room. There Nul sat with a whetstone, working on the daggers. The pika had been right about one thing: the cool sounds that metal made against stone were in a language that even Jeremy could easily understand.

Barach came back some time later, looking troubled. He closed the door, took a few shriveled, blackened dried fish from a bin near the fireplace, and stoked the blaze with them. "I have little to report, I fear," he said to Nul and Jeremy. "The other ship is the *Carosar* and it seems to be just a trading vessel—cargo of fabrics, furniture, and metalwork. It has been in the harbor for two days now and will leave soon. There are no Valley people in town at present, though they come fairly often; indeed, a small party of them left only the day before yesterday."

"Before or after other ship come?" Nul asked, with a glance at Jeremy.

"Shortly after. But I could learn nothing about that. Anyway, I asked for a guide, and the young woman who showed us here from the quay said she would take us as far as the Gray Falls for a few silvers. I told her that would do. We should leave, I think, tomorrow if possible."

Jeremy nodded his agreement.

"Where are our sedimentary friends?" Barach asked.

Nul explained—an explanation that Jeremy found hard to follow. Both of his companions seemed to forget his disadvantage when they began talking to each other, much to Jeremy's annoyance. He finally interrupted with a plaintive demand to be remembered, and Nul apologized.

Barach stroked his beard. "Well. I have arranged for provisions and some transportation. It will take us about three to five days, depending upon the weather, to get to Three Rivers, the first major town in Twilight Valley. The Valley is protected from snow, and it will hardly be as cold there as it was out on the ocean, but we will be in for some uncomfortable nights."

"And nights are so long," Nul complained.

"Nothing for that; whatever cannot be transmuted must remain the same, as the saying goes. Jeremy, how do you feel?"

"Like a fool," Jeremy said, wondering if the words came out as thickly as he seemed to hear them. "Can't talk well. Otherwise, I am the same as ever."

"Try a very small spell. Nothing dangerous, mind; nothing with fire or great moving power. Just something easy and harmless." Barach glanced around the room. "There is a pillow on the bed there. Try to levitate it."

Jeremy thought in English, and after a moment he said, "The air pillow—it isn't filled with air or light as air; it actually floats on air. An incredible bargain if you act now. Just watch it go."

The pillow remained just as lumpish and gravity-bound as before. In his clumsy Presolatan, Jeremy said, "Sorry. It didn't work."

Barach shrugged. "Your Earth magic is so capricious.

I thought there was at least a chance that it would not be affected by the mazerite. However—"

"Sorry," Jeremy repeated.

"Nonsense; nothing to be sorry about. It is not your fault."

But later that evening, when they turned in for sleep, Nul cried out in shocked surprise as he lay his head on the pillow. Jeremy, about to blow out the candle he held, gaped. Nul's head had sunk *into* the pillow, and only his cheeks, nose, and chin were outside. The pika reared up, his eyes wide.

Barach, frowning, tried to lift the pillow from the bed. His hands passed through it. "What was your spell?" he asked Jeremy.

Jeremy, avoiding visualization to prevent the re-stated spell from operating, translated what he had said into Presolatan.

"Hm." The old mage scratched his shaggy head. "The pillow did not float on air, but it seems somehow to have *become* air. And I do not know what to do with it."

They could not move it, and when Jeremy tried another spell, one designed to give the pillow substance again, it seemed to have no effect. "I'm not really surprised," Barach said. "Physical-alteration spells are very difficult to manage. You succeeded the first time precisely because you were not trying. The second time . . . well, the mazerite obviously warps Earthly magic, too."

In the end Nul folded an extra blanket, placed it on (or rather inside) the illusory pillow, and did well enough. But Jeremy wondered what sort of local reputation the inn would achieve in future days. Not many establishments, after all, could boast the presence of a ghostly pillow.

Their departure was delayed the next day by unexpected bad weather—not snow, but a terribly thick fog. Busby and Fred had returned at dawn, as they promised, but dawn was nonexistent, and Barach gave the two gargoyles permission to spend another day in the foothills if they wished. Both did, for it appeared that the igneous rock formations of this far northern country were immoderately absorbing, and while away from civilized eyes the gargoyles could comfortably revert to their proper sizes.

Barach, who had been up even before dawn and had spoken with their guide, said that since they had extra time he would go out to secure delivery of a few extra provisions he had already arranged to purchase. The old magician had set aside his brown monk-like mage's habit, and now was a strange spectacle in a heavy blue flannel shirt, short black coat, dark brown trousers, and boots. To Jeremy it was a bit like seeing Santa Claus in civilian dress.

After Barach left, Jeremy and Nul decided to go for a walk. Days of being confined to the ship had made them both irritable and edgy, and now that they were on dry land again, they found it almost as hard to walk as they had during those first awkward days aboard the *Gull*. Nul, bundled well in his woolen jacket and hood, did look a bit like the youngest Fridporters, if you were not close enough to gaze at his face, and Jeremy in a long fur-lined coat (he did not want to wear the magician's robe for fear of attracting attention in this magic-shy land) was indistinguishable from any of the sailors.

The sun must have been somewhere above the eastern mountain rims when the two of them stepped into the street, but it was lost in palpable gray fog, incredibly thick, a fog that lay heavily in the lungs and coated the skin with an unpleasantly cold sheen of moisture. Jeremy had seen something like this in the Hag's Valley, but that had been a conjured mist, created by the Hag to shield her works from prying eyes; this was just a normal fog, though it would have accomplished the Hag's purposes quite as well.

There was no sightseeing on that walk, for Nul's and Jeremy's vision could penetrate only a few feet in every direction. All the buildings seemed to be constructed of the same purplish gray stone, all the streets to be made of flat flags of the same material—and the green slate roofs of all the buildings were lost in the enveloping fog. The streets, too, were unusually quiet. Most Fridporters, it appeared, felt content on such days to warm them-

selves by their odorous firesides. Only a few ventured
into the streets, and they were quiet and withdrawn as
they hastened along with turned-up collars and turned-
down eyes.

Jeremy sympathized, and so did Nul, seemingly. They
walked together slowly, Nul favoring his bad leg, and
neither spoke. They shared a sort of common stolidness
that, in some ways, was more companionable than talk
could have been.

At length Nul and Jeremy came to a stone bridge
arching over an invisible river. "Here where Friddifor
come to sea," Nul pronounced. They walked across the
bridge, and it occurred to Jeremy that it was probably
the most ambitious structure not raised by magic that he
had seen on Thaumia. The arch was fairly steep. At its
apex Jeremy estimated they had come a third of a mile or
thereabouts. Leaning over the weathered wooden parapet, he could hear just the faintest sound of water below.
The bridge was high as well as long.

A rumbling of iron-bound wheels on stone came from
the dim downslope of the arch, and Jeremy and Nul
stood close by the parapet. A child about Nul's height
came trudging along, holding a lighted torch in his hand.
Close behind him came a two-wheeled cart, drawn by a
dispirited mule driven by a well-bundled man. The clatter died quickly as boy, mule, cart, and driver disappeared into the enveloping fog.

"Want to go on?" Jeremy asked.

"Yah. Little way at least."

"Hope we can find our way back."

"Damn fog have to lift sometime."

They descended to the other side of the river. The
buildings here were smaller, more spread out: private
houses, Jeremy surmised. They strolled for quite a long
time, saying little, each wrapped in thought as both were
wrapped in mist. At length they turned and retraced
their steps. It was past noon, and the fog had thinned
considerably: now they could see perhaps two hundred
yards ahead.

They recrossed the stone bridge, and this time Jeremy
could appreciate just how much of an achievement it

was. Nearly a mile long, framed in great heavy beams of some dark wood and resting on huge narrow arches of stone, it spanned a broad, slow-moving river and was tall enough to permit the passage underneath of small masted fishing vessels.

Once back on their own side of the river, Jeremy and Nul quickly became lost. They struck out in the direction of their inn—or so they thought—and continued until they reached the waterfront, where the boats rested idly. "We missed it," Jeremy said. "Let's find the *Gull* and start from there."

The ship was still tied at the pier, and there alone they found some activity. Evidently the cargo had already been unloaded; now dockworkers were busy trundling cartloads of kegs to the ship and loading them aboard. "Think we better ask captain?" Nul asked.

On deck, Redeker turned the fog blue with an explosion of curses directed at some hapless stevedore. "I don't know about that," Jeremy said. "Do you think you can find the way to the inn?"

"Maybe. It about as hard to see now as it was last night." Nul and Jeremy attempted to follow the path to the inn they had taken on disembarking the day before, but once again they found themselves in a maze of unfamiliar streets.

"Think we one street, two streets, too far to west," Nul muttered at last. "Maybe go over that way?"

They followed a narrow side street to the east, only to find that it ended in a blind alley. "Damn," Jeremy sighed. "Guess we'd better ask for help, if we don't want to be here all night."

They retraced their steps and paused at the mouth of the alley. "Someone coming," Nul said.

A group of five or six men in a loose group, heads hunched down, hands in pockets, trudged toward them. When they were close enough to speak to, Jeremy said very slowly and carefully, "Excuse me. We're lost. Could you—" he broke off as the two men in the lead looked up.

"Well," the shorter of the two grinned, rubbing his forehead. "If it ain't the man with the monkey."

*   *   *

"Run!" Nul yelped as the two sailors lunged for them.

Jeremy was just quick enough to elude the tall man. He heard Nul's running footfalls dying through the fog and followed, the sailors close behind. In less than no time, Nul was both out of sight and out of hearing, leaving Jeremy completely lost.

He ducked into an alley, found a low stone wall, vaulted over it, landed, crossed into a different street, and pounded along it. It seemed to be a street of small shops, for heavily bundled women, baskets on their arms, stepped out of his way and gave him disapproving glares as he dodged them; but from behind Jeremy still heard sounds of pursuit, so he dared not pause.

The fog, though lighter than it had been, had become his ally, confusing things, distorting figures, offering some cover. When he began to pant, Jeremy dodged into the recess of a shop doorway and flattened himself against the wall. Seconds later, the two sailors—he wondered where the others had gone—rushed past, not giving him a glance. Someone tried to open the door, and Jeremy had to move. He stepped into the shop, still breathing hard, as an elderly woman pushed past him.

"Yis?" said a stocky man who stood with his back and ample buttocks to a good fire.

Jeremy sniffed. The shop was aromatic with fruity, yeasty smells. As his eyes became accustomed to the dimness, he could make out open crates stocked with produce, small red apples, ruddy-skinned pears, small purple onions, brown potatoes. "Yis?" the man said again.

"How much are, uh—the apples?" Jeremy asked.

"Wha?"

The language problem. Fridporters spoke their own dialect of Presolatan, and it was not an easy one for foreign ears to understand—doubly hard for Jeremy. Jeremy held up an apple. "How much?"

"Affle," the man said, scowling.

Jeremy gave up, felt in his pocket, and produced a copper. The man held out his hand for the coin, took it, and nodded. Jeremy slowly and deliberately ate his purchase. It was hard and tart, not to his taste at all, but it bought him five minutes in the shop. He finished, tossed the core into the grate, and left.

Though the fog was perhaps a bit lighter, the street was darker now, the sun headed down behind the western rampart of mountains. Jeremy backtracked but somehow missed one or more of the turns. Before long he realized he had passed the outskirts of the town and was striding along a road leading west, the broad brown river at his left hand, open fields at his right. He turned again and promptly lost himself in the labyrinth of twisting streets.

Three people whom he asked for directions ignored him. He plodded on aimlessly. Finally, just as lights began to show in the windows, he found himself in a somehow-familiar street. He followed it, found a turn that he seemed to recollect, and took it. It was only the blind alley that he and Nul had blundered into earlier.

Cursing under his breath, Jeremy turned—and almost ran into the two sailors.

"Thought ya'd be back." The short one, the one Nul had brained, grinned. His breath was foul.

"I have no quarrel with you," Jeremy said, wishing he'd brought a weapon of some kind with him.

"We got one wiv you, though. Bust my head, bust a messmate's toe, would ya?"

The tall sailor gave Jeremy a rough push, making him step back. The fact that the tall one limped a bit when he stepped forward was very small comfort. "Thought ya'd get off poundin' me an' my friend, uh?" he said.

"I didn't—"

"Close it, mate. Ya've a lesson to learn."

The fist came from nowhere, smashing into Jeremy's stomach, doubling him, knocking the breath clean out of him. Before he could straighten again, a knee crashed into his forehead. He fell to the dirty flagstones of the alley, groaning. The two sailors stood over him, wary but not attacking. Jeremy huffed for breath, found it at last, and got up on unsteady legs. "All right," he said. "Get it over with."

"Here," the tall sailor muttered. "Ya're talkin' funny,

like. Sound a bit like a Bakalona Islander, ya do." He
gave Jeremy a light shove, staggering him back against a
wall.

"Well, fight back," the shorter sailor said.

Jeremy's head throbbed. "What's the use? There're
two of you. You're going to beat the shit out of me no
matter what. Get it over with."

The two sailors exchanged a startled glance. The taller
one said, "I don't know about this, Willum. Don't seem
right, somehow, if he just lets us do it."

The shorter man thought it over. "Look here, you wiv
th' monkey. What if just Grice here fights you alone?"

Jeremy looked up at the tall sailor, a head at least
bigger than he was. "What if I just pounded my head
against the stone wall there until I broke it? That'd
accomplish the same thing."

Grice scratched his head. "Slagged if I understood half
o' that. Look, man, what's wrong wiv ya? The monkey,
he jumped Willum here, and he was smaller to Willum
than you are t'me."

"He isn't a monkey," Jeremy said. "He's a pika. His
name's Nul."

"A what? Peeker, did ya say?" Willum asked.

"Pika," Jeremy panted. "Did you catch him?"

"Nay, he scrambled away. Look, you all right?"

"My belly is kissing my backbone," Jeremy grunted.
"Your friend there has quite a punch."

"Aye," Grice said comfortably, holding up a fist the
size of a cantaloupe. "Put m'hand through a solid oak
door once. Remember, Willum?"

"The girl in Debalosha," Willum said. "What took yer
coppers and then wouldn't let ya in her bedroom."

"I got in, though."

"That ya did, Grice. And wa'n't she mad, though?"

They both chuckled. Jeremy, bent at the waist, concentrated on getting his breath back.

"Ah, well, that was a time, eh, Grice? And what d'ya
think about this fella's words?"

"What words is that, Willum?"

"Why, one word: pika." Willum said. "Grice, wa'n't
that the word t' lad kept jabbering about t' th' master?"

"Aye, Willum, it was, if I recollect aright. Pikas and the Twilight Valley, it seems it was."

"What lad?" Jeremy asked. He could now almost stand upright; at least he had achieved a stooped Groucho-Marx posture.

"T' lad we gave passage to on th' *Carosar*. Awful vexed he was to find the *Gull* at sea already; but t' master told him our craft could overtake her, and so we did."

Willum added, "He come right on t' deck wiv magic. He seen t' master and paid him an almighty bribe, I'd guess, t' leave port a day early. Owners'd turn a pretty pale green if they knowed what he was about, I'd lay. T' old ship wa'n't even three-quarter laded when we put out, was it, now, Grice?"

"Not near three-quarter," Grice acknowledged. "But t' master decided t' put out t' sea anyways, 'count o' that lad."

Jeremy tried to straighten completely and found it a waste of effort. "Who was he? What did he look like?"

Willum glanced at Grice, who raised his shoulders. "Master give'm t' little cubbyhole where cabin boy sleeps when we have one. He didn't stir out the whole trip. But of a night t' captain would talk wiv'm, and sometimes we'd overhear. 'Gotta get t' th' Twilight Valley. You know anything about pikas? Can we catch t' *Gull*?' "

"Did you see him?"

"Not more'n two, three times, never t' speak to. Didn't really get a good look at'm."

Willum took up the story: "I did. Just a lad, maybe seventeen, thereabout. Not big built. Wore a cap and a heavy cloak. Talked kind o' hoarse, like."

"What happened to him?"

"He left, he did, headin' west, up t' river. Now. Ya better?"

"Yes, a little."

"Good." Willum looked him up and down. "Now. Tell ya th' truth, ya've shamed Grice and me. It wa'n't right for the two of us t' fight one landlubber, and him a small one. 'Twas unsailorly behavior of the both of us, and we're sorry."

Jeremy's breath was still coming in painful hitches.
" 'S all right."

Willum nodded. "Good. So you an' me will fight it
out. Ya ready now?"

"Fight it out?"

"Surely. 'Twouldn't satisfy our honor, now, not t' have
a bit of a fight, would it, Grice?"

" 'Twouldn't indeed, Willum."

"Oh, shit."

Willum put up his hands and began to dance in and
out. "Come on, then, lad. I'll go easy-like till ya get ya
wind back. Let's get it over wiv. Here we go."

Willum was a good twenty years older than Jeremy,
but he moved fast, dodged easily, and seemed hard as
stone. They fought for five minutes, got hot, and Willum
companionably suggested that Grice could hold their coats.
They shucked the coats off, joined again, and slugged at
each other for maybe ten more minutes. Willum concentrated on body blows—once after Jeremy had struck him
hard on the forehead, he paused to give some instruction: "Now, look. Ya hit somebody on t' head, ya gonna
break ya hand."

"Specially," Grice put in with a grin, "somebody hard-
headed as my messmate here."

"Arr," grunted Willum. He slapped his flat stomach
hard. "Th' belly, see? If ya got a rock or a stick, it's t'
head. If ya ain't, it's th' belly and chest. Got it? Go
again."

Despite Willum's evidently well-intentioned advice, Jeremy was knocked down twice. When he rose the last
time, Grice quietly suggested, "If ya've had enough,
mate, it's no disgrace t' say so."

"I had enough when we started," Jeremy grunted.

"Well, then!" Willum held out his hand for the
Thaumian handshake—a quick grasp like that of arm-
wrestlers and a side-to-side movement—and laughed.
" 'Twas a good fight, and I'm fully satisfied if you are,"
he pronounced formally.

"Oh, yes," Jeremy said, pressing his left hand to his
bruised and throbbing chest.

"Here, ya're a mess." Willum slapped the moist sand

and dirt from Jeremy's back and trousers. "Have a drink wiv us?"

"Uh—thanks. But I'd better get back to the inn. If I can find it."

Grice held out Jeremy's coat and helped him slip into it. "What inn'd that be?"

"I don't remember the name of the place," Jeremy confessed.

Willum said, "Probably th' Durenskans'. T' master of t' *Gull* sometimes puts up there in t' summer, when he's in port a longish time. That's t' one he'd recommend t' ya, sure's sheep-shanks. Have a bit of a drink wiv us and we'll take ya back."

Jeremy hobbled with them to a dim and smoky grog-shop, where the sailors insisted on toasting him with some sort of distilled hellfire the color of molten copper. He got a couple of drinks down and started to feel lightheaded. He gave the sailors a wide grin which hurt his damaged left eye. He closed the eye and reeled a bit in his seat. They looked at him with what seemed to be honest concern.

"Probably a mistake t' drink wiv maybe green and purple bruises way down on t' inside of ya," Grice advised. "Sit quiet for a spell. When ya're better, we'll find t' inn."

"Why are you so friendly all of a sudden?" Jeremy asked through a haze of alcohol and aches.

Willum shrugged. "Why not? We just wanted t' finish what we started back in Dale Haven's all. Bad luck t' take a blow and not ever return it, ya know. But we got nothing against ya, mate. And ya're a game one, for all that ya don't know nothing about t' fist-fighting."

At length, well after dark, the three of them started off in search of the inn, Jeremy in the middle, Grice on his left, Willum on his right, their arms around each other's shoulders. Grice and Willum needed the steadying influence; Jeremy needed the support.

They were still a little way from the inn when Barach found them. He was at first thundery, but when Jeremy assured him that things had turned out all right, he took over the support duties and bade the sailors a curt farewell.

"Nul?" Jeremy asked as they lurched toward the inn.

"Is in the room. He finally found his way back two hona ago. I walked the streets looking for you, went back just now to make sure you had not turned up, and was just setting out again when I met you. Here we are."

It was agony to ascend the five steps to the front door, but Jeremy made it. "At least our room's on the ground floor," he grunted.

"When we get back to Whitehorn, I'm asking Fallon to start you on a course of unarmed self-defense. This is shameful."

"I entirely agree," Jeremy said.

They limped down the corridor and into the room. Nul leaped up as they came in, grinning at the sight of Jeremy—but his grin quickly changed to kindly solicitude and then to anger. "Should find sailors. Hit head again," he raged.

"No, it's over," Jeremy said, easing himself onto his hard bunk. "And listen, there's news." Briefly he sketched in the story of their pursuer and his interest in the pikas that might be in the Twilight Valley.

"This is bad," Barach said. "I had no idea that anyone else would even be interested. And the mischief of it is that I can't even speak to Tremien; these cursed mazerite mountains prevent that."

"We'll have to leave early tomorrow," Jeremy said. "Fog or no. Whoever he is, he has a head start."

"We will leave early. That is, if you feel up to making the journey."

"I'll be all right. I'll have to be."

Barach sighed. "What a shambles this is turning out to be. There's one small blessing at least—your use of the language is getting better."

Closing his eyes, Jeremy said, "Begging for mercy must be very good practice."

CHAPTER 6

JEREMY WAS DISCOURAGINGLY achy the next morning, but Barach was eager to set out, and the younger man did not admit the effort it cost him to slip into the straps of his pack and shoulder his crossbow. Barach, who had transferred almost all of his belongings into another pack, considerately placed both dwindled gargoyles in his own carpetbag and so spared Jeremy the added weight of Fred, at least. "Come," he said, taking the lead out of the inn. "Dawn is almost upon us. Our guide will be ready to go."

The woman, Bessora, was waiting for them already in the street. Short, like all the other Northlanders, and even more heavyset than most, she had nearly black eyes and jet black hair that glistened in the golden light of a torch she carried. She greeted Barach with a rattle of quick words. Jeremy found her language absolutely impossible to understand, but Barach was a patient interpreter. "She says there are horses for both of us in the stables, together with our pack pony. I hope you're up for a good day's ride."

"Oh, yes," Jeremy said, thankful for small favors. "I'd much rather ride than walk."

It was perfectly true, for though Jeremy had never sat on a horse before coming to Thaumia, there he had learned to be a pretty fair horseman. True, his very first experience, with a gentle mare named Whisper, had left him with saddle sores and a disinclination ever to ride again; but training had improved things wonderfully, though at times he had complained that a true wizard should never have need of such a thing as a steed.

Truth to tell, Jeremy had even begun to enjoy horses. He and Kelada had even gone on several pleasure rides in the long, mellow afternoons of autumn, their mounts rocking easily along under the eaves of the forest, and eventually Jeremy had come to feel comfortable in the saddle. He was not prepared, however, for the sight that met him in the warm, dung-scented stable. "Those are horses?" he asked, blinking at the huge creatures waiting patiently for them.

"Northern horses, made for work, not pleasure rides," Barach said shortly, already busy lashing bedrolls and packs to the pony.

Jeremy walked around the three animals. They stood very tall, their massive shoulders above his eye level, and they were correspondingly heavily built, with enormous thick legs like those of Percherons supporting barrel-shaped bodies that were covered with thick shaggy dark-brown hair. The three horses stared back at him placidly, their large, liquid eyes half concealed behind crinkled drooping manes. Next to them, the pack pony, similarly shaggy but a light dappled gray and a great deal more delicately built, seemed positively dwarfish as it stood patiently beneath the bundles of provisions that Barach had lashed to its back.

"You take the horses. I think I'd better ride the pony," Jeremy said.

"No, sorry. Little Thistledown has to carry our provisions."

"But these damn things are so big—are they really ours?"

"Only the pony is; I bought him. But the others must return with Bessora once we reach the Falls. We will make the rest of the journey afoot."

Jeremy had seized the reins of one of the horses. With a dubious look at the faraway saddle, he asked, "How do we mount these behemoths?"

"Carefully," Barach advised with a quirk of his mustaches that just might have been a smile.

In the end the combination of the horses' size and

Jeremy's bruises proved too much. He was reduced to the ignominy of having to lead the horse he had chosen next to a wooden gate, clamber up the ladderlike bars, and swing on that way, much to Bessora's ill-concealed amusement. Nul, who was to ride pillion, climbed up similarly, but even with the help of Jeremy's outstretched arm the pika had difficulty getting onto the animal's back. "Ugh," he grunted, settling into place behind Jeremy. "Like sitting on a table."

Bessora swung up onto her mount with an easy, almost insolent movement, and even Barach managed to get into the saddle without assistance, though the old man was by no means as graceful about it as their guide. She said something, and they followed her out of the stable, the pony, tethered to Barach's saddle, clumping along behind.

The morning was still dark and fairly misty, though not nearly as foggy as the previous day had been. They clopped through the echoing, deserted morning streets, occasional lighted windows making bright yellow smears off to their left and right until there were no more windows and no more houses. The narrow cobbled street became a broad unpaved road; from off to their left Jeremy could hear the murmur of the Friddifor River.

At first the rocking, swaying ride was uncomfortable for Jeremy, his strained muscles and bruised flesh protesting at every heavy step of his lumbering steed, but before long he fell into the animal's rhythm and tried to adjust his seating—though his legs still felt uncomfortably wide apart, straddling that monster back. Eventually he found that he was actually beginning to enjoy their progress.

The mist lightened to pearly luminescence with dawn and fled entirely when the yellow sun at last peeked over the eastern mountains. The countryside, revealed as by a rising curtain, seemed to spread itself out around them. Nul, who seemed much more ill at ease than Jeremy on horseback, squirmed as he took a look around from the high vantage of the saddle and muttered, "Big wide valley here."

It was indeed. The Friddifor, broad, brown, and slow-moving, stretched more than a thousand yards across at this point, and the valley on the other side continued in a gentle series of rolling hills, lightly forested with conifers, until the forbidding gray-blue mountains began again. Similar country on their right hand bore many signs of cultivation and tilling, with a few isolated stone farmhouses now and again spewing smoke aromatic with fish fat. Jeremy was just as happy when these fell behind them and the only odors on the air were the clean scents of fir resin and moving water.

Their pace was steady, though unhurried, and by midmorning they had put perhaps ten miles behind them. They stopped at a small country inn, really hardly more than a tavern, to refresh themselves and the mounts. The proprietors, a stocky, swarthy married couple (anyway, Jeremy thought, they *look* married) served them a pale bland ale, slabs of hearty brown bread with butter and honey, and of course smoked fish.

Again Jeremy needed some assistance getting into the saddle. This time the innkeeper gave him a leg up, almost tossing him over the horse; but he settled somehow into the saddle and reached down for the pika, who declined the innkeeper's assistance. Nul grunted up behind him uncomfortably, and with the pika's spindly arms gripping Jeremy's waist, they set off upriver once more. Barach had been engaged in deep conversation with Bessora for most of the morning. Now he allowed Jeremy to draw alongside of him.

"Our guide tells me we shall be at the Falls an ona or so before sundown," he said. "She thinks it would be best if we climb the Gray Stair this evening and rest in the upper valley tonight."

Jeremy's grasp of the language was improving, but he was unsure he had heard the name correctly. "The Gray Stair?"

"Yes. You will see what that is when we get there. How are you holding out? Are your injuries still troubling you?"

"I couldn't win a race, but otherwise there's no permanent harm done."

"Never want to ride horse again," Nul chimed in. "Too big around for pika legs."

"Not so good for man legs, either," Jeremy returned. "The upper valley that you mentioned is our destination, I suppose?"

"Mm. The Friddifor flows for many tens of leagues east to west in the Twilight Valley, which really is the upper valley, all that part between the Gray Falls and the headwaters of the river. It is much broader than this section, and thanks to a freak of geography it is also much warmer. More sunlight, for one thing, and for another the mountains keep most of the snow off. We are traveling specifically to a town called Three Rivers, where two great tributaries join the Friddifor. It is the only settlement of much size in the valley, and beyond a doubt it is the place where the fur traders go in trading season. Despite my studies, I know but little of the area. However, from Bessora I gather that the town is a good walk upriver, perhaps three or four days westward from the Falls." Barach frowned behind his beard, appeared to be on the verge of saying something more, and evidently thought better of it.

"What is it?" Jeremy asked.

For a few moments Barach was silent, appearing irresolute. Finally he shrugged. "Nothing for certain. Only we shall have to be circumspect. Travelers are surpassingly rare in the Valley, and we, obviously from the Southlands, will be conspicuous. Remember that those of the Valley deeply distrust and fear all magic; they will likely regard Nul with extreme suspicion."

" 'Extreme suspicion'? What that mean?" Nul grunted in a combative tone.

"Only that they have never seen a pika, friend Nul. They will not understand what you are—nor will they be eager even to try to understand, if I know human nature. We must therefore travel as quietly and as cautiously as possible. I fear that will mean some nights in the open."

"That doesn't seem so bad," Jeremy said. "At least if the weather holds."

"In some ways it is not bad at all. As for the weather, I think we shall be warm enough—the pony is carrying our bedrolls, and they are good ones—but there are strange animals in the Valley, Bessora says, and if the traders' story held any truth, there may be unnatural things as well. We shall have to keep careful watch."

"I watch," Nul said. "And any hob I see—damned be he that cries 'Hold! No more!' "

Barach chuckled as Jeremy shook his head.

The horses, seeming to be absolutely indefatigable, clopped ahead at the same steady pace. The sun reached its zenith, though that point was still quite low in the southern sky, and began to slip down toward the mountain rims ahead. Gradually the river grew narrower and more agitated, its color changing from an earthy brown to black streaked with white, rushing faster over a bed of loose, well-rounded black rocks as the land rose and the valley walls began to close in again. At last they rode a narrow track between steep hillsides, and from ahead came a distant thundering sound that increased in volume as they neared.

"The Gray Falls," Barach said. They had fallen into single file, and Jeremy, bringing up the rear behind the pack pony, leaned far out to see around the old mage. It was a sight worth seeing: a heavy curtain of water tumbled into spray and foam from a height of perhaps a hundred and fifty feet, spilling over a forbidding rampart of stone and shouting with a voice like twenty earthquakes. Jeremy began looking for the Gray Stair, whatever that was, with no success.

They were deep in the shadow of the cliff before he spotted it. The right wall of the canyon had become almost perpendicular. Carved into the gray granite, the work of many hands over uncounted years, was what had to be the Gray Stair: a zigzag path, more than man-high and perhaps two feet deep, running in a dozen or more stretches up to the top of the cliff. There was also something more intriguing: a wooden derrick, small at this distance but unquestionably enormous in reality, projected a short way over the cliff edge above, and from it hung a heavy rope, looped and doubled. "What's that?" Jeremy shouted over the roar of the falls.

Barach looked back at him, then in the direction of his pointing finger. "The lift," he yelled over his shoulder.

"The same mechanism the traders use. How else did you suppose we were to get this pony to the top?"

"We have to lift him?" Jeremy asked incredulously.

"It's only fair. Poor little Thistledown could never make the climb alone."

The basin of the falls was somewhat wider than the rest of the canyon; the river, slowly eating its way back through the rock, had broken down enough cliff and had piled enough debris to make a sort of flat shingle beach on the right side. As long as they were in single file and on horseback, conversation was impossible; the very ground shook from the thunder of the water. A fine drifting mist filled the air, silvering the horses' shaggy brown backs and forming droplets like spiderweb dew in Barach's eyebrows and beard. At last they stopped and dismounted, Jeremy sliding off awkwardly first and then giving Nul a hand, at the foot of the Gray Stair.

Barach, already on the ground, bent his head close to Jeremy's ear. "I'm afraid you'll have to be the one to make the climb. The derrick is simple to operate; when we see you at the top, we'll arrange matters for Nul, then the pony."

Jeremy nodded, though he felt absolutely no eagerness to undertake the steep climb. He paused only long enough for a deep drink of icy water straight from the foaming river. Then, with a sickly smile and an unenthusiastic wave to the others, he set off up the stair.

The rock underfoot had been carved into steps, well worn in the center from years and years of tramping feet. They inclined up the cliff face for perhaps a hundred feet before reversing. There was no hand-hold and no safety rail; and the steps were no more than two feet wide. Jeremy felt terribly exposed as he began to climb, not the least because his path on the first leg took him closer to the roaring falls.

Halfway up a disturbing thought came to him: at the switchback, the stairs going up would be well over his head. Was he expected to jump for it? He was already high over the riverbed, and the prospect was more than daunting.

His legs began to ache and tremble even before he

reached the first landing. Worse, the moisture in the air collected on the stair, making it slippery and encouraging a thin, slick growth of green moss; only the center was worn clean, and Jeremy had to keep his head down to direct his steps aright.

He grunted and puffed along, and as he neared the switchback he became aware that the stair seemed to end in a slanted wooden partition of some type. It puzzled him a good bit until he actually reached it; then he saw that it was hinged at the bottom. He pressed back, and it swung away from him and down until it lay flat on a ledge cut level in the manner of a landing. After a moment, Jeremy understood. He walked over the wooden partition and found that the landing widened out just beyond it—here the carvers had gone deeper into the stone, leaving a recess all of three feet deep. Jeremy turned, raised the wooden partition again, and closed it. Cleats on this side made it possible to climb up to the next long line of carved stone stairs.

But he had to rest first. He sat on the mist-cooled landing with his back against the stone cliff and looked down, where Nul, Barach, and Bessora appeared to be talking. Barach glanced up, shading his eyes; Jeremy gave him a weary wave and set off again on the long climb.

His legs seemed almost dead beneath him long before he reached the top. He stumbled more than once, feeling a thud as his heart, which seemed to realize even better than his head just how high they both were, leaped in alarm. Caution and desperation drove him at last, and when he finally emerged onto a great level plateau at the top of the stair he felt like weeping with relief.

But the sun was already very low in the west, giving him no time to rest. He approached the wooden derrick and found that it operated by means of a block and tackle, driven by a double-handled windlass. A complicated-looking harness of leather lay on the edge of the drop, tucked under the protecting overhang of the derrick platform but tied securely to the long, heavy rope. Jeremy pushed it off and found the restraining chock for the windlass. He drew it out, and the weight of the harness made it drop down to the riverbed below.

Jeremy lay flat on his stomach to look over the edge. Nul, it appeared, would be the first passenger. A tiny and foreshortened Barach tied him to the harness, also affixing a bundle or two for good measure, and then gave Jeremy a wave.

The pika was very light, but then the rope was very long. Jeremy's shoulders began to throb with the effort of turning one of the two cranks. At last the dangling Nul hove into view, body spinning slowly in the harness, huge orange eyes tightly closed and face looking most unhappy. Jeremy chocked the windlass carefully, held onto the derrick platform, and leaned far out. "Give me your hand."

It seemed to be an effort for the little pika to release his grip on the rope, but he stretched out a long, spidery arm and Jeremy caught his three-fingered hand in a sturdy clasp. Leaning back, the young man pulled Nul to the edge of the platform. The little creature's feet scrabbled for purchase, and finally Nul was able to stand. Barach had tied Nul securely, and it took a minute or two to free him.

Nul immediately edged away from the drop. "Too high," he said with conviction.

"What's next? Barach?"

"Pony."

"Thistledown? How am I supposed to manage him?"

Nul nodded toward the bundle that had been attached to the harness. "Brought help."

He had brought Fred and Busby. Jeremy saw the idea immediately. The gargoyles, freed from the carpetbag, inspected the windlass, caught on to its principle of operation, and began to enlarge themselves, swelling with a series of slow pulsations almost like breathing. Nul, meanwhile, retreated to a safe distance from the edge of the chasm.

Jeremy let the harness go. Again he looked over the edge of the drop until Barach waved; then he turned. The gargoyles, full-size again, waited for him to give the word. "All right, fellows. Now."

With Fred at one crank and Busby at the other, the windlass creaked steadily on. The stone talons had been equipped with an opposable thumb of sorts, no doubt a thoughtful gift from the sculptor-magician who had first formed the gargoyles, and they gripped the metal handles with no difficulty. They looked odd, the two stone monsters, as they moved with the untiring precision of a machine, but they unquestionably did a better job than Jeremy's exhausted shoulders could have.

The pony came up looking resigned but not startled. Jeremy gathered from the little beast's patient stare that he had made the trip before. This time it was a bit trickier hauling the harness aboard; Busby held the windlass in place while Fred, with his superior reach, snagged the harness and pulled it to the derrick. Busby gave just enough slack to get the pony safely onto the platform; then Jeremy freed the animal, led it to where Nul sat, and sent the harness down a final time for Barach. Just as the gargoyles began to crank the mage up, Jeremy, leaning over the edge, saw their guide setting off downriver on her own horse, the two others in tow. By now the valley was a place of deepening purple shadows, though here on the rim a wan sun still shone a little way above the mountains.

"Here we are at last," Barach said as he freed himself from the harness. "And none of us the worse for it, though I fear you will feel the effects of your climb for some days to come. Where's Nul?"

"Back there somewhere," Jeremy said with a jerk of his head. He had taken the time to look around while waiting for the others to reach the top of the cliff. They were clearly at a boundary of sorts: to the west, the upper valley opened out into a wide, rolling landscape, heavily forested with evergreens, while the mountains retreated on either side of it, spreading out to a much more hospitable distance than in the lower valley. The sky overhead was going salmon with the incipient sunset, but it was clear and cold-looking.

The pony seemed no more nervous of the gargoyles than it had been of the horses—which, when Jeremy came to think of it, were about the same size. Barach and Jeremy walked behind the two creatures of stone, leading the pony behind them, on a path that led down from the derrick platform into the valley proper. There they found Nul, squatting with his back to a low, partly roofed-over semicircle of roughly laid stones, a small pyramid of wood in front of him and an iron tripod with a fairly large black cauldron on it resting over the wood. "Finally," he said as they approached. "This look like place for camp. Good windbreak built here. Cooking pot. Fires have been here. I pick up dry driftwood from down close to river. All right?"

"It's a fine place to camp," Barach said. "You did well to collect the wood, and we shall have fire in just a moment, if steel, flint, and tinder can summon an elemental to this magic-forsaken place."

The fire magic, at least, worked. With a cheery blaze to encourage them, Jeremy and Nul between them hauled the cauldron down to the river's edge for a thorough cleansing, a scrub with clean sand, and a final rinse. Then they brought it back a quarter full of water.

Barach, though no cook, at least managed a hot supper of sorts, dried meat and vegetables cooked into a bubbling and fragrant stew along with steaming-hot herb tea. Jeremy nodded over his cup, and somehow he fell asleep without even realizing he was getting sleepy. He jolted awake once, aware that he was trembling violently; then he realized that everything was. "What—?"

"Earthquake," came Busby's complacent voice. "Small one."

The rumbling shudders died away. "No harm done," Busby grated.

"There is a deep magic here," Barach said uneasily. "That was no ordinary tremor."

"Magic—in this valley?"

Barach, his face ruddy in the campfire light, shrugged. "Not verbal magic, Jeremy. More like elemental magic, I should think. But it's over now. Sleep. And be grateful that it did not happen when you were halfway up the Gray Stair."

Jeremy shivered. "Thank you for the thought. Now I don't know if I *can* sleep."

He was far too tired not to sleep, however. Barach, Nul, and the gargoyles took watch duty. The remainder of the night passed quietly, and it was just as well. Nothing short of a real earthquake or an all-out war could have awakened Jeremy.

The next day's sunrise came cold and clear. "Good morning!" Barach called as Jeremy crept out of his bedroll. "Hot water for a quick wash, if you want it. Nul and I have already made our toilet."

Jeremy tipped enough hot water into a natural depression in the rock—"bathtub," Nul named it—to give himself a quick sponge-off, the only kind of bath he'd had since embarking on the *Gull* some eleven days earlier. He shivered in the cold, and the water itself rapidly lost its warmth. His ablutions were very cursory.

Back at the campfire Barach had reclaimed the cauldron and was cooking up some kind of porridge in it. Jeremy's protesting muscles had stiffened in the night, and he did a series of slow-motion stretches as Barach prepared their breakfast and Nul sat sharpening his short sword. The gargoyles had gone to the river and, despite the nearby falls and the rushing white water, were sporting in it, leaping and diving. When Barach called him over to eat, Jeremy nodded toward the two stone figures. "I suppose they're too heavy to be washed over the Falls."

"I should think so," Barach said, looking at the two. "They're mainly interested in the stones on the bottom, anyway, and they won't stray far enough out to get in the worst of the current."

Nevertheless, Fred and Busby were quite a sight, wading in the rush of water, sometimes where the current was strong enough to dash a sheet of spray over them, ducking under the surface for long minutes, then emerging a little farther upstream.

The flesh-and-blood travelers made short work of breakfast, as did their pony, and before long they had extinguished their campfire and had set off west again. Fred and Busby, rejoining them on the path, bubbled with news about the valley: it was all basalt, they said, clearly the product of a volcanic eruption not long ago.

"How long ago?" Jeremy asked nervously.

"Recently," Busby said. "Not more than ten thousand years back, we should judge."

"Oh," Jeremy said, breathing easier.

The track here in the upper valley was by no means as well traveled as that below the Falls; indeed, it was scarcely more than a narrow strip of turf worn clean of grass. The river formed its western boundary, and a dense fir forest the eastern one. The trees, though fairly tall, crowded so closely together that Jeremy could see only a short way into the wood. A similar forest grew on the far side of the river, and beyond them, but farther away now, were the familiar bare pinnacles of the Fridhof Mountains, their tops uniformly snow-crowned. Before the group had gone far along the trail, the gargoyles, engrossed in a discussion of magmas and lavas, took up the lead, and gradually they left the sound of the Falls behind them.

"I doubt if we will encounter anyone," Barach said. "Winter is upon us, and that is a time of little trade or activity in Twilight Valley. But as we draw closer to Three Rivers, it would be as well for our stone friends to dwindle themselves again; in a country that fears and hates magic, they are a little too magical for comfort."

Jeremy agreed. Though he still felt some discomfort from the pounding he had taken from the sailor, Willum, and from the long climb up the Gray Stairs, soon he had walked a great deal of it out and had fallen into a steady pace, not fast but almost restful. He estimated they were making about three miles an hour. The sun, climbing higher in the sky to their left, gave them a sort of half-hearted warmth, not springlike certainly, but at least not the harsh chill of winter; and before long Jeremy actually began to hum.

"Sing song," Nul said suddenly.

"I can't sing," Jeremy grinned.

"You sing well enough," Barach answered. "And there are no ears but friendly ones to hear you. Come. Favor us with a song in that weird tongue of yours."

"Well—hm. All right. Here's one my mother used to sing." He cleared his throat, hoped he could find something like the right key, and began:

Alas, my love, you do me wrong
To cast me off discourteously—

He sang all the way through "Greensleeves"—a properly medieval piece, he thought, for the strange land of Thaumia.

When he had finished, Barach said, "Very nice."

"What do you mean by that?"

"Just that; the song was very nice."

Jeremy shook his head. "No. You don't understand. 'Very nice' is what you say when you don't want to hurt anyone's feelings."

Nul grinned. "Well—"

"I'd like to see you do better, you animated dust bunny."

Nul licked his lips with his odd round tongue. "Not know any human song. Can sing pika song. That do?"

"Lay on," Jeremy said.

In a voice quite a bit softer than his normal speaking tone, Nul began to sing. The melody was unadorned and plain, a long, drawn-out line of simple variation, and the words were of course entirely unintelligible to Jeremy. Still, there was something like a charm in the plaintive, chantlike lyric. When the words had ended, Nul looked away and coughed. "Song finished. That all I remember."

"It was wonderful," Barach said.

"Better than mine," Jeremy admitted. "What was it about?"

"Just pika song. List of different kinds of gems, how they look, what good they are. Not much of a song." Nul gave Jeremy a shy sideways glance. "Funny. I not think of old songs for years and years. Then Jare die. Songs come back to me."

"Hold on to them, then," Barach told him. "I begin to see that pikas are not just interested in food, drink, and sleep after all. They have a music of their own—and a very lovely kind of music, at that."

"You next," Nul grinned. "Old Barach sing song now."

"Good heavens, my voice would frighten the pony."

"Sing," Jeremy ordered. "Sing or your beard's nothing but a rat's nest."

"See here," Barach said sternly but with a lurking twinkle, "I've worked hard to grow this ornament and I will *not* have it insulted by a stripling like you. Why, your own beard's not a hand's breadth yet, you pup."

"Sing!" Nul and Jeremy chorused.

"Very well, but give me time to think of something appropriate."

They walked along for a few hundred feet before a song came to Barach. Then, with a surprisingly clear and strong baritone, much like the voice he had used in his days of power to sing potent spells, he began:

I knew an old man who lived alone,
With a heigh! ho! din-dowly;
Had no women in his home,
No women all his life,
No sweetheart had he ever known,
No sister and no wife . . .

The rollicking tune did not leave the lonely man alone for very long; while practicing a magic spell the unlucky old fellow summoned up a very amorous and very naked nymph, and then he had the utmost difficulty in dealing with her sweet wishes and urgent demands. Jeremy, surprised at this earthy streak in his teacher, began to chuckle when the nymph cornered the lonely but desperately chaste man in bed, laughed louder when she caught him in a hayrick, and whooped when she at last had her way with him on a food-laden table during a high feast, to the shocked surprise of the diners.

Barach, however, didn't crack a smile, but continued until he reached the very last stanza, which concerned the old man's closest friends visiting him at his sickbed to commiserate with him—and demanding to know the exact wording of the spell that had misfired. As the last note died, Barach gave Jeremy a mock bow. Then he snorted, choking with laughter.

"You old scoundrel," Jeremy howled. "Prim as an archbishop all this time, with such filth in that gray head of yours. What would Tremien say?"

"He—he," Barach began, gasping. He took a deep breath. "He taught it to me."

Jeremy collapsed again. Nul shook his head. "Human mens," he muttered. "Make such fuss about mating." But the laughter was infectious, and before long even he was laughing, or barking out the short *urf*ing sounds that passed for pika laughter.

Their trip upriver progressed almost without incident. On the second night, something dark and skulking came close enough during Jeremy's watch to make the pony nervous, but Busby stalked out into the darkness, clashed through some low-growing brush, and connected solidly with something that yelped and ran away. The gargoyle did not identify the creature except to sniff, "Couldn't even take a little lash of the tail."

Aside from that mild excitement, the journey was simply a steady march in the cold, made worse only when, as on the morning of the third day, a drizzle fell. By then Fred and Busby had dwindled down to cat-size again, and they, riding in packs on the pony's back, did not complain. Nul and Barach, however, found it dismal going as the path underfoot changed to sticky mud and their clothing became soaked. Jeremy, snug in Tremien's gray robe (which seemed waterproof as well as warm), felt a bit guilty—though not guilty enough to take off the robe.

Late in the afternoon of that day they saw signs of life: smoke from chimneys on either side of the river. Near sunset they glimpsed a distant farmhouse, made of stone but not as squat as those of Fridport and with a lower, more rounded roof. They saw no people around it. By then the rain was a steady, miserable sprinkle, so cold that it was almost gelid. "I believe we should stop for the night," Barach said. "We're making slow headway in this. And besides, it would scarcely further our purpose to arrive with an ague. Let's just see what sort of hospitality we can expect in Twilight Valley. Nul, perhaps you should lag behind a little until we can prepare these people for your coming."

The farmhouse was some distance off the trail. Before they had even come close to it, Jeremy began to sense something amiss: no smoke drifted from the chimney, and the place had a curiously forlorn look about it. As they approached they could see that the domed, wood-shingled roof was charred and holed in several places, and soon they saw that the door was off its hinges.

"Looks bad," Jeremy said.

"I agree. Nul, you had better wait here with the pony. Jeremy and I will see if there's anyone about."

"Call if hobs there."

"If hobs are there," Barach said dryly, "we won't have to call. You'll know."

They approached cautiously, though openly. Jeremy caught the scent of burned wood from a hundred feet away. "I'll look," he said.

Some birds the size of pigeons, but longer in the leg and colored a uniform reddish brown, stepped and pecked in the farmyard mud. They formed a single-file line and went sailing away around the building as Jeremy neared. He came up to the gaping doorway, looked into darkness, and finally took a step inside.

The only light came from the doorway itself and from a gaping hole chopped in the ceiling. The room evidently had been the kitchen: a great stone fireplace, dark and cold now, stood in the wall to the right, and a splintered, broken table reared on its two good legs. Jeremy paused, listening. There was no sound, aside from the soft patter of rain on the roof and the steadier, louder *plop plop* of drips from the overhead hole into a growing puddle on the stone floor. Without turning, Jeremy waved Barach over.

The older man was at his shoulder in a moment. "I'm going on in," Jeremy told him. "You might want to wait here."

"Be careful."

Jeremy stepped carefully over broken, scattered rubble, fallen shingles, broken crockery. He found a window, the stout shutters securely fastened with iron pins. Jeremy drew these out and threw open the shutters to let in more light. He stared hard at the windowsill. It bore deep, fresh cuts, as if someone outside had been hacking at it with an axe.

A short hallway led from the kitchen to the rest of the house. One room, a bedroom, had been gutted by fire; the roof overhead was almost completely burned away, just skeletal charred beams left. The bed was a ruin, itself scorched and heaped with soaked black ashes. A door opposite that room was closed. Jeremy tried it, found it barred from the inside, and opened the last door, at the end of the hall. He quickly closed it again, gagging on the stench of decay.

He stumbled back to the kitchen. "Something back here," he said. "And a locked room. We need light."

Barach had one ready; he had come into the kitchen and had retrieved a fallen candle, now burning. "I'll come too."

They stood in the doorway of the last room staring in at a sprawling horror. "What is it?" Jeremy asked.

"A hob. Or what is left of one. Three days dead, I should say."

The body lay on its belly just inside the door. It was manlike, but apelike too, with huge, sloping shoulders and a small head. The creature lay with its feet closest to them. It was large, probably more than six feet from crown to sole. The back of its head, its neck and shoulders all bore pale brown hair, curly and coarse-looking. The right arm had been almost severed at the shoulder, and the body adhered to the stone floor in a thick paste of dried blood. It wore only a sort of tunic, partly dirty beige but mostly dark brown with congealed blood, that left its arms bare and came down almost to its knees; the feet, large and splay-toed, were bare and dirty. The slaughterhouse stench of corruption was overpowering.

"The family tried to stand them off in here," Barach said, his hand pressed to his face and his voice muffled. "They broke in through the ceiling, I think. The people retreated from the bedroom or kitchen to here—and accounted for that one, at least."

"There's a locked door."

"Let's see."

Barach tried the door, as Jeremy had. "Yes, barred from the inside," he murmured. "No marks on the door.

Let's see." He rapped very lightly with his knuckles. "Is anyone there?"

He provoked no response but silence. "I think we ought to make sure there's no one inside," Jeremy said.

"I agree."

Jeremy went to the door and yelled for Nul. The pika led the pony to the farmyard. Before they were very near the house, Thistledown's nostrils flared and his eyes rolled. The pony set his legs, stopping Nul. After a moment, the pika simply tied the pony's lead to a bush, then clumped over to the house, his sword drawn. "What happen?"

"A fight, looks like. One hob here—and it's dead."

"Too bad," Nul said grimly.

They rejoined Barach. "I can see through the crack here," he told them. "There is a bar that we should be able to lift, if we can get any leverage."

Nul brandished his sword. "I try."

The sword blade slipped through the crack easily enough. Nul caught its tip beneath the bar and pressed up. The bar rose, slipped, and fell back in place. "Almost," the pika grunted. "I try again."

On the second attempt the bar came free and clattered to the floor. Jeremy pushed the door open.

A howling demon flew out.

Jeremy, caught by surprise, staggered back, borne against the door frame opposite. Talons tore at his face and throat, hooked in his short beard, tried for his eyes.

Barach yelled something, stopping Nul's sword in mid-descent.

Jeremy caught the claws in his own hands, tumbled to the floor, got the squirming creature under him—

And the human girl, not more than fifteen, began to scream in anger and grief.

CHAPTER 7

A WINDOWLESS STONE hay shed behind the house had escaped burning and ransacking. The girl slept there, wrapped in blankets, after Barach had managed to make her swallow a little broth and a great deal of sleeptea, a calming and soporific herbal brew.

Evening had brought no letup in the rain, but at least they had some shelter from the cold, constant shower. The gargoyles, at full size and completely indifferent to any kind of weather, kept a lookout, one of them just outside the shed and the other a little way off, to the north of the house; Nul, Barach, and Jeremy sat around a very small, almost smokeless fire built under the overhanging roof outside the shed's only door. "Did you learn anything from her?" Jeremy asked as Barach returned from checking on the girl.

The old man sighed, settling down into a knee-popping crouch between Jeremy and Nul. "She said but little, and even that was disjointed and difficult to understand. The trouble happened three days ago, it seems, about the time we were rising after having scaled the cliff. The creatures came in the early-morning darkness. Her father had come outside to look after some sheep that were crying in the fold over there—no use looking, they're all gone now—and came hurrying back in at once. He and her mother barred the doors and the shutters. The hobs pounded and shouted and at last broke through with fire and axe, and the girl retreated into her own bedroom. She keeps calling for her mother. What became of her parents she does not know, though I can guess."

"If she was all alone in the house, why didn't the hobs get her?"

"Who can say for sure? Possibly the coming of sunrise drove them away. They have never had any love for the light; I recall no fight with them that took place during full day. Possibly they had by that time . . . well, let me just say that possibly they were no longer hungry."

Nul shivered. "Things like that had Jare."

Jeremy had checked the workings and string of his crossbow. "Will they be back?"

Barach, staring moodily into the fire, shook his head. "Impossible to say. On the one hand, they left nothing here that they would be interested in, as far as I can see. On the other, who can know their reasons or their thoughts?"

Jeremy eased the crossbow string back, then released the tension gradually. "Three days. The girl stayed in the dark room all that time?"

Barach nodded. "She said little about that, but I believe she must have done so. It is hard to think of her there alone, afraid of the sounds of fighting, so long as they kept up. And afterwards perhaps even more afraid of the silence. It's certain that she has had nothing to eat or drink for several days; and precious little sleep, I should think. We'll take her with us to Three Rivers, of course."

"Of course."

Nul picked up a long twig and poked at the glowing fire, sending a few sparks spiraling like tiny glowing birds out into the heavy dusk and the steady rain. "Where hobs come from? How they get here, to farm?"

"From underground, surely. I wonder if the quake we felt had anything to do with this."

"Are the things that powerful? Could hobs cause an earthquake?" Jeremy asked, frowning.

"Alone, no, they surely could not. However, they may not be completely alone. The Great Dark One was known to work with greater forces than most magicians would dare try to control. Whether the hobs have some remnant of his ability with them now, I have no way of knowing."

Nul snapped the stick he held and tossed it onto the fire, which crackled eagerly to receive it. "But what I want to know is this: where hobs go after leaving here? Where is way to underground from here?"

Barach held out his hands to the warmth. "That I cannot say. Derilis would not know—that is the girl's name, Derilis—and it's far too dark tonight to try to pick up any sort of trail, even if the rain has not spoiled the traces. Nul, did you see to Thistledown?"

Nul nodded out into the dark. "I put pony over there, under the sheep shelter. Just fit."

"Good. We surely cannot be far from Three Rivers; we should try for an early start tomorrow, if Derilis is able to travel. Do you think the two of you could manage to carry the bedrolls and a pack apiece?"

"I could," Jeremy said. "I think I'm more or less recovered from fighting Willum—and from climbing the Gray Stair."

The pika, too, grunted his assent, his orange eyes flashing in the light of the fire. "Nul take two, three packs, if it mean we get to find hobs sooner."

"Well, it shouldn't come to that. I believe our friends Fred and Busby should be small and well concealed when we come near to town, or we'd use them to help carry. If you two can assist me with carrying the pony's load, though, I think the young lady should ride Thistledown."

"I think that's a good idea, too. Nul and I can handle the load."

Barach eased himself down from a crouch to a sitting position. "Even with heavier packs, it shouldn't take much longer to get into town. If what Bessora told me is accurate, I believe we should arrive there sometime late tomorrow."

"Sooner the better," Nul murmured.

They sat for some time around the fire, not speaking, each lost in his own thoughts. At last Barach sighed. "It is said that Ulm of Skandarovon once adventured disguised as a young mercenary, though his skill was all with magic and not with fighting. On a dark and windy night his captain, who knew nothing of Ulm's powerful magics, ordered him to stand watch. Not wishing to lose his sleep, Ulm cast a potent and deadly spell that would instantly destroy any creature that moved to invade the camp. Then he went to sleep."

"And what happened?" Jeremy asked.

"Unfortunately his captain decided to check on the sentry. The moment he stood and moved, a bolt of lightning blasted him to cinders. The next morning Ulm complained that the noise and the ensuing uproar of the soldiers kept him from getting any sleep at all that night."

Jeremy, grinning to himself ruefully, shook his head. "In other words, tonight we mount a full guard, despite having Fred and Busby along to help us."

"I think keeping guard would be wise."

"I'll take first watch."

The shed, tightly built and with a fine wooden floor well off the damp ground, had been a place of storage for hay—the family cow, along with the sheep, was missing—and was still half full of dry, crisp, sweet-smelling straw. The girl slept in the far corner, Nul and Barach just inside the door, burrowed down into the aromatic hay. Jeremy, warm inside his robe, stood watch outside the shed but under the protective overhang of the roof. Fred, a few paces away, crouched like a sphinx in the dim night, hardly more than a shape, motionless and impassive even in the cold rain. A hob, or any other intruder, come to that, would have taken him for a statue; which, Jeremy reflected, he was, difficult though it had become to think of him as stone.

For a sentry on duty, time passed slowly. Jeremy lost himself in a reverie: it would be early December back on Earth, back in Atlanta; he had first left his own world nearly a year ago. December 21 it had been, the first day of winter, and coincidentally a time of exaltation in the peculiar magical configurations of the Thaumian universe.

He had not been translated directly to Thaumia. Before arriving there, he had spent long weeks in the Between, the bizarre and deadly emptiness that linked all universes (or so Thaumian science taught), the "place" where all dreaming beings went during sleep. It was there he had first met Kelada, exiled thief, a young woman filled with hatred for the world because she did not love herself.

How far they had come in that one short year. Briefly he thought of his dark twin, Sebastian Magister, he whose powerful spell had first made possible the exchange between Earth and Thaumia. Sebastian was still in Atlanta, as far as he knew, filling his place at the advertising agency—and elsewhere. For Sebastian was now married to Cassie, Jeremy's former lover.

Despite himself, Jeremy smiled. Sebastian, the unfulfilled mage, had discovered a natural talent—and a real love—for, of all things, business. Keen-witted and ruthless, he had plunged into the advertising world and within six months had worked his way to the top in Taplan and Taplan, the agency that employed him under the impression that he was Jeremy. The last Jeremy had seen of Sebastian, the rascal had been planning to branch out with his own consulting firm. That had been in June; by this time, Jeremy supposed, Sebastian was probably pulling in defense contracts. Five-hundred-dollar hammers and thousand-buck screwdrivers somehow seemed just his line. More than likely Taplan and Taplan was now a wholly owned subsidiary of SebastiCo, Inc. And surely Sebastian voted the straight Republican ticket.

Well, Jeremy hoped that Cassie and Sebastian were as happy as he and Kelada had been. Would be again, he trusted. Funny—at first Jeremy had thought himself in love with beautiful, raven-haired Melodia, the quiet healer who had been one of Sebastian's many feminine conquests on Thaumia. But the two of them were far too different in temperament and spirit ever to have a real love. Only when he had thought his life was lost had Jeremy realized how much and how deeply he cared for Kelada—and how much the waif who thought herself ugly had come to care for him. The simple realization was magical enough to give her true beauty, or rather to let the true beauty that had always been inside her to show through. Jeremy's love for her swelled his heart . . . even when, as tonight, he began to doubt the wisdom of his choosing to stay in Thaumia.

For, to tell the truth, even now he sometimes felt

misplaced on this strange world; there were still times when he missed Earth, when he would like to speak with his friends, his family, or with Cassie. Even times when he remembered what a Big Mac tasted like and missed it.

Tonight was such a time. What had he to do with this business of keeping watch against some improbable monsters from the depths of the world, with preparing for combat in a most medieval fashion? What right had he to practice magic, and to miss it sorely when it no longer worked for him? Standing in the shelter of the shed roof, staring into darkness, hearing the chatter of the rain, Jeremy had the odd feeling that somehow he was still dreaming: that none of this, none of the whole year, had been real. With a sharp little pang he thought to himself that he needed to see Kelada, to touch her, to hold her warm and alive in his arms, just to reassure himself that it all had really happened, that he was still here in Thaumia, and that he still loved her and she him.

No, taken all in all, he could not say that his life with Kelada was something he would have willingly missed.

Driven by a chilly west wind, the rain lashed harder, blowing under the overhang of the shed in sharp spiky darts, stinging his face. He took a step or two back. The fire in front of the shed door had smoldered down to dim red embers. They hissed as the drops reached them, steamed, and died. The water elemental riding down on the rain, Barach would have said, had chased the fire elemental back to its own plane, away from their offering of dry wood. Elementals had existed since the first chaos, and in some ways they still yearned for disorder, still hated each other, and still combatted each other, even if only in small ways, in the *tsst!* of cold water against red-hot embers.

At one time Jeremy would have smiled at such talk. But on that terrible day when he had faced the Hidden Hag of Illsmere, an elemental, of all things, had saved his life: a tame fire elemental, something so surpassingly rare that not even a sorceress like the Hag could have foreseen to defend against it. Jeremy wondered where golden-hot Smokharin was now; with Melodia, he supposed, because the fire spirit was as firmly under her spell of beauty and kindness as the moon was under the gravitational spell of Thaumia.

Elementals. That sent him off into another consideration: the mysterious stone mazerite and its anti-magical properties. Elemental magic seemed to work here; why not verbal magic? He supposed that Busby and Fred, themselves made of material favored by the elementals of rock and soil, found themselves welcome here. Perhaps it was that humans had invaded Thaumia as outsiders from magic-poor Earth, had slipped through dimensional windows in the past, coming from all over: Africa, the Americas, Asia, Europe. Were there any Australian-descended Thaumians? He didn't know; certainly he had neither seen nor heard of marsupial animals here.

But perhaps mazerite was a sort of defense mechanism of this world, a way of keeping some part of it safe from the invaders and their ability to change the order of things by the arrangement of words of power. There were times when Jeremy sensed that all of Thaumia was alive, one organism. It might not be beyond all possibility that the world was in some fashion aware of the humans who lived like parasites upon it and that Thaumia had found ways of protecting at least some of her secrets from the puny invaders—whereas native beings, like elementals or even the hobs, might be safe from the subtle protective forces.

In the crackling hay inside the shed Barach stirred, rose in the dark, and came to the doorway. He stood sniffing the cold air, listening to the harder drumming of rain on the shed roof. "It is time for your relief, I think. I see the weather has worsened. That's good."

Jeremy yawned and stretched, feeling the mail that he wore beneath the robe lift and fall, a sobering weight. "You have peculiar ideas of goodness."

"My young friend, hobs dislike getting wet about as much as they dislike the light of day. I'd say the storm only makes us safer."

"You may have a point there."

"Get some sleep."

"Thanks. Did you sleep well?"

"I thought too much to sleep," Barach said. "I pondered long about those farmhouses we saw at a distance. The smoke from their chimneys."

"What about them?"

"The smoke may not have been rising from chimneys."

Jeremy shivered despite the robe. "You'd better wrap yourself in your blanket," he said. "The fire's been out for a long time, and it's wet and cold out here."

"I'll be all right. You will need the bedroll for yourself; I gave two of our heavier coverings to Derilis."

"No, I have the robe. Here." Jeremy stepped into the shed, felt in the hay, shook out the blanket, and returned to spread it cloaklike around Barach's shoulders.

The old man pulled the makeshift garment a little tighter around his neck and patted Jeremy's hand, an indulgent grandfather thanking an officious grandson. "Thank you, Jeremy. Most considerate of you. Get some rest now. I'll awaken Nul when it is his turn."

Jeremy removed the robe and found the air was really cold inside the shed, so cold that he wondered if the rain might actually be sleet. But he removed the mail, dropped it to the floor, and in just his shirt and trousers burrowed a little way down into the hay. The ample robe was large enough for him to spread it out and draw it over himself like a blanket, and even like that it maintained its virtue of warmth. He snuggled into the straw, closed his eyes, and was asleep.

He awakened to a still gray dawn and a tantalizing smell. Rising from the hay, Jeremy looked outside. The rain had ended, though the roof of the house still glistened with it and the eaves were hung with finger-long icicles. Barach looked up from a more respectable fire than they had risked the night before and said something unintelligible.

"What?" Jeremy asked.

With a frown, Barach said, "Are we back to that? You seemed to understand well enough up to this morning." He spoke slowly and distinctly, and yet Jeremy was unsure whether he had completely understood the old man.

"Something is wrong. I— Wait." He went back into the shed, picked up the robe, shook straw from it, and

donned it. Then he went back. "Now," he said. "Say
something else."

"What would you have me say?" Barach demanded,
and this time his meaning was clear.

"It's the garment," Jeremy said. "I should have noticed the difference before. Somehow wearing it makes
the language easier for me."

"Ah." Behind his heavy beard Barach smiled. "Tremien's
gift. I wonder if he suspected it would be somewhat
proof against the mazerite of these mountains? But of
course he did; the old man is deep in the ways of magic."

"What are you cooking?"

"Eggs! Nul found the hen coop—though these pitiful
little creatures hardly deserve to be called hens—and a
three-day supply. I trust you are hungry."

"Starving. Is the girl—"

"Still asleep. I have asked Fred and Busby to dwindle
and pack themselves. Nul is feeding Thistledown. I suggest we eat first; then I'll awaken Derilis and try to get
her to have something."

Nul returned just as the scrambled eggs were ready.
Barach had brewed tea—not sleeptea, but a hearty brown
infusion almost as strong as coffee—and had toasted
some dry biscuit on an improvised fork made from thin
twigs. Jeremy, dressed again in his mail, boots, and robe,
piled the scrambled eggs on the biscuit and devoured
them eagerly. "It's good to have fresh food," he said.

Nul, whose wide mouth had already taken care of two
of the biscuits, reached for a third. "Good not to have
fish," he added.

As soon as they had finished, Nul went to harness the
pony, and Jeremy began to redistribute the bedrolls and
packs. Barach woke the girl. She came trembling into the
light, a thin, dark young thing with haunted eyes and a
haggard face. She bolted for the house; Barach stopped
her and spoke kindly in a voice too soft for Jeremy to
catch. At last she sat just inside the shed door, her legs
warming at the fire, and munched toasted biscuit and
eggs, not seeming to notice what she ate. But she drank
the tea greedily, two full, steaming cups of it.

Barach took Jeremy aside. "She will need heavier clothing," he said. "If you wouldn't mind searching for some in her room—"

"No," Jeremy said. He walked across the muddy yard and into the house.

With more light coming in through the broken roof, he could see better the desolation inside. The puddle of water in the kitchen had almost covered the floor and had skimmed over with ice. Everything there had been overthrown or pulled from its place. The rank smell of rot in the hallway was even stronger than it had been. He ducked into the room quickly.

It was very dim inside—there was no window here and he had not lit a candle—but enough light spilled through from the great hole in the roof across the hall to let him see. The bed was narrow and simple, another straw mattress pad on a low tablelike affair. A carved wooden chest stood against the wall beside the bed. Rummaging through it, Jeremy found a well-worn pair of sturdy, comfortable-looking boots, some heavy canvaslike trousers, flannel shirts, and a thick woolen coat. Farm clothes. He took these out to the shed.

Barach led the girl inside, spoke something kind to her again, and came back out. "I think her mind is still shocked," he said. "She will do what I tell her, but she will be slow about it. Give her a few simi to dress herself."

Perhaps ten minutes passed. At last the girl opened the door and stepped outside, almost shyly. She had changed into the trousers, shirt, and boots, and the coat, dyed a faded golden brown, was thrown loosely around her shoulders. She asked Barach something in a plaintive voice.

The old man replied in the same sort of dialect. With his fussy old-man's hands he fastened the coat. Nul, who had gone to the sheepfold for the pony, came leading Thistledown. Derilis cried out at the sight of the pika and shrank back. Barach spoke quietly to her once more, his arm around her shoulders. He turned to Jeremy. "She did not see the hobs. She thinks Nul may be one of them. Show her he is our friend."

Jeremy walked to Nul and put his arm on the pika's

shoulder in mimicry of Barach's pose with Derilis. "Smile at the girl," he said.

Nul did. The smile could be frightening enough, given Nul's huge expanse of mouth and sharp teeth, but there was something reassuring in it, evidently. A faint answering smile flickered on the girl's face, like sunshine flashing when cloud-shadows race across the countryside. Thistle snorted and shook his mane. Derilis looked at the pony, her eyes for the first time showing interest. She took a few steps forward and put a shy hand on the animal's cheek. Thistledown nuzzled her.

"Help her on," Barach told Jeremy.

The girl was used to riding. She sat the pony bareback easily and with skill; they were able to put some of the blankets behind her. From the moment they began to travel, her whole attention was on the animal. With quiet delight she patted his neck, stroked his mane, and whispered into his twitching ears as the party resumed its westward trek.

The day wore on without getting any lighter, but at least without rain or snow. The heavy clouds swagged over their heads, and the wind in their faces was bitter and chill, but they made good progress. The river ran more or less west to east here, with a few sweeping, sinuous bends and once in a while a tributary stream to negotiate. They forded the shallower ones, often having to step carefully over ice-glazed stones at the edges of the streams, and found that the people of the Valley had erected low stone bridges, simple arched structures, over the deeper ones. They saw a few more farmhouses, but they all seemed deserted: no smoke, at least, showed from their chimneys—or their roofs. "It looks as if Twilight Valley is under siege," commented Barach, leading the pony. "I wonder what we shall find in the town."

"How far?" Nul asked.

"I am not certain. Not too much farther, surely. It is already afternoon."

But it was early evening before they finally saw the town of Three Rivers in the distance. There was no mistaking it: a bridge, the largest they had seen in this country, arched the stream perhaps a league ahead of them, and off to the right they could see a similar bridge over an unseen tributary stream. The town itself was walled, with no castle as such visible, but with many defensive towers built into the stone wall itself. Here there was smoke in plenty—and woodsmoke, from its smell, not fish smoke. The town was large, though not quite large enough to be a city even by Thaumian standards. From this side, it looked to Jeremy perhaps half the size of Dale Haven. The protective wall was dark gray stone and about twenty feet high, except for the towers, but what he could see of the roofs beyond seemed to be wood-shingled and steeply pitched.

They approached the bridge to find it guarded by perhaps a dozen men in light scale armor and metal-studded leather helmets, swords at their sides, quivers of blue-feathered arrows strapped to their backs, and short bows in their hands. Barach approached them first, his hands out and open. After a brief parley with a group of them, he returned to the others. "It is as I thought. The hobs have been plundering the farms, and most of the people in this part of the Valley are behind the walls. These men are suspicious of us, but I have persuaded them to let us pass inside. Nul, you will appear strange to them; control your tongue and hold your temper. Jeremy, I will speak for us all. Let us go in."

The soldiers gave them hard looks as they crossed the bridge, and they got more from another detachment guarding a high gate—though a runner from the bridge had prepared the way for them. As they approached the gate, Jeremy could hear sounds of construction, sawing, hammering. Or at least he assumed it was construction, until they actually passed within the walls. He saw that he had been mistaken when they entered the town: the sounds were those of houses and shops being taken down, not put up. The structures were right against the inside of the wall—indeed, the wall itself served as one of their walls—and they were all being destroyed. "Precaution against fire, I suppose," Barach said to Jeremy's inquiring glance. "Fire-arrows can do great damage in such a situation."

A young man, clad in heavy red woolen trousers and a blue jacket, met them and spoke to Barach. Barach nodded and replied. To the others he said, "This lad will take us to the town master. Be on your best behavior, please."

Jeremy gaped at the incredible scene of a town besieged as they followed the youth. Tents and lean-tos, many of the latter cobbled up from the material of the destroyed structures near the walls, were everywhere, and in their shelter sat men, women, children, infants. Grim eyes scrutinized the party, voices fell hushed at their passage. Campfires burned everywhere, and families cooked meals over them. The streets smelled of crowded humanity. The buildings, most of them ancient structures of dark gray stone and wood bleached to ash-color by years of sun and weather, seemed shabby in the gathering dusk of evening. The lights inside the narrow, high windows were very dim, as if one candle had to do for an entire huge room.

They came at last to another wall, this one more than man-high, and again soldiers saw them through a gate. Barach spoke to their guide for a moment. "The girl is known here," he explained to Nul and Jeremy. "She has relatives, an aunt and an uncle, in town. The lad will find them for us. Now we are to see the town master and explain ourselves. Ready?"

"I suppose," Jeremy mumbled.

Derilis dismounted, gave Thistle a kiss on his long nose, and followed them in docilely enough. They came into a sort of conference room, a fire bright at one end, a heavyset elderly man sitting at a table. Barach spoke to him, and the man gave a curt response. "Sit," Barach told the others.

They did, all except the girl. She stood before the fire, staring into the flames. The man said something to Jeremy; Barach responded, and the old man nodded. Then, much more deliberately, he said, "I am Thendenis, Master of Three Rivers. You have come from the world outside. If you bring help, welcome. If you bring magic, we do not want you."

"I bring no magic," Jeremy said. "I know your laws."

"Our sacred beliefs, you mean. What is that?" Thendenis pointed a stubby finger at Nul.

"This is a pika," Barach said. "He is a speaker and a thinker, as men are, and a creature of nature, not of magic. One of his kind was killed near here not many months ago. We seek news of this one and of any others."

Thendenis made a curious gesture, a slow sideways nod, his chin coming up and moving toward his left shoulder and then back again. "No," he said. "I do not know of this kind of being. Only of the hobs."

Barach's speech picked up speed, and Jeremy lost the thread. But Thendenis made that same strange gesture now and again, and from Barach's tone Jeremy gathered that it meant "no." A knock on the door interrupted them; the town master barked some short invitation, and the boy who had guided them opened the door. Behind him were a short, stocky man and woman. "Derilis," the woman cried out.

The girl flew into her ample arms and began to weep, great gasping sobs wrenched from deep inside her. The woman led her out. The man stayed behind, his face red, his eyes teary. "My brother," he stammered. He waved a thick hand. "Would not come. Thought he was—he was safe. I—thank you."

"The girl's uncle," Barach said as the man abruptly turned and hurried away. The boy closed the door again.

Thendenis sighed. He pushed himself out of the chair with some difficulty—he was not an undergrown man— and began to pace the floor. He wore, Jeremy saw now, a dark green cloak trimmed with some white fur over an embroidered tunic. Gold chains hung on his neck and gold rings gleamed on his fingers. His hands locked behind his back, the town master turned on them.

"Outlanders," he said. "We have our own troubles. The hobs have grown bold this past year; the very ground shakes with their devilish work. Buildings in town here have been damaged, and in the countryside fear walks abroad. And now unbelieving foreigners are coming to disturb our peace. Know this, travelers: we do not want you. We must face our troubles in our way. You will go back, tomorrow. I will send a guard one day's march with you. That is all I can do, and more than I ought to do."

Nul stirred, but Barach put a quieting hand on the pika's arm. "We mean no harm to you or your people," Barach said. "You saw how the girl felt upon meeting her relatives. Think of Nul; think of his need. He feels even as a man would do—or a girl of Twilight Valley."

Thendenis set his jaw. "One, ah, person, is nothing," the town master said. "The hobs bring fire and blade from beneath our very feet; the valley is fighting to survive. You must see that, facing such a threat, we have no time for you or your troubles." He held up a hand, silencing Barach's objection. "You will return tomorrow. That is my decision. You may rest here tonight. That is all."

Barach sighed. "Very well," he said. "But allow us some time at least to rest. Some time at least to seek news of Nul's brother, who died here. A few days. For the sake of our common losses to the hobs."

Thendenis wavered. "One day," he said finally.

"Only one?"

"Even that," the town master said, "is far too generous."

The town of Three Rivers boasted no such thing as an inn or a hotel. Nor was there even a private house with room for them. Instead, Town Master Thendenis sent the three travelers to the north gate of Three Rivers, where a sort of tent city had gone up on what had once been the market square.

The bivouac was a place of soldiers, or of what passed for soldiers in that besieged hold; most of the inhabitants of the tents had been farmers, workmen, artisans, until the troubles with the hobs had begun. Now they were evidently preparing for a long wait. At least, there were far more tents in the open square than there were soldiers to occupy them, and when their young escort had spoken to a captain—the only thing distinguishing the man as an officer was a red armband, for he wore the same country home-spun as the others—the man readily found them a tent space.

Nul and Jeremy pitched the tent while Barach led Thistledown away on some private errand of his own. The tent was of an odd, squarish design, and pitching it took the two of them some little while. Nul's odd appearance attracted a number of the soldiers. Jeremy's difficulty in understanding them was great, but their curiosity led the men to huge efforts of language and gesture, and eventually they devised a half-spoken, half-acted sort of language.

Jeremy, as well as he could, explained to the curious bystanders what Nul was. Nul, for his part, growled in his throat as with a heavy little mallet he grimly went about the business of pegging down the tent.

"He talk? Like men?" asked one of the soldiers, an unkempt youth of perhaps seventeen. The notion seemed to be amusing, for the speaker and several of his friends broke into unbelieving laughter. "Make talk."

"Nul's not a performing animal," Jeremy objected. When the others looked at him with no understanding, he said, "Nul is a—a person. He has feelings. Not like a dog trained to do tricks."

That was no good. Dogs were not common in the Valley, and the men jabbered among themselves about some supposed relationship between the half-mythical dog and this clearly mythical pika. The young man scratched his lean chin (he was just starting to sprout scattered and bristly whiskers) and said, "That the kind of little thing sometimes fights for the hobs?"

Jeremy, instantly alert, glanced at Nul, but the pika, busy with a peg and the hard ground, evidently had not heard. "What do you mean?"

The young man held his hands out, palm-up, in a gesture that had no significance for Jeremy. "Just up at Highfields something like him killed last year."

"Who knows about this?" Jeremy demanded, glancing around. The dozen or so men who had come over evidently misunderstood, for they stepped back, and one or two fingered weapons. "No. No harm meant. But who knows of the thing like Nul that was killed at Highfields last year?"

There was a quick conference, and one of the men turned and strode off. "Kasten family knows," the young man said. "He bring back one of them. It won't talk for us now?"

Nul had finished with the pegs. "I talk," he snarled, hurling his mallet down with a crash. "I, Nul, talk. What you want to hear?"

A murmur went up among the men, mingled surprise and amusement. The young soldier crouched to be more nearly on a level with Nul. "You are—what you call him? Peeker?"

"Pika," Nul corrected. "Pika of Bone Mountains. I look for family now, in this place, this valley."

The young man's face split in a grin that was missing only two teeth. "Talk good," he said. He struck his chest with a fist. "I Hlovis Daymartin. You Nul?"

"Nul," the pika agreed. To Jeremy, he complained, "Where Barach gone? Need to begin looking for family. Dark soon. Have only one day."

Dusk had fallen. In the tent city campfires already burned here and there, and the gray sky overhead was fading toward dark. A commotion attracted Jeremy's attention to a side street, a narrow lane between two rows of close-built stone houses. Four or five men, several of them carrying ruddy torches, nearly skipping in their evident excitement, strode along there, making toward them, Hlovis Daymartin stepped back. "Here Farlis Kasten. He tell. He tell."

"Nul," Jeremy said quickly, "this man may know something about your brother. It was his family that—that dealt with the trapper. We—"

Nul hissed, a sharp intake of breath between even sharper white teeth, and again some of the soldiers took a half-step away.

"No!" Jeremy put his hand on Nul's shoulder, found the pika trembling. "Nul! Calm, now. I will talk."

The pika tightened all over, but then grunted, "You talk," just as Farlis Kasten and his retinue came up. Kasten was a tall man for an inhabitant of Twilight Valley, easily matching Jeremy's height, and he wore a heavy fringe of black beard. Since the whole front of his head was bald, with a mane of black hair running backward from behind his ears, the effect was something like seeing a large head-shaped egg in the nest of some great bird. Kasten's clothing, brown leather and green rough-

textured wool, was mended and held together with random strips, wooden pins, patches. He spoke first to Hlovis,
then turned to Jeremy: "They call for me. I here now."
His eyes were on Nul.

Jeremy introduced Nul, not taking his hand from the
pika's shoulder, and said, "His family is missing. Hobs
took them, we think. They say you have seen one like
him."

Kasten squatted on his heels, looked at Nul eye to eye,
and stood with bowed head. "Yes. Saw it. Year ago
almost. After big battle with hobs. One like this dead on
our farm. Father took the skin."

Nul stirred, and Jeremy gripped harder. "It was Nul's
brother," he said.

Kasten's eyes, nearly buried under heavy upper lids,
were level and pitiless. "My sister. My mother. Dead.
Hobs. We come here after. Father dead now too. Gray
one not only one dead. Many die."

"Where is Highfields?" Jeremy asked.

"Home."

"No, you don't understand—if we wanted to go to
Highfields, how would we get there?"

One of the men said something, the others laughed,
and Kasten turned to snarl a quick sentence that cut
them off. Slowly he turned back to Jeremy. He jerked
his head toward the group behind him. "They laugh. No
more Highfields. Gone. Hobs burn all, break all. But
used to be north and west, up Little River, in hills."

Jeremy became aware of a bulking shadow at his elbow. Barach had returned. "This man knows—"

"I heard," the old magician said. "Let me speak with
him." For some minutes the two held a colloquy. The
men who had come to gape at Nul grew bored and
wandered away. Before long, only Kasten and Hlovis
remained. Nul stood breathing hard. At length the heavy
farmer and the reedy young soldier turned away, too,
and Barach herded Nul and Jeremy into the low tent.

"It is some distance from here," he said. "Two or
three days' walk, anyway, along the course of the Little
River. We shall go there as soon as we know more."

"What more?" Nul demanded.

"Why, whether the hobs are still there, for example," Barach snapped. "And perhaps where they came from. They evidently have a system of tunnels and caverns underlying the Valley, but who knows where the outlets are? From what I've picked up in town, they've even been digging about close to here. At least there are fresh holes in the riverbank just north of town, though no one knows whether they are natural or made by hobs. There are other indications of their nearness, too: a provision party with many people and several animals is overdue here. It must be the one that started from the lower valley just ahead of us."

Jeremy stirred. "The one that the other southerner accompanied. The young man. Could he have been a spy?"

Barach merely shook his head. "I have no way of knowing. But having dealt with hobs before, I suspect that any human save the Great Dark One would be looked upon by the hobs only as food, not as an ally. Certainly there seem to be a great many hobs in the Valley now; an army of them, it appears. And if we go to confront an army, it would never do to go on our own. We will need help."

"The town master didn't seem disposed to offer us any."

"No, Jeremy, he did not. Perhaps now that we're stranded we may get more assistance."

Nul frowned. "Stranded?"

Perhaps beneath his beard Barach was smiling. "Derilis loved Thistledown so. I sought out her aunt and uncle and gave the pony to her. I'm afraid they might have believed that Thistle belonged to her parents. My command of the language is not complete."

Jeremy grinned. "And naturally we'll have to ask permission to find another pack animal."

Barach shrugged. "I am afraid so. And, alas, I have noticed that such beasts are in remarkably short supply in Three Rivers."

Nul nodded. "So trying to find one give us maybe two, three more days—"

"To raise a force—"

"To start to hunt—"

Barach held up a quieting hand, stilling both Jeremy and Nul. "We have time only to try. To *try*, my friends. It may not be easy. But we are here; we have at least heard some little news of Nul's family; and we may at last begin to hope, in a judicious way. Remember what Welidale the Wise said of hope: too much of it makes one insane. Too little of it makes one despair. And the difference between too much and too little is so small that no scale can measure it."

Nul was enormously excited that evening, speaking in feverish snatches of the pikas he remembered, of his own family, of the chances that his father and mothers might yet be alive. They made a campfire and, sitting around it, ate their own provisions, for the resources of the town were strained just to feed the refugees inside the walls without sparing food for outsiders. Nul seemed to take little notice of what he ate. At length, long after sunset, they settled in to sleep, though again Nul, very excited, tossed and turned for much of the night, and that kept Jeremy awake.

For his part, Jeremy began to consider the problem. If they were to descend into the caverns in search of the hobs and their presumed captives, there should be more than the three of them. But the people of Twilight Valley seemed so taciturn, so hostile, that he doubted the party could ever secure their friendship or their aid. Unless the common enmity of the hobs could bring them together.

At last Nul stopped shifting and his breath hissed regularly and shallowly, as it always did when he slept. Barach had dropped off immediately upon retiring, and his soft snores, muffled by his beard, had been going on for what seemed hours. Just as Jeremy himself was on the verge of sleep, a soft grating noise brought him bolt awake, the hairs on his arms bristling. "Can we come out?" gritted a soft voice.

"Fred," Jeremy said, relieved. He dropped his voice to a confidential whisper: "Yes, come out of the packs if you want. But we're in a town now. You won't be able to regain your full size. And they hate magic here. You can't show yourselves outside the tent."

"It's a strain to stay small," Busby grunted, emerging from his own pack. "And we don't sleep."

"It's very dull in the packs," Fred put in. "All alone in the dark, no company."

Busby agreed at once: "If we could be together in the same place at least we could talk."

"Quietly," Fred added in a wheedling tone.

"You wouldn't even hear us."

"All right, all right," Jeremy whispered, his voice wavering with suppressed laughter. The gargoyles, for all their geological age, were much like children in some respects. "Here. Both of you into the carpetbag. That'll muffle your voices. I have to step outside for a minute."

"What for?" Fred, the ever-inquisitive, asked.

When Jeremy told him in one succinct phrase, Fred immediately lost interest. "We don't do that," he said, creeping into the carpetbag.

"We do, though." Jeremy rose and went outside into the chill to visit the latrine trench—as he passed by other tents, a few soldiers standing guard glanced his way—and relieved himself. Enough fires burned here and there to throw the camp into dim illumination. He saw a good many sentries on the walls. Well and good, he thought. Always best to keep on guard.

He was on the way back when a red streak cut the heavens above him.

A falling star, he thought, before realizing that the night was still overcast.

A soldier on the walls shouted something in a voice gone soprano with alarm.

Jeremy's mind corrected itself: not a falling star, but a fire arrow—

The hobs were upon them.

CHAPTER 8

JEREMY'S SHOUT TO Barach and Nul was hardly needed; the entire town erupted in a cacophony of shouts, screams, and the clatter of running feet. The pika appeared first, wearing only his trousers, his short sword firmly gripped in a three-taloned hand, his daggers thrust into belt scabbards. The gray fur on his neck and head stood up alarmingly, and his orange eyes glared in the light of flaring torches. "Where?"

"The eastern wall, I think." Jeremy dived past him into the tent. Barach had grabbed his black coat; he shrugged it on over shirt and trousers, tied it closed, and reached a broad hand for his ornate, silver-headed staff, normally a walking stick but at need a formidable weapon.

"Here," Barach said, tossing the gray robe to Jeremy. "Its virtue *might* help in battle, too."

Without bothering with its fastenings and buttons Jeremy slipped the garment on and hastily knotted the sash. He seized his crossbow and a quiver of bolts and followed Barach outside into confusion.

Many fire arrows had followed the first, not really aimed but just sent in at random to find what targets they might; at least three of the scores of tents in the market square blazed, and the roof of one of the taller buildings nearest the wall was afire. A row of men had taken positions on the wall walk of the eastern wall, and from them came the twang of released arrows as the archers fired out into the night.

Barach's hand closed on Jeremy's shoulder. "Where's Nul?" Barach bellowed into Jeremy's ear.

"Don't know. He was here as I got back to the tent."

"See what you can do on the wall. I'll look for him."

Jeremy headed for one of the defensive tower doors, left open in the excitement. He was still several yards away when the ground rolled beneath his feet, accompanied by a rumbling like the world itself caving in. Jeremy staggered, lurched into another man, and lost his footing altogether. He fell hard to the compacted soil of the market square, grunting as he hit on elbow and hip.

Through his flesh he felt the vibration and shuddering of the quake. The fires and torches were just strong enough to give dim illumination to the figures high up on the wall walk—bad situation, Jeremy thought, they're silhouetted and the enemy is in the dark—and from the ground Jeremy saw them reeling, clutching at the parapets or each other as the wall itself shook.

He pushed himself up to a kneeling position. Things seemed to happen very slowly. A man toppled, screaming, backward off the wall walk. The ground rose up in a rolling swell more vicious than the rest, reminiscent to Jeremy of those bad moments aboard the *Gull* just before their final landfall. Men shouted. A horse shrilled out a scream somewhere in the distance. And the wall broke.

Jeremy gaped. Away to his left and about fifty yards distant the wall bulged, cracked in a crazed pattern of zigzag rents, and began to collapse. The stones at the base rolled inward or fell out into darkness, and the edges above it bowed toward each other, buckled, slid into a miniature avalanche. In a moment a billowing crowd of gray dust concealed the ruin.

"The wall!" someone shouted, panic sending his voice into the upper registers. "To the eastern wall! A breach! A breach!"

Jeremy was on his feet again and running into the dust cloud, aware of others on either side of him. He tripped and stumbled over loose rubble, heard the clatter of stones still dropping from the edges of the break. A hand clutched at his ankle. "Help me," pleaded a voice, guttural in the Northern fashion but filled with weak despair.

Jeremy stooped to pry loose a huge stone, then another and another. The archer still clutched his broken bow. His legs had been caught in the fall, and in two places jagged bone penetrated the flesh, the blood looking black in the uncertain light from the fires.

"Here," a woman said at Jeremy's elbow. "Go. No, leave'm to us; we'll care fr'm. To the wall."

Jeremy left the archer behind. Combat swirled ahead, the fighters standing or stumbling on the mound of rubble that had been the wall. Squinting against the dust cloud, choking on its dry taste at the back of his throat, Jeremy readied his crossbow and waded in.

The hobs were fighting hand-to-hand with the men of Three Rivers. Even in the gloom and blur of dust it was clear which side was which: the hobs towered over the men, great slope-shouldered hulking shapes wielding heavy clubs. One of them had drawn back a cudgel almost as long as a man was tall and was about to smash it down on the head of an injured man on all fours.

Jeremy dropped to one knee and sent a bolt into the hob's armpit. It blossomed there like a strange stiff flower, the red feathers its bloom. The creature howled and staggered, dropping the club; almost at once another man was at it with a long sword. Jeremy reloaded, a tedious business when battle raged around him.

Another hob materialized out of the darkness ahead, moving with incredible speed for something so large. Jeremy staggered away from a swashing blow of a club, feeling the wind of it on his face. He loosed the crossbow bolt into the thing's body at point-blank range, but the hob never even paused, following through with the club's movement, bringing it back and up and starting a backhand attack.

And suddenly Barach was there, wielding his own staff as if it were a baseball bat, arcing its silver head around and up in a terrific uppercut that caught the hob where its chin should have been. Jeremy heard the crunch of impact and saw the hob topple backward, its club flying free to clatter away somewhere off to the right.

"There he is!" Barach shouted. For a moment Jeremy's confused thought was that the old magician was exulting over the fallen hob; then he realized that Barach meant the pika.

Nul had found a vantage point atop a fallen stone the size of a hogshead barrel. He had evidently huddled there, his coloring and proportions enough to disguise him as another rock. As Jeremy looked, Nul's sword flashed in a roundhouse sweep that caught a passing hob just below the left shoulder blade. The creature bellowed and lurched, and Nul, his sword still gripped tightly in his hands, toppled off the boulder.

Jeremy had managed to load another bolt. He sent it into the staggering hob, which seemed to be trying to lift its club to smash Nul, out of sight on the ground behind the fallen stone. The bolt connected low, about kidney-height, and the hob, its fighting spirit gone, screamed, dropped its club, and scrambled off into the dark.

"They flee!" someone shouted from above.

The dust was settling and thinning, and Jeremy for the first time became aware that not all the men on the wall walk had fallen; on the unbroken parapets a good many archers still occupied their stations, and they had steadily been sending shafts down into the massed horde of hobs outside the breach in the walls.

The defenders of Three Rivers cheered. Jeremy had paused to reload his crossbow, but now he climbed a loose rampart of fallen debris and slid down the other side. He saw dark shapes, hobs, retreating into the darkness outside the walls. And there was a shorter figure, too. He squinted. Yes, there was the flash of a short sword.

"Nul!" Jeremy cried. "Let them go! Come back!" He started forward.

Someone grasped his arm.

He turned, trying to bring the crossbow up.

"Nay," a gruff voice said. It was a man, not a hob. "Come wi' me."

"But my friend—"

"In th' dark you'll get a shaft in your back, like enough. Inside. Now."

Jeremy twisted free. "Nul's chasing the hobs. I—"

Something pricked him under the ribs. " 'Tis a sharp blade, fellow. Shall it go deeper?"

Another man had appeared and, before Jeremy realized what was happening, had wrenched his bow out of his hands. "Do as th' captain says, now," this one advised.

They climbed the fallen stones again, back into the town. Jeremy could now see that the break in the wall was not a terribly large one, perhaps twenty feet across at the top and ten at the bottom. "My friend the pika—" Jeremy began.

"We saw 'm," one of the two men said. "We couldn't stop 'm. Just you. On wi' you."

They walked through dark streets to a familiar building. Jeremy found himself in the anteroom to the town master's council hall; and there, too, was Barach, himself guarded by two townsmen with red armbands. Barach gave Jeremy a weary smile. "Where is—"

"No talkin'."

Barach glared at the guard.

Jeremy shivered and yawned. The room was very dim; a single hanging lamp overhead gave illumination, making the tapestry covering one wall a dark abstraction of shadowy shapes. Jeremy noticed a small pool of oil directly beneath the lamp. He guessed that the quake had spilled it.

"In," a new voice said. A fifth red armband, this one older than the others, had opened the door to the town master's hall. Jeremy and Barach were seen through and into Thendenis's presence.

The town master, his garments ill-sorted as though he had tumbled into them hastily, sat brooding at the head of his table, his hands clutching the arms of his chair. A candelabrum with six lighted tapers aided the hanging lamp in this room—Jeremy noted another dark splash of oil on the table beneath the lamp—though Thendenis's features were still half in shadow.

The town master glared at them through droop-lidded eyes. "So," he said in his thick voice. "Here you are."

Barach spread his hands. "Here we are, Town Master. Why are we here?"

"Because you did not escape with your friends."

"I do not understand you. Our friend Nul—"

"Not him. The big ones. The hobs."

Barach scowled. "They are no friends of ours. Ask your soldiers if you have doubts. Jeremy and I fought side by side with the men of the city—"

"I have no knowledge of that. But the young one there and the little fellow were seen escaping through the wall. The small one got away; this one was caught."

Jeremy said, "I was only trying to reach Nul. He—"

"Silence." Thendenis straightened in his chair, his bulk making the wood squeak. "I felt there was something wrong about you—magicians—earlier. I curse my foolishness in not acting. I let sorcerers from the south into town, and in reward for an act of kindness they throw down my walls."

Barach stirred. "We did nothing—"

"Of course you say that now. But it is clear enough: you were permitted to sleep in the northeastern market; that very night the wall is cast down by magic. Your guilt cries out from the stones themselves." Thendenis stood. "You will be thrown into a cell tonight. Tomorrow the town council will decide how to execute you."

"Execute us?" Jeremy said, outraged.

"That," Thendenis said in his coldest voice, "is what we always do to spies."

The eastern sky showed the first flush of sunrise. Already men were at work clearing away the fallen stones of the wall, preparatory to sealing the breach. The undamaged wall walks above were thick with bowmen; but they looked out on a landscape empty of movement.

Two of the townsmen had grunted and groaned their levers beneath a huge piece of masonry and stone and had at last succeeded in rolling it outside, away from the wall. They paused a moment, leaning on their levers and breathing hard. "How many dead?" one asked.

The other shrugged. "Nine, ten maybe. We were lucky. The hobs not so. Sixteen dead, I heard. Seven inside the walls, the rest with arrows through 'em."

"Any taken alive?"

"Ah, no. They ain't like that. They get hurt bad, they

kill themselves somehow. My old dad told me once they melted, like, but these don't. Just lay there dead. You never take one alive. What is it?"

The other man had turned to peer behind him, back at the pile of rubble that still partially choked the breached place in the wall. "Thought I heard something down the slope there. Stone scraping."

"The women with their baskets. How long to patch this?"

"Week, maybe, they said."

"Hobs'll be back tonight."

"They don't usually come again that quick. If they do, we'll just have to— There it is again."

"Maybe somebody under some stones?"

"Better see."

The two of them climbed partway up the hill of debris and started to clear away stones, tossing head-sized rocks back into the town. "Must've been settling," the one who had heard the noise decided.

"Must've been—hey!"

"What is it?"

The other man scrambled up the slope.

The first one followed. "Oy, what is it?"

"The stone moved in my hands!" the second man said. "I picked it up—"

"Well, of course it moved if you—"

"Nay, it squirmed in my hands!"

"Are you daft?"

"I—look at that!"

The first man looked down the slope. A pale shape was scrambling down, clattering over loose rock. "What is it?"

"Th' stone!"

"Shht! D'ye want people to think you've no brains—there's another!"

The two men looked at each other, then down at the slope. Two somethings, creatures perhaps the size of cats but pale reddish yellow in the dawn twilight, scampered away into the gloom.

"D'ye think we should tell?"

"Nay. I think we should—we should—"

"What?"

"Move another rock."

And with their levers and several anxious glances around, they did just that.

"This," Busby said, "is wrong."

Fred had begun to swell. "Barach and Jeremy were taken away by those men. I saw them. Nul is out here somewhere. If Barach and Jeremy are in trouble, we have to find Nul to learn what we should do."

"How do you know they're in trouble?" Busby began to enlarge, too. They were well away from the town walls, where they had almost been captured themselves— one man had actually lifted Busby briefly—and it felt good to release the confining shrink spell.

"The same way we know Nul came this way," sighed Fred.

"Hotheaded young shale."

"Old schist."

"I am not—"

"I know, I know. Mm. Off to the northwest here."

Busby sighed, or gave as good an imitation of sighing as an unbreathing creature could. "I trust your horizontal sense of direction. But what are we to do if Nul is—"

"We will settle that," Fred said, "when the time comes."

They passed through a curiously abraded countryside. Busby commented once that the land had the look of a lava flow frozen by air and time, and Fred absentmindedly grunted an agreement. But if the rock had been lava, it had been so many ages before, as measured at least by short-lived humans; now it was a tangle of conifers, brush, and grass. The sun came up in a cold blue sky as the two gargoyles clambered up a steep hillside quite a good distance from the town. They emerged on a flat ledge at last. "Look," Busby said, staring off into the distance to the west.

The river flowed below them, passing the hill they were on off to the north; three miles or so away was a bridge over it, and past the bridge was the town itself. "They'll repair that wall all wrong," Busby continued, gazing at the distance-dwindled crack. "Good strong granite would do it. But they'll pile up these chunks of basalt again, not grading the sizes properly, and—"

"He went in here," Fred said.

Busby came to join him. The two of them stared into a dark opening in the side of the hill. "Lava tube," Busby said. "Worked out a little, but natural in origin. Deep, too."

"Do we go in?"

"You were the one who wanted to find him."

Fred looked at Busby. "What if he's been taken prisoner?"

"Do you think we can free him?"

Fred turned to gaze down the tunnel again. "Of course we could. If they didn't kill him first."

"They are so fragile."

"Mm."

The gargoyles had spent more than a lifetime of man guarding the gates of Whitehorn; they had never once faltered, never once been surprised. But now, all their attention on the dark hole ahead of them, they were for the first time in their existence taken completely unawares.

"Well," said a soft voice behind them, "what have we here?"

The hulking ones had fled into a dark mouth in the dark earth, hunched forms stooped over, yammering in heated snarls and words like coughs. He had pursued them, limping on his bad leg, across the hillsides, up the slope, and to a narrow ledge just below the tunnel mouth. There Nul paused, gasping for breath, shaking partly from the cold and partly from anticipation.

He felt the fur bristling on his head and neck, the old fear-anger reaction of his race. Which was it now? Was he afraid of these creatures, even larger than the big people? Did he rage at them? A little of both, he decided, listening to the voiceless words of his pounding heart. With part of his mind Nul knew that the thing to do was turn back, wait for daylight, come with his friends and such help as they might find in Three Rivers; but a deeper part of him urged him forward, into the round opening, down to whatever he would find there.

Snuffling in the cold morning air, Nul caught scent of something only half-remembered: a warm scent, faintly musky, redolent of underground waters, new-dug gems, the hard bones of the world, the rocks. It was the scent of pikas.

Standing irresolute on the ledge of stone, Nul whined his frustration. If only he had had the presence of mind to shout to Jeremy, to ask him to follow—or to Barach. But in the heat of the moment he had taken out after the hobs on his own, and now he was alone beneath a lightening sky, staring into darkness.

Go back, his mind told him.

They are there, said his heart.

With a hiss, Nul scrambled softly up the slope and came to the very mouth of the tunnel. The hob-scent was strong here, strong and pungent, the smell of a creature that ate nothing but flesh: and under that, a weak counterpoint, lay the faint half-known scent of pikas.

Strong as the hob-smell was, it was not absolutely fresh; hobs had been there, yes, and within the last few simi. But they were not near now, and the tunnel stretched empty ahead of him. Nul stepped inside, orange eyes wide and darting.

Firemoss grew in scattered patches on the walls, not much of it here so close to the surface. But the very faint glow that it sent out (all but invisible, Nul felt sure, to any but pika eyes) was sufficient to cast a thin orange illumination, shadowless and depthless, on the walls of the tunnel. Deeper down the moss would grow thicker, its light more intense. Nul could remember banquets, feasts, in underground halls ablaze with the stuff, light pouring from stone walls cushioned in centuries-thick growths of firemoss.

Here, though, he had to pick his way carefully through the tunnel, given only the faintest aid by the scanty moss. The tunnel floor was roughly even, though it slanted downward. The ceiling hung with ropy tails of stone, solidified there ages ago when the hot lava that had passed through the tunnel drained away somewhere, leaving driblets behind to twist their way downward. Nul had not gone far into the tunnel before something odd struck him about the firemoss. It all seemed to grow at about the same level.

He inspected a patch the size of both his outspread hands. It adhered very weakly to the wall, and the edges, instead of showing new growth, were dried and dark.

It has been planted here, Nul thought to himself. And from the height of it, planted by my people.

And now that he was noticing such things, it was clear that pikas had been at work in this tunnel, removing obstructions, smoothing the floor, widening constrictions. Parts of the wall and floor showed obvious signs of work—with marks too small to be made by any tools likely to be wielded by hob hands.

He sniffed the patch of moss. It smelled only of itself.

Nul put on more speed. The tunnel trended northward and downward. Before long he became aware that he was passing from natural tunnel to artificial and back again; the pikas had evidently used the lava tubes whenever their courses allowed, but for some reason of their own (or more likely of the hobs', Nul thought grimly), they sometimes had cut through the hard basalt. What work that must have been! Nul's back and shoulders seemed to recall the days when his father had put him and his brothers to the task of quarrying out great blocks of sandstone, soft stuff and easy to cut, but heavy and tiring.

And this was much denser, much heavier. Pika shoulders and backs had surely screamed in agony at cutting and lifting this stone.

Nul caught a strange scent and checked his almost noiseless progress. The moss had begun to grow a little thicker, and now his eyes, accustomed to the dimness, could make out a good stretch of the tunnel ahead. Nothing seemed to lurk there, and yet there was an odd smell in the tunnel; not of hobs or pikas, but of—of—

"Pine?" Nul murmured to himself in a voice too soft for anyone else's ears.

Yes, pine. But where—

Nul looked up and grinned. A neat round hole pierced the tunnel roof directly overhead. It led up, perhaps for hundreds of paces, through rock and soil to the surface.

A ventilation hole, such as his folk made to bring air and occasionally sunlight down into their underground abodes. Wan daylight showed far up the shaft, but it bent enough so that Nul had no direct view of the sky. Still the cool air sinking into the tunnel had brought the scent of pines with it, and a reproachful memory of his friends.

But his people were ahead. He all but knew it.

Taking one great lungful of the air from outside, Nul hurried on northward, deeper into the tunnel, closer to the hobs and to whatever they held captive.

The town of Three Rivers evidently had no regular dungeon. The room Barach and Jeremy had been thrown into was perhaps ten feet on an edge, stone-walled and stone-floored, and it smelled powerfully of flour. Traces of flour lurked in the corners in inch-thick drifts, no longer white but dirty brown with age; and when the heavy wooden door slammed shut, locking them in darkness, more flour flew, choking them into a coughing fit.

"A private warehouse," Barach said when he could get his breath. "The whole building is a granary; this room held the flour supply of some well-to-do family of the town, I'd guess."

Jeremy had shoved at the door. It was immovable, solid wood a good three inches thick. The quake or age had settled it a bit, so that a long, slender triangle of light showed at the top of it and another, standing on its point, showed at the hinge side. But the door itself was secure, probably barred on the outside, and without window or opening. "What will they do to us?"

"Here are our beds, I take it." Jeremy heard Barach ease himself down in the darkness. "Do with us? Execute us if they can. I expect Thendenis is only waiting for the work on the wall to be finished. That will be a job requiring many hands, and until it is done all the soldiers will have to remain alert. But once the wall is in shape, then Thendenis will execute us. Probably publicly, from what I know of the Valley people."

"You seem to be taking it calmly enough."

"Jeremy, a wise mage was once traveling by sea to a distant land. The ship he was on came to grief and began

to sink. It carried no boats, and the mage's magic was
not powerful enough to keep it afloat. The captain of the
vessel saw the mage come out of his cabin stark naked,
carrying a handful of soap. 'What do you intend to do?'
the captain asked. 'Die clean,' the mage replied.''

Jeremy kicked the heavy door. An invisible cloud of
ancient flour choked him, burned dry in his nostrils,
stung his eyes. "Looks like we'll die breaded."

"If it is our time to die. I am not convinced."

"Why not?"

"The town has worries more real and more dangerous
than ourselves. Hobs are not bright, but if they have any
kind of a real force they will attack again this evening,
before the wall can be fully repaired. Or the ground may
quake again. Or Nul may return. There are many impon-
derables between us and the stake, Jeremy. And in the
meantime, we have time to think and plan. I should be
very slow to think that all is lost."

"You've cheered me up."

"Settle down. You're stirring up this infernal dust."
Barach sneezed, a sound almost as loud as a gunshot in
that small, closed space.

Jeremy left the door and groped toward Barach's voice.
His shins collided painfully with a low platform. "Damn!"
he grunted in English. Then he felt the thing he had
bumped into. "This is a bed?"

"Evidently."

"It's nothing but a little wooden table. No mattress, no
blanket, nothing."

"The Valley people are fighting a war," Barach reminded him. "You should be snug enough in that robe of
yours."

"Want it?" Jeremy asked guiltily.

"No, thank you. I find the atmosphere in here a bit
stuffy, actually."

Jeremy sat on the bed. "No flour on this, anyhow.
They must have put these in specially for us."

"Remind me to thank them."

"Do you think—"

"Frequently," Barach said. "You should try it sometime."

Jeremy lay on his back and sulked. Despite everything,

in the close, warm room he became drowsy—he had had little sleep in the past two days—and before he realized it, he was indeed asleep and dreaming.

He dreamed of himself in the Between, the netherworld, the point of consciousness where all universes somehow met. He saw himself trudging across the featureless gray plain, under the evenly lighted gray sky of that place, dressed in his old red pajamas and the electric-blue boots of a thief named Niklas File.

His dream-self waved ironically to him. *He's not real*, Jeremy thought. *I made him up out of the dream-stuff of the Between. And he knows he's not real.*

Was I real when I was there? Maybe I was there then only because now I dream I was there.

Jeremy's mind chased itself in circles, and the dream drifted away from him. He dreamed only once more, and then very briefly: he imagined that the Valley was quaking again.

But immediately he was awake and aware of Barach's shaking hand on his shoulder. "Meal time," Barach said.

Jeremy swung his legs off the bed and sat up. "They brought us a light."

"Yes." Barach moved the lamp, a little clay vessel with a small, very smoky wick protruding out the end. "And our food. Thin fare, I'm afraid. Here."

Jeremy took a chunk of coarse bread from Barach. "Is this evenly divided?" he asked suspiciously.

"I assure you. And here is a cup of water, too."

"Bread and water. If either of us had our powers, we could have a feast instead."

"Don't try anything."

"I won't. I remember the pillow." Jeremy bit into the bread. It was stale and about as palatable as a sponge, but he choked it down, trying to quiet his suddenly inquisitive stomach. The water helped only a little.

As he ate, Jeremy looked around their cell. His bunk was against the left wall, Barach's against the right. Overhead a few straggling cobwebs drifted, dusted with the flour to visibility, stirred into movement by the heat currents over the wretched lamp. "Nothing to work with in here," he said.

"I had observed that earlier."

"We might try to overpower the guard when we're fed."

"Yes. We might try to break down the door by hitting it hard with our heads, too, but I wouldn't recommend it. There were three guards, Jeremy, two of them quite well armed."

"It was a thought." Jeremy finished the bread and water. "How long will the lamp last?"

"Not long. It must be dark outside, or nearly so. Hard to tell in here. But for half an ona or thereabouts we should have light, such as it is."

Jeremy looked at the old man's face, grave above the tangled gray beard, yet somehow serene. "You really have no ideas?"

"None that we could possibly put into practice. Jeremy, do not be impetuous; something will happen."

"There's not even any soap here," Jeremy said.

"How's that?"

"We might as well die clean."

Barach grunted. In a way, his grunt frightened Jeremy more than anything else: more even than the nightmare hobs had done, more than the Hidden Hag of Illsmere or even the Great Dark One; for in the curt response to his admittedly feeble joke Jeremy read something like despair. And Barach never despaired.

For a long time Jeremy simply sat on the edge of his bunk, staring at the smoky red flame of their pitiful lamp. It flickered and smoldered, but it seemed alive, somehow. If only, he thought, Smokharin were in that flame, now. The fire elemental would give us a fighting chance. He could even—

"Burn down the door!" Jeremy said aloud.

Barach, who had been lost in his own brown study, started. His eyes flashed red, reflecting the lamp flame. "I beg your pardon?"

"We could burn down the door. It's wood. We could, ah, peel splinters off these bunks to get things started. The fire elemental would—"

"Suffocate us with the byproducts of burning. No, thank you."

"It—was an idea."

"Of a sort." Barach smiled. "Full credit for trying, Jeremy. But I'm afraid that what you suggest is not practical. Perhaps if—*shh*. What's that?"

Jeremy bowed his head and listened. "I don't—yes, I do, too. A sort of scratching noise?"

"A scraping. What's doing it?"

Jeremy got up and took the lantern in his hand. The noise faded as he neared the door. It seemed to come from the center of the room—and yet there was nothing in the spot but bare floor, close-set squared stones, their interstices mortared with tamped-down flour.

"There," Barach said.

Jeremy stared. One of the stones of the floor lifted fractionally, subsided, rose again, grinding, fell again. Barach rose and dusted himself. "I suggest, Jeremy, that you help with the stone."

"But what's raising it?"

"That," Barach said, "is an excellent question. If the stone moves, we find out."

"And if it's hobs?"

"Then," Barach said, slapping more flour from his robe, "we die clean."

He had been moving for hours without rest, food, or water. His bad leg throbbed. Yet Nul did not slow or slacken his pace; his bare feet found the best of his way through the dark tunnels (lighter now, with a heavier growth of firemoss to give a dull glow to his path), pausing only at cross-tunnels to sniff his direction.

He was deep underground. With some sense that he could not explain, and of which he was only half aware, Nul knew that tons of soil and rock lay overhead, stretching far up to the surface. Here the air was warm and unmoving, the floor underfoot softened by sand and the smoothing of many passing feet over many years. But the hobs had left the smell of their passing on everything, and he could still follow them with his nose.

They had moved fast, faster than he could move. The scent had faded from the strong reek it had been near the surface, was now merely unpleasant and heavy. He had not lost the pika scent, though; it lingered there still, thin against the heavier smell of hob but there. And now and again Nul found small tokens.

There was a bloody arrow, very short, for example. It smelled faintly of Jeremy's hand: a crossbow bolt. And one that had found its mark. There was a club, cast aside by some fleeing hob. There were, at wide intervals, dark splotches of blood.

And still the hobs fled onward and downward. Nul's throat burned; his stomach felt hollow. But he had snatched up no food, no drink, only weapons. There was no help for his thirst or his hunger, and so he did his best to ignore them, trotting on as best he could.

He fell into an almost mechanical pace, trying to become mindless, to ignore the throb of his twisted leg, the demands of his body. The sword he carried in his right hand was real, and only that was real; and its thirst, more than his own, he was determined to satisfy. He recalled the evil castle of Illsmere, the domain of the Hag, and of her servants, mindless brutes fashioned of dead bones and the slime of a swamp. Those things moved without tiring, existed without having to eat or drink; and he was better than they. He should be able to subsist for a while, too, without food or water.

So much water. There had been so much of it in the Hag's valley, ponds of it, rivers of it; the very ground was saturated with it, soaked to the point of dissolving and more. Even in the torture chamber there had been water, water oozing from the foul dark stones, spreading in a black pool over the floor. Even as the Hag's servants had turned the great wheel, had wrenched his limbs and twisted his sinews, he had smelled that damnable odor of water.

And now he smelled none at all, though his tongue swelled thick in his mouth and his very eyes felt dry. No help for it, no help: there was only the downward path, ever downward.

His leg hurt him cruelly. Had he cried out much when the Hag's torturers had popped the joint, when they had snapped the bone? Nul could not remember. He could recall little of that bad time, just pain and darkness and the clammy touch of the vilorgs, the Hag's living servants, not bone and muck but twisted parodies of humans, raised from the amphibians of the swamp by the Hag's fell magic. And one other touch.

Jeremy's.

For the longest time he had thought the touch no more than a dream, a delirium, a hallucination brought on by pain, rage, and fear. There had come a time, in the red light of that hellish torture pit, when Nul had—gone away. That was the only description for it. He had slipped into a bottomless pit and had started to fall.

And then Jeremy was there, searching for him, calling his name, from up above.

And Nul had begun the climb upward, not expecting or even wanting to live any more, just hungering for one more touch of the familiar, for one farewell from the world he was leaving. Oh, that climb had been hard, up steep walls and slippery; and at last he had heaved himself out to find Jeremy receding, fading. But Jeremy had been there, in his secret place, in his head; and he had called Nul back from the brink of death—perhaps from beyond.

He awoke to pain.

The vilorgs stood gaping, opening and closing their stupid mouths. They wandered here and there, bumped into each other. Someone, not Jeremy, burst through the door, toppled the creatures one upon another—they offered no resistance—and cut Nul's bonds. Gareth it had been, the captain who had accompanied Jeremy, Nul, and Barach into the swamps.

Nul had faded then. When next he knew himself, he lay with his back propped against a shattered tree stump, staring over the black waters of the Hag's Well as the entire castle shivered, slumped, toppled, the walls breaking, the stones falling. Melodia was there, the healer, speaking words to him, singing, taking some of the pain away from him and into herself. And—Nul remembered now how he had laughed—from the ruin of the castle Kelada had come, carrying, impossibly, comically, *carrying* Jeremy in her arms, leaping from stone to stone, wading through mud.

And Jeremy had been cut, bleeding. Nul knew now that Jeremy, too, had been in that dark bottomless pit, and that Jeremy, too, had fought his way back into the light. They had spoken of Jeremy's attempts to find Nul; that, Nul knew now, was the voice he had heard. Jeremy believed at the time that he had failed; he had thought Nul dead. For some reason, Nul had never been able to bring himself to confess that Jeremy had succeeded, had summoned him back.

But, he told himself in the tunnel, he would tell him. He would tell him soon. He would tell Jeremy everything, just as soon as—

Nul stopped, panting almost silently, every nerve alert. Something had moved ahead, around a blind bend in the tunnel; he knew it. Yet now he could hear nothing.

The sword hilt was cold and heavy in his hand. Nul took a cautious step forward, then another, and another. He edged his way around the turn.

For a puzzled moment Nul believed himself mistaken: there was nothing visible down the tunnel but the everlasting rock walls and a few loose tumbles of stone, such as might have been cast down by the shaking of the ground during a quake.

But one of the stones moved, stirred, gave out a groan.

Nul hissed in surprise. It was a small dark huddled shape, not a stone, and too little to be a hob—

The familiar scent flooded his nostrils. In four steps he was beside the dark fallen figure. In the faint glow of the firemoss he saw the smooth gray fur, nearly black; the spidery limbs, clutched tight against the body now. And he heard a small groan.

Nul knelt by the fallen pika. The face was very thin, the layers of fat that ordinarily padded out a pika skull and made a round ball of the head long gone. The eyes bulged under shrunken lids; the cheekbones showed in harsh relief. "No," the pika moaned in pika-speech.

"It's all right," Nul said in the same language, astonished at how smoothly it came off his dry tongue. "I am a friend. It's all right. You are safe."

"S-safe?" The eyelids fluttered, the orange pupils rolled and jittered, unable to focus. "Safe? Wh-who?"

"My name is Nul."

"Nul. Used. To. Know."

"Your name? Your name?"

"Gr-Grall . . ."

Grall fainted. Nul stroked her face, frowning, lost in memory. Grall—that had been a clan-mate's name, not of his family, but a cousin older than he. But this shrunken body was no more like hers than— The pika was stirring again. "Help me."

"How can I?"

"Water. Some water."

"Where?"

"I can. Show you. Help me stand."

Nul helped—or, more accurately, did all the work himself, pulling Grall to her feet, getting her arm over his shoulder, taking most of her weight on his hip (his bad leg screamed), half-dragging her as she weakly pointed to a side tunnel.

Nul staggered into the tunnel, nearly lost his footing on the suddenly steep slope, barely recovered himself. We'd better not run up on any hobs, he thought to himself. I'd have no chance at all of drawing a weapon like this.

Grall tried to help, taking weak steps when she could, but for the most part merely keeping her feet on the ground. Before long the tunnel became even steeper, and soon Nul smelled water. "There," Grall groaned. "Careful. Now."

The tunnel ended, intersecting with a vertical pipe of rock through which water trickled into unknown depths. Nul managed to get Grall to a sitting position, wedged in a corner between a fallen stone and the tunnel, and then he filled his hands with water. Most of it trickled through, but Grall's tongue found some of it and she slurped it into her mouth. "More," she begged.

Nul had no sort of container—but then he thought of the daggers, both fixed to his belt in good leather scabbards. He took one scabbard off, slid the dagger out, and filled the scabbard with water. Grall drank eagerly, and again, and again. Finally Nul himself drank, but not from the scabbard; he braced his long arms against the walls of the tunnel, leaned far backwards, and let the water fall on his upturned face, into his open mouth. He drank until he could drink no more.

"Still thirsty?" he asked Grall.

"No, no," she said. "Nul. Do I live? Are you here?"

"I am here. Come to save you. Come to save all our clan."

"No, no. You are not."

"Here. Feel." He gripped her arm, wincing inside as his three-fingered hand entirely encircled her wrist. "Nul is real. The time for freeing the pika-folk has come at last."

"Too late," Grall said and began to cry in the curious pika way, a faint ululation of the breath, without tears but wrenching. "Ah, too late!"

"Never, while there is still hope."

"No hope," Grall sobbed.

"But Nul is here."

"No hope, none! The elementals, the elementals—all is lost."

"What do you mean?"

"They do their bidding now."

"I do not understand. What—?"

"Fire and stone," Grall wept. "Fire and stone. They serve the hobs. All is lost. All will die. All."

CHAPTER 9

THE PAVING STONE, flat on top, its sides roughly round, and not much bigger than a man's head, rose, settled, and grated back upward again. In the flickering red light of the smoky oil lamp, Jeremy gave Barach a dubious look. "Did I understand you? You want me to *help* move the thing?"

Barach sat at ease on his bunk, his hands folded across his considerable stomach. "I would like you to do that, if you're at all curious about what is below. I confess that I am."

"Well—I'm curious in only a theoretical sort of way. It could be trouble, you know."

Barach spread his hands apart. "The stone is obviously going to be moved, with or without your aid. If there is trouble beneath it, I for one would just as soon see it right away and have it over with. Besides, perhaps it isn't trouble. There is one way to find out."

Jeremy took a deep breath and knelt beside the stone. A few inches of it projected above the general level of the floor now, wriggling back and forth with faint grating sounds that seemed hollow in the echoing emptiness of the cell, and he tried to get a grip on it. The stone was rough, but its sides offered him no good purchase and were somewhat slippery with a fine coating of old flour into the bargain. He tugged and pulled ineffectually, and when the stone subsided an inch and pinched his little finger in the process, he leaped to his feet and did a little dance of agony—but in silence.

He shook the pain from his finger and looked down at

the floor. The stone was rising again; it lifted a little
more this time before grinding to a halt. With a reproachful glance at Barach, Jeremy knelt to his task
again. After a sudden heave and a lurch, enough of the
stone became exposed to give him a somewhat better
grip, and when the pressure from below eased this time,
Jeremy was able at least to hold the stone in place and
prevent its subsidence. In a moment the rock started to
rise again, quite a bit faster this time, pulled by Jeremy
from above and pushed by—something—from below.

When at last the stone slipped out of its socket, it did
so with disconcerting suddenness. Jeremy grunted, scrab-
bling at the solid weight of the rock, easily fifty pounds.
It turned treacherously in his grip as he rolled it aside,
and he barely managed to get his left hand away before
any more fingers were crushed. The stone thudded on
the floor and was still. From the hole it had occupied
came a surprise. A sandy-colored, vaguely raptorlike head
popped through the opening, swiveling about on a ser-
pentine neck. "At last. And here you both are."

"Fred!" Jeremy laughed, though quietly. "Startle us
next time, won't you?"

"Startle?" The dwindled gargoyle squeezed through
the opening and shook like a wet dog. Loose particles of
soil and sand flew everywhere, rattling like miniature hail
on the stone floor. "How did I startle you?"

"Coming up through the floor that way. How in the
world did you get here, and where did you come from?"

Fred, sitting on his haunches, was licking his forepaws
clean with his raspy stone tongue. He paused long enough
to answer: "I tunneled in, obviously, and I came from
the yard outside this building. The tunneling was no real
problem; the soil here is quite porous, a mixture of
volcanic sands and loam—probably alluvial, from the
river, don't you know. And the building doesn't have
foundations anywhere near deep enough for such a large
structure, particularly in a quake zone. Anyway, I knew
you were in here—"

Barach, his eyes dancing in amusement, raised a hand
to quiet Fred's chatter. "A moment, a moment, if you

please. How did you know that we were in this particular room, my good sandstone?"

"Oh, it's common knowledge in town. A couple of wizards shut up in an old storeroom in the flour and grain mart. In a little crowded place like this town, it's awfully hard for humans to keep secrets—"

"I see," Barach said, raising his great bird's-nest eyebrows in skeptical inquiry. "You simply strolled up to an ordinary shopkeeper and asked him what was happening about town, and he told you all about us, eh?"

"Well—no, it wasn't like that, Mage Barach. I mean, it's obvious that *I* couldn't ask about you; people here are not used to magic and all, and heaven knows what they'd think of a walking, talking gargoyle. But you'll soon learn how I found out. I'll show you. Come on, we have to leave now."

Jeremy had taken the earthenware lamp from the foot of Barach's bunk and was peering down into the tunnel beneath the loosened stone. "Leave? I don't see how. We can't possibly get out by this route, at any rate. Barach and I lack your shrinking ability, you know."

Fred gave an impatient final shake of his head and neck. "Of course not that way. Even if you could shrink, how would we get your things if we left that way?"

"Our things? Our clothes and weapons? You know where those are, too?" Jeremy looked up from where he squatted at the edge of the hole.

Fred had climbed up onto the foot of Barach's bunk. "Well, certainly I do; it's no greater secret than where you were held. Not much imagination in these town folk. Your bags and things are just next door, in another storage room."

Barach's warm brown eyes twinkled in the uncertain light of the lamp. "And I suppose you picked up that information in town, as well."

"No." Fred looked a little embarrassed, so far as stone was able to express the emotion. "To tell you the truth, I found the gear when I was looking for you two—I broke through the floor in there first and saw all the stuff piled in the corner behind the door. That was why I took so long to get to you in here. But how was I to know exactly which room you were in?"

Jeremy rose, his knees popping. "This is all beside the point. We're still locked in, and Barach and I certainly can't tunnel out, like you. So knowing where our gear is does us no good that I can see."

With an irritated flick of his tail, Fred jumped to the stone floor, clattering a bit. "Just follow me," he said, stalking across the floor and grumbling *sotto voce*. "Human beings. Always making things more complicated than they are. Call *us* hardheaded. Next to a human's, a gargoyle's head is like—like—butterstone next to flint!" Jeremy and Barach, who had risen from his bunk, followed Fred to the doorway. The wooden door was set in a slight recess, perhaps six inches or so, with wooden jambs set flush against the stone of the walls. Fred took up his stand there, standing parallel to the door. "Get ready to go. You'll know when."

Fred began to enlarge. In a minute he was three feet long and filling the door recess, his hind feet braced on one doorjamb, his front talons on the other. Still his size increased. The door made a crackling, snapping, dry-wood sound.

"Just like a jack," Jeremy said, lifting the lamp high to give Fred more light.

Fred paused in his exertions to give Jeremy a quizzical over-the-shoulder look. "A what?"

"Never mind. Just keep doing what you're doing."

The gargoyle resumed his task, his paws compressing the thick oaklike wood of the jambs. "If I had enough space in here, I'd just pound it down. But there's no way—ugh!—to get a running start at any decent size. Good hard granite, these walls are. Nice and solid, good tight grain, evenly spaced small inclusions. None like it anywhere close to town. Probably—argh!—they quarried it somewhere off in the mountains. There!"

With a crack and a shower of ancient flour, the door split suddenly, a floor-to-ceiling rent an inch wide appearing on the hinge side. Fred leaned hard against the door, and it swiveled outward, pivoting on its lock, then crashed to the stone floor outside, raising a choking billow of flour dust. "Hurry," Barach urged. "That racket is sure to bring guards."

Fred had tumbled out through the opening, barely fitting now that he was almost full-sized, and Jeremy followed hard on his heels. They emerged into a great open space that looked as if it had once been a main warehouse floor, broken here and there at regular intervals by arched stone pillars supporting the low vaulted ceiling. The huge room was dimly illuminated by a dozen or more scattered torches in wall sconces. Barach stepped gingerly over the fallen door, teetering a bit as the door rocked on its handle. Fred backed off a dozen gargoyle-paces, then came galumphing head-on at a neighboring door. It didn't even slow him. With a report like a cannon firing, the wood broke apart, showering and clattering about in a rain of slivers, splinters, and kindling.

"Quickly," Barach said.

Jeremy, still holding the small flickering lamp, stepped inside and grabbed up two packs from the floor just inside the broken door. "Give them to me," Fred said from close behind Jeremy, and he took the straps in his mouth and squeezed through the open doorway.

Jeremy snatched the carpetbag and his crossbow. He slung the crossbow over his shoulder, wondering if his quiver of bolts was anywhere about; he didn't see it, but it could easily have been slipped into his pack. "Here." He passed the bag out to Barach, then seized the magician's staff, leaning against the wall. "Got it all," he said, stepping out of the storeroom and handing the staff to Barach. "Let's go."

"Me first," Fred mumbled around the straps he held in his mouth. "Doesn't matter if they see me now."

"After you," Barach said, pointing to the distant opposite wall of the warehouse. "The large doors directly across open into the street, I believe."

"Right." Pausing only to maneuver the straps over his head so that the packs slipped down his snaky neck and dangled loosely at his chest, Fred crouched to begin his run.

A clamor of pursuit made Jeremy look around. From a stair to the left came a clatter of feet and a confusion of excited male voices. Three guards burst into view, running headlong. "Here! Stop!" the one in the lead cried, drawing a glittering sword.

Fred, from his stand halfway across the floor from the guards, turned, reared on his hind legs, and bellowed in a horrible high-pitched screech, the sound rapidly deepening to a vibrato that shivered the stones of the floor.

"Holy name of God!" one of the soldiers screamed, turning on his heel.

The three guards were nonplussed long enough for Fred to pound his way across the floor and dive headlong through the twin doors. This time they did not completely shatter, perhaps because they had not been locked and barred as securely: they merely broke apart and flew wide, banging loudly against the outside wall. "Run!" Jeremy shouted, giving Barach a helpful push.

One of the soldiers, the one in the lead with the red armband, had begun a charge, his sword raised. Jeremy brought the crossbow up. "Stop or you'll have an arrow through your eye," he said in a level voice full of even menace.

The soldier stopped five paces away. He was older than Jeremy, perhaps forty, with short bristly graying hair and a seamed, experienced face. "Nah, son," he said in a sorrowful, reproachful tone. "You won't shoot me."

Jeremy grinned, as flat and savage an expression as he could muster. "Ah. But how do you know?"

" 'Cos you ain't got no arrer in that thing."

"Oops."

"So wot you gonna do, eh?" grinned the soldier.

"Uh—catch!" Jeremy said, and hurled the lighted earthenware lamp.

With a curse the man tried to dodge, but the lamp caught him fairly on the forehead, shattering in a spray of pottery and oil and making him sit down hard, the hilt of his sword clanging against the stone floor. The other two guards had retreated up the stair; Jeremy didn't waste time looking for them, but fled out through the open door into the night streets of Three Rivers.

He stumbled on something just outside the door: the

outstretched legs of yet another guard. The man must have been standing with his back to the door when Fred burst through. Jeremy bent over the fallen figure, but he heard the man groan and felt him stir and did not pause to administer any kind of first aid.

"Here!" Barach cried from somewhere off to Jeremy's left. "This way."

Jeremy followed the sound through a quick zigzag of narrow alleys. From somewhere behind them came cries and shouts and the footfalls of pursuit, echoing off the building fronts in the twisting streets. In a few moments Jeremy had caught up to Barach, who was making excellent time indeed for a man who had already passed his hundred and sixieth birthday. They trotted over the cobbles of a dark street, the only light coming from a dim window here and there, serving more to show them where the walls of the houses were than to give their path any actual illumination. Ahead of them Fred ran in great catlike bounds, noisy enough to be easily followed if he did not outstrip them by too much. "Where are we?" Jeremy gasped.

"No idea. Was lost when we got outside. Follow the gargoyle," Barach returned.

At last a light glimmered ahead of them, the ruddy glow of campfires and torches in a large open space. "Looks like the market square."

"I believe you're right."

They flew out of a narrow alley like a large cork and two smaller fragments popping out of a bottle. Jeremy had a momentary view of the field of tents, of men leaping to their feet, of wide eyes reflecting firelight, round mouths in perfect black *O*'s of surprise. Then they were running through the tents, Fred not even bothering to swerve around the canvas. The first tent he ran through made a sound like a blown-up paper bag being burst, and men spurted from either end of it like peas forced out of a pod. By the time Fred hit a second one a few yards farther along, all the tents in the yard were empty, and running men were shouting and screaming in great confusion.

Jeremy saw the idea: Fred was making for the breach

in the wall, half-mended now. From the wall walk the archers had stirred to life and were loosing shaft after shaft. Fortunately for Barach and Jeremy, they were inconspicuous in the swirling human chaos—at least compared to a galloping stone statue the size of a healthy horse—and the metal-tipped arrows were all aimed at Fred. They clattered harmlessly off his shoulders and neck, one or two striking sparks from him but otherwise causing no damage at all.

A few brave souls on their level hurled spears, most of them flying wide of their mark, and one great bearded giant of a man stood his ground and struck Fred a tremendous slashing blow with a sword. Flesh and bone would have been severed; but the sword broke against Fred's hard shoulder, and the man cried out in pain, thrashing his injured hand wildly as Jeremy flashed past.

Fred had reached the break in the wall. It had been repaired to a height something above man stature. Hunkering for a moment on his haunches to gather his strength, the gargoyle gained the top with an easy feline leap. "Come on!" he urged, pausing there, a hellish figure in the reflected glare of the campfires.

Arrows rained around him. "We can't," Jeremy panted. "We'll be hit—"

"Oh, go under," Barach said. "That's what he's waiting for, you see."

Jeremy saw. But, from the scant shelter below Fred's flashing tail, he boosted Barach up first. The mage crawled beneath Fred's belly, protected from the arrows by the gargoyle's solid bulk. Jeremy leaped after him and followed on hands and knees, his back scraping the gargoyle's carved stomach plates. They slid down a rampart of rubble and were outside the city.

Fred scooted down after them, from the sound of it bringing half the loose stone with him. "I'll bring up the rear," Fred roared. "Get away into the dark!" Something—it must have been an arrow—whisked past Jeremy's head, and he needed no more urging to break into a run again.

It was dark indeed in the open away from the town, and before Jeremy knew it, he had blundered thigh-deep into a cold, fast river that tugged hard at his left leg, trying to pull him in and under. "Not that way," Barach said, gripping his arm and dragging him ashore. "This way. Follow me." The mage promptly ran into a tree.

Jeremy helped him up and they staggered and limped somehow or other until they had left the town behind them and off to their right. They paused for breath, Jeremy staring back into the darkness to the town walls, vaguely outlined by the dim red glow of the campfires. "Think they'll follow us?"

"Not likely," Barach said, ruefully rubbing his nose. "They didn't the hobs. Anyway, I think we've passed their last outpost—that would be the bridge yonder. Here comes Fred."

The gargoyle, a more solid shape in the general darkness, loomed up. "All right?"

"Both of us are fine, thank you, Fred," Barach answered. "And you?"

"Lost a bit of a chip from my right shoulder when that man hit me with the sword. Not bad; no cracks from the place. But I feel the loss of a small part of me."

Jeremy ran his hand over the gargoyle's surface until he touched a pitted depression. "Yes, here it is. Piece about the size of a walnut seems to be missing. Does it hurt?"

"I'm not sure that I know what pain is. I'm stone, you know; and stone feels things differently from flesh. But I really don't know."

Jeremy gave the stone flank a fond pat. "Well, at least you don't bleed."

"No," Fred acknowledged. "But that tiny part chipped off from me is itself living stone, and has something of its own intelligence. Well, may it fare well! And I hope its small thoughts and memories are occasionally of Fred and his companions. A glorious adventure, wasn't it?"

Barach had wandered a little way off. Jeremy heard the hiss of water as the old man relieved himself. "Hard on the kidneys, I'd say." He grinned in the dark.

Barach returned a moment later. "I heard that insolence, apprentice. Consider my delicacy of timing: had you noticed, the Valley folk had made no provision for our comfort or for the sanitary condition of the cell. Had I not waited—"

"Point taken," Jeremy said.

"We'd better move," Fred told them. "We have quite a long way to go."

"Where are we going?" Barach asked.

"Ah. That is a secret."

Jeremy said, "Where's Busby?"

"He's where we're going. Here, I still have your packs around my neck. Do you want to take them now, or should I carry them for you?"

"I simply want to get started," said Barach. "But do you suppose you could manage some of our luggage? It's rather heavy for the two of us alone."

"Surely. And are you tired, Mage?"

"Exhausted," Barach confessed.

"Well, gargoyles are not usually beasts of burden, but if you could bear my back, I would be pleased to bear you."

"An excellent idea, and very solidly suggested," Barach laughed. "Here, old stone, be still. I am not so good a bareback rider as I once was."

"Oog," Jeremy moaned. "I had no idea you were fond of puns."

Barach had achieved a precarious sort of seat at the base of Fred's snakelike neck. "Well—I am barely acquainted with them, at any rate."

Fred laughed like a loon, and even Jeremy, protected by the kindly cover of night, grinned.

As they made their slow way through the invisible landscape, Fred was as silent as any Earthly stone on the subject of their destination, though he was talkative enough on other topics. The gargoyle confessed feeling great uneasiness about Nul, who had plunged straight into a hob-hole, as nearly as Fred and Busby could judge from the signs. "Do you think he's a prisoner of the hobs?" Jeremy asked.

"Don't know. His scent is there, though, right at the entrance of the tunnel. Busby thinks that maybe the hobs thought he was one of their other pikas—"

"Others?" Barach, who had been complaining intermittently about Fred's lumbering gait, had at last felt sufficiently recovered to slip off the gargoyle's back and walk alongside of Jeremy. "How do you know there are others?"

"The scent," Fred said, his voice patient. "Like Nul's, but not Nul's. And different individuals. Several of them, Busby thinks. Anyway, it could be that the hobs seized Nul and dragged him away, thinking him one of their own captives. Or perhaps Nul went of his own accord. We cannot tell. But he is certainly underground now."

"And in dangerous company, if it's a hob-hole," Jeremy said uneasily. "Barach, what must we do? Even with the gargoyles' help, the four of us cannot stand against an army of hobs, not in full force."

"As usual, Jeremy, you are moving too rapidly. First we have to reach the tunnel opening," Barach said. "Then we shall decide what to do."

Jeremy squelched along miserably in his wet left boot. "How's your head?"

"Unfortunately, not nearly as hard as Fred's here. I have a small lump on my forehead and the end of my nose is sore, but there's nothing seriously damaged."

"I'm sorry you hurt yourself."

"My fault entirely. I should have seen the tree."

Jeremy grunted. He was warm enough inside the robe, but his left foot, soaked through, was freezing. "I should have seen the river. Wonder if I could stop and change boots? I've another pair in my pack."

"I don't see why not."

It was difficult in the dark, but Jeremy identified his pack by touch and pulled out his second pair of boots, lower-cut and not really intended for serious walking. He shucked off his soaked walking boots and his hose and dug a pair of dry socks out, or rather what he hoped was a pair. "My arrows are here," he said. "That's a comfort, anyhow."

"Then put on the quiver. They'll do you little good in the pack."

"I learned that," Jeremy said, tugging his boot on, "back in the prison. There. Let me tie these boots together so I can carry them over my shoulder, and I'll be ready. Got it." He rose to go, marveling at how much better a dry boot made him feel.

As they resumed their march, Fred broke the silence with an impulsive remark: "One other thing that Busby and I noticed—the hobs are starving."

"Starving?" Barach's voice sounded as if the old man were quite taken aback. "Are you sure?"

"Yes, Mage. Living flesh has a distinctive odor when it is badly nourished, an unpleasant sort of yeasty, fermenting scent. The hobs have that bad smell about them. Busby thinks they were raiding the town only for food."

Jeremy, remembering the hobs' diet, shivered. "Busby seems to be doing a lot of thinking," he said.

"Well, he's older than I am, of course, and he's had some eons more practice at thinking. The old fellow has a very weighty mind, actually. I like to chaff him, but Busby has a solid head on his shoulders—"

"Please," Jeremy said.

"I beg your pardon?" Fred's voice held so much surprise that Jeremy wondered if the gargoyle had even intended the stony puns. But a moment later he heard Fred's barely suppressed snicker. "Sorry about the foolery. I suppose it's all the excitement tonight. But truly, Busby is a careful thinker, and he has wonderful judgment."

"Then it was Busby and not you who planned our escape tonight?" Barach asked.

"Oh, no, Mage." Something like concealed glee lurked in Fred's easy words. "We had nothing to do with thinking that up. That was not a gargoyle plan at all."

"Then whose plan was it?"

Fred's reply was complacent: "You'll see when we get there. It isn't far now."

But the night was exceedingly dark, with a thick overcast hiding moon and stars, and their progress was very slow. Jeremy was grateful that Fred was along, for following behind the gargoyle he managed to keep his bearings and his footing—and the low brush that lurked in their path was stamped flat by the stone feet, which left a serviceable lane for the human feet to follow. The air had the damp, clammy feel of impending rain, though at least the temperature was relatively warm. The biggest problem was the darkness. At length they reached an incline—a hillside—and began to climb. "There," Fred said. "Up on the ledge. See the firelight?"

Jeremy, peering around the bulk of the stone creature, did make out a dim orange glow several hundred yards ahead of and well above them. "Is that you?" came a familiar grating voice from that direction.

"Here we are, and all safe," Fred returned. "How goes it here, Busby?"

"As before. We've still had no sign of hob or pika. Come along, the three of you, and quickly. We'll have some food for you humans."

Barach and Jeremy toiled up a steepening slope, dropping at times to all fours to grope for handholds on the scattered brush and projecting stones to help them along, until they reached a narrow ledge of hard, bare stone. Jeremy's first glance was at the round mouth of the tunnel, easily tall enough to accommodate the hobs. His second was at the campfire, where a thin hooded figure, back bent, facing away from him, sat in silhouette against the embers. On the far side of the fire, against the cliff wall near the tunnel entrance, Busby reclined, forepaws crossed, eyes half closed, looking something like a satiated lion and something like a brooding eagle. "There you are at last. And for your escape you may thank this fellow sitting here by the fire—the knavish young rascal who followed us by ship and then passed us on land."

"Well," Jeremy said, striding toward the fire and the figure, "I don't know who you are, boy, but we certainly do owe you our thanks—"

The youth leaped up, whirled, and grabbed Jeremy. Before the startled young man could pull back, he was kissed, hard, on the mouth. For a moment he was literally shocked; it was as if an electric current had immobilized him.

Then he sputtered.

Then he gasped, "Kelada?"

Throwing her hood back from her fair hair, she grinned at him. "Hello, husband. I couldn't let you come alone on a fool's errand like this, now could I?"

*   *   *

"What did you say it was?" Thendenis, eyes raw from lack of sleep, demanded of the guard with the bruised head.

"I didn't say," the injured man grunted stolidly, rubbing his palm over the goose-egg lump that crowned his left eyebrow. "Because I don't know."

" 'Twas a dragon," the other guard quavered in a thin, fluttering-leaf voice. "A great, huge, fire-breathing, rampaging dragon it was."

"A dragon," snarled the first guard. "Fat lot you'd know about what it was or was not. Took one look, you did, and it was up the stair with you and Peleter alike. Dragon, ha! You wouldn't know a dragon if it bit you on the—"

"Ramp," warned Thendenis. "This is no time for arguing among ourselves. If Coster here did not get a decent look at the—the thing, at least you did. What was it?"

"I don't know, I tell you," Captain Ramp insisted angrily. "How can I tell you what it was if I never saw the like of it before in my life, now?"

"Then describe it for us," Thendenis said with unconcealed impatience. "Perhaps I will know what it was by your description of it."

"It was big. It was light-colored. It moved fast. It busted through three doors with its head and just kept on going. Now, Town Master, you tell me what manner of beast could do that, and I'll tell you what it was. Fair enough?"

"It was a dragon," Coster insisted. "Scaly it was, with a great snakelike head, big huge teeth, flashing eyes, and brimstone smoke pouring from its mouth. A wonder you wasn't roasted alive like a spit pig, Captain, sir."

"Aye, it were a wonder," Ramp returned in a surly voice. "A burning lamp broke open on the head of me, and my front all drenched and doused with oil. I stink of fish oil yet! But only the oil and no dragon would've done the roasting of me, you witless—"

"Sir, the dragon attacked us. Perhaps you didn't see what happened. It bit poor Peleter on the leg, and it

busted poor Captain Stadlakis's brains out of his head
with one blow of its tail. Its horrible teeth—"

"Oh, stow it!" roared Ramp. "Stadlakis is all right
except for a whopping great lump on the back of his
head, and Peleter stumbled on the stair and you run right
over his legs, and that's what's the matter with Peleter.
That and the dung he dropped in his trousers."

"Magic," Thendenis said. "It has invaded the Valley at
last. We're dealing with magic."

The other two fell silent at hearing the forbidden word,
giving Thendenis an uneasy gaze. The plump town master, thanks to the alarms and excursions of the last couple of nights, had a somewhat shrunken appearance, and
his hair stood up wildly. He was clad only in a faded blue
brocade dressing gown, and he sat clutching the arms of
his chair as if fearing another quake. "It was magic, men,
beyond all trace of doubt. Some abomination from the
world outside, called in by these sorcerers. Alas! Our
teachers have always said that no spoken magic from
outside the Valley can hold here; but that seems no
longer true. I doubt not that these devilish magicians are
in league with the hobs. Spies, that's what they were;
traitors to the human race. And now we—you—have
foolishly lost them."

Coster stared hard at his toes and began to mutter in a
miserable tone: "We tried to stop 'em. Not our fault if
they had a monster to help them."

Thendenis waved a weary hand. "You are at least
partly right. We had no way of knowing that their accursed spells would work here; but we should have taken
precautions all the same. I blame myself."

"Aye," Coster said helpfully, but he fell immediately
silent under the glare of the town master's indignant eye.

"Don't agree with me too quickly. I blame you, too,"
Thendenis added coldly. "To flee from escaping prisoners—why, man, for any kind of a soldier that is a disgrace."

"I didn't flee," Captain Ramp insisted.

"No, and you didn't stop them, either," Thendenis
shouted. "Do you perhaps want a medal for letting them
go?"

From between tightly clenched teeth, Captain Ramp answered, "No, sir."

Thendenis, his elbows on the table, interlaced his fingers and rested his chin on his knuckles, red-rimmed eyes staring off into vacancy. "We've made the one mistake, and one mistake is too many. We cannot merely stand by and let them make good their escape."

"But they're clean away, out in the Valley beyond the river someplace," Coster protested. "They've gone, sir."

"And we must go after them. I see that now. There is no citadel, no fortress, no town, safe as long as the hobs and the damned magicians are free and in league together. They must be hunted down and slain, and that as quickly as ever may be. Why, they're the cause of the quakes, beyond a doubt; we've had them before, but never as strong as in the last weeks, and none like the one that cast down the wall—when they were actually inside the town. Men, I have a feeling that if we destroy the old wizard and his young helper, we will rob the accursed hobs of more than half of their power."

"I don't know about that, Town Master. Hobs were here before ever these outsiders came," Ramp pointed out. "Never seemed to need their help before this."

"Hobs!" snorted Thendenis. "One look at the hobs should tell you they haven't the brains for half the mischief they've done us. Who thinks for them, hey? I'll tell you: these magicians, that's who. And now that they have most of the Valley bottled up here in Three Rivers and in the other towns, in Mountain Hold and West Fork and Greenfields, why, now they come into the Valley themselves, to take charge themselves of our final destruction. The hobs never had the nerve or the wit to attack our cities before. Why do they now, if not for the fact that the strangers guide them?"

Coster cleared his throat, making the other men look at him with expressions of faint surprise, as if they had forgotten his presence. "There was—there was that girl they brought with them. What was her name . . . Derilis. What about her? Should we get her, too?"

Thendenis shook his head. "No. Derilis is one of our people. There are town folk who know her and her family well, and her uncle is an old and trusted friend of mine. Obviously, these foul wizards brought the unfortunate lass to our town just as a trick, as a way of gaining our confidence. Think of the brazenness of it! They undoubtedly killed the girl's father and mother themselves, then brought her in with their lying story of hobs and massacre. For that, if for nothing else, they all deserve to die."

"What do we do, then?" Captain Ramp asked. "I'm willing to take my part, whatever it be—but what do we do?"

Thendenis pushed himself up from the table and began to pace, his hands locked behind his back. When he spoke again, his voice was deliberate, each word carefully measured and weighed: "We must send out a fast hunting patrol. They will move as swiftly as possible. They will track down these fugitives, find them, and deal with them."

"And what of the big animal?" Ramp demanded. "Them at the wall says it just shook off their spears and their arrers, and Captain Claymor has a busted hand from trying to slice into it with his good broadsword. Whatever the beast is, it ain't natural. We ain't about to be able to kill something the likes of that."

Thendenis paused before the dead fire, lifting a finger in admonition. "We will not have to. If the wizards die—yes, and their little gray creature, too, the Nul thing—then the monster will beyond all doubt become powerless. Indeed, I don't believe it to be a living creature at all—"

"You never seen it breathe fire," Coster put in. "You never heard it roar."

"Coster! It is not living, I tell you, but rather some ungodly abomination conjured up by the magicians. You saw the hole in the floor of the cell. Too small a hole, by your own description, to be the way that huge beast got into the room. But what if they somehow raised it from the stone and soil beneath them?"

Ramp's dark brown eyes narrowed. "It did have a kind o' stony look about it, now that you mention it. I think you may be right, sir. It may be naught but clay and rock somehow made to move and look as if 'twere alive."

"Yes, exactly. And when the wizards are dead, the beast will in all likelihood drop lifeless as well, a—a puppet with no strings to animate it. So there is the mission: the patrol must follow the fugitives, find them quickly and silently, and from a distance—from a good safe distance, mind you—kill the humans and the gray beast. That will mean archers."

"I'll go," Ramp said. "Give me a hunter or two to track, five good accurate archers to shoot, and I'll go after them. Get me good men, mind; the best we can spare from the walls here. Make sure they're all of them real soldiers, not these blasted farmers with hands made for plows and not for swords, and I'll do my best."

"That won't be sufficient if you fail, Captain Ramp. Before I send you, I have to know that you'll succeed."

"How can I promise that, Town Master? But you can rest easy in your mind that I'll give it a good hard try, my best try. I've a score or two of my own to settle with that impudent young fellow." He rubbed his forehead.

Coster coughed. "I, ah—if you don't need farmers—I mean, I'm a soldier, but I'm not really all that good with a bow—"

"You are excused from the mission, Coster," Thendenis said with a sigh. He settled back into his chair and smiled. "I have another place in mind for you."

"What's that, sir?" the soldier said, visibly brightening.

"Why, you're going to take the place of the prisoners in their cell, as soon as we get the new door up. Ramp, get your men. Leave before dawn. And don't return until the cursed sorcerers are dead. I want their heads, and the head of their little pet, all three of them. Do you understand?"

"Yes, sir," said Ramp, and his smile was a grim one.

CHAPTER 10

NUL HAD BEEN almost afraid to leave Grall alone:
afraid that when he returned he would find her dead. But
she had fallen into a fitful sleep, full of mutterings and
uneasy twitches, and at last he did leave her, long enough
at least to forage for something to still his clamoring belly
and to offer Grall, who seemed on the verge of starvation herself. He recalled from the old days that where
firemoss will grow other things will grow, too; at a pinch,
even firemoss could be eaten, though it was but poor
nourishment, dry and bitter in taste even when properly
cooked.

He had to explore only a little way from the water
shaft before he began to make discoveries: the puffy,
pale mushrooms the pikas called darkbread, for one,
growing in great abundance in the drifts of soil near the
walls of a little-used tunnel that had hardly been worked
by pikas or any burrowers. These mushrooms ranged in
size from small ones the size of a pika's clenched fist to
fully grown ones larger than Nul's head. And below
them, in the soft mold that the fungus favored, he found
some billygrubs, as he almost always had when searching
similar spots in the caverns of the Bone Mountains as a
child.

The grubs, not really grubs at all but rather golden
yellow finger-long pupae, were forbidden snacks; for their
adult forms, slithery many-legged insects that scuttled in
the dark places of the world, carried the darkbread spores
with them and spread the beneficent fungus. Here, however, Nul didn't mind cutting into their numbers some-

what; and besides, the crunchy pupae had a pleasantly nutty taste.

He brought a heaping armload of darkbread mush- rooms and a double handful of the grubs back to where Grall rested near the trickling water. She lay curled on one side, her head pillowed on her outthrust arm, and seemed to be breathing a little more easily. Grall awak- ened and stirred as Nul squatted near her. "Hungry?" he asked, his voice hushed.

Grall replied with a slow eye-blink, the pika gesture of agreement. To Nul it was strangely touching, familiar and yet odd. He himself had long since picked up the human habit of nodding. "Hungry. Yes. They do not feed us often."

"Here. Can't cook it, but darkbread's good raw, too. And try these." Nul fed Grall a few of the grubs, and she managed to sit and munch on a large darkbread by herself. Nul gave her all the billygrubs and ate only a couple of the smaller mushrooms himself; they seemed to fall into a bottomless pit inside him. Then he drank again, very deeply this time, and brought Grall more water.

"Billygrubs," she said after sipping the water. Nul noticed that her hands trembled from exhaustion or weak- ness. "I have not eaten them in . . . oh, since I was little. Thank you. I feel better now."

Nul settled next to her, sitting with knees bent on the stone floor of the tunnel. "Can you talk?"

"Yes. Are you really Nul?"

"I'm Nul. Remember me?"

"Yes. It was so long ago." Grall reached to touch his forearm lightly, as if to assure herself that he was really there and not a dream in the darkness. "I remember you when you were very young, you and your brothers. Where have you been all these years? Your speech is strange. And why do you wear men-clothes?"

"The pika tongue is not one I have spoken in these many changings of seasons. I have lived among men. And, yes, I wear their clothing," Nul admitted, though he felt indecent, sitting here beside a female of his kind with his lower limbs sheathed in fabric. Pikas, both male and female, wore clothes ceremonially or decoratively, or they might simply go naked, dressed in their own sleek gray fur. Their clothing, when they did wear any, generally consisted of sleeveless jackets and simple loin-wraps, not trousers.

"It is strange," Grall said.

"Never mind the clothing. I want to hear of our people, of what happened to them. And of the hobs."

"The hobs? I do not know what a hob is."

Nul cast about for a way to explain the word: "The bigger-than-people things that caught you."

"Oh. The firvolkans."

"Firvolkans?" Nul frowned. The name had meaning in a tongue he had some little acquaintance with, an ancient tongue of magicians that Tremien sometimes used. "What does that mean? The first ones, is it?"

"That is what they call themselves. Firvolkans. The old ones, the ones who came first. And you call them hobs?"

"Men call them that." Grall had not finished one of the larger darkbreads. Nul reached for it and munched it thoughtfully, his stomach still demanding food. When he had finished eating the mushroom, he hesitated for a long time. At last he cleared his throat. "What of Vall?" he asked softly.

Grall turned her face away from him. Her voice was kind, but her words chilled him: "Dead, Nul. Dead long ago."

Nul nodded, feeling a pang as if his heart had been pierced by a thorn. "I feared so. I think deep inside I knew so. My mother, Yaret?"

"She still lives. And your brothers Zaf and Tol—Tolinar. Many of your sisters. But many others have died, Nul. Chag, a long time ago; Zolisat; and then Jare, your full brother. He died trying to escape from the firvolkans only last—"

"I know how Jare died. His death brought me here."

Grall looked back at him, her orange eyes enormous in the faint light of the firemoss. "For what?"

"To save the pikas."

Grall reached to touch Nul's face, a grooming gesture,

maternal. "Nothing can do that, Nul. We are a lost people."

"I do not believe that."

Grall sighed. "You should leave this place. You are strong enough to reach the outside. Go far away and never come back."

"I am here to stay," Nul said. "If I have learned odd habits in the world of men, I have learned some useful ones, too; and some of what I have learned can help me fight the hobs. Do you feel stronger?"

"Better. But not strong."

"I know. Are you able to talk?"

"Yes. If nothing else, I can at least talk."

"Then tell me," Nul said, leaning forward, his eyes intent on hers. "Tell me of our people. Of their loss. Of their despair."

The tale Grall spun out there below the surface was a cruel one and a weary. The first part of it Nul knew already: the sudden appearance of the hobs, a ravaging and incomprehensible army. The pikas had been taken quite by surprise, as Grall told him. One moment all was peace and tranquility in Zarad-zellikol, as the pikas had named their domain beneath the Bone Mountains, the calm of life far underground; the next all was blood and chaos.

"They were surprised at first," she said. "They did not know the caverns were inhabited. But when they saw how small we were, and when they felt how strong they were in relation to us, they moved quickly. Many pikas were killed in those first hona of fighting; the rest of us were rounded up and penned in our own caverns."

Zarad-zellikol, in the pika tongue, was "the place where storms never come." But the tempest had truly broken with the coming of the firvolkans, and many pikas died before its merciless winds. Before a full day had passed the pikas of the Bone Mountains were either dead or captive; and that evening the firvolkans had forced the living to carry the dead deeper into the mountains, into caverns and passageways the pikas themselves had never explored. The dead were taken because the hobs had one idea about the pikas that was quickly dispelled. "They tried to eat some of the fallen," Grall whispered. "They could not. Their stomachs would not accept the flesh. If not for that, no pikas would be alive now."

At first the firvolkans were only roaring, shrieking animals, their speech as unintelligible to the pikas as the roar of a fang-cat. The pikas, nearly two hundred of them, were herded in a series of desperate dashes from cavern to cavern, even outside and overland at times, always at night, as the hobs retreated to the mountainous north. The northern caverns were uninhabited, the pikas having found the surrounding surface land too poor for their type of agriculture, but the hobs made use of them. And at length they came to unknown caves, caves through which black rivers flowed to unseen seas, caves where even the pikas' small magics ceased to work.

There the hobs called a long halt. In those earliest days there had been something more than a thousand of the hobs, male and female alike. The pikas were always watched and never had a chance of escape. With the passage of time, the pikas had begun to learn the hob language.

"They are a sad people," Grall said of them. "They served the Great Dark One because they thought he would bring the end of life more quickly."

She explained in halting tones that the hobs worshiped the spirits of their ancestors; and they believed that living things grieved and tormented those spirits. "Every human being is a danger to them," Grall said of the spirits of the dead. "And every pika too, I guess; and every bird that flies, every fish that swims, every billylegs that creeps. The ceaseless activities of the living grate on the dead, rasp them in their afterworld, burn into their senses like fire."

Nul could hardly understand. He had become aware of the human forms of worship, and he remembered the simple pika formula of gratitude to the maker of all things for the blessings of earth, for snug caverns underground and for the sunshine and rain to grow the crops above; and he remembered the Journey of the Dead, the journey that he had sent Jare on by singing the song he recalled. But to pikas the dead traveled to a far happy country, where no affair of the living could possibly reach or trouble them; the spirits of their ancestors did not linger behind to be troubled by the rumor of the living, as the firvolkans thought.

The hobs, believing this, had come to worship death, Grall said. They saw death not as release, not as a journey, not as a transition to another world, but as a goal in itself, as the greatest good imaginable. "The last peace, they call it," Grall told Nul. "They believe that when all that live have died, then the spirits of their ancestors, and of themselves, will be at peace forever and will be happy. At that time, only the spirits of all the firvolkans will possess the world and its good things. Until then, they are driven to kill."

That drive had been well harnessed by the Great Dark One, who had come upon the firvolkans in a southern land far away. The Great Dark One had promised the firvolkans exactly what they passionately desired: a dead world, an empty world, a world where the spirits could rejoice amid desolation, where they could feast to their fill on shadows without fear of being disturbed by any living creature. They responded to his call and became soldiers; they were by no means the powerful wizard's only troops, but they were among his best, absolutely unheedful of their own lives and incapable, when captured, of living long themselves. A firvolkan in despair quickly died, by some process that Grall could only describe, not explain.

The hobs who had invaded the Bone Mountains were a small detachment of a much greater army. Their goal had been to destroy the people of a valley between two arms of mountains. That had been impressed on them time and again, along with its utter urgency; and so when they had been defeated by arms and had fled into the caverns, the hobs had not despaired and died, as their folk on the surface had. They still hoped, somehow, to carry out the wishes of their master and to bring death to the people of the valley.

But their leaders, the ones who knew the location of the valley, were all dead. In the years since the war, the hobs had discovered Twilight Valley, a place that seemed to fit the description of their target: a broad valley with a river through it (many rivers, in fact), and tilled by humans. Thirty-eight years earlier the hobs had decided that this was the place that must be destroyed. They had set to work then, and they were still working now.

Nul stirred uneasily. He knew of another such valley, between the hospitable arms of the Wizard's Mountains, dominated by the high spired citadel of Whitehorn Keep. It had been Tremien's home that the Great Dark One had in mind, he felt sure; that, too, fit the description. But with the passage of time the hobs had shifted to the Twilight Valley, and now they desired its subjugation and the destruction of all those who dwelled in it. More, as Grall continued to explain, the hobs had forced the pikas into their service toward this end.

"They learned we were diggers," Grall said. "We were useful. We could shape stone and remove it, could make tunnels that would not fall of their own weight. The firvolkans cannot do such things. They needed us to perform these services. We became their slaves, and so we, some of us, have lived this long. The firvolkans would kill us all, if they could; they despise us. They call us the plant-eaters. They eat nothing but—but meat themselves."

The hobs had been forced to move slowly against the people of the Valley. For one thing, there were fewer hobs left by the time they arrived in their final hold, the volcanic tunnels under the Valley: probably about eight hundred or so. There seemed to be many thousands of people in the Valley, and the hobs could not move directly against them. And so they bided their time, drove the pikas to make a living place for them in the bowels of the mountains, raided the surface for the meat they required—and bred.

"Firvolkans do not live long," Grall explained, a faint line of puzzlement between her eyes. "By the time a firvolkan is as old as you, Nul, it is an ancient creature, feeble and grizzled; and none that I know of has lived to be as old as I. These now are the children and grandchildren of our first captors, but none the less cruel, and still devoted to bringing calm to the spirits of their ancestors."

The firvolkans had multiplied radically, for they foresaw a terrible fight on the surface of the world. It became a part of their mythology and their religion, the last great battle on the surface of the world; and some of them seemed to believe that the Valley was the last hold of humans on Thaumia, that when the ones above were dead, at last their holy goal of universal death would be realized.

And so the firvolkans bided their time and nursed their unending hatred for all that breathed, for all who walked the surface. At first they lived clandestinely, taking a sheep from one farmer, a cow from another; and they were spread out, in their caverns underground, from one end of the Valley to the other. But now the firvolkans numbered in the thousands, and in the past few years they had grown more and more desperate for sustenance, more and more bold in their raids to find it.

The people of the Valley had reacted, too, gradually coming to realize that the night raiders who decimated their sheepfolds and despoiled their cattle pens were more than the wild animals of the mountains. Skirmishes began, quick bitter fights that often sent firvolkans underground wounded and dying but even more often found them bringing human flesh into their lairs along with that of animals. The firvolkans faced an awful irony: by the time they had bred enough soldiers to be sure of overthrowing the hated humans above them, their numbers would be too great to support by ordinary raids; they would be so weakened by hunger that they would be unable to fight—and, more, the humans would be fully aware of them.

The dilemma they had never resolved, and having no resolution, they stuck with stubborn determination to their old plan, to the only plan they knew. They continued to breed in the dark and visited the surface for their food, apparently not knowing or being capable of inventing any other plan. At least, they had pursued their original idea until recently, when they had blundered into an approach even more brutal than the notion of overwhelming the people by sheer numbers. . . .

Grall, who had been shivering with weariness, fell silent and only a moment later nodded off into sleep.

Nul rose beside her and paced. He took another deep draught of water. He thought of shaking Grall awake again, but the sight of her worn, thin body, curled up like a child's, stayed his hand. He sat near her, his sword drawn and close at hand, his head spinning with weariness and confusion. He wondered if he could possibly bear Grall all the way back to the surface; wondered if he tried, what would happen to the pikas in the deeper caverns, helpless at the hands of the hobs.

Nul sighed. He felt as if the whole enormous weight of the mountain above him were resting on his shoulders. Shoulders too weak, he thought to himself, to bear such a crushing burden.

Kelda, by stretching her supplies, had managed a hearty meal of stew and wine. True, the wine had to be diluted with water to go around, but even at that the supper was far above stale bread and water in a town cell. Jeremy, seated on a stone with a bowl of the stew cupped in his hands, would eat a bite or two, look down at the ground, scowl, and then look up with that angry expression on his face—only to break into a happy grin when his eyes met Kelada's.

"You're trying to be angry with me," Kelada observed from her place next to him.

"I *am* angry," Jeremy insisted, but again he could not keep the smile off his face. Fred, lying across the fire next to Busby, chuckled, apparently enjoying immensely this intimate look at human customs. Jeremy ignored him. "You have no business here. What about our child—"

"Here." Kelada dished more steaming stew into Jeremy's bowl. "You men. What if you had come up here only to be killed? You never asked yourself that, did you? Then what would I tell our son when he asked about his father? That I let him go to his death without giving him my help and skills? No, thank you."

"But now you're in danger, too." Jeremy turned to appeal to Barach, seated on another stone and tucking into his third helping of stew. "Tell her, Barach."

Barach, carefully sweeping his mustaches back from his mouth, merely shrugged. "What would you have an old bachelor say to a young wife, Jeremy? The ways of the heart are a mystery even the greatest magicians have never penetrated. I wouldn't dare presume to tell Kelada that her presence here is unwelcome; after all, think of where we would be without her and the gargoyles."

"Thank you, teacher," Jeremy snorted, shaking his head. He took a deep drink of watered wine and began again, trying to make his voice serious and straightforward: "Kelada, truly, you don't know what danger you've come into. The hobs are—"

"Hush," she said briskly. "I probably know more about the hobs, or at least about these particular hobs, than either of you two men. I've fought them, evaded them, and tracked them over the past few days. Been inside their camp once, while they were sleeping. Have you been so close?"

"Of course we have. Why, I shot some, and Barach knocked the teeth out of one."

"Oh. I do beg your pardon, learned wizard. I'm sure you learned much about their habits and ways from so close a connection."

Jeremy felt his face burning. "At least we found the place where they've taken Nul—"

Kelada laughed. "*Who* found the place?"

"Well, Fred and Busby, but that doesn't—"

Fred piped up brightly: "We weren't the first here."

Jeremy gave Kelada an inquiring look.

She smiled at him. "I was here nearly three days ago. I saw the hobs returning from the city early this morning and hid myself away, for safety. Somehow I missed seeing Nul; but the gargoyles are hard to overlook." She nodded toward the tunnel opening. "This seems to be the way to a big nest of hobs. There are others; I found them downriver from here. But all the hobs seem to be gathering here for some reason. And taking as many people with them as they can kill."

Barach came to the fire, where a cauldron of steaming water rested on the coals next to the almost empty stew pot. He cleaned and rinsed his flat wooden bowl and shook the last droplets of water from it. "I'd be most interested, my dear, in hearing about your experiences with these creatures. Well learned is well armed, they say, and if we are to go in after Nul, we shall need the best arms we can bear."

"She's not going in."

Kelada squeezed his hand. "Hush, Jeremy. I'll tell you what I know. Busby says that you thought I had gone to spend some time at Melodia's farm. That is partly true: I did leave with Melodia. She then used the speaking spell to arrange with the captain of a ship, the *Carosar*, for my passage northward. And when she had done that, she used her own travel cantrip to send me directly to the ship."

"Hence fooling Tremien," Barach observed. "Very clever. Tremien would have sensed your own use of the spell, since your cantrip is newer and stronger than Melodia's. He might not have understood exactly what was afoot, but his suspicions would have been aroused. Well managed, Kelada."

"Thank you. I had taken enough golders to buy quick passage. We passed you, though I did not realize the ship was yours until after I met the gargoyles and talked to them. Of course, once we made port I knew that I had arrived before you; and from the people of Fridport I learned enough of the lay of the land to know that only by being well upriver, far past the Gray Stair, could I be so far into the Valley that you would be unable to send me back when you caught up with me.

"In Fridport I fell in with a party of traders from the Valley. They were trading for arms—did you know that? The Valley people have great need of arms just now, and they are giving up much of their stored grain and food in exchange for swords, bows, and arrows. Anyway, there were more than a dozen of the traders, with a whole string of pack ponies, and they didn't mind taking me along. They lifted me up the Stair on their pulley-thing— did you do that? Wasn't it fun?"

"It was interesting," Barach smiled.

"It was *dangerous*," Jeremy insisted. "A pregnant woman shouldn't—"

"Oh, hush, husband. I've known women who paused in their job of unloading fishing craft, had their babies, and then picked up their baskets again. And those baskets weigh half as much as a woman does!"

"But you—"

"Please," Barach said. He turned to Kelada. "I wish you would tell us what happened in the Valley, my dear. From things we saw along our way, I gathered that your party was attacked."

Kelada leaned forward, her arms crossed beneath her breasts, and stared into the fire. "Yes, we were attacked. It was the second night we were in the upper valley; we had taken shelter in a barn, with the permission of the farmer. We kept watch, of course; but even so the hobs surprised us. They come very silently, and they seem to prefer the hours of darkness.

"It was not long before dawn. I was asleep in a corner of the barn. Something woke me, and I sat up and looked around. We had posted a sentry in the doorway, and the first thing that bothered me was that I could not see him.

"The next thing that bothered me was seeing two hobs slouch in. The things are quick! Before I could even cry out, they had slit the throat of a sleeper and were dragging him out. I shouted then, and the men of the trading party sprang up. The hobs had taken the sentry and two others already, without waking anyone; then they attacked us in earnest.

"We had a supply of daggers that the Valley folk had bought in town. I broke them open and threw them— knife-throwing is one of the skills that Niklas File taught me, and I learned it well—and killed at least one of the creatures. We tried to break from the barn, for the farmer had several large sons who could aid us in the battle, but there were too many of the hobs. And I don't know if any of the sons were still alive, for the farmhouse was in flames."

"We saw something similar," Jeremy said grimly. "But we arrived long after the hobs had come and gone."

"You were fortunate. When it became clear that the hobs were about to fire the barn as well, I began to look for another way out. There was one, a single small window high in the back wall. It took a bit of scrambling, but I got to it. None of the men would follow me—they thought the back would be watched, and we'd be killed one by one as we tried to leave by the window. I smashed out the lattice and hung by my hands before dropping. It wasn't a very long drop, fortunately, because the barn had been built back into the side of a hill.

"I was out of the barn, but poorly armed, and alone. The hobs had all concentrated in the yard between the barn and the house. I scuttled away as silently as I could, though I think the hobs, with all their yattering, could hardly have heard me had I worn bells. I found a dense tangle of low brush and trees and wriggled in there. I was hidden well enough, and I could see what happened."

She paused for a long time. When she resumed, her voice was low: "What happened was a massacre. The hobs sent in showers of fire arrows and got the hay in the loft alight, and soon the barn was boiling with smoke. Some of the men came staggering out, driven by the flames, and the hobs struck them down. They were like animals, like wolves: four and five of them upon each man, pulling them to ground and killing them. Inside the barn I could hear the ponies screaming. It was terrible. The fire burned itself out after two or three hona of this—the walls of the barn were stone, and the hay smoldered instead of bursting into flame. The roof did not catch.

"At the end, some of the hobs went inside the barn and came out dragging more bodies, the men and even the ponies. The hobs are incredibly strong; I saw one pile the bodies of three ponies on a drag, then haul them away single-handed. The creatures went away as the sun rose. When I was sure they had gone for good, I crept back to the barn and retrieved my pack and equipment. There were two dead hobs there; no dead men, no ponies. They had taken the bodies away with them."

"We know," Barach said gently.

Kelada nodded absently. "I tracked the hobs. They are not subtle, these creatures; they take the most direct route always, even if they have to break through brush and scramble over stones. They left a trail Blind Mat could have followed. They had gone away from the river, to the south. They camped in a dense grove of trees not far from the farm and rested there during the day. That's when I raided their camp; I had to know if any of the trading party were still alive. None were. I slipped back out of the camp empty-handed, and when the hobs moved again, I followed their trail. They traveled all the night long. The next morning I found their hole, a cave opening much like this one. I did not venture inside.

"That is about all. I knew from the traders that a city lay up the river. It took me about a day to get back to the river; then I simply kept walking to the west. I dared to move only in the fullest light, and from that night on I avoided the homes of men, for they were clearly the targets of the hobs. I had no provisions to speak of and had to hunt, though I'll confess to raiding a farmhouse or two along the way. It was no real theft: no one was left alive in the houses to miss what little I took. I was still a good half-day's march away from the town when a small party of hobs, twenty or thirty of them, passed me early one morning, hurrying along and jabbering.

"I had climbed a tree and saw them from across the river. They had a few pikas with them, maybe half a dozen or so; I could not tell from that distance if one of them were Nul. Again I followed the hobs. From their trail, I guessed that they joined a second, larger party, and the whole group went north.

"I came across other hob trails. They all ended here, at this hillside. The hobs are gathering down below for some reason. I kept well out of their way and saw more parties come in, sometimes with a few pikas, more often alone. Then last night many of them left with full darkness, oh, five hundred or more; they made for the city yonder.

"By then I supposed that you were probably in the Valley, though I did not know that you had actually reached the city. I did not dare to stir with so many hobs about, and so I kept close. I saw the hobs straggle back, many of them wounded, few of them bearing human bodies, and gathered that a battle had been fought. As I said, I missed Nul somehow, though he must have passed not far away from me; and long after the hobs had disappeared into the tunnel, these two stone behemoths came clambering along. I spoke to them, learned that the two of you had disappeared somehow, and made my way into town."

"And that was a braver action than you might expect. They are not fond of strangers," Barach said.

Kelada tossed her head. "The people of Three Rivers thought me no stranger. A thief learns languages quickly, and her tongue can twist itself to any accent. I went into the city in the guise of a peasant woman driven in from the countryside by the hobs. The guards did not even notice my entrance—it's a good thing for them that the hobs are the clumsy creatures they are, and not trained thieves!—and before long I was gossiping with other women who had fled to safety behind the city walls. There I heard about the quake—"

"Heard about it?" Jeremy asked, raising his eyebrows. "You mean you didn't *feel* it? It was strong enough in town to break down a good part of the wall!"

"It did not shake the hillside here."

Barach stroked his beard, a troubled look on his face. "A very strange kind of a quake, to be so localized. Not natural, obviously. I sense some magic at work."

Kelada shrugged. "I cannot say. At any rate, within an ona I knew you must be the two outlanders who had been taken prisoner and blamed for the hob raid. I heard that you were in the granary and even found the building before I slipped back out of town. I came back here to the gargoyles, we put our heads together to devise a plan for your escape, and the rest you know."

Jeremy, following Barach's example, rose and cleaned his and Kelada's bowls—the gargoyles, of course, ate nothing—and slipped the rinsed bowls into Kelada's pack. "I can't say that we're not grateful for what you did. But from here on, things will get dangerous."

Kelada laughed.

Scowling, Jeremy continued, "I mean really dangerous. The people of Three Rivers are no friends of ours,
and we can't rely on them for help. I think we have to go
into the tunnel. Barach?"

"I wish we did not," the old mage said. "But I agree,
Jeremy. Nul, whether prisoner or free, is in there somewhere, and we have a duty to him. No, I see no other
course."

"And," Jeremy said, "I'm not about to let you go into
that tunnel, alone or with us. Maybe you can slip back
into town—"

"If you keep me from going in with you, I'll only
return after you've gone and follow you. You can't keep
me away."

"But it's dangerous!"

"So is living, Jeremy. Don't you know by now that
without you I would not want to go on? Go where you
will, I will be there."

Jeremy had settled briefly on the stone beside Kelada.
Now he got up again and paced, his head down. "Then
we won't go into the tunnel at all. Nul is my friend, but
you're more than that to me. If I have to abandon Nul to
keep you safe, then I will."

"No, you won't."

"Kelada—"

She sighed. "You know you will go in after Nul; I
know it, Barach knows it, even the gargoyles know it.
You wouldn't be Jeremy if you could walk away from a
friend in peril. And I wouldn't be Kelada if I did not
follow."

"You make it sound as if we have no choice at all."

"I do not believe we have much of a choice in this
situation," she said. "Do you, Barach?"

Barach, still seated on his own stone, his arms crossed
over his chest, shook his head. "Do we ever have a
choice? A man in a maze may take any turns he wishes,
but until he finds the end, he is in the maze still. For my
part, Jeremy, I think you should give in. Kelada has lived
all of her life in a very demanding profession, and she's
learned a trick or two about keeping her skin whole.

Nothing about that has changed. She is in no more peril than you or I, and possibly less, for I am growing old and you are a newcomer to this world."

Jeremy heaved a sigh. "You would have to be logical at a time like this. Very well. I give up. But I want you protected when we go into the tunnel; the gargoyles will lead and be the rearguard. I'll come next, then you, then Barach."

"You may need me up front to track."

Jeremy gave Barach a despairing look. "There is no spell," Barach said kindly, "that can make marriage easy."

Havoronas had been a hunter and trapper in the days before the hobs had become so troublesome; then he found himself a soldier, hating the life, hating the regimentation. When Captain Ramp came to his tent on the southwest side of town with the offer, he had taken it at once: to be a hunter again, under the open sky, outside the walls, meant more to Havoronas than all the military glory, all imaginable medals, in the world.

Indeed, his only disappointment this night was that the task Ramp had set for him was far too easy. Following the escaped men was no task at all, in fact; it would have taken harder work to miss the signs of their flight. They had an animal, and a big one, with them, and the beast had plowed a furrow through the undergrowth.

"Two men," Havoronas had told Ramp when they came upon the first traces, just north of the bridge along the bank of the river. "One of them is young. About twenty measures or so in weight, fairly tall, about your height. The other is a good deal older, heavier, twenty-five measures I'd guess, and a hand shorter. They have a strange beast with them."

"You'll do," Ramp had said.

"The animal—what is it?"

"Haven't you heard the rumors from the men in the Merchant Square bivouac?"

"Don't listen to rumors, Capt'n. Don't much talk to the men in the other outfits, neither." Havoronas had risen. "Damn strange creature, this is."

"What do you make it to be?"

"Tracks like a fang-cat's, but thrice the size. And the hind tracks are more like some big bird's. Hanged if I can guess what the thing is. But it left a clear enough trail."

"That's all we need to know about it, then." Captain Ramp seemed satisfied. "Follow the trail."

He had done just that. Even with no moon or stars to help, aided only by the thin light of a muffled lantern, the tracker had followed the trail, never once losing it, not even when it crossed bare, rocky patches. Behind Havoronas Captain Ramp led a company of half a dozen archers, hard men and experienced soldiers who kept silence. Ramp stayed always about twenty paces behind, and the bowmen, well disciplined, kept behind him; no blundering about and ruining the trail here.

The men they were chasing had broken out of their prison during the first ona of full dark. Another ona had passed while Ramp spoke with the town master and assembled his force. The trail, though certainly not cold, was still not absolutely fresh. Yet the tracker knew that the soldiers were moving a good deal faster than their quarry had moved, and he expected that, if the escapees kept up their line of march and did not increase their speed, the soldiers should catch up to them by first light at the latest.

Havoronas paused at a point where the animal and the men had swerved slightly to the east of north. He knelt and traced the surface of the ground, moving very slowly; at last he stopped altogether, head bent, considering. After he had remained in that posture for a few moments, Ramp came to crouch beside him. "Anything wrong?"

"Naw," the tracker grunted. "Decided to mend their path a bit here's all. Didn't speed up or nothing."

"What does that mean?"

Havoronas grinned in the dark. He did not like soldiering, he did not like soldiers, and to tell the truth, he did not much like Captain Ramp. "Means a couple of things. Means they got a place in mind to go to—not just running blind through the night. Since they didn't speed up, they don't know they're being chased. They ain't marching like they expect trouble, neither; not in file or anything like that. Sometimes one of 'em's on one side of the beast, sometimes t'other is." The tracker rose to his feet. "We're catching up, too. Let's move along some."

They went along in quick-march time, gaining on the fugitives all the way. Finally they emerged from the dark tangle of a brushy forest and Havoronas paused, one foot on a fallen tree trunk, knee bent, eyes intent on something in the distance. Again Ramp appeared at his elbow. "What is it now?"

"Look ahead yonder. Up in the air, like. Not far up, though. See anything?"

After a pause, Captain Ramp's voice was tentative: "Is it a light?"

"Aye. Not much of one, neither. You got good eyes."

"A torch, do you think?"

"Nah, Capt'n. Ain't moving. Guess again."

I don't know. A signal of some kind?"

"Ah, now, Capt'n. You reckon they'd try so hard t' get away and then put up a come-all-ye for us to see?"

Ramp lost his temper. "Damn you, you're the tracker. What do you make of it?"

Havoronas scratched his chin. It was prickly and made a rasping sound inside his head. They had made him shave off his hunter's beard in the army, so that no hob could grab it and jerk his chin up long enough to cut his throat. That's what they told him, at any rate. Officers, he noticed, often wore beards. He found himself sometimes sympathizing with the hobs and wishing them well. At length he said, "Capt'n, if I was to have to guess, I'd say it was a bit of campfire. If you concentrate real hard, you can smell the vittles."

Ramp leaned forward, as though trying to pierce the distance and the darkness with his eyes. "Them?"

The hunter wrinkled his nose. He could smell Ramp's sweat, and the odor overpowered the traces he had caught from the ledge. "Must be them. Who else would it be away out here?"

"Must be expectin' us. Looks to me like they've taken the high ground."

Havoronas made a tuneless whistling sound between his teeth.

The soldier, still leaning forward, did not even look around. "What do you think we should do?" Ramp asked.

"Me? Capt'n, I'm naught but a hunter. I find 'em, you deal with 'em. I done my part already."

After a very long pause, Captain Ramp said, "Assume that these people are animals that you been hunting. Now you got 'em at ground up on the hillside. You want to get close enough to put an arrer in 'em without giving yourself away. Now, hunter, put the case like that, and what would you do?"

Havoronas shrugged. "We ain't in a bad spot here. Got the wind t' our advantage. Can't rightly see the hills, but if I remember where we are, there's a kind o' path running along the shoulder of yonder rise. I'd guess they're up on that. Now, if it was me, I'd go off to the right a ways and climb the hill along the top o' the ridge. Nah, it's too dark to see, never mind looking that way. Just take my word for it, it can be done. Come in downwind of 'em that way, and get above 'em before they know it, if you're lucky. You got good bowmen then, maybe you can get them both before they know you're on 'em. If they're all alone up there."

"What do you mean?"

Havoronas pulled his nose. "Hobs've been all through here, Capt'n. Hundreds of 'em. Some come through days ago, some of 'em is the ones what run from the town earlier. Their traces are plain as plain. Been seeing 'em all night."

"You think maybe it's a trap? Think there could be hobs up there with them?"

"Could be, Capt'n. But you never said my job was looking for hobs, so I never paid the traces much mind."

"Damn you," Ramp said again.

"Well," Havoronas said, grinning to himself, "it's your time to make up your mind now, Capt'n. Yonder they set, with an army o' hobs around 'em—or yonder they set, all alone. From here I can't tell you which way it is at all. Guess you have to decide just how it is, and how you mean to come at 'em."

"Can you get close enough to see?"

The hunter considered the question in silence for a few moments. "Don't know. Might be able to. Used to slip up on banrips without them hearing me. 'Course that was back when I was naught but a hunter, not a soldier-boy."

"Go on then."

"What? And maybe get skewered when I come back, from your boys thinking I might be a nasty old hob?"

"Then give us a signal. Make a sound like a bird or something."

Havoronas snorted through his nostrils. "Hang a sign on my back, why don't I." He grunted, tiring of the game. "I'll go have a look, Capt'n. No worry about shooting me. Your men there won't know I'm back till I choose to let them know. You stay right here; don't stir a pace from this spot. Else we might make a mistake in the dark ourselves, the two of us."

"You and me, you mean?"

"Nah," grunted Havoronas. "Me and my knife." He faded into the night, moving with quick agility, catlike springs and scrambles. He found loose stone and avoided making one grain grate on another; he grasped stems of brush without stirring one dead leaf or rustling a twig; he followed the trend of the ridge up and up the hillside, deliberately, slowly, but moving all the time. Only a few simi had passed when he slipped silently up to a perch on a boulder and was able to peer down at the ledge, a very short bow-shot distant.

His eyes narrowed. The fire was nothing but embers now, but it gave off enough of a glow to see them. There were the two men, right enough: the heavier old one, bearded like a grandsir, and the slimmer, active younger one, his face keen above a short brown beard, the kind of beard Havoronas himself had once worn. But there was a woman with them, too. They were moving about, breaking camp, evidently, but with no hurry.

The hunter bit his lip. The three appeared to be alone, without a hob in sight. No doubt Ramp would be pleased. And yet . . . a woman . . .

He was just about to slip away when another movement caught his eye. Something was all but hidden just out of his sight, below the edge of the hill. He cautiously lifted himself.

And felt the breath catch in his chest.

He looked down on an animal. *The* animal.

The size of a good sturdy draft horse. Hindquarters of a dragon. Forequarters of a cat. Falcon's head.

Magnificent.

Havoronas had a hunter's heart. He lost it then and there.

A magnificent animal.

Just magnificent.

CHAPTER 11

IT HAD TAKEN several trips, for Nul was worried about Grall and fearful that the hobs were not as far away as she seemed to think; but at last he had brought a considerable store of darkbread to where she rested. He had even found an exceptionally large mushroom, well past its prime, with a tough, leathery outer rind. He hollowed this out with one of the daggers and produced a rough sort of water skin. Ungainly, lopsided, and all too apt to collapse and spill what it carried, at least it held water without leaking when he tried it.

She awakened again as he was preparing to leave her. "What are you doing?" she asked, her voice a little stronger after the food and the rest.

"Getting food and water for you. I have to go now. I want to scout ahead, find the other pikas if I can. When you feel stronger, try to make it up to the surface. You can find your way, can't you?"

"Yes. I was in the work party that opened the tunnel through to the world outside. But I am too weak to go so far."

"I am sorry. I can't take time to help you now. After I've seen the others, I'll come back for you."

"No." Grall's voice was mournful and resigned. "You cannot return. You will die if you go into the caverns. You do not understand."

Nul rinsed his hands beneath the trickling flow of water, rubbed them on his trousers. "I know that our people need me. That's enough for me to understand."

"No—wait." Grall lifted a hand to her head. "I do

201

not remember. I told you of the firvolkans and the elementals—or did I?"

Nut sat near her. "Elementals? You mentioned them. But what about them?"

Grall shivered. "They are terrible creatures. The firvolkans were sent here with a fire elemental, one somehow enthralled by the Great Dark One, a slave of his. The firvolkans speak to it. I think maybe they even worship it. And then, not long ago, they encountered another elemental, one of stone. It was our doing."

"Tell me."

Grall hesitated for a long time. Then, in a tentative, halting voice, she took up the tale: "We were digging out a passage between two chambers. They were living quarters for two groups of—of our masters. The firvolkans wanted them connected. Pikas worked many a weary ona cutting stone and digging soil. At last we came to a sphere of very hard stone, too hard for us to break or move without our magic. But the firvolkans drove us, insisted that we break through. We tried, failed, and tried again; and when at last we did break through the stone, it proved hollow, like a great egg. And from it came the stone elemental.

"It was—oh, I can't tell you what it was. A creature of mineral, a giant, even beside the firvolkans; and it could have killed us in an instant. It had slept long in its stony shell, had slept through long ages of the world, I think. It did not fear us or hate us or love us; it was not even curious about us, only terribly indifferent.

"I think if the firvolkans had not been allied to their own elemental, it would have crushed us all, or perhaps torn us to pieces, pikas and firvolkans alike, out of idleness and desire for some small activity. Some things that I have heard tell me that the stone creature fell asleep long ago, when the world was different and different creatures walked upon it. We were strange to it: not of interest, exactly, but different from what it had seen before. That is all.

"But the fire elemental somehow communicated with the stone one. The elementals do that, though it is true that they do not often speak; and when they do communicate, it is not often in a friendly way. But this time it was different. The fire elemental somehow won over the stone one. Now the stone elemental is helping the firvolkans with their task."

Nul shook his head. "Elementals almost never fight against humans or other living creatures. They may destroy us, but as you say, it is almost always through indifference or simple ignorance of our existence. That I have learned from great magicians."

Grall tugged at his arm. "These elementals are different, I tell you. There are fires deep below this valley, fires of stone; and the two elementals have agreed to loose them on the world above."

Nul stared hard at her in the dim light from the firemoss. "Fires of stone? I cannot understand."

"I hardly understand myself. But there is a place, far underground, where stone becomes so hot that it is liquid."

"Yes. I have seen one volcano, and I have heard of others."

"The valley above us was formed by volcanic forces. They still rest far below ground, deep under the surface. The elementals have agreed to release these forces."

Nul frowned. "Make—a new volcano?"

"Yes. Fill the valley with melted and burning stone. That will sweep all before it, or reduce the entire valley to dead ashes. The burning stone will purge the valley of life."

"And that is what the hobs desire." Nul rose. "I still must go. Get to the surface if you are strong enough, Grall. Try to find a human named Jeremy, or one named Barach. They are friends. And if you cannot find them, then try to follow the river downstream as far as you can."

"Nul, do not go. There is nothing you can do for us now. Save yourself."

"I am trying to do that," Nul said. "Farewell, Grall! Remember the names: Jeremy and Barach. Strange names for a pika's tongue, but good friends for all that. Take care."

He left her then, driven by a new sense of urgency and a despairing notion that time was getting away from him, that he had hesitated too long already. Nul returned to the main tunnel and ran silently along it, feeling its smooth floor beneath his bare feet, noting how the firemoss grew thicker and brighter as he went deeper into the heart of the world. Once he took a heavy spill. The breath went from him for a moment, but he was not seriously hurt.

Nul got up carefully, fearing that the noise he had made would bring hobs down upon him. He had stepped into a deep hole. When he retrieved his dropped sword and looked at the place that had tripped him up, he saw it was a ventilation shaft leading farther down into the tunnels, a shaft far too small for him to wriggle through. But he stretched out on his stomach and pressed his face against the opening. Breathing deep, he smelled warm air, a strong scent of hobs, and the old lingering odor of pikas, many of them.

Nul pushed himself up, took a tighter grip on his sword, and resumed his trotting run—though this time he looked more intently at the tunnel floor, noting where he put his feet.

"Got away!" Captain Ramp was livid, his voice ringing with indignation. He seized the hunter's jacket and shook him. "You let them get away, you—"

"Easy, Capt'n. Start by letting go of me." Havoronas felt the grip on his jacket loosen. "That's better, now. You don't want to get so heated up, Capt'n." They stood in the cool lee of the pine thicket; Captain Ramp, as he had promised, had not stirred a foot from the spot while Havoronas had been gone. The hunter kept his voice even: "Did I say they'd got away? No words of mine. That ain't what I said, Capt'n, and you know it."

Ramp swung his short, curved sword, chopping off a spray of pine needles from mere frustration; the sharp scent of fresh pine sap spiked the air. "No. 'Got into a cave' is what you said. But it amounts to the same thing."

"Not a bit of it." Havoronas scratched his chin and looked up at the sky, a ragged gray mass of dark cloud a little brighter in the east. " 'S a bit lighter. Be getting on to dawn before long."

"Look," Captain Ramp said, "if they got inside a cave, they're as good as gone. I ain't got the men to go chasing into a hob-hole."

Havoronas spat. "Nah. I reckon you ain't at that. Got six archers, but archers ain't the type that loves to go running into hob-holes, now, are they? Anyhow, what good'd them bows do down in the guts of the world, huh? Not hardly no space to draw 'em, naught but long tunnels t' shoot down; no village greens there, no fair open space to a big painted target, eh? And I reckon that soldiers like yours yonder wouldn't feel right about going under the ground anyhow, huh? Probably a little too confined for them, I guess."

Captain Ramp had dragged a rag from a pocket and was using it to wipe his blade. In the incipient dawn the cloth seemed to float on its own, invisible in his darker hand. "You're up to something, hunter. What is it?"

"Me?" Havoronas put innocent surprise in his voice. "I'm naught but a hunter. No policy in my head, there isn't. What would I be up to, now?"

"Tell it." Ramp put the cloth away and sheathed his sword, its blade making a cool slicing sound as it slid home in the leather scabbard at his waist.

"Well, 'tis my guess the town master'll be none too happy wi' you if you come back without the men you went after. Am I right there?"

Ramp grunted a short agreement. "Thendenis wanted their heads. He'll have mine if I go back without them."

"Aye, Capt'n. I figured he must want 'em pretty bad, to send us out at night after 'em. But, like you say, they've gone down a hob-hole."

"And you have a way to get them out." When the hunter did not reply, Ramp demanded. "Is that it? You know how to smoke these men out of their cave?"

"Ain't saying that, Capt'n. Not exactly."

"What are you saying, exactly, Havoronas?"

"Put it this way. Once when I was, oh, a good bit younger than I am today, my old father—he was a hunter, too—ran a shag bear into a cave. You know shag bears?"

"I heard of 'em."

"Yah, but never saw none, I warrant. Ain't none to see no more, not in these here mountains. All killed off when I was still a youngster. Might have got the last one myself, for all I can tell about it. Sport, they was! Strong as any six men together, wily and cunning, and not afraid of demons and spirits riding on dragons. Anyway, this old black and brown shag bear, near as big as a pony he was, he'd got himself snug back into a cave. And my ol' dad says, well, there goes the kill. Meant a lot to us, you know, month's eating, maybe, fur to sell, and that. All lost, my old dad thought, because of how the bear had run down into his lair. But I said as how I thought it might be possible to get old bear out of the cave. So my dad, he sent me in. And I got the bear out, too."

"How?"

"Piece at a time," Havoronas said laconically. "That's what I reckon we got to do now, Capt'n; go in after 'em and bring 'em out a piece at a time. Only it's likely to be kind of squeezy-tight in a cave. So we won't be needing the archers. They'd just get underfoot in close quarters, anyhow."

Ramp turned and gazed away toward the archers. Havoronas knew he saw nothing; they were invisible in the predawn gloom. "Then what am I supposed to do with them?"

"Send 'em on back to town."

"Just you and me."

"Yah. Should be enough. If it ain't, well, who's to miss us, hey? I ain't got no woman. You?"

Captain Ramp did not answer. Instead he strode away, spoke something sharp and low to the archers, and then came back. "Let's go."

Havoronas grinned. "Thought you'd give me a bit of an argument."

"No point. You know what's probably in the hole as well as I do. I told the town master I'd hale 'em back, and that's what I'll do, if I don't die trying. Let's go."

"Right you are, Capt'n."

Havoronas led the way up the slope to the tunnel entrance. The two men paused on the ledge. Havoronas looked around from that vantage point. He could make out the town, way over toward the river, by the few lights it showed. To the east the clouds were growing lighter, though this looked as if it would be a day of all clouds and no sun. Well, the light where they were headed wasn't likely to be bright, either, he reckoned. "Got torches?" he asked. "This here dark lamp won't hold out very long now."

"I have seven. Mine and the archers'."

"Collected the soldiers', did you? Good thinking, that. They can find their way back to town in th' dark, can't they now?" Havoronas rubbed his mouth with the palm of his hand. "That gives us, what, maybe four hona of light? Means we'll have to move fast."

Captain Ramp had already lit one of the torches. He held it close to the ground, frowning in its yellow light. "Here. What's this?" The flame illuminated a shallow footprint, nearly twice the length of a man's, the dark shadows cast in it by the low angle of the light making it seem deeper than it really was. "What made this?"

The hunter smiled down like a priest who had just sent out a blessing into his congregation. "Now, that's a question, ain't it? What would you suppose it to be, now?"

"Hanged if I know. Looks like a dragon's print."

"Close, Capt'n, mighty close. That's beastie that was with 'em. Saw it from the ridge. That's one thing I want, Capt'n, I'll leave the men to you, and the woman, too—"

"Woman?"

"Aye."

Ramp frowned. "The town master said nothing about no woman. I don't like killing women."

"Do what you want with her. She's yours, for all of me. Her and the men both; you can have 'em all, free gift from me. Except only I want the beast. It's mine, understand?" That's what I claim."

The wind played with the torch, making a whipped-rag sound on the morning air. "You can have the beast," Ramp said. "I don't care about the beast. But if you want it, you kill it."

"Aye," Havoronas said easily. "That's what I expect to do."

* * *

"Ugh," Fred grunted. "Mazerite all around. Feel it squeezing at me."

"Are you all right?" asked Jeremy, just behind the gargoyle.

"Yes. But I don't think I could dwindle now. The influence is too strong. It's trying to slow my life-magic; it's like wading through thick mud. Never felt anything like it."

Barach, who was behind Kelada but ahead of Busby, said, "I think we will not need the torch, Jeremy. I see firemoss on the walls, enough to give us a kind of light."

"Good," Jeremy said, his breath coming more shallowly than usual. "I was nervous about carrying a torch anyway. How do I put it out?"

"I'll put it out if you just drop it," Fred said. Jeremy tossed the torch to the floor of the tunnel and the gargoyle stepped on it, snuffing it instantly. The reek of pine pitch and smoke filled his nostrils. The dark descended at once, gripping Jeremy in its impalpable black hand, soft as midnight velvet but merciless. He gasped.

"Jeremy? What's the matter?" Kelada whispered.

"Uh, nothing. I'm—fine," Jeremy said, having to grunt to force the words out of his constricted throat. He was intensely aware of the tons of stone and soil above him, though he could not see so much as his hand before his eyes. The enormous dead weight of it seemed to stop his breath in his throat, to squeeze his lungs and his heart. "Where—where's this light, Barach?" he said, his voice squeaking a bit.

Barach's quiet and reassuring voice was too soft to give rise to any echo: "It is there, Jeremy. Your eyes are not used to the gloom yet, that's all. You'll soon see."

Fred had not paused, and Jeremy groped after him, stumbling over his own feet, fighting the ridiculous notion that the floor of the tunnel was irregular, that he was about to step off an invisible subterranean precipice and fall forever. His breath panted shallowly in his own ears, and he felt sweat breaking from his forehead, rolling down his sides from beneath his arms.

"It's all right," Kelada said, touching his shoulder with

a soft hand. "Don't look straight at the walls. Look away and notice them from the corners of your eyes."

Jeremy did, though he hardly knew where he was looking. He gradually became aware of a dim phosphorescence, a faint green-yellow speckled glow like a crowd of minute fireflies, at the edge of his sight. "See it," he gasped.

"It will grow stronger as your eyes adjust," Barach said. "Put out a hand to the wall if you need to steady yourself. Fred, are you still on Nul's track?"

"Oh, yes, Mage. The scent is clear as anything. No hob has been this way since Nul passed here."

"Good," Barach said. "That means Nul is probably safe."

Jeremy, fighting the urge to shuffle his feet along, searching with his toes for the nonexistent edge of the imaginary drop, said between tightly clenched teeth, "How—how do you make that out?"

Barach's voice held no nervousness; it came as calmly and as reasonably as if he were sitting in the library at Whitehorn, discussing some arcane volume of lore. "Why, if he were a captive, a hob or two would be holding him so, and his scent would be mixed with theirs. But Fred says Nul's scent is quite distinct and plain, with no overlay of hob to it. Therefore, he is following the hobs, as we follow him; he is not a captive but a hunter."

"That makes sense," Jeremy said. "Do you think the floor's becoming steeper?"

"I don't think so," Fred said. "Feels much the same, anyway."

"Feels like it's tilted more to me."

"Jeremy," Kelada said again. "What is it?"

Jeremy attempted a weak laugh. It was, as laughs go, a complete failure. "Don't really know. Just a touch of claustrophobia, I guess."

"Of what?" Barach said.

"Claustrophobia. English word. Means that closed-in places make me frightened. Funny, I didn't even know I had it till I got in here."

Barach's voice was knowing and full of comforting warmth: "You probably didn't have it. Imaginative peo-

ple sometimes have trouble in tight, dark places like this.
In the Wizard's War something like this happened. Some
of the Great Dark One's forces had sealed off a small
city. The magicians they had working for them confused
the travel-spell and disrupted it, so that the spell was
useless; I told you what happened to me when I left
Jalot. Anyway, a little band of soldiers, only five or six of
them, decided to go for aid the only way they could:
through a drainage tunnel beneath the town. Their leader,
whom no one could call a coward, was fine until he
dropped into the tunnel; and then fear took him and
locked his limbs. The same fear you describe with your
English word, Jeremy."

"What happened?"

"He forced himself to go on anyway. Had to; they
were all single file in the drain, with not enough room for
someone to get around him or even to turn around. They
could only go forward, not backward; and so he made his
legs carry him even though they wanted to collapse."

"Did he, ah, make it?"

"Oh, yes, in good time. The soldiers got free of the
city, summoned aid, and broke the siege."

"Good for him."

"You should tell Captain Fallon that when we get back
to Whitehorn."

"Captain Fallon?"

"He was the young soldier."

Jeremy gritted his teeth. Fallon was a tough old fellow,
solid and scarred as if he'd been carved from a stump of
oak with a dull hatchet; there was nothing soft about
him. It was hard to imagine the old soldier trembling in
the dark—trembling anywhere. Fallon's being afraid was
as unthinkable as the notion that the sun wouldn't rise in
the morning. Jeremy forced himself to take a deep breath,
and then another. He picked up his pace a bit. "We'd
better go faster," he said, noticing that he could now
make out the bulky silhouette of Fred against the firefly
glitter of the moss. "Nul may need us."

The insidious velvet fingers around his throat never let
go completely, but they loosened a bit. The party went
on for some time, doggedly following the trail, and the

firemoss grew denser and somewhat brighter as they did so. Eventually the patches of moss gave enough light so that Jeremy could make out the dull orange-brown expanse of Fred's back and the reflection of the moss in the blade of his drawn sword. He looked back. Kelada's face was a pale blur behind him, Barach's beard a whitish-gray wisp of cloud floating over her shoulder. Busby, too far back to make out in any detail, was a heavy black shadow partially eclipsing the firemoss growths.

"Here's something," Fred said, suddenly checking.

Jeremy, caught off guard, almost blundered into the gargoyle. He put out his hand and touched Fred's flank. "What is it? What did you find?"

"Obsidian," the gargoyle said. "Volcanic glass. A big slippery patch of it. Be careful."

"I thought you had found something."

"I have! It's a very unusual mineral—"

"Quiet!" The word itself was spoken softly, in the stone-grating-on-stone voice of Busby.

"Yes," Barach said. "This is no time for a mineralogical—"

"You, too," Busby said sternly. Barach fell silent, and they all paused. After a moment Busby said, "Someone is behind us, and not far."

"Hobs?" Jeremy asked.

"I do not know. But I hear someone, still far back and very faint. Coming our way, I believe. I think we had better pick up our pace."

They moved faster, though Fred complained that it was harder for him to trace Nul's scent that way. But they hurried onward and downward, the firemoss growing even thicker and brighter—"We're now more than a thousand paces below the surface," Busby said brightly at one point—as they descended. They had already passed the mouths of several tributary passages when Fred suddenly stopped short at an intersection. "Strong!" he breathed.

"Nul?" Barach asked.

Jeremy became aware that he could see Fred in fair detail, could see the long bent neck, as graceful as a swan's, and the huge head lowered to the floor of the tunnel as the stone nostrils snuffled. "Nul. And another."

"A hob?" asked Kelada.

"No. No. Strange scent and yet familiar. A pika? I think a pika!"

"Follow it."

"The track is very confused in this place. Nul's traces are strong here. He was here and then moved away and came back again. What is this?" The gargoyle was nuzzling something small and round, the size of a tennis ball. Jeremy squeezed up to his head and picked it up.

"Ugh. Something soft and squishy."

Barach had drawn abreast of Kelada. "Let me see." The mage, his dark brown robe invisible but his hands and face floating pale in the luminescence, took the cold object from Jeremy's hand and sniffed it. "A mushroom. Edible, I should think from the smell, and quite recently picked."

"This way," Fred said, veering to the left. "They both went this way."

Jeremy fell in behind the gargoyle once again. "Don't run away from us."

"Sorry." Fred moved faster now, stalking forward in his impatience the way a cat will stalk a bird, with long thrusts of his forelegs, stealthy but quick at the same time. "Water ahead. Someone's there."

Jeremy pushed past again, aware of Barach at his shoulder. "Where? I don't see—"

A small stone, weakly flung, bounced off the tunnel wall near his knee. Jeremy squinted into the dimness. "Where did that come from?"

Ahead of him shadow moved, and another stone fell short. "Let me past, Jeremy," Barach said.

The shadow hesitated. A flat, high-pitched voice said, "Jer-e-mee?"

"It is a pika," Barach said with a quick intake of breath. He rattled off something incomprehensible in a speech full of hisses and buzzes.

The small shadow answered in the same peculiar tongue. Jeremy caught the name "Nul" at least twice. Barach said something else in what evidently was pika-talk, and then said to Jeremy, "This is Grall, a pika of Nul's tribe. She has long been a captive. She was left for dead by the hobs, and our friend found and nursed her. He left her only two or three hona ago; we must be very close behind him now."

"I need more light," Kelada said. She had slipped by Jeremy without his noticing her—good thief that she is, he thought—and was bent over the dark form of Grall.

Barach plucked a patch of moss from the wall and breathed on it through his open mouth. The moss glowed brighter, and he breathed again, and then again. Before long it was at least as bright as a candle. "Here," Barach said, passing it to Kelada. "The radiance won't last long, but the firemoss loves heat and moisture. If it fades too much, give it a few breaths to bring it back."

Jeremy stooped to peer at the pika. He felt shock wash over him: Grall, unlike sturdy little Nul, was emaciated, the thinness of her arms and legs not offset by a husky body. Except for her natural coat of sleek gray fur she was naked, and Jeremy saw the flattish mounds of four breasts on her wasted chest. Her great orange eyes, much like Nul's, were sunken and somewhat feverish. Kelada had run her hands over the pika. She glanced over her shoulder. "Nothing broken, no wounds. Just ill-treatment and starvation."

Grall said something to Barach, and the old mage murmured something reassuring. He had never relinquished hold of his carpetbag. He opened it and rummaged inside. At last he found what he was after and passed a small stoppered bottle, no longer than his forefinger and no thicker than a pencil, to Kelada. "This is a cordial that should help her. Give it to her when I tell you." He said something else to Grall, and she replied weakly. "Now," Barach said, "give her about half the bottle. Slowly, almost drop by drop; if she should choke or cough, stop."

But Kelada tilted the bottle against Grall's lips and the pika lapped and smacked as a thick, dark liquid flowed out. Kelada checked the level in the bottle once, gave Grall a little more, and then replaced the cork. "It has a minty smell. A mixture of Tremien's?" she asked.

"It is an older remedy than that. This is the liquor of the eternity plant."

"What!" Kelada laughed. "If I were still practicing my old profession, I could keep this to retire upon. My God, what thief has ever held in her hand something so precious?"

"What is it?" Jeremy asked.

"I thought all mages knew about this," Kelada said, holding up the vial before handing it back to Barach.

"Not ones from Atlanta. Barach—?"

The old mage held the glass tube up for a moment, gauging how much of its contents Grall had taken, before he stooped to put it back in his bag. "This liquid is a very precious extract from an extremely rare plant, Jeremy. Wizards, you may have noted, live somewhat longer than most people. The elixir here is the reason."

"What is it? A—a youth potion?"

"Not exactly; it is a natural nectar that does not restore youth but rather lessens and delays the ravages of age. I take a drop once or twice a year; so will you, when you reach your normal middle age and begin to feel aches and twinges. There is but little of the elixir available, and it has its greatest effects on wizards. Tremien has consumed quantities of the stuff in his time. And I imagine the Great Dark One, who fears old age and death so much, bathes in it."

Grall was breathing more deeply and more easily now, and she had risen to a sitting position.

Jeremy glanced at the pika. "Then she will live to be five or six times normal pika-age now?"

"I doubt that. Unless one has strong inherent magic—which pikas do not—the nectar refreshes and strengthens, but does not rejuvenate."

"She does seem much stronger already," Kelada said.

"It works that fast?" Jeremy asked.

"It has immediate effect. Grall will continue to improve over the next days," Barach said. "The elixir will give her a temporary kind of strength, but her body needs rest and food more than any magical concoction. If she does not get them, she may be worse off a week from now than she is at this moment." He spoke to Grall, then

helped her up. As she tottered to her feet, Jeremy noticed that she, like Nul—like all pikas, he supposed—had
a short stub of tail. "She thinks she can walk now,"
Barach said. "If not for Busby's fear that someone is
back there behind us, I would send her out of the tunnels
altogether. Let us go after Nul."

Fred and Busby could just squeeze around to change
direction, but, unable to shrink themselves because of
the mazerite in the tunnel walls, in the narrow passageway they could not pass by each other. Busby took the
lead on the way back to the intersection. They had just
entered the main tunnel again when a gleam of yellow
light burst forth on their right. Jeremy, his eyes fully
accustomed by this time to the dim glow of the firemoss,
was dazzled by torchlight. But he recognized the voice
that cried, "There they are!"

It belonged to the soldier he had hit with a clay lamp.

The depths glowed with an eerie luminescence, as bright
as the light of a full moon—if the full moon could be pale
green. Nul had found steeper paths than the main trail,
had descended once down a long, rough, and almost
vertical shaft, until now he moved along a deep, deep
tunnel, its walls smoothly rounded, its floor flat, glowing
in the light from great clinging and hanging bunches of
firemoss.

How far he had come he did not know, nor had he any
clear idea of just where he was. He could find his way
back, of course, assuming that he could climb back up
the steep, unworked shaft that he had almost tumbled
down; but he had lost his orientation and no longer had a
clear trail to follow.

Hob scent was everywhere, thick and clinging, the
ammoniac reek of meat-eaters. They had come to this
level, and here they seemed to have milled and scattered.
When he paused and became still, Nul could hear occasional sounds now—faraway echoes of harsh gabbling
voices, the booming ring of metal against rock—muted
by distance and the twists of the tunnels. But he could
not accurately guess their direction or even their dis-

tance; that faculty, almost inborn among his kind, had left him long ago.

He clenched his teeth and cautiously negotiated a long bare stretch of tunnel, one with no hiding places anywhere. He made it through and came to a maze, a network of smaller tunnels, many of them irregular, with chest-high masses of stone jumbled about as if from recent falls. These stretches were darker, too, with less firemoss growing on the walls. Nul gripped the hilt of his short sword and listened again. There were sounds of rock work going on, perhaps a little nearer now, but from which direction did they come? Nul explored a side tunnel for a little way, until it seemed that the clatter and clang of steel on rock had become a bit softer, and then he retraced his steps and tried a different direction.

This time there could be no mistake: the sounds grew constantly louder until the clang and clatter seemed only a few hundred paces away. Nul moved toward the noise, finally having to drop to all fours and creep through a very small passageway, too small for any human and barely large enough to allow him space to move. This little tunnel was unworked and almost wholly dark, with only one or two ineffectual glows of the firemoss splashed on its ceiling; but the mouth of the passage, when it came in sight, gave onto a larger space that seemed well lighted. Nul crawled very quietly to the lip of the opening and with great caution peeked out.

His heart fluttered. Pikas—three, five, six of them— toiled at a rock face a good way below and opposite him. He was gazing into a vast domed chamber, probably artificial, that stretched perhaps sixty man-paces in diameter and rose to a vaulted roof some forty pace-lengths above the black-sand floor. Nul's opening was nearly halfway up one wall. Looking down from it, he could see the mouth of a far larger tunnel at floor level and, standing in the opening of that passageway, a hob guard, hulking and stoop-shouldered, with a long, stringy mane of dirty gray hair falling from its neck and shoulders. It was naked, as were the pikas: they wore not even the loin wraps that work parties had always donned. Nul looked from face to face without recognizing any of them; but all looked wizened by time and hard work, and he could not be sure that they were strangers.

The pika work party had scraped out a rough recess in the wall nearly opposite Nul's vantage point. He saw that they worked with short-handled picks, hammers, and metal spikes. The picks seemed to be the traditional type, probably forged by the pikas themselves. Perhaps the picks, Nul thought, were even old ones, ones that his uncles may have made years ago beneath the Bone Mountains. But the hammers were obviously of human make, far too large for the small three-fingered hands. The pikas worked in utter silence, a circumstance that made Nul feel deep unease. He had been on digging parties before, when he had grown large enough to carry baskets of stone and dirt, and he could not remember one that did not pound along merrily to the rhythm of a sturdy work song.

The hob in the doorway seemed completely indifferent to its charges. It shuffled about, leaned on its club, scratched itself. Nul began to get a glimmer of an idea. In the dark he shucked off his trousers, being careful not to let his daggers or sword clatter against stone. Then, naked, he edged to the lip of the opening and looked down. The drop was steep, but not precipitous, and the walls of the chamber were rough, studded with projecting knobs of stone. Nul glanced back up. The hob was busy searching for a flea in the springy hair of its thigh. Nul studied the wall again and swung himself out. Head down, he scrambled to the floor of the chamber, the noise of his descent lost in the clamor of picks against rock. He scuttled across the sandy floor and came into the midst of the pikas. The hob looked up dully, studied the work party, yawned, and resumed its search for the insect that seemed to be annoying it.

The pikas looked at Nul with wide orange eyes, but not one of them murmured a word of surprise. Nul took a pick from an older pika, whispered, "Move stone for awhile. I will explain." He attacked the black basalt wall with terrific vigor, sending down a rattling rain of broken stone. "My name is Nul," he said during the flurry of noise. Another blow of the pick, more noise. "I have come to help you." Another blow. "Tell me how."

They carried on a sporadic conversation in this way, their words masked by the deliberately timed sounds of digging. Only one of the pikas, the older one whose pick Nul had taken, remembered Nul; this was Sard, who was almost as old as Nul's father would have been. Nul groped for Sard in memory and found a dim recollection of a hearty, food-loving fellow, one of the surface farmers, an expert in polishing and shaping gems. For a pika, the Sard of Nul's memory had been almost fat, a jolly barrel of a fellow with thick upper arms and legs. He had changed in the interim. After forty years of hob captivity, Sard was sadly wasted, a walking skeleton almost; but spirit burned in his eyes as he heard Nul whisper of what had taken place in the world above the caverns.

The other pikas, Nul was shocked to discover, were all younger than he. Of the six in the party, four were females of about forty, just the age to find mates; but with their dispirited demeanor and starved bodies they would have but poor prospects—at least in normal times. Nul wondered at the drive that kept the pikas mating and reproducing their kind even in captivity. If Grall were right, it contrasted starkly with the despair felt by the hobs, they who were driven to reproduce only in hopes of bringing an end to their races and to all who lived.

In their intermittent talk, the others told Nul that the hobs wanted this chamber connected with the one where the stone elemental rested; that in a huge chamber on the other side of a thick wall a great many other pikas toiled in similar work, digging toward them; and that their own stint, many hona long, was almost over. Before long another group would be brought in to take up the labor.

"How many guards?" Nul asked.

"Just two of them," Sard told him. "One there. One in the tunnel."

"And you haven't attacked yet?"

"It is hopeless."

"Why?"

Sard waited until Nul had struck another blow with his

pick. In fits and starts, he told Nul that until recently the pikas had been much more heavily guarded by the hobs; many times over the years pikas had tried to escape, but on every occasion the hobs had caught and killed them and had displayed the heads to the others. Recently, however, the hobs, themselves weakening from hunger, had been forced to reduce the watch.

"It does not matter," Sard said. "We can no longer find our way in the tunnels."

"Are you sure?"

"Our magic does not work here."

Nul swung the pick harder, more viciously. "You don't need magic to find your way!"

"We do. We do."

Nul grimaced as he dug. He had thought to stir the pikas to some sort of revolt, to an attack on the guard and to flight; but now, in the face of Sard's hopelessness, he wondered if any plan had even a remote chance of working. "Where do you sleep?"

"In a pen. A large cave." Sard paused. "I think we all are kept there. All who are left alive."

"How many of you?"

"Perhaps a hundred and twenty."

Nul's heart fell; the number was less than half the population of the clan he remembered. That meant that few of the pikas he had known were likely to be living. He worked on at the rock face, thinking furiously. "I will return with you," he said at last. "Perhaps there is something we could do."

"I do not think so."

"Still—" Nul grunted as he swung the pick—"there must be some chance."

"I fear—"

A gabbling, croaking voice startled Nul. The hob in the doorway had come up behind the party and, brandishing its club in one hand, it stood scolding old Sard. Sard cowered and groveled, and the hob, with a vicious sweep of its free hand, struck him across the face. Sard fell to his knees as a spray of blood, nearly black in the greenish-yellow light of the firemoss, flew from the little creature's mouth.

Nul roared in rage. The hob, caught by surprise, whirled and brought up its heavy club. Nul rushed him, coming inside the circle of the club before the big creature could begin its blow. Nul hacked with his pick at the knees of the thing, connecting solidly, drawing a gush of blood. Tottering on its good leg, the hob bellowed in fear and pain, and another of its kind came through the tunnel mouth, a spear in its hand. Nul maneuvered to keep the first hob between himself and the new adversary. "Help me!" he shouted to the others. "Hobs can be killed!"

Nul leaped aside, barely avoiding a thunderous smash of the hob's club. He swung his pick overhand and buried its head to the haft in the hob's broad, hairy chest. The creature reeled back spasmodically, gurgling in its throat, pulling the pick out of Nul's hands.

The second hob thrust at Nul with the spear. Nul feinted as the spear reached him, grabbed it by the shaft just behind the point, and brought his knee up. The spear snapped across it. The hob paused stupidly to stare at the broken wood, and Nul swept his arm down, throwing the head as if it were a knife. It struck one of the hob's eyes, bringing a shriek of pain from the creature. "Help me!" Nul shouted again, and this time the stunned pikas rallied.

The first hob had collapsed to its knees. Two of the pikas fell on it with their own picks. One seized a good-sized stone and hurled it at the blinded hob, catching it behind the knee and sending it crashing face-down to the floor. The others, including even Sard, attacked at once.

It was over within moments. "There," Sard proclaimed, wiping a drooling string of blood from his injured mouth with the back of a hand. "We've killed two, at any rate. Now let them kill us."

"No," Nul said. "Can you all climb?"

No, none of them really was in shape to climb; but they all had to. He went first, found a projection big enough to stand on, and gave the others a hand up into the small passageway. "Go through," he said to each. "Wait at the other end."

He came last of all himself, gathering his trousers and

weapons on the way. He found the others huddled, shocked and lost, at the far end. "Where?" Sard asked.

"There is a way out. It is to the left, with many turns and twists. If I tell you, can you remember it?"

Sard grimaced. "I do not know. My head is not good. I fear not."

Nul danced into his trousers. "You must remember. I have friends on the outside who will help us. Listen carefully—"

As if in mockery of his words, there came a deep booming down the tunnels. "Drums," said Sard. He sighed. "We killed two of them. That is something."

"We will account for more."

"No. You do not understand. The drums—they are speaking."

"Speaking?"

"The firvolkans behind us are using them to speak to all the others throughout the tunnels. They know. They have discovered their dead."

CHAPTER 12

"NO LAMPS TO throw here, boy," the soldier said, grinning at Jeremy, his words deliberately mocking the tone he had himself used back in the granary-prison. "So wot you gonna do, hey?"

"Put away your weapon," Barach said quietly. He and Jeremy were closest to the two newcomers; the others were behind, at the intersection of the water tunnel and the main passage, their way blocked by the two gargoyles. Barach took a step toward the man, carefully, offering no threat. "We have no reason to fight you."

The soldier rubbed his forehead, still grinning. "Ain't you, though? I got a reason to fight you, though, haven't I? That's enough, old man. Stop right where you stand. Havoronas! Back me."

"What's the animal?" the lean, hawk-faced man asked. It was he who held the torch, a pace behind and to the left of the soldier. He seemed oblivious of the quarrel and was trying to peer past Barach and Jeremy at the bulk of one of the gargoyles. "Head of a bird, neck of a serpent, forelegs of a great cat, hindquarters of a dragon. I never see the like of it."

"Havoronas!"

The other man still did not stir. "Fight your fight, Capt'n. I found 'em for you, didn't I?"

"I will deal with you later." The soldier, sword at the ready, edged toward Jeremy. "You got a man's weapon now, I see. Use it!"

Jeremy raised his own sword, shifted his stance, got

ready to parry. "This is wrong," he told the soldier. "I don't want to fight you."

"Yah. I bet you don't." The soldier lunged suddenly, his sword whistling in a controlled, economical slash, a quick but hard attack in the tight surroundings of the tunnel. Jeremy gave way half a step, barely fending off the blow, stumbling to one knee with the ringing impact. The soldier, his follow-through spoiled by the tunnel wall, frowned and took a step to the side. "Havoronas!" he barked again.

The man with the torch merely stood his ground and shook his head. "They're yours, Capt'n. I only wanted the beast, remember? And here be two of 'em."

"I'll kill you next, hunter, right after I settle with these two," grunted the soldier. He turned, his right side close to the tunnel wall, the sword still at the ready. "Old man! Here is my only offer. If you will surrender yourselves, I will pledge myself to talk to Town Master Thendenis on your behalf. If not, I'll kill this youngster."

Barach said, "I think not."

And Kelada, who had worked her way behind the soldier without his even noticing, pressed the tip of her dagger into the man's ribs. Jeremy rose to his feet, ears ringing, his sword arm trembling, feeling almost numb from the sword blow.

The soldier scowled without looking around. "You can cut out my kidney, you behind me. But see if I don't open this young fellow's throat before I die,"

"We have reached an impasse, it seems," Barach murmured. "You, sir—what is your name?"

The captain's weapon did not move and his eyes remained steady on Jeremy even as he spoke to Barach: "Melkior Ramp. I ain't ashamed of it."

"Well, Captain Ramp. You have followed us, I take it, on the orders of Thendenis of Three Rivers?"

Ramp nodded. " 'S right. He sent me after you."

"Why?"

The soldier frowned. "Must've had his reasons. He said it was because you're in league with hobs. Because you broke the wall of the town."

"That," Barach said, "is wrong. We oppose the hobs,

just as do you. We have a friend who is their captive. Does that not change matters?''

Ramp had a soldier's iron concentration. Not once did the tip of his sword waver, not once did his eyes leave Jeremy's. "So you'd say anyway, to save your skins. Might be a lie. Probably is. How can I believe you?"

Barach sighed. "I don't know how to convince you. Except this way. Jeremy, lay down your sword."

Jeremy, immediately obedient, bent his knees and carefully laid his sword on the ground.

"Kelada."

The thief's gray eyes seemed to flash in the light of the torch. "Never!"

Jeremy said, "Kelada, please do what Barach asks. If it's the only way."

A storm of emotions, doubt, anger, fear, crossed Kelada's face, troubling her stormy gray eyes. At last the thief stepped back from the soldier and dropped her blade. It clanged on the rock of the tunnel floor.

"Now," said Barach, spreading his arms wide and letting his own staff drop to the floor. "We have put aside our weapons. We are at your mercy."

For only an instant or two did they stand that way, the captain still obviously distrustful, still at the ready. Then without warning the tableau broke. Ramp sprang at Barach, his sword drawn back for a quick and deadly thrust. At the same moment a huge form knocked Barach to one side, met the soldier's charge head-on. Ramp cried out, his blade ringing off stone a second before he was borne back into the wall by the charging bulk of Busby. There was a crumpling impact. The other man, the one with the torch, had dropped to one knee and had thrown a dagger; it, too, bounced harmlessly off the gargoyle's side.

Busby backed away. For a second Ramp stood with his back against the wall, knees bent, eyes closed, his chest collapsed on one side where the stone head had struck him, had pressed him against the tunnel wall. Then with a wordless groan he fell forward onto his face.

Barach lifted himself up and went to stoop over the

fallen man. He gently turned the body over, felt for a pulse at the neck. "He is dying," he said.

Kelada had recovered her knife. Breathing hard, her weapon held before her, her weight balanced on the balls of her feet, she faced Havoronas. "You next."

The man shook his head, his rapt eyes on Busby. "What is it?" he breathed. "Yonder animal. If you're going to kill me anyhow, before you do it, just tell me what it is."

Barach's voice took on a whiplike snap of command: "There will be no more killing!"

Ramp, on the tunnel floor, shuddered, coughed, gasped, convulsed once, and was still. Jeremy had retrieved his blade, but now Barach and Busby were between him and Havoronas. Kelada stood to one side, just beyond Busby's head.

"Made all of stone, ain't it?" Havoronas asked. "Not real flesh at all. No wonder it left no droppings, no traces. A magic beast?"

"The beast has its own magic," Barach said, his voice suddenly old, bitterly weary. "I know what your people think of such magic, but the gargoyle is our friend and our protector, and he is not evil. Go! Tell Thendenis that his prisoners have made good their escape. And tell him that only fools thirst for the blood of their friends."

"Can I touch it? The animal? Just to feel the stone?"

"What is wrong with you?"

Havoronas had risen to his feet. He held out his open hands. "Look. I ain't got no other weapons but this." He unstrapped and dropped a short sword, still in its scabbard. "Capt'n there was hot to kill you, but not me. I could've killed you outside, quick as thought, when you stood beside the cave and I was up above; but I didn't, did I? I just wanted a close-up look at the beast, is all, and a chance to get at it. I had both. I'm a hunter, see? And such a beast as this I never hunted before."

"Keep him away from me," Busby said in a low, troubled voice. "I do not wish to harm another."

"It talks," Havoronas said, a childlike delight dancing in his words.

"Hunter, go back to your world," Barach said. "Go with your life. Take our message to Thendenis."

Havoronas appeared to consider for a moment. "Nah, old man, I think not. Never liked the army much, nor it me. And see where it's got Capt'n there. Always one for orders, he was, and just see where his orders has brought him at the last. If you'll take me, I'll go with you. For the sake of a sight of the beast. For the only thing yet I seen that I can hunt but never kill."

"Why should we take him?" Kelanda snarled. "Why not just kill him where he stands?"

The hunter himself answered: " 'Cause I can follow a track. 'Cause I can kill when I have to. 'Cause if you don't, I'll just follow along behind, anyhow—unless you do want to kill me, and I don't think the old man there much does, somehow."

Barach was quiet for a long moment there, deep in the tunnel beneath Twilight Valley. At last he took a long breath. "I believe you. Very well. But be warned: we are going to face hobs before this is done. You have seen what they can do."

"Yah. But let 'em do their worst, they can still do no worse than kill me. Can I—?" The hunter gestured toward his dropped weapon.

"Yes. I think you had better come behind Busby."

"No," Busby said. "I don't want to be near him. Let me lead. Put Fred in the back."

It was arranged. They dragged the body of Captain Ramp into the side tunnel, and with Busby in the forefront, they continued their exploration of the underground with two new members: Grall, who rode on Fred's broad back, and Havoronas, who followed Fred quietly.

"I have never killed before," Busby said in a voice so soft that only Jeremy could hear it as they headed down a new turn.

"Barach was in great danger," Jeremy responded, wondering that this stone behemoth could apparently feel remorse. "You had no choice."

"There is always choice," Busby returned shortly.

Fred grumbled a bit when Busby took a few turns that

he thought ill-advised, but for the most part they traveled in silence. At last they came to a halt near a gigantic opening in one side of the tunnel, an opening that dropped almost sheer for a good long way. "He went down this way," Busby announced, sniffing the edge. "Nul climbed down there. No other pikas, no hobs; only Nul."

"Then we must do the same," Barach said, peering over the edge. "It will be difficult."

"I can make it," Busby announced. "And Fred; we were made to be good climbers. The rest of you must be very careful. Do you have rope?"

Barach opened his bag again. "I brought some that I had off Captain Redeker of the *Gull*. A quarter-thousand coil."

"You will have to use it. I will go first; let Fred follow. Then the hunter, I think."

"As you think best."

The gargoyles clambered down the drop, clinging miraculously to the sides like enormous lizards creeping down a garden wall. The firemoss grew profusely here, and watching them descend, Jeremy saw that they left behind them a broad dark wake where their legs, bellies, and tails scraped the walls clean of the moss. Havoronas disdained the rope and went down feet first, hugging the stone, following the same path the gargoyles had and moving with wonderful dexterity. Jeremy went next, but he made good use of the rope, and even so had a bad moment or two when the wall suddenly became vertical for short stretches, leaving him dangling and twisting slowly. Barach lowered Grall after him, and then Kelada. Last of all the old mage came down himself, hand over hand, grunting a bit from the exertion. At the bottom of the incline, he gave the rope a couple of sharp snaps, and it slithered down to his feet. He coiled it around his arm and shoulder. "I hope we have no more of that. I am far too old for such athletics."

The cavity they had dropped into broadened at the base, like a somewhat squashed inverted funnel. Two passages led off from it in opposite directions—or more likely one passage that simply intersected the opening led both ways. The gargoyles had sniffed both and had decided on one almost at right angles to the way they had been proceeding earlier.

Jeremy said, "I—"

A sound cut him off, a deep booming sound echoing through the tunnels.

The sound of drums.

"Back," Nul said, spreading his arms, trying to herd the pikas before him like a flock of frightened hens. "There were no hobs this way. If we run—"

"Look! They come!" a young pika shouted, her voice shrill with alarm.

Nul took a hasty look back, but no one was coming. "Don't jump at shadows! They are not here, but they will come. Run," he said, pushing and shoving. The six pikas stumbled forward, hesitated, and at last began to move. More drums took up the thundering counterpoint to the pikas' flight, their direction and distance impossible to gauge, but a great many of them sounding out— beaten, no doubt, by a great many hob hands. Nul had seized Sard's arm and was half-dragging the older pika. The others, accustomed to following Sard, were trotting along in an ill-defined formation, some of them already stumbling from weariness or sheer fright. "Through here," Nul said, taking the lead through the dangerously straight and unbroken stretch of tunnel. Fortunately, no hobs lurked there—at least none that he could see. "Quick!"

The stone beneath his feet trembled a bit, a gentle quivering that passed as quickly as it came. "The elemental," Sard panted in despair.

"What do you mean?" Nul asked.

"It senses everything that lives and moves beneath the surface. It searched for us. Its mind touched us, made the stones seem to vibrate. The firvolkans will know where we are now. No hope, none at all!"

"Let them come. We may have a surprise or two for them." More loudly, he called, "To the left at the cross tunnel. To the left!"

The shuffling, gasping, staggering band of pikas stayed

with him somehow. He let himself fall back to the rear
briefly, listened, and then urged the others to more exertion: from the distant patter of running feet, Nul judged
that they were being pursued.

Ahead of him, Sard suddenly cried out in fright. Nul
fought his way through the pikas, who had come up
short, clinging in terror to one another. "More ahead,"
Sard said, grasping Nul's arm. "They are on both sides of
us."

Nul cursed, drawing his sword and both of his daggers.
He gave one knife to Sard, another to one of the female
pikas whom he did not know but who seemed to be in
control of herself. "Use your claws, use loose rock," he
said to the others. "When the hobs tell the story to
others, make them call this a fight!" He, too, could hear
the heavy sounds of running feet now, coming from
ahead of the band. They were indeed cut off with no
possibility of retreat or sleight. "There is an open place
not far ahead. Let us make for that as a place to stand
and face our enemies—we will be able to fight better
there."

They ran with him; tired as they all were, sick with
fear as they had to be, the pikas fell into place and ran
alongside Nul, trusting him. They reached the open spot,
a juncture of six tunnels well lighted by thick firemoss,
and there they paused.

"We could take a side tunnel," Sard said.

"No. We would become lost, and they would still find
us. We make our stand here. Take the wall to the right,"
Null ordered. "Get behind the fallen stone there. Stay
between the tunnel openings. If any of you sees a chance
to flee for the surface, take it!"

The band from ahead of him came into view far down
the tunnel, shadowy huge forms hurrying toward the
pikas, cutting Nul's words short. The pika brandished his
sword and howled, a tight, high sound of rage. Beside
him Sard tensed as from the tunnel mouth an impossibly
large creature ran into the open space.

"Fred!" Nul shouted in disbelief and joy. The gargoyle
pulled up short, sand flying from its backpedalling feet,

thrown stones already bouncing off its chest and neck.
"No!" Nul called to his pikas. "This is a friend!" In
Presolatan, he shouted, "Jeremy! Barach! Friends!"

But the reunion was short. Another pika screamed
something, and Nul turned to see hobs, a dozen of them
or more, tumble from the tunnel his band had just left.
The hobs had small eyes not well adapted for dark places,
but in the creatures' shock and surprise at seeing the
interlopers, their eyes flew nearly as wide as the pikas'.
Jeremy had just enough time to send a bolt from his
crossbow into the leg of one of the leaders. It hit with a
solid *thwack.* The injured hob screamed and toppled
sideways, and the others charged.

Nul hacked at the thigh of one of them, laying it open
and making the creature go sprawling to the ground. As
they had with the guards, the pikas fell on the downed
hob to end it. Nul was already attacking another.

Barach wielded his staff now like a club, now like a
spear, now like a sword, smashing, thumping, turning the
hobs' heavy clubs away from him. He parried a killing
blow from a hob nearly twice his size and returned such a
stroke to its neck that the creature spun away from him,
screaming in pain. Kelada was there, too, evading heavy
clubs and using her knife in a series of quick, vicious
slashes. And a man whom Nul had not seen fought
beside her, a lean, tough sort of fellow with a fell smile
on his thin face, who wielded a wickedly whistling sword.

The gargoyles acted more as shields than weapons,
moving quickly to protect Barach or Jeremy or Kelada
when hobs seemed to threaten, but not fighting much
themselves; indeed, Nul saw only one blow from them,
when Fred smacked an attacking hob away from Kelada
with one careless swipe of a forepaw.

The hobs, once their initial astonishment had worn off,
fought with determination and stubbornness. The pikas
retreated to the narrow space between the fallen stones
and the cavern wall, where the overlarge hobs could not
get directly at them; but the huge creatures tried none-
theless, snatching the stones away from the wall, pounding their clubs into the recess.

Nul weaved in and out among them, seeking to hamstring the creatures, to run them through, to harry and delay them. There came a moment when the way was clear, when the last hob threatening the pikas had been struck down. "Now!" Nul shouted. "Run! To the passage out—there!"

Five of them ran. Sard did not. He lay beside the rampart of stone on his face, his skull crushed by a hob's club. Nul saw the others go and turned just in time to see another club descending toward him. He dived to one side, almost out of the way. The club gave him only a glancing blow, but it was wielded by a heavy hand. Nul crashed to the cavern wall, his arm numb, the sword dropping from his grasp, and for a moment he lay stunned, unable to get his breath. He was only dimly aware of a hand grasping his ankle and dragging him over the stone floor of the cavern.

Then Jeremy was above him, sword in hand, swinging at the hob that held Nul. Nul saw everything slowly and as through a smoky film, felt his limbs only from a great distance. He saw the hob seize Jeremy's arm, wrench it cruelly until the sword went flying, saw the creature throw Jeremy against the cave wall, saw another grab Jeremy's ankle, as the first had grabbed his own, and drag the young man away.

Then the hob holding him was running through the tunnels, dragging Nul over the rough stones. Nul twisted, but his head banged into the floor of the tunnel, sending an explosion of light through his skull, and then all was darkness.

Havoronas rose from beside the small gray body. "This 'n is dead, hit hard by one of them clubs. Is this here animal the one you come after?"

Barach, still shaken, looked at the body of Sard. "No. I saw Nul during the fighting, but this is a different pika, a strange one to me. Kelada!"

She paused in the very mouth of the hobs' retreat tunnel, her knife still out, her arm and blouse splashed and stained with blood. "They took him! I'm going after them."

Barach crossed to her, put a hand on her arm. "Not alone. Jeremy would not wish that." Kelada gave him a hot-eyed glance, but she stepped unwillingly back from the tunnel. To Grall, who had slipped off Fred's back and was now at the center of the milling group of pikas, Barach called, "Where will they take Nul and Jeremy?"

Grall considered and then answered at some length. Barach nodded his understanding and translated for the others. "The hobs will probably go to a chamber some way below and ahead of us, Grall thinks. They have at least one of the elementals there. It is a great open chamber, a gathering place for them. We will have to see if we can get to the place by stealth, not by charging blindly ahead. There are thousands of the hobs deeper down; this was only a scout party."

"Then let's go," Kelada said, anguish in her face. "You know what those things do with the humans they capture!"

Havoronas had retrieved Jeremy's dropped crossbow. "Good weapon," he said, looking it over. "And the young fellow made right good use of it. Too bad it's such a slow one. Them creatures is fast, to be so big."

Kelada screamed in her frustration.

"Mage," said Busby, "let me take the lead again. I can find my way through any vertical stretch of stone; that power has not deserted me. And I'm sure I can scent out Nul and Jeremy."

"Go, then" Barach said. "Though what we can do against so many I do not know." He turned back to Grall and in pikish said, "Nul wished you and the others to get to the surface. Can you lead them?"

"Yes," Grall said in the same language. "But it is far, and they are very weak."

"Go with them. You know what waits below."

Grall shuddered, but said in a surprisingly brave voice, "We will try, for that was what Nul wished us to do."

"Let's go," Barach said to the gargoyles and the humans. They stepped over the bodies of fallen hobs and started for the depths; behind them, Grall led the surviving pikas upward on the long trek toward the light.

* * *

They had dragged him for a hundred years, and then they bounced him against a stone wall. At last they tumbled him like a sack of potatoes onto a sandy floor that grated against his face, filled his mouth, stung his eyes. Jeremy coughed, spat sand, and groaned.

The place stank, stank with the predator-stench of the big-cat cages of a zoo. He opened his eyes. He could see the legs of hobs, many of them, shaggy, bandy, muscled. He could see Nul, sitting up, rubbing patches of glittering brownish-black sand from his round head, blinking in evident confusion.

"Are you all right?" Jeremy asked.

Nul nodded, his orange eyes glazèd. "Think so. Bruised a little." His hand stole to his belt, but the daggers and sword were gone. Jeremy stared around him. He was in a warren of the hobs, clearly; at least a hundred of them stood or squatted around him, their small eyes intent on his every move. They chattered together in a dialect Jeremy could not recognize.

"They eat you," Nul muttered. "Eat human flesh."

"They brought me this far without eating me. And they didn't try to kill me," Jeremy said. He got to his feet, feeling almost as shaky as he had following his fight with Willum, though a part of that might have been his lingering feeling of being trapped far underground. "They look like they're starving," he said, more to himself than to Nul.

It was true: the hobs, taller than any but the tallest of men, were desperately thin, some younger ones with distended bellies. All were naked and most were filthy, their clay-white skins smeared with mud or feces, their shaggy arms and legs matted with tangles of hair. When Jeremy swayed slightly, they moved his way, without particular menace but watchfully.

"Careful," Nul said. "If they hungry, they more dangerous for you."

"I don't see how they could be much more dangerous than they are already," Jeremy replied. "What happened to the others? Did you see?"

Nul rubbed his skull again. "Got hit hard. Saw nothing then."

The hobs seemed to be following the exchange, or trying to. "Why did you bring us here?" Jeremy asked them. They merely stared back at him with their small, dark eyes, although a few of them muttered together in voices too low for Jeremy to hear distinctly.

"They not talk our talk," Nul said. "Used not to, anyway, if what mages say is right."

"My God," Jeremy said, again to himself. "They look awful. And this place—"

The enclosure, a nearly circular cavern, was lighted with heavy growths of firemoss. As his eyes became accustomed to the soft glow, Jeremy felt his stomach heave. The sandy floor was littered with scores of bones, most of them animal—a cow skull was almost underfoot, and near it the foreleg of a sheep, with some skin and fleece still attached—but there were also scatterings of other bones, ribs, the long bones of legs, that looked human. "Why don't you do something?" Jeremy asked them.

Again there was no response, but he felt their tension, their watchfulness. They were waiting for something to happen.

Or for someone to come.

The steep path was impossible, but Grall had been on a work force that had been driven daily into the upper reaches of the cavern to break through to the outside ledge, and she knew other ways. Her most difficult task was simply to keep the weary pikas moving, keep them all together. She found herself filled with unexpected reserves of energy, the result of the wizard's nectar she had sipped, she supposed, but it was fragile: she felt that at any moment strength could be replaced with weakness, that if she paused to rest she would never rise again.

"This way," she said. She could not lead, for the others were too far gone to keep track of each other. From the rear it was difficult to tell if those in the front had taken the correct turn or not. It was most vexing.

But somehow or other they kept moving, up and up,

following a darkening path as the firemoss became more scant—she herself had planted some of the newer growths here, months ago, when the pikas first began driving a shaft from the volcanic tunnel to the surface—but for all its darkness a familiar path.

They came to the water passage, and she herded them in. They drank, the stronger of them in Nul's way, by leaning back into the flow of the stream, the weaker by cupping their hands tightly and sipping the discouragingly small amounts they could trap. "Must rest," Varkal, one of the youngest of them, panted after having drunk. "Too tired to go on."

"Only for a little while," Grall said. "Firvolkans could return any time."

"Who was he?" asked Hast, a pika Grall knew only slightly. "The one who came for us?"

"His name is Nul," Grall said. "He was of our clan once. He has come to save us all."

"All?" Hast asked, blinking in the dim light at the six of them huddled there.

Grall felt sudden unreasoning anger well up within her. "Yes, all! He is down there now seeking the others."

Hast shook her head. "Too many. Too many. The firvolkans are too strong for us, too strong for the humans. They are lost. We are lost."

"Then stay," Grall almost spat. "The rest of us are going to the surface, as the great Nul ordered. Who else will stay with Hast?"

The pikas stirred uneasily, edging away from the unfortunate Hast. "I did not say I would stay," she complained. "But where will we go? Even if we reach the world outside, where will we go?"

"To our home," one of the young males, Trel, said suddenly. "To our old home in the Bone Mountains, the one the elders tell us about."

"That's right," Grall said, suddenly feeling that it *was* right, somehow. "That is where we shall go."

"Oh," Varkal said in a voice gone light with wonder, "is there such a place?"

"I lived there," Grall said. "And Nul." She had sat on

a stone: the very one, she recalled, that Nul had occupied while nursing her. "That is where we will go. Home."

"Tell us about it," Varkal begged.

"We must go."

"Then tell us as we walk."

Grall touched Varkal's cheek, so gaunt. She is a baby,
Grall thought with something like surprise. Once she
would have been nothing but a little child, too small for
digging. "Let us walk," she said. They stirred themselves. When they turned into the main passage, Grall
began to speak: "The caverns under the Bone Mountains
are beautiful. Not like this, not black with night and hard
with basalt, but streaked with all colors. The walls are
smooth and high, the air always clean. Water flows there
in great abundance. And jewels glitter underfoot. . . ."

She spoke on and on as they walked, hypnotizing the
others almost, indeed putting herself under the same
kind of spell. The place she described was a wonderland,
a home of abiding beauty and peace. At last it seemed to
her that they all had died back in the lower tunnels, that
their spirits now trod the path to the happy place, the
light and shining caverns where the dead found content-
ment.

That seemed to be the place she was describing.

Their home.

Someone in the lead cried out in sudden excitement.
Grall tried to shake the weariness from her head. The
others clustered around, their fur smooth and gray in the
cool pale light of—

Day.

They had reached the tunnel mouth.

Trel—it was he who had cried out—ran ahead of them,
laughing, stretching his arms forward as if to embrace the
light, to gather it to him. "Come!" he called, almost
dancing, framed against the brilliant light of an overcast
day. "Come and see! Come and see!"

Grall pushed through the others, feeling her throat
fluttering in the pika way of weeping. She heard a sound,
not a loud noise, but more like a soft slap.

Trel turned toward her, a dark shape against the

light, his orange eyes wide, his mouth open in surprise.

"We will make it home," Grall said, laughing and
weeping at once. "Oh, Trel, you have never seen the
surface. It—"

Trel fell to his knees and collapsed sideways, his voice
whistling horribly in his throat. One of the other pikas
screamed. Grall felt the world lurch beneath her feet.

An arrow had struck Trel in the chest, probably penetrating his heart. A little blood came from his mouth. He
tried to say something, shivered, and died.

"No!" Grall cried in despair.

No firvolkan used bow and arrow, except for the clumsy
fire-throwers. And this arrow, smooth-shanked, feath-
ered, black, was no work of firvolkan hands.

It had been made—and used—by humans.

The firvolkan leader was in no way distinguished from
the rest: he was just as naked, just as wretched as any of
them. But he spoke, after a fashion, Presolatan.

"Come," he told Jeremy. "This way. Now."

"Where are you taking us?" Jeremy asked. He and
Nul were not bound, and their guards carried no weapon
more formidable than the clublike staves most hobs seemed
to carry, but he had no hope of escape. They were too
far down, too lost in a maze of branching tunnels, for
that.

"Come. He send. You come."

"Who?" Jeremy repeated. "The Great Dark One?"

The hob leader growled deep in his throat. "Not Master. No. Him, Stone spirit. Come."

"Elemental," Nul grunted. He was still shaken and
had some trouble keeping up with the hobs' long strides,
or with Jeremy's shorter ones.

"Please," Jeremy said. "There's no need. Listen to
me. The Great Dark One was defeated in the war—"

"Master told us. Master want human-folk in valley
with river all dead, all. Were to burn them. Now will do
Master's bidding."

Jeremy was prodded into movement. "Your Master

lost the war," he said again. "You have to understand.
War over, finished. All your kind have—ah, gone away.
You don't have to fight human folk anymore."

"Time draws near," the hob said. "Hurry."

"But the Great Dark One has been beaten. He—"

"End, end all," chattered the hob. "Sleep, all rest.
Final rest. Last night of world. Great promise. Fire and
stone. Much dying."

They had been shuffling through a low passage, uncomfortably low for the hobs, who had to stoop at the
hips and duck their heads to get through, and small even
for Jeremy. He could walk erect without bashing his
head, but just barely, and he could not escape the suffocating feeling that the walls were ready to collapse inward on him, to bury him under choking tons of soil and
rock.

"This pika tunnel," Nul said suddenly. "Dug out of
hard stone. Not long ago."

"Here," the hob leader said. The passage gave into an
immense open space, with more, many more, hobs already there. Hands reached for Jeremy, seized his arms,
the claws biting his flesh, and they passed him forward,
through a stench of carrion-flavored breath, dung, fouler
things.

"Nul!" Jeremy cried as he was propelled forward.

"Here. Behind you." Nul evidently was receiving similar treatment.

One of the hobs gave him a hard shove between the
shoulder blades, sending him staggering and then sprawling facedown onto a cold stone floor only lightly strewn
with sand. Nul came hustling after, his short legs moving
quickly to keep himself from taking a tumble. "Great
hall," he said with an impressed intake of breath.

Jeremy pushed himself up. They were indeed in a huge
space, as large as a cathedral at least, the high ceiling
hung with great streamers and trails of the firemoss, the
curved walls dense with it. By all rights, he should have
felt more at ease here; but somehow even in the great
open space he was acutely conscious of the intolerable
weight of rock above them. His breath came shallow and

tight, and he had to swallow hard to keep from yelling in simple panic. The hobs stood all around them, their voices raised in a monotonous rising and falling chant. At the far side of the cavern, perhaps a hundred yards distant, was an enormous figure.

They prodded him again, shoved him, showing him that they wanted him to approach it. Jeremy walked slowly, Nul at his side. "What is this place?" he asked.

"Not know. Meeting place of many, many hobs. Strange stone."

The stone, where it showed through breaks in the moss, was indeed different from that of the tunnels. Instead of a glistening or dull black, this was pale gray, marblelike, with spiderwebs of darker gray shot through it. "Mazerite?" Jeremy asked.

"Could be. Never see that kind of rock. I not know."

They had neared the colossal sitting figure. Jeremy had taken it at first for a natural formation of stone; as he neared, he saw it had roughly humanoid outlines. It was, then, an idol.

Or so he thought until he stood a few paces away from the towering bulk of the thing.

That was when it moved.

And spoke.

"They are gone," Busby said. "All of them."

"Are you sure it isn't an ambush?" Barach's worried eyes scanned the dark reaches of the tunnels ahead.

"No. The hobs have been here—you can see their sleeping pallets, their fires, the remains of their food. But they are not here now. They have gone elsewhere. I can't imagine why."

Kelada said, "What about Jeremy?"

Busby dropped his head. "I cannot find a trace of him. I am sorry."

They stood in a large cavern, its floor littered with clubs, scattered bones, blackened pieces of firewood. The drums had ceased some time before. Both gargoyles had taken turns at trying to ferret out the scent of Jeremy and Nul; they had lost the way some time back, when a tremor had collapsed the walls and ceiling of a small passageway. In trying to find a way around the blockage they had indeed come across many signs of hobs, but the human and the pika seemed to have vanished.

Barach asked, "Which way have the hobs gone?"

"Down," said Busby.

"To the right," said Fred.

"Then let us go that way. Jeremy and Nul will be, I fear, where the hobs are thickest. We will try to find traces of them toward the hobs."

They went on, not as cautiously as before, but alertly; Havoronas was all nerves, it seemed, his eyes darting, his ears quick to hear the least sound. The gargoyles might have been hunting dogs, vastly overgrown. Kelada strained ahead. Only Barach restrained them all from rushing headlong into darkness and danger; and he seemed increasingly uneasy as they passed through more tunnels where hobs had been but which now stood empty.

"I smell him!" Busby suddenly announced. "Here!"

Kelada was first to his side. "It's only a ventilation hole," she cried.

Busby could barely get the tip of his nose into the opening. "But he is there: almost below us, I think, perhaps a hundred of your paces. And Nul, I believe, though his scent is fainter."

"But there is no way!"

Barach said, "There may be."

Busby gave him a long look. "Mage, I cannot."

"Will you try?"

Busby stared back at the small, vertical stone tube. "I cannot."

"I will," Fred said suddenly, trying to push forward.

"No," Barach murmured. "You are not as old as Busby. You have warm feelings, but not as much of the old deep magic of stone. It must be Busby, or no one."

At last, reluctantly, Busby said, "I do not think I can. But I will try."

They watched, Havoronas with cries of wonder, as Busby slowly shrank. "It is very difficult," the gargoyle groaned when he had lost half his bulk. "The mazerite is all about us."

"If you cannot—"

"I will try."

It took a long time. At last the dwindled gargoyle was no larger than a cat. "Can you keep that size?" Barach asked.

"If not," Busby said, "I will become a part of the Fridhof Mountains forever. Here I go." He squeezed into the opening of the ventilation shaft. His hindquarters seemed to stick for a moment; then his dragon-legs scrabbled for purchase and he dragged himself in, his tail slowly withdrawing into the darkness.

The others watched anxiously. "I think he may make it," Barach said.

And then the quake shook the tunnel.

CHAPTER 13

THE GROUND SHUDDERED. Jeremy tried to keep his balance, failed, and fell onto a surface of bare stone scattered with loose black sand. Another quake? No; it was like a quake, and yet different. It was—

It was the giant.

His arms trembling at the exertion, Jeremy pushed himself up from the floor of the cave. The giant was there, sitting, its hands on its knees. If they were hands, or knees.

Vaguely human in outline, but clearly made of craggy stone, its elongated head something like those of the giants of Easter Island, the creature inclined its heavy features and the ground shook again. Though there was no sign of movement where the mouth should be, the giant was beyond all doubt speaking. Jeremy managed to roll to a hip. He half-sat, half-reclined on his arm. They were surrounded by the hobs, hundreds, maybe thousands of them: the far reaches of the cavern were lost in distance and darkness, though he had a sensation of vastness. "Nul," he said, his throat rasping partly from thirst and partly from long-sustained anxiety. "Are you all right?"

"Hurt head," he grunted. "Damned hobs! You?"

"Shaken up a little, nothing broken." Jeremy forced himself to breathe more slowly, more deeply. "What is that thing?"

"Elemental. Stone elemental. Never seen one."

The giant had tilted its misshapen head as if listening.

It rumbled something else. "Think it talks to us," Nul grunted.

"Let's see." Jeremy shouted, "We can't understand you! If you want to speak to us, speak Presolatan!"

The giant raised a hand, or rather a talon: five fingers and a thumb, with great hooked stone claws. The hand almost seemed to change form and outline, as if the rock were malleable and changeable. The giant, whatever it was, had none of the carven shape of the gargoyles. It made a gesture. "Now," it said in a voice that still shook the stones, "we can talk."

"Yes," Jeremy said, thinking furiously. What had Tremien said? Verbal magic would not work, but inborn magic might. And evidently the giant carried a powerful store of inborn magic.

"Let us kill them," a harsh voice demanded. "We hunger, O great one."

Jeremy twisted. The speaker was the chieftain-hob. He had pressed through the crowd and stood not far away.

The earthquake-voice of the giant said, "Should I allow them to eat you, creature?"

"I hope not," Jeremy said. "I think, as you; I move, as you; there is no reason for one thinking creature to eat another."

"You are what they want me to destroy. To burn, along with their fire demon, and then to bury under stone. You look weak to me."

Jeremy painfully got to his feet. "Compared to you, I am weak."

The giant's stone face was inscrutable. There were no visible eyes, and the mouth did not move, and yet a voice came from it. "Once large creatures roamed the surface of this world, creatures as large as I; but made of flesh, and therefore weak. I tired of them. I slept. I wake to find the world given to small creeping vermin. Why should I not join with my brother of fire and wipe them from the surface?"

"Why should you?" Jeremy returned. "For the sake of these creatures?" He swept an arm back, indicating the massed hobs. "Why should so powerful a being serve such weak and cringing things?"

"I serve no ends but my own," the giant answered imperturbably. "I amuse no being save myself."

"It is not amusement, mighty one!" cried the tallest hob, the leader. "It is the way the world must go, for the sake of the spirits' peace!"

Jeremy looked at the hob, noticing now in the better light that the creature only seemed somewhat human. Its head was small and pointed, the eyes little and close together over a brown bud of a nose. The mouth was a savage gash, not as wide as a pika's, but lipless and drawn back at the corners. "My friends did not begin the war," Jeremy said. "Your people did."

"No war! It is no war to slaughter harmful beasts, nor thievery to take what is by right our own!" The other hobs began to murmur agreement. The leader extended a clawed finger to point at Jeremy. "Thousands of turnings of seasons ago, his kind came to our world, despised and hated us, killed us by the score. This is theft, this is war; and it must be punished."

Nul, still seeming dazed, had risen. "They believe living things injure the spirits of their dead," he said to Jeremy. "Grall gave the whole story to me. They want all that live to die, for the peace of their ancestors."

Jeremy gave the pika a surprised look. "Your way of talking has changed."

"Has it?" Nul considered. "What tongue do we speak? I thought it was pikish, but it is not."

"It seems English to me—"

"It the language of thought," rumbled the voice of the stone giant. "A gift to all of you, so that we may understand each other clearly. Such matters are trivial. Our concern here is with life and death."

"Their death, O great one," the hob chief insisted.

Jeremy said to the hob, loudly enough for all close by to hear, "I have never struck a blow against your people, except to save myself or my friends. Not once have I sought you out to kill you or to eat your flesh. The hobs must answer for this, not humankind."

"Unnatural flesh!" the hob shouted back. "From worlds not our own. We consume you as the world shall consume all, before the great peace descends at last."

Jeremy rested his hand on Nul's shoulder. "My friend here is of this world, and all his kind. Yet you enslave them and kill them. Where is the justice in that?"

The chieftain made a throwaway gesture with his cupped hand. "The great always prey on the weak, the hunters always on the hunted. We are right to rule the small ones because we are greater than they; so the great one there deserves to rule us, for his strength is more than ours. That is the justice of the world. That is the justice of the firvolkans."

Jeremy looked at the impassive face of the elemental. "You hear what he says. You deserve to rule these creatures. Do you find joy in this dominion?"

"No joy," came the unemotional earthquake-rumble of the elemental's voice.

"Do you sorrow in their oppression?"

"No sorrow."

Jeremy took a step toward the great stone being sitting like a brooding idol in the vast underground cavern, knees bent, long arms wrapped around them, chin sunk on breast. He felt an impalpable and yet real resistance, a strong magical ward, and realized that he and Nul were protected within the circle of the elemental's will. He could not move out of it, nor could the waiting hobs move in to get at him. "Tell me," he said to the stone being, "do you need the works of the firvolkans' hands?"

"I am sufficient to myself."

"Do you need the flesh of their bodies?"

"I need nothing."

"Do you desire them to accomplish some tasks for you?"

"I desire nothing."

Jeremy gave the chieftain the merest hint of a bow. "I apologize to you and your people. I had believed you the most evil of creatures. I was mistaken. You at least have excuses for what you do; you kill to soothe the dead and feed the living. Your evil is nothing to this thing's wickedness."

The chieftain cringed. "The great one is good and moves for the good of the firvolkans!"

"Are you good?" Jeremy demanded of the elemental.

"Good and evil have no meaning for me."

"You move; you think; you live. Is that not a good?"

"Movement is purposeless. Thought is annoyance. Life is endless boredom. Are these things good?"

"Then why live at all?"

"Because I cannot die, human. I wearied once before of unceasing life, and I slept. But these beings have stirred me from sleep and promise some little amusement before I rest again. Should I not avail myself of it?"

Jeremy looked down at Nul. "Don't stop," Nul whispered. "You have him talking."

"But I don't know what to say," Jeremy admitted. "I have no magic here. And this creature can't be convinced with words."

"There is magic in words!" Nul insisted. "Magic in your plays, in your writings. Find it. Use it."

Jeremy sighed. "I will try," he said. To the patient elemental, Jeremy said, "I would like to know one thing. There is no reason for you to explain it to me, but there is no reason not to explain."

"Ask."

"Why am I alive?"

The stone merely stared at him in its mute and eyeless way.

"I see," Jeremy said with a rueful grin. "You told me I could ask my question, but promised me no answer. Let me put that a different way. You could have killed me, or allowed the firvolkans there to kill me. You kept me alive, and my friend here. To what purpose?"

"I told you. The firvolkans want me to destroy your folk above. I wished to know what I will be destroying."

"I have studied a bit about elementals," Jeremy said. "May I tell you a story? You can comment or not, as you wish." When the being did not reply, Jeremy resumed: "I will speak until you wish me to stop. Here is the story I have heard: in the earliest times, when the universe was new, all was magic, powerful, concentrated, and undifferentiated. But the universe exploded, the learned ones say, by the will of the God of all things."

"I have seen no god."

"Then say because it was the only thing the universe

could do. Four powerful magics awakened to consciousness in that first moment: the magics of stone, fire, air, and water. And in an instant they were torn asunder, splintered, shivered into a billion billion fragments of themselves. And since that time the elements have warred, have combined imperfectly, but have never recovered the first unity."

Jeremy paused and the silence drew itself out, longer and longer, until at last the being rumbled, "It may be so. Or something like that."

"That is our tale," the hob chief cried. "Our religion teaches that: all is in disarray, all in conflict, until the great peace descends; and then all is one again, all quiet, forever."

Jeremy looked at the hobs around him. "You all work for that end. You all desire the great peace. Look at you. Driven underground, living wretched lives in the dark, masters only of the small and weak, servants of a great indifference. Are these things good? Are your dead pleased? Do they speak to you to show their gratitude? Or do they seem to sleep, unquiet though life is?"

"The dead are restless!" a wizened hob shouted. "The stirring of an insect disturbs them. The whistling of air in a bird's nostrils is agony to them. I am a priest! I know the dead!"

"You will be silent." It was more of a statement than an order, but the hob that had spoken dropped to its knees, clutching its throat. The others tried to edge away from it as much as they could. To Jeremy the elemental said, "I will hear your reasons. I think the other should be here, too." It gestured with a finger. The ground broke open.

Jeremy almost fell. A fissure had appeared not ten paces away from him, narrow at each end but so wide in the center that he could not have jumped across it. Steam and smoke, red and billowing, boiled forth, and a moment later a shining presence rose. "I am here," it said in a voice that sounded like vast flames whipping at the wind.

"The other elemental," the stone giant said. "I have

released it from the firvolkans' hold. We will hear your argument, human. And we will both decide your fate."

Jeremy licked his lips. "The hob said that the fire being serves the Great Dark One."

"Yes-s-s," breathed the living flame. "He trapped my essence. I do the wizard's bidding."

"Even now?"

"Yes-s-s."

Jeremy shook his head. "What use is it? If one of you is convinced already, I cannot hope to win a decision you both must make."

"Then we will do as the firvolkans wish," the stone elemental said.

"No. Wait," Nul said. To Jeremy, the pika said, "Try."

"I don't know how to go about it," Jeremy protested. He thought for a moment. "Tell me," he said, "does the fire being communicate with the Great Dark One? Is the wizard directing the fire elemental even now?"

"No," the fire elemental sighed. "The mountains prevent that. I have been alone for the time the firvolkans brought me here."

"I created a special stone," the stone being said, "to protect my sleep from disturbance. No magic works here, save by my will alone."

Jeremy took a deep breath. "All right. I will try."

The hobs murmured among themselves. The stone elemental straightened a little in its place. "Very well. But before the trial commences, I sense intruders in this, my domain. They must be dealt with first."

And magic flowed from the giant in an almost palpable wave.

"He is stuck fast," said Fred, panic making him shrill. "The passage has closed around him."

"Can you help?" Barach asked.

Fred groaned. "I am younger than he and not as strong. I cannot shrink. I have tried. I am not strong enough with the mazerite so near."

Barach lay at full length on the tunnel floor and reached his arm far down the passage. "I cannot feel him. Perhaps he has freed himself."

"I know stone," Fred insisted, nervously shifting from foot to foot. "The stone shifted; the air shaft has closed farther down. He cannot turn back in the narrow passageway. What are we to do?"

"I have no answer, good gargoyle," Barach replied, slowly getting to his feet. "Save that we might try to discover the place that the shaft led to by other means, and perhaps from there—"

"I don't know the way!" wailed Fred. "I can find my path on this level, but not from one level to the next."

"We must do our best," Barach said firmly. "For that is all that is left to us. Now. Try to find a trail—a trail of pika or of human. That is our only hope now."

Kelada said, "If he is dead, I want to die, too."

"Now, now," Barach muttered. "Too soon to be talking like that; we don't know what might lie beyond. And he would not want you to speak that way."

"Here," came a voice from far down the tunnel, making both of them start. "I think I have found something." It was the hunter, Havoronas; they had almost forgotten him in their concern for Busby.

They hurried to him. "Looks like another water shaft," the hunter said, standing beside a murmuring recess in the tunnel wall. "Only this'n is bigger. Lots bigger. We could fit through."

Barach stared into the depths of the opening. It was another open pipe, a good shower of water spilling through, tumbling to unseen depths. "There is some light very far down," he said. "The water is not a torrent; we might be able to descend with the aid of the rope."

"But is it the right place?" Kelada asked.

"How should I know!" Barach snapped. "I am as far in the dark as you." After a moment, he said, "I am sorry. You are worried, and so am I; but that is no reason for anger." He sighed. "It is clear that this must open somewhere below us, and perhaps on the same level as the place the air shaft led. We can only try. Fred, it is too small for you unless you can dwindle a bit."

"Not even a little bit," the gargoyle moaned.

"Then you must remain here. I'll tie the rope around

your neck, and you can lower us. Be here in case we need you to pull us up again, quickly. Will you do that?"

"Yes. Will you—will you try to help Busby if you can find the air shaft?"

"Of course we will; he is our companion." Barach had taken the coil of rope out. "Here," he said.

Fred suddenly stiffened. "Mage—something is happening. Some great magic has just touched us."

"Aye," said Havoronas, who had sprung suddenly to his feet from where he had knelt by the water passage. "I felt something too."

Barach frowned. "I sensed nothing. Perhaps I am without my magic, but I can still *feel* magic. I—" he broke off in confusion. "What under heaven?"

Kelada cried out. Both Fred and Havoronas had vanished, quite suddenly, like blown-out candle flames. It was as if they had used the travel-spell. "What happened?"

Barach switched the coil of useless rope against his leg. "A great magic indeed, and a deep one. I think, Kelada, that an elemental is at work here. It seems to have summoned our friends."

"I feel it now!" Kelada cried out, reaching for him.

Barach grabbed her arm—and his hand closed on nothingness. He was alone in the passage.

For some time he waited, but nothing further happened.

He stood irresolutely for a little more. At last he set about securing the rope to an outcrop of stone. He threw the coil down the water shaft, saw it fall, unrolling, straightening itself into a plumb line down into the unknown. The water played over it, making the rope twitch a little—and no doubt making it slippery as well.

Barach tested the strength of the rope and of its anchor. He hesitated.

He seized the rope firmly and set one foot on the rim of the water passage.

This time he felt it: the tingling, itchy sensation of magic playing over him. He even felt himself beginning to fade.

And just before he vanished he breathed a sigh of relief.

*   *   *

Grall and the others did not dare venture too close to the tunnel opening, and yet they felt through the soles of their feet vibrations, shudderings of the world itself, that frightened them almost more than the archers. They clustered many paces back in the tunnel, staring toward the mouth, invisible behind a turn of the shaft but making its presence clear by the gray-blue radiance of daylight.

Grall felt despair, a deep aching despair, but together with that, almost to her surprise, she felt something else: fury. It was infuriating to have come so far, to be so close, and at last to be denied escape not by the hated firvolkans, but by humans, whom she had never hurt, whom she had only rarely in her life seen. At that moment, had she had the power, she would gladly have destroyed the town of Three Rivers and all that lived within the walls, just as her people had been destroyed.

But the pikas lacked power, she reflected bitterly; they always had. A small people, an inoffensive people—except for Nul, who seemed to have become a warrior in his absence from them—they had never contemplated war, let alone practiced it. She did not know what to do in the face of this new challenge. Clearly the archers were quite near, and deadly in their accuracy. She could not hope to approach them without being hit. And, as far as she knew, there was no other way out of the warren of tunnels.

She started from her thoughts suddenly, struck with a sensation of her hair standing on end, feeling an electric tension in the air; and then it was gone.

The other pikas began to wail, almost in unison.

"Quiet!" Grall snapped.

"It was he!" screamed someone, her voice too distorted with fear to recognize. "The stone giant!"

Grall grimaced. She had never been in the presence of the elemental, but she had worked near his chamber, and there she had felt something like the sensation: a close brush, a caress, almost, of magic. "He did not hurt us—"

Her breath was snatched from her lungs. Grall felt a giddy sensation of sudden movement, as if the ground itself had fallen away beneath her feet, as if she were falling headlong down a great, dark void. Then she staggered and fell, a roaring in her ears. Her head spun. Hands touched her.

She tried to fight them off, but there were more and more of them, too many. The world steadied itself, and she saw pikas all around her. "What—where—?" She lay on her back. She raised her head and saw that she was in a familiar place, a low hollow in the stone set aside for a pika dormitory by the firvolkans. And she saw more: her companions, all but one, lay sprawled and dazed here, too.

"You appeared," an old pika male told her. "You and the others. There was a feel of magic working, and you appeared in our midst."

Grall could not reply. Her throat was clutching and unclutching in the pika manner of weeping, and she was overcome by frustration, fear, and grief.

Nul stood by his friend's side. The stone elemental had gestured for silence before Jeremy had even begun, and for several simi they had stood before it. At last the mighty stone hand fell. "There. The intruders have been confined. Three humans, five pikas, two most unusual creatures. I think we shall have them here."

Without fuss or noise, Fred and Busby materialized a few paces away from Jeremy and Nul. Nul blinked. Fred was full-sized, Busby very small—but the dwindled gargoyle immediately began to swell, and in moments was his own size again.

"Living stone," the stone elemental murmured. "Yes, I remember the creation of it; a brother of mine to the south amusing himself. And has your long life brought you no more wisdom than to serve humans?"

Busby glared at the stone being, his features sharply etched in the flaring light of the silent fire elemental. "We serve those who are our friends," he said.

"Stone and flesh," the stone elemental rumbled. "How curious. I am almost interested. My brother of fire, are you interested?"

"I burn," the other whispered. "I yearn to destroy."

"We could do it, you and I. We could unite, as the firvolkans wish, and give the stone a fire so hot that it would melt, run, turn to vapor. No life then! What say you, stone?"

Busby could not look at the stone face. "We value life," he muttered. But in a stronger voice he said, "Though we value friendship more."

The stone elemental was ominously silent. "One of the humans," it said at length, "prides himself on his killing skills. Firvolkans! Which of you is the mightiest hunter?"

The hobs muttered. Nul, sweeping his gaze over them, felt sick. They were all huge, all strong, compared to a pika. But one stood forward, bigger than the rest, scarred in a half-dozen places. "I," the firvolkan said.

"Then, human," the elemental said to Jeremy, "your eloquence may not be needed. Here!"

Jeremy fell to his knees again, and Nul had to clutch him to keep from tumbling himself. The floor of the cavern had opened once more, but this time in a trench perhaps shoulder-high to a human, though deep enough to conceal a pika entirely. The firvolkan vanished from where he stood and a moment later reappeared in the trench.

"And the human," the elemental rumbled. The hunter, Havoronas, materialized opposite the firvolkan, his hand already reaching for a weapon that was no longer there. "The two of you will try this matter by combat," the elemental said. "Neither armed, neither aided. Let the winner decide my action. Fight!"

"It is not fair!" Nul cried.

"It is my will."

Nul looked back at the trench just in time to see the hob charge. Havoronas, still apparently disoriented, was pressed back against the wall at the end of the trench, the hob clawing for his throat. He dropped completely out of sight, and for a moment Nul thought he had been thrown to ground by the hob; but an instant later Havoronas rose behind the creature, struck it hard across the back, and danced away.

The combat was constricted in that narrow trench, but it was ferocious. The hob had strength and size on his side; the human only speed and dexterity. The crowd of hobs shouted and stamped encouragement for their own;

Jeremy and Nul remained silent, except for shouted warn-
ings that seemed neither needed nor heeded. Havoronas
handled himself well.

Both hob and man were breathing hard, both bleeding, after only moments of battle. The hob, infuriated,
roared and rushed the hunter, arms spread as wide as the
trench would allow to enclose the man. Havoronas feinted
right, dived left, and barely got past the hob. In passing,
he gave the back of the hob's knee a terrific kick, and the
creature, howling, went to its knees.

In an instant Havoronas had kicked hard again, this
time in the center of the hob's upper back. The hob fell
face forward, head jammed against the trench wall a few
inches above the floor. Havoronas launched himself into
the air, coming down with both feet on the creature's
neck.

It snapped audibly.

The hobs screamed in rage.

"It is not exciting," the stone elemental said with a
careless wave of its hand.

Nul cried out as the ground moved again, and Jeremy
started forward, but too late. The trench closed with a
shudder on both victor and vanquished. There was not
even time for a scream from Havoronas.

"Soft humans," the elemental said. "You die so easily.
You will have to try to convince us, after all."

Jeremy was shaking. "Convince you! You promised
that the combat would decide!"

"There is no promise. Talk. Amuse us."

"No!"

"Yes," Nul said. He felt the elementals' attention turn
to him, stony cold and fiery hot. "Yes. My friend will
speak for us. But only if all are here. My people, his
people, all of us."

"Easy enough," the stone elemental said, and there
they all were.

Nul blinked. He had never seen so many of his people
at once, not even when the clan was whole, unless at
some half-remembered great feast when he was very
young: they stood and knelt and lay in a vast throng, well
more than a hundred of them, and among them he saw

Grall. He cried out to her, took a half step toward her, and felt himself held fast. The pikas, behind Nul and Jeremy, seemed similarly trapped—and similarly protected from the wrath of the hobs.

Nul turned. Barach was there, now, to one side, with the gargoyles, and with him Kelada, who was crying out soundlessly, struggling without success to move to Jeremy.

"All are here," the elemental muttered. "Now. Convince."

Jeremy ran a hand through his brown hair. "What could I say to an eternal being?" he asked.

"Tell him about us," Nul said. "You, me, Kelada, Barach, Busby, Fred, all of us. All different, but all alike. I do not know the words. You do. Tell him."

For a long time Jeremy stood silent, the elementals bending over him like waiting birds of prey. Then at last he sighed. "The Great Dark One promises rest," he said slowly. "A world of peace, of final quiet: but it is a lie. His offer is an offer of death, of cessation. And life was not meant to end in such a manner.

"You, elementals: you have been on Thaumia since Thaumia began. Your memories are long. Do they go back to a time when there were no elementals, no life at all as it is today? To a time when stone, fire, air, water, were one, a unity? Is that what you want now?"

"To be one," breathed the fire elemental.

"The need and desire are always with us," the stone being agreed. "The desire to find what we have lost, to make one those which are many."

"And the Great Dark One twists that desire, as he twists the desire of the firvolkans to find the great peace," Jeremy said. "He does not offer life for the spirit, but death for the body; not renewal and growth, but an end to growth. He wants a great stillness, ruled over only by his own mind. But that is not peace."

Nul studied the stone face, but saw no flicker of agreement or disagreement there, no sign even that the giant was listening. Jeremy had begun to pace, as much as the confining circle of magic would allow him. "You look at us and see different creatures, firvolkans, pikas, humans, even living stone. But are we so different? You despise us because we are weak, small, scattered, individual. But are we not all part of life? You want unity, to be one again with the other elementals. Are you not already?

"Consider: we live in one world, in one universe. Use your magic however you may, can you go outside that universe? Can you travel to some other place where elementals are one? No?

"Then do you not see that you have that unity? All belong to Thaumia, all are her children. Look at us: human and pika and gargoyle, not many but one in purpose and in spirit. And that is the gift of life, not of death. When life ceases, that is not unity, but only a part of unity; for life is the spirit of the universe, and death is only a part of life, not the whole end of it."

The stone head inclined, not much, but a bit, as if the elemental were listening to some far music. "Then you believe that I am wrong to seek rest?"

"No," Jeremy said. "But you are wrong to impose it on others. To live together in peace, though we are all of different kinds: that is the goal. You see my friends: pikas, humans, gargoyles, all. We do not hate each other because of our differences. The differences are what make each of us special; the individual is as important as the group."

"And yet humans war."

"We do. We know the right, but do not always live according to its rule. That is our burden and our woe. But our failures do not mean the idea has failed, only that we have. Do you not feel the unity of all creation? Do you not feel the wonder that comes in beholding a different creature and in speaking with it? Do not plants draw life from the soil? Do animals not gain life from plants? Does the world not reclaim her own when the animals return to her in death? A world is brother to an ant; a cloud is the child of the ocean; bones are one with the stones of the world. All, all are one. If not, my words mean nothing. But search your feelings; search your need to be at one with something other than yourselves. Then you will find the truth. If you find none, then destroy us. But if truth is there, then hold your hand."

"And what," rumbled the elemental, "do the firvolkans say?"

The chieftain stepped forward. "Our wishes do not change. Kill the humans and all their works!"

"No," the stone elemental said, and Nul breathed a sigh of relief. "No. Here is what we will do instead: human, take the female of your kind. We will send you to a place of safety. All the others—the living stone, the other man, the pikas, the firvolkans—must die. But the two of you live."

And Kelada was there, inside the magic circle, embracing Jeremy, weeping on his shoulder. Nul saw Jeremy's anguished eyes. The pika swallowed. "Go," he whispered. "You have helped me find my people. Go now."

Jeremy kissed Kelada tenderly. Then he turned to the elemental. "No," he said, his voice scarcely audible. "We will not."

"Yes!" Nul cried. "Go now, while you may!"

Kelada took Jeremy's hand. They stood like two children before the immense stone elemental. "No," she said, tears in her voice. "Jeremy is right. We will not leave our friends."

The stone head nodded once. "Then take all your friends except the living stone," it said. "The old man, the small furry ones. I will send you all to safety; but I must have the living stone."

The gargoyles reared their heads high, looking fierce and proud. Jeremy gave them a long look. "They, too, live," he said softly. "And we will not leave them to you."

Again the giant gave a single nod. "Then we will destroy only the firvolkans," it said. "And all your party will go free."

"No," Jeremy said, his voice stronger now. "Not even them. Enemies though they have made themselves to us, they too live. And it is as wrong to destroy them as to destroy us."

"Kill them!" cried the hob chieftain. "Kill them, O mighty ones, even if you kill us, too! The dead demand it!"

"There," said the stone giant, "is your answer. All must die. It is decided."

"Wait!" Nul cried out. "Please."

"Yes?"

"Please," Nul said again. "If we must die, let us all stand together. It is a small thing to ask."

"It is of no consequence."

There was a moment of disorientation, and then Nul found they were indeed all together: pikas, gargoyles, humans. Barach stood to his left, Jeremy to his right. Both men put their hands on his shoulder.

"We join," the stone giant said, rising slowly. Its head barely cleared the lofty ceiling when at last it stood. "We unite for death." It strode into the heart of the living flame elemental, and the fire played over the stone surface. In a heartbeat the stone glowed dull red; in another, it had begun to melt and run; and then the two beings were one, a giant of molten stone, so bright that it dazzled the eyes.

"At last," sighed a voice that was a combining of stone and fire. "One. One. Now we rise."

Nul trembled. The glowing stone pulsed, became even brighter, and the heat of it was scorching. Then it reared, flattening, a wave of white-hot lava, and from the fissure through which the fire elemental had come more lava burst, rising, curling over hobs and humans, pikas and gargoyles. Some shrieked as the burning death crested, rolled over, and came crashing down on them.

CHAPTER 14

THE FIERY WAVE broke.

Jeremy, his mouth open in a shout that not even he could hear, held tight to Kelada's hand. The white-hot magma toppled him into searing pain; the world flared away in fire, and then there was only silence and darkness.

It's cool, Jeremy thought in wonder.

A tremulous voice, Kelada's voice: "Jeremy?"

"We're alive!" he cried, and echoes from faraway walls sent his words ringing back to him.

"So we are," Barach said, and suddenly the darkness was filled with laughing, shouting, screaming pika voices. "Quiet, please! *Beskara lettimu!*" The noise subsided suddenly under that order shouted in pikish. Barach took a deep breath. "First things first. We need to know where we are—and who is here. Fred? Busby?"

"Here!"

"Here, Mage!"

"Nul?"

"Here. Wherever *here* is."

Fred's voice grated above the resumed murmur: "Mage Barach! We are away from the mazerite!"

"Are you sure?"

Busby broke in: "He is right. I feel none of its influence."

"Light here," Nul said. "Not much. Hard to see after the fire. But some firemoss, I think."

"My eyes are dazzled as well," Barach said. "But if we are truly away from the mazerite, why, then we may have a little light. Jeremy?"

259

Jeremy, in an undertone, spoke in English his private cantrip for wizard light: "It's the wonder light from nowhere that will shine a million times just for you. And if you act fast, it's free, free, free! Let all be bright."

Light burst on them: not the pale luminescence of firemoss, not the glaring incandescence of molten rock, but a good steady wizard-light emanating, it seemed, from the very walls. Jeremy gasped. Except for the elemental's den, the volcanic tunnels under the Fridhof Mountains had been twisted, constricted, suffocating. Even the place of the elementals had seemed somehow cramped, partly because of the crowd there and partly because of the elementals' imposing size. The cave in which they stood now, though, was a cathedral by comparison, an enormous cavern with high-arched sides gleaming, streaked with color, hung with sparse growths of firemoss: and from above hung a thousand stalactites, glistening, gleaming, every imaginable hue, rust red, jade green, cool buttery yellow, deep copper blue. "Home!" Nul gasped. "Is home!"

The pikas had seemingly gone mad. They leaped, capered; some dropped to their knees and sobbed without tears, the husky, breathless sobs of broken-hearted children. Small clusters embraced each other. Still others wandered solitary, dazed, touching the walls with fingers grown tentative and shy.

A hand fell warmly on Jeremy's shoulder, and Barach gave him a gentle fatherly shake. "You saved us. You and your words worked a magic beyond any I have known."

Jeremy shook his head. "No. I didn't save us. You all did. Even poor Havoronas did his part. I think it was our standing together in the end; the elementals had some sense of what that meant, of unity. They, after all, are fragments of a whole. I think that our singleness of purpose impressed them somehow. They sent us here."

Kelada shivered. "What of the hobs?"

Nul murmured, "They wanted death. Do not think elementals disappointed them."

Barach nodded. "I fear you are right, friend pika.

Though such a death I would not wish even upon our enemies." In a sober voice, he added, "And the people of the Valley? Did the elementals destroy them all?"

Jeremy shook his head. "I have no sense of the Valley or of the magics that may have worked there. I simply can't tell. I hope not. My words seem to have convinced even me: life is too precious to be snuffed out."

"Even the hobs' lives?" Kelada asked.

"Yes," Busby said quietly. "Even theirs."

They were all silent a moment, each with his own thoughts. Barach finally clapped his hands together. "Well! Jeremy, use the communication spell to speak to Tremien. He will want to know the outcome of our adventure."

"I've lost track of time," Jeremy warned. "It may be night at Whitehorn."

"Even so. Serve the old man right, there warm at home while we were off questing."

Jeremy shook his head again, but he crossed his arms and spoke the activating cantrip. Tremien's voice instantly came from the air before them: "At last! And I sense that you are all there, and more besides. Barach, my old friend, how did it go?"

The old wizard bowed his head. "As everything goes, Mage Tremien; with some sorrow and some joy. But we are safe, and Nul has found his people at last. How has Whitehorn fared?"

"Well, thank you. We look forward to the turning of a year tomorrow. We have had no word of troubles from anywhere in the land. The valley is blanketed in snow, and quite beautiful. Will we have you home for the feast?"

"Assuredly."

Jeremy broke in: "Tremien, we have over a hundred small folk here. We were sent from the Fridhof Range back to their home beneath the Bone Mountains by magic—"

"Magic?"

"Yes, elemental magic. It's a long story. I'll explain it all when I see you. But they came naked, Tremien, and without even food. They are in desperate need."

Tremien did not even hesitate. "Of course! But they return to their old homes at a most fortunate time. The kitchens here have been going for days, preparing the new year's feast. Allow me a few simi to make arrangements, and Nul's folk shall have food in plenty for the time being. We will see to their supply for the future a little later. I know how independent pikas can be, but they will need our help at least through next year's growing season."

"Thank you, Mage," said Nul.

Tremien's voice was solemn and kind: "No, Nul. It is the least I could do for one who was content to call himself servant but for so many years was truly a friend. May all blessings come to your people, brave pika. I give you joy to crown your quest."

They spoke a bit more, not for long, and soon Tremien made good his promise. Tables laden with every imaginable dish, from fish to pheasant and back again, appeared in the cavern with an audible *pop!* as the master of Whitehorn emptied his holiday kitchen for the pikas, who shrank away from the unexpected apparitions, still shy and confused.

Nul, meanwhile, had been passing among them, speaking to them, touching one here and there. He came back finally to Jeremy. "Have two brothers here, and mother. Other brothers dead. Father dead long time ago."

"I'm sorry, Nul."

"Nah, nah. Is more than I expected after so long a time." He sighed. "They all hungry; but afraid. Won't eat until they know is all right, until they have permission. Pikas have been hurt badly."

"Slavery hurts all creatures," Barach said. "It even hurt the hobs, who wrongly thought themselves masters. Well, good Nul, tell your folk to eat, for I am starved myself. If I get to the tables before them, they may yet go hungry!"

But there was no fear of that; Tremien had sent so much food, indeed, that the pikas were safe from hunger pangs for at least a week. With Nul urging them on, they shyly sampled the food, then tucked in with great eagerness, some weeping even as they ate. Jeremy saw Busby quietly walk to a distant, dark nook of the cavern. After a moment Kelada followed him.

Jeremy filled a plate—Tremien had even sent along the coiling-dragon pattern, his best china, he saw—and took a glass of pale surry, a bracing fruit drink that Melodia the healer had always liked, over to Kelada. She stood with one hand on Busby's face. "Here," he said.

"Thank you. Busby's not feeling well."

Jeremy nodded. "He killed a man."

"Yes," Busby said morosely. "I did not mean to; but he would have hurt Barach."

"It was right to kill him," Kelada said fiercely. "He had his chance to leave in peace."

"No," Jeremy said. "Busby knows the truth. He was wrong to kill Captain Ramp."

"Jeremy!"

He held up a hand. "Listen. When I spoke to the elementals, I was trying to use my skill with words. But, damn it, I wound up saying what I believed: all life is precious. It's wrong to kill.

"But sometimes, Busby, we find ourselves forced into wrong. It may be that we are serving a greater good; but that doesn't change matters or our feelings about them. Wrong is wrong, and I'm glad you feel sorrow for the man's death."

Busby nodded thoughtfully. "Life. I have had it for so long; for eons. And yet it has not made me wise, or strong, or happy."

"Maybe life doesn't do those things of itself," Jeremy said. "It just makes wisdom, strength, and happiness possible. But now that you feel you lack them, at least you can begin to search." He paused. "I wish I could offer you comfort. I have killed, too; and yet before I did, I never considered myself a killer. You will see yourself differently from now on, Busby. You will feel differently. But you have friends to speak with—and one in particular." He nodded toward Fred, who had perched on an exceptionally large stalagmite and who surveyed the feast with an air of remote loneliness. "You are the same at heart; give him a chance to hear your woes. And never forget the pain that killing brings."

The gargoyle nodded gravely. Jeremy took a deep breath, hoping that he himself could live up to the scant comfort he offered his friend.

They spent the night in the caverns beneath the Bone Mountains, Jeremy and Kelada nestled together in a snug little nook. He spread the wizard's robe over her and slept with his arm around her waist, his hand spread on the gentle curve of her belly. He dreamed of loving her and of the unborn child waiting beneath his palm.

The gargoyles shared a spot in the main cavern, the only place big enough for them in their undwindled state. They did not sleep—they never did—but passed the time in low conversation. Some of it was trivial talk about the minerals in the walls. Much of it, for a change, was about other things, and was more serious.

Barach slept in a bedroll placed on the cool sand of the cavern floor, breathing easily, a smile lurking on his face even in repose. Before long he began to snore. A few young pikas, aroused by the odd noise—one not usually made by sleeping pikas, certainly—came and stood around him for a long time, wondering what it meant.

Only Nul was wakeful. He talked far into the night to his brothers and his mother, until they, still weak and half-dazed by the events of the day, fell asleep. Nul paced the cavern and shooed away the youngsters who were standing around Barach, holding tufts of moss in front of his mouth to see them flutter when he snored. Nul told the pikas a tale of wizardly wrath that would, he hoped, keep them well away from the old mage.

He walked on, head down, pondering. He explored the well-remembered passageways, discovering memories even in the feel of the loose, clean sand beneath his bare feet. He found some of the passages partly blocked by stone falls or intruding roots, others much the same as he remembered them. He went down a slanting tunnel to an underground pool where he and Jare had come to swim and fish for the white-fellows, albino creatures that lived here beneath the mountains and had a sweet, delicate flavor when roasted.

The pool was still there, more oval than circular. A stream coming from underground fed it and another carried it away under the mountains, so a slight current stirred its waters. The pool's surface gleamed in the light of a thick growth of firemoss on the barrel-arched ceiling of stone above it.

Nul stood on the sandy rim of the pool for a long time as he thought of the pikas who had returned and those who, like Jare, were never to return. His heart felt as heavy as stone in his chest. It would take a long time before the pikas could be anything like a whole people again. Some of them, the old and weak, might yet die. Only a very few of the young had much vigor about them. Grall did; but that, he thought, was probably the result of the magic potion that she said Barach had given her.

Thinking about Grall, Nul sighed deeply. The water before him was a smooth dark enigma, beckoning and yet mysterious. Giving in at last to its call, he pulled off his trousers made by human hands, dropped the garment on the shore, and waded into the pool. The water was cold, delicious on his skin. Nul gasped as it came slowly up to his belly, then his chest. He waded to a point where it lapped just under his chin, then ducked under the surface. The cold water whispered secret things in his ears.

He came up dripping, the water beading on the fine fur of his head and face. His legs ached a bit from the old injury, but even that seemed welcome, an old friend returned. He lay flat on the water and tried a clumsy stroke or two.

Pikas did not swim much, as a rule; only the young ones really liked water that much. But in the days of adventurous youth he and Jare had had races here, from the shore to a moss-cushioned ledge opposite and back again. Nul pushed off the bottom and splashed his way across the expanse. He grabbed the ledge, his hand finding the familiar deep growth of moss, and heaved for breath. Some water got into his windpipe, making him cough. He was no longer the young pika who could swim across, reverse direction, and reach the shore without even breathing hard. Now his heart hammered in his chest so hard that it hurt. He lowered his face to the water and took some in his mouth, cold, somehow sweet, tasting of home. He drank deeply.

At last he swam back, though much more slowly, glad when at last his feet touched bottom and he could wade the rest of the way. He felt somehow as though Jare had returned with him, as though they had silently shared the ledge for a moment or two; but now his brother was gone. For good, he thought to himself. He had a moment of shock when he saw a dark form ahead of him on the beach—but it was not Jare.

Grall waited on the shore for him. "I remember when you and your brother did this foolish thing."

For a moment Nul felt embarrassed, standing in water up to his hips and reluctant to go any farther, even though pikas did not feel about clothing the way that humans seemed to feel. "We did not think it foolish at the time," he said. "I sought him here."

"He has gone along the paths of the dead."

"And others. We must sing the old songs for them."

"We have already, in our hearts. But we will sing them again."

He splashed out. "You are sitting on my trousers."

"Yes." Grall herself, he could see now, was no longer nude. She had wrapped a scrap of cloth about her, the way that courting females had always done. Never mind that this piece was old and tattered, found no doubt in some family niche where it had lain ever since the hobs had taken the pikas away into bondage.

Nul sat beside her on the sand. "I am cold," he said. She held him.

They all woke the next morning in a different frame of mind. The pikas, over the first delirium of homecoming, were subdued now, the older ones speaking of what had to be done to prepare for the growing season, to make the caverns a place of life again, the young who had never seen this fabled homeland asking a million questions. All had grown timorous and fearful; the least noise was enough to make them cringe, as though they thought it all a dream, one from which they would awaken again.

Nul led Jeremy and Barach up a larger exit tunnel, one that let them walk fairly upright, to a doorway made of worm-riddled wood bound in rusted iron. "May not open," Nul said. "Could be roots grown into it."

But he and Jeremy leaned hard against the door, and it grated slowly open on squealing hinges, the soft wood crumbling a bit as it rubbed against stone at the bottom edge. They opened the door to dazzling white light and a burst of cold air. "Snow," Nul laughed.

Jeremy looked out. The door had opened from the side of a gentle hill, and for as far as he could see the hills rolled on and on, pure glaring white beneath a high blue sky. No seam showed on that smooth face, no interruption until, far on the horizon—the southern horizon, Jeremy supposed, seeing the position of the morning sun—a great forest was sketched in lines of black and white.

"Arkhedden," Barach said, his breath misting as he raised his arm to point away toward the forest. "Jeremy, thirty leagues south from here is the great forest road, part of which we traveled once. And away there somewhere—" he pointed somewhat south of east— "is Whitehorn Mountain. Now that we know just where we are, we may use the travel-spell to return."

"At last," Jeremy said.

Nul said nothing.

They returned to the cavern. The pikas were gradually organizing themselves, falling into twenty-five or thirty small family groups. Nul spoke to many of them, and to one, Jeremy noted, in particular: Grall.

Jeremy spoke again to Tremien, and soon the arrangements for the pikas' survival through the hard winter were complete. Whitehorn would send regular supplies of food and in the spring would add seed to that; the pikas should gradually be able to resume their lives again, to take up almost where they had left off so many years ago.

But not completely. Too many had died at the hands of the hobs, or of starvation and abuse, for that to be so. Still, there would be pikas in the Bone Mountain caverns once more, and that seemed to be a good thing. And, Jeremy suspected, the pikas would be more friendly to the big folk of the surface this time, if they did not look upon humans as they did upon hobs. He hoped the friendship would take root and flourish, for the sake of the small folk and the great alike.

Barach and Jeremy had just finished speaking with the gargoyles, who had been told to shrink down to cat size for the journey, when a shout from the pikas made them turn. Nul stood before a group of them, waving his arms. What he said, though, was drowned in their enthusiastic chant.

"What is it?" Jeremy asked, unable to understand the pikish words.

"They want him," Barach said, smiling, "to be their king."

Jeremy found it suddenly hard to swallow. "Oh."

The tumult kept up for some minutes. Making his way over to them through the crowd, Nul spoke to the two men, looking unhappy. "Never thought this," he said. "They want me for chief, like father. Didn't ask them—"

"Of course not, Nul," Jeremy said. "You saved them. That's why they want you. And they're right."

"You think I should stay?"

"I can't say. You must do what is right for you."

Nul shook his head. "Have so many friends at Whitehorn. But this—this home."

"You'll always have friends at Whitehorn," Kelada said. "As long as Tremiem is there, or Barach, or Jeremy. Or me."

"Hard choice," Nul said. "Hard choice."

But it was a choice that had to be made. In the end, Jeremy, Kelada, Barach, and the dwindled gargoyles traveled to the tunnel entrance together with Nul; but he, dressed strangely in a simple white loin wrap and a sleeveless white jacket, made by the women pikas from one of the tablecloths Tremien had sent, stayed inside when they ventured out into the knee-deep snow. "Cheer up," Jeremy said, not in truth feeling very cheerful himself. "You can visit whenever you want."

"And you always welcome here," Nul said miserably. "Wish Nul could be two people, go, stay at same time."

"No, my friend," Barach said. "You must be one person. And that one must rule as well and wisely as possible. Remember the case of—"

"One good reason to be king," Nul said. "Now I can tell you to go and take stories with you." In a quieter voice, he murmured, "Joke only. Bad joke. I will miss the stories, Mage Barach."

"Then I shall save them up and tell them all to you when I see you again, Your Majesty."

Nul's orange eyes grew pale, a pika way of blushing. "Not call Nul that," he said. "Just Nul."

"And that," Barach said, his own voice suspiciously thick, "is itself a title of honor."

They stood there awkwardly for some moments. Then, his voice unsteady, Jeremy said, "Well. We should go. Farewell, Nul, and come to see us soon." In pikish, he added a sentence that he had painstakingly learned from Barach. *Nasg karl somi, sed sed bas:* part of our hearts stay with you.

He pronounced the travel-spell cantrip, and the shifting colors of no-space enveloped the humans and the gargoyles. The travelers did not speak much to each other.

Tremien's study at last wavered into place around them, dark-panelled and odorous of leather-bound volumes. Tremien himself stood before the fire, a thin, stooped figure in a carmine robe, his grave dark face lightened by a broad smile. "Here you are," he said. "A band of friends returned once more. A good omen on the first day of the new year!"

"What happened in Twilight Valley?" Jeremy asked, for that had been much in his mind, and Tremien seemed to have ways of knowing things that no other person could discover.

"I have learned nothing of their fate," Tremien said. "However, that is probably good news. Had there been a calamity, surely someone outside the Valley, away from the influence of the mazerite, would have noticed and informed me." He narrowed his eyes at the gargoyles. "And are you two prepared to resume your, ah, neglected duties?"

"Yes, Mage," Fred said. "We've seen much; we have a great deal to remember and to talk about."

"And to think about," Busby added in a more subdued voice.

"I am glad you enjoyed yourselves," Tremien said. "Well, if you are quite ready—"

He led the way through the crowded main hall, where soldiers and courtiers made a path for them. It seemed that he had not completely exhausted his holiday larder, for the aromas of a banquet warmed the air. Jeremy and Kelada spoke to some of the younger couples, smiling and touching hands, and they fell behind. When the two of them reached the courtyard and the main gate, the gargoyles were already more than halfway up their pillars and were swelling rapidly to full size.

They reached their stone globes, crouched over them, and clutched them in their forepaws. Tremien spoke a brief spell—a warding spell, to aid them in their vigilance— and then stepped back. Fred and Busby held their poses, staring down fiercely at the courtyard, at the road beyond, and at the snow-covered valley. "At last," he said, surveying the gargoyles in their places. "Whitehorn looks like home again."

The winter passed away in peace. Banquets were held, and feasts of revelry. When Jeremy attempted to return the gray robe to Tremien—another of its virtues seemed to be that it was no worse for the wear, not even needing to be cleaned—the old wizard declined. "You have earned a better gift from me," he said. "I have never had a son. Stand in my son's stead and accept it from me now."

"I am more honored than I can say," Jeremy responded, truly flattered. But, he thought, he would not often wear the robe, wonderful though it was; for it would always remind him of Nul. He could not lose that memory even in the midst of feasting and rejoicing. Nor, as he quickly discovered, would long days of hard work erase thoughts of the pika from his mind. Barach, never an easy taskmaster, began Jeremy's lessons again barely a week after their return; and life went on. Kelada fretted that she was becoming fat as the child within her grew. Jeremy smiled and kissed her and told her that no pregnant woman was ugly. She accused him of practicing advertising on her.

Later in the winter, when a few ships had managed to slip through the ice and visit Fridport, news came to them from Twilight Valley: there had been a great earthquake there, and the Friddifor River had changed its course somewhat, but for the most part the cities were intact. The river wall of Three Rivers had fallen almost completely, they heard, and some houses were damaged, but there seemed to be few casualties. At least, with their long-accustomed independence the people of the Valley declined all offers of help from the outside.

The hobs seemed to have disappeared entirely, though Jeremy was never to know whether they perished in the white-hot lava or whether the elemental had transported them, too, away from the caverns. As he had told Barach, Jeremy found himself hoping that, somehow, the hobs had been given a chance at life; but his nightmares were of their terrible death in the white-hot tide of molten rock. He wondered as well about the elementals: was the fire spirit, now unified with his stone brother, free at last of the Great Dark One's controlling spell? And the stone elemental: had it encased its new, white-hot being once more in mazerite, to protect itself from the Great Dark One's troublesome magic, to dream away the eons of the world? Some questions, alas, could not be answered.

Jeremy, after the first few weeks of feeling relief at merely being home again and in one piece, found the long winter evenings somewhat lonely. In an effort to recover himself a bit from Captain Fallon's instruction—as Barach had promised, Jeremy now had an hour of un-armed combat each morning—he took to closeting himself in a small study for an ona or so each evening, working, as he told Barach, on his next play. "Which is this one to be?" asked Barach, who had discussed the problems of translation with him several times before. "*Hamlet* or *Romeo and Juliet*?"

"I may surprise you," Jeremy said.

Weeks passed. One morning as Jeremy and Kelada walked in the courtyard, she suddenly cried out and pointed at a flower bed. Through a thin crust of snow— Tremien never allowed more than a few decorative inches to fall on his castle—a bright-red flower showed, a tiny cuplike hurry-spring. Jeremy noticed then that the snow was melting more quickly than new flakes fell. He stood alone in the gateway later that afternoon, looking down on the valley. The dark river snaked through a white field of snow, but there were gray patches where the snow was melting, and he saw no glint of ice on the river's surface. The trees, too, were dropping their bur-dens of snow and stood stark and black against the white background. "Spring is on the way," a stony voice said from overhead.

Jeremy glanced up. "Yes, it is, Busby," he said.

Fred, his hawk's head turned a bit to the left, gave Jeremy a roguish wink. "We know what spring does to you flesh beings when it comes," he said.

"I hope someone uses that chip off your shoulder for a door stop," Jeremy shot back. The gargoyle only laughed.

Spring was, indeed, on the way, though it took its slow, sweet time about coming. Though most of the snow in the valley had melted, the season still had not com-pletely arrived many days later when a soft tapping sounded at Jeremy's study door early one evening. He put his pen crossways in his mouth, laid a book on his manuscript to keep the pages from blowing off the table, and rose to open the door. The pen dropped to the floor when he cried out, "Nul!"

The pika grinned literally from ear to ear. "Hello,

Jeremy. I back." He stooped to retrieve the pen and held it out.

Jeremy took the pen from him and then stepped away to take a good look at his friend. Nul was resplendent in gray velvet trousers, a white shirt with bloused sleeves embroidered with a whole field of flowers, and an ornate sky-blue vest decorated with gold braid and buttons. "You look every inch a king," Jeremy laughed.

Nul dropped his gaze. "Nah, nah. Nul no king. Pikas get over being rescued, they start to argue and disagree. Do this, do that, do the other. King take this side, king take that side. Make Nul mad. I make brother king in my place; I come back home."

Jeremy held the door for him. Nul limped in, glancing about curiously. Closing the door, Jeremy said. "I'm glad to see you, Nul. But is this what you really want?"

Nul climbed up into a chair and sat with his legs dangling, his bare feet swinging back and forth. "Is enough," he said in a serious tone, "to know that pikas there, in old home under Bone Mountains. That Grall there. That I can go there whenever I want." He spread his hands. "What good Nul as king? Not ever been king. Not have patience. Not know most of new pikas. One day will go back to live. Maybe one day will try to make peace between pikas of Bone Mountains, other pikas, if we can find them. But not yet. Want to help Mage Tremien for little while more. Want to travel with Jeremy little bit more. Want to see Kelada's child. Even to hear Barach's stories. Nul's life with friends not finished yet."

"May it go on for a long time," Jeremy said.

"Yes. Sorry for knocking on door, bothering you. Barach say you writing play. But I want to see you very much."

"I'm glad you did. And the play is finished, except for printing. Here it is." Jeremy picked up and straightened an untidy pile of paper.

From his chair Nul craned to see it. "Which one you do? The man who kill his brother and nephew make revenge, or the young ones who love and die?"

"I decided not to do either of them. They belong to another man. This is something of my own."

"Good," Nul said. "Told you you should. Good play?"

"I hope it is. I've done my best with it," Jeremy said, laying the bundle in Nul's lap. "Here. For you."

Nul picked up the title page in his three-fingered hands and read it silently. "Actors will do this?" he murmured.

"If they want any more of my plays, they will. And after all, it has excitement, romance, adventure; I think it will be a success. How do you like the title, Nul?"

Nul's whisper was a little choked. "It a fine title, Jeremy. A wonderful title."

And he set the title page aside and began to read act 1, scene 1, of *The Pika King*.

Brad Strickland has been writing science fiction, fantasy, and horror since 1982. In addition to *Moon Dreams* the first novel in the Jeremy Moon series, he has written *Shadow Show,* also available in Signet editions. His short fiction is widely published, including a story in *The Year's Best Horror XV.* Brad lives in Oakwood, Georgia, with his wife, children, and numerous pets.

In the vast intergalactic world of the future
the soldiers battle

NOT FOR GLORY

JOEL ROSENBERG

author of the bestselling
Guardian of the Flame series

Only once in the history of the Metzadan mercenary corps has a man been branded traitor. That
man is Bar-El, the most cunning military mind in
the universe. Now his nephew, Inspector-General
Hanavi, must turn to him for help. What begins as
one final mission is transformed into a series of
campaigns that takes the Metzadans from world to
world, into intrigues, dangers, and treacherous dip-
lomatic games, where a strategist's highly irregular maneuvers and a master assassin's swift blade
may prove the salvation of the planet—or its ulti-
mate ruin . . .